HUNTING & HOME
in the
SOUTHERN HEARTLAND

HUNTING & HOME
in the
SOUTHERN
HEARTLAND

THE BEST OF ARCHIBALD RUTLEDGE

Edited by
JIM CASADA

University of South Carolina Press

Copyright © 1992 Jim Casada

Published in Columbia, South Carolina, by the
University of South Carolina Press

Manufactured in the United States of America

Library of Congress Cataloging-in-Publication Data

Rutledge, Archibald Hamilton, 1883–1973.
  Hunting & home in the southern heartland : the best of Archibald
Rutledge / edited by Jim Casada.
      p.   cm.
  Includes bibliographical references.
  ISBN 0–87249–822–0 (alk. paper)
    1. Hunting stories, American—South Carolina.   2. South Carolina—
Social   life   and   customs.   I. Casada,   James   A.   II. Title.
III. Title: Hunting and home in the southern heartland.
PS3535.U87A6   1992
813′ .52—dc20   91-43713

THIS WORK IS DEDICATED to Irvine Hart Rutledge and to the memory of his brothers, Archibald Rutledge, Jr., and Henry Middleton Rutledge IV. The bond between "Old Flintlock" and his sons was a wondrous one, and theirs was the good fortune to live much of what he wrote.

Contents

Acknowledgments

A number of individuals have offered their advice and encouragement in the course of this work's compilation. Foremost among these has been Judge Irvine Rutledge, who is ever eager to have his father's work available to the reading public and to whom the work is dedicated. I have benefited from correspondence and conversations with Rob Wegner, who has a special interest in Rutledge's passion for hunting whitetails and the many stories he wrote about the animal. The interlibrary loan staff of Winthrop College's Dacus Library have been helpful in obtaining information and copies of obscure books and articles. Warren Slesinger, Acquisitions Editor at the University of South Carolina Press, helped me launch this project and see it through some uncertain moments.

My family, as always, have been firm bastions of support. To my parents, Anna Lou and Commodore Casada, I owe a lasting debt of gratitude for implanting and nurturing in me a love of the outdoors which has always been a sustaining feature of my life. Finally, to my wife, Ann, and my daughter, Natasha, I tender heartfelt thanks for the patience and understanding which have made not only the present work, but also my literary labors in general, possible.

A Note on Selection

Selecting the "best" of a writer as talented and prolific as Archibald Rutledge is difficult. In the course of his career he published untold hundreds of stories, and to date nothing approaching a comprehensive bibliography of his writing has been compiled. However, there are some parameters which guided the editor in selecting pieces for inclusion in the present work. First of all, this is the initial volume of a projected trilogy. The titles of the two succeeding volumes—*Archibald Rutledge's Great Deer-hunting Stories* and *Archibald Rutledge's Great Turkey-hunting Stories*—are self-explanatory. Accordingly, the present work does not include any of his delightful tales on these two subjects. Likewise, no poetry is included.

At present, only one or two of Rutledge's books are in print. It should be noted, however, that in 1986 his sole surviving son, Judge Irvine Rutledge, compiled a fine anthology, *Fireworks in the Peafield Corner*, which is still available. This collection focuses primarily on hunting tales. With the sole exception of "Why I Taught My Boys To Be Hunters," I have opted to look outside its pages in choosing pieces for the present book. Beyond that, all I can claim for what follows is that my choices are ones which appeal to me as a student and admirer of Rutledge. They do, however, constitute a reasonably representative cross section of his work. Chronologically they span the whole of his career, and collectively they touch on most of the themes which run as constant, colorful threads through the body of his work. Most important, the pieces are enjoyable. Those who are already familiar with Rutledge's writings will likely encounter old favorites along with a sprinkling of previously unread tales, while newcomers to his world have a rare treat awaiting them.

Each of the selections included in this volume is identified according to the book (or in some instances, books) in which it was published. Of course, virtually all of the pieces first appeared in periodical form. Brief editorial commentary, intended to provide a backdrop for the subject of that particular section, introduces each of the work's six parts.

HUNTING & HOME
in the
SOUTHERN HEARTLAND

Archibald Rutledge:
Sweet Southern Scribe

No one has sung the South's sporting song with the same alluring sweetness as Archibald Rutledge. A proud son of the Southern soil, with roots reaching deep into the Carolina Low Country's past, he was a man born to love nature. Rutledge ranks as one of America's most popular and prolific outdoor writers. His lengthy, multifaceted career was that of a Renaissance man, and the primary purpose of this book is to make some of his sparkling literary achievements available to the public once again.

Rutledge was born at the family's "Summer Place" in McClellanville, South Carolina, on October 23, 1883. If one judges from the contents of several of his books, his was an idyllic childhood. During most of the year the family lived at their ancestral home, Hampton Plantation. Annually though, when mosquitoes, humidity, and the dog days of late summer made life unbearable and malaria a real risk, they would beat a temporary retreat to the Summer Place or to the North Carolina mountains in search of comfort.

The line from which Archibald Rutledge was descended was a long and proud one. His ancestors included a signer of the Declaration of Independence, a chief justice of the United States Supreme Court, and a South Carolina governor. His father, Henry Middleton Rutledge, was the youngest Confederate soldier to attain the rank of colonel in the Civil War, while his mother, neé Margaret Hamilton, was a lady possessed of all the finest attributes of Southern womanhood. Rutledge pays a moving tribute to his parents in *My Colonel and His Lady* (1937).

Rutledge's halcyon days of youth at Hampton came to an abrupt end when he reached his teenage years. When local educational opportunities could no longer meet the precocious lad's needs, in

1896 he departed Hampton to enroll at Charleston's Porter Military Academy. Four years later, although younger than most of his compatriots, he graduated as class salutatorian. His outstanding academic performance earned him medals in, among other subjects, French and English. His prowess in these fields suggests that even at this juncture there were signs of a writer in the making. Much later he would recall, with a pardonable degree of self-satisfaction, his graduation awards: "It pleased me to have gathered enough gold and silver medals to survive a depression." His overall achievements earned him a prestigious Lorillard Scholarship to attend Union College in Schnectady, New York.

For a son of the South this period far from home must have been exceedingly difficult, although he later wrote: "During my four years at Union, I met only a single person, from the highest to the lowest, who was not gentle and courteous." That sole exception was a heartless fellow student who threw a letter from Rutledge's mother into a mud puddle. An altercation ensued in which Rutledge's nose was broken. For the rest of his life his nose, which mended at a bit of an angle, bore vivid testimony to the way he defended a trivial insult to family honor.

Constant homesickness and this one incident aside, his college years were good ones. He was devoted to academic excellence despite grinding loneliness which was never completely dispelled until finally, many years later, he returned home to Hampton for good. He completed his studies for a bachelor's degree at Union College in the standard four years, graduating with honors in 1904. The honors were but a small part of what he accomplished, academically and otherwise, in college. His days and nights were filled with frenetic activity, establishing a work ethic that endured all his life.

Rutledge was an outstanding member of the Union track team, and his native wit and eloquence made him a powerful orator. Along with excelling in his studies and extracurricular activities, Rutledge showed a rare talent for making friends. This was a characteristic which he would carry with him throughout his life. Perhaps drawn by his innocence and transparent goodness, several professors took the bright-eyed, intelligent young man under protective wings. During the summers of his college years he worked for General Electric, and while so employed he came under the influence of that company's head, Charles Steinmetz.

Rutledge described Steinmetz as an "elemental genius"; the two became fast friends. Through Steinmetz's good offices he met a number of famous men—Thomas Edison, Henry Ford, George Westinghouse, and John Burroughs. The last, perhaps the greatest naturalist of his day and certainly a man with rare gifts for communicating the outdoor world, made a deep impression on the young man. Many years later, when Rutledge won the John Burroughs Medal for his natural history writing, he must have looked back on the glad occasion of their initial meeting with warm reflection.

Shortly after his graduation from Union, Rutledge accepted what supposedly was an interim position teaching English at Pennsylvania's Mercersburg Academy. He was still shy of his twenty-first birthday, and when the wife of William Mann Irvine, the headmaster, met him, she unthinkingly blurted out: "He will never do—he's too young." As matters turned out, Mrs. Irvine's snap judgment proved inaccurate on several scores. The "temporary" post launched a teaching career at Mercersburg which stretched over the next thirty-three years. Moreover, in 1907 the young man who had been greeted with such skepticism married Florence Louise Hart, Mrs. Irvine's younger sister. Florence Hart was a lovely Southern belle who, as a published poet, shared her husband's literary interests and made him an ideal helpmate for the twenty-seven years they were together.

Those busy, bustling years at Mercersburg were in many ways filled with joy. The three sons to whom the present work is dedicated were born, and from all accounts Rutledge proved a masterful, immensely popular teacher. In fact, most of the Hampton bucks he killed over the years fell to a cherished Parker double-barrel shotgun which was a gift from admiring students. Nonetheless, Hampton Plantation remained constantly in Rutledge's thoughts, and regular visits to the place of his roots marked Christmases and summer holidays. Particularly after the deaths of his parents in the 1920s, each return renewed Rutledge's vision of the day when he could again truly call Hampton home.

Meanwhile, he wrote in every spare moment. Necessity was one impulse underlying this literary outpouring, for a growing family and the dream of a restored Hampton posed financial demands which far outstripped his salary. The key to his productivity, however, lay in the fact that the muse which moved deep within him was the single most important motivating factor in his life.

Eventually his poems and magazine pieces would number in the thousands, and in collected form they constitute the basis for all but a handful of the books, more than fifty in all, which he published during his lifetime. In time, Rutledge's literary endeavors earned him considerable renown. By the conclusion of World War I he was already well on his way to becoming a nationally recognized writer on natural history, outdoor sports, and the South's way of life. At an early stage in his literary career he began winning prizes in essay and story contests, and from the 1920s on honors were bestowed on him with great regularity. In the course of his career Rutledge would be awarded at least a dozen honorary degrees and was elected to membership in the American Society of Arts and Letters.

A real watershed in Rutledge's literary career came when he was named South Carolina's first poet laureate in 1934. At this juncture he began thinking seriously about a permanent return to the Palmetto State and getting on with the massive project of restoring Hampton Plantation to the glories of bygone days. Several factors coalesced to strengthen his resolve in this regard. The death of his first wife in 1934 turned his thoughts even more longingly toward Hampton, as did his subsequent marriage, in 1936, to a childhood sweetheart, Alice Lucas. Then too, his three sons had all reached manhood, and their departure from home eased the financial burden which a return to Hampton would involve.

Still, the move back to Hampton in 1937, coming as it did while the Depression held the country in its deadly grasp, was a daring one. There would be a small stipend coming to Rutledge as state poet laureate, and presumably he had accumulated some retirement benefits during his years of teaching. He could also count on royalties from his books, and the post-Pennsylvania years would see no noticeable abatement in the appearance of new books and the articles from which they were shaped. Still, it took strong resolve to retire from Mercersburg and make that final pilgrimage back to Hampton.

Rutledge spent most of what remained of his life, save for a period in his final years when poor health saw him move to Spartanburg to live with a sister, at Hampton. There he wrote, supervised the restoration of the plantation home (which dated back to the mid-eighteenth century) and its grounds, hunted, hosted countless visitors, and lived to the hilt the life of a Southern squire.

It was a portion of Rutledge's life which had plenty of gladness, but there was sadness too. Prince Alston, his beloved black friend who had been a constant companion in childhood and always the first to greet him when he returned to Hampton, had died. So too were many of the other "henchmen" to whom he frequently pays tribute in his work.

Indeed, in speaking of Rutledge and his black friends, it is important to recognize that modern sensibilities may be offended by the manner in which he writes of the blacks who were such a prominent part of life at Hampton Plantation. We live, however, in different times, and to judge the mores of the past from the perspective of the present is unfair. For those who might be inclined to condemn Rutledge on this score, some of his words from *God's Children* (1947) are worth pondering:

> Of what America will be in the days to come, and of what the Negro will be, I have no knowledge. Tomorrow in tremendous night reposes. I only know that the strength and beauty and glory of our country as we know it today have been in part due to a race originating in the Dark Continent, long held in slavery and now free to work out its own destiny. Its past has many flowing, if humble pages. If its future, with its superior opportunities, shall achieve even as much as its past did with its severe limitations, there will be made to our nation's history an inestimable contribution.

To Rutledge, blacks were part of an extended plantation family. The old "huntermen" taught him well the ways of wild creatures, opening up before him "the pages of nature's gigantic green book," and he felt a debt of gratitude to them which he expressed time and again in his writing. And Prince Alston was his closest friend. He called Prince "A Comrade to My Heart" and wrote that he "brought to my heart a peace the world could not give."

The loss of Prince deeply saddened Rutledge, and after his return to Hampton, other cherished aspects of his earlier years faded away. Even the glories of the Hampton Hunt, which Irvine Rutledge has poignantly described as "a period of twenty shining years," came to a premature end. Middleton Rutledge was killed in a traffic accident in 1943, and at the same time the winds of World War II carried young Archibald and Irvine Rutledge to duty overseas. Even after the conflict was over, with one member of the inseparable quartet gone the Hampton Hunt's postwar years were not the same.

Yet each day brought its bright moments, many of them centering on the pilgrimages Rutledge's readers made to Hampton. There they were ever assured of a warm welcome. Similarly, the daily mail brought letters from admirers, always faithfully answered. For exercise, there was the pleasure that a ramble about Hampton's grounds provided. Schoolchildren came to admire South Carolina's gentle patriarch of letters, there were still members of the Alston clan willing to share a hearty laugh or drop whatever was in hand for a hunt, and memories of the past were there to provide comfort in the present.

As Rutledge eased into octogenarian status the years began to take a physical toll, but the fires which fueled him as a writer still burned brightly. As late as 1970 one of his finest books, *The Woods and Wild Things I Remember*, was published. That same year also witnessed an event which gave Rutledge great pleasure while assuring the preservation of his beloved Hampton. He sold Hampton Plantation to the state of South Carolina with the stipulation that the home and grounds be maintained and open to the general public. In a touching indication of how much Prince Alston had meant to his life, the agreement also specified that members of the Alston family were to be employed as staff as long as they desired.

Three years later, on September 15, 1973, just five weeks shy of his ninetieth birthday, Rutledge died. Fittingly, the end came at the Summer Place in McClellanville where he had been born, thus completing the full circle of his life in a fashion one can only admire and envy. The sweet Southern scribe who was Archibald Rutledge now belongs to that world we have lost. Yet he still enriches us with the music and magic of his words, and the sedate, stately columns of Hampton still stand to form a tangible link with the past. The enduring wisdom of his words and his evocation of all that was good about the plantation way of life are Rutledge's gifts to posterity. All who love beautifully crafted literature and Southern tradition should be grateful for his legacy.

PART I
FAMILY AND FRIENDS

Archibald Rutledge was a sociable soul, a man blessed with an exceptional gift for cherishing the companionship of both family and an ever-widening circle of friends. In his later years he welcomed all and sundry to Hampton, genially embracing them as an extended family. Throughout his long life he also conducted a voluminous correspondence, and even after his fame brought him a flowing, growing stream of letters, he faithfully replied to all who wrote him. It was typical of the man's generous nature that, once he had achieved some degree of renown, he had small cards printed with several of his favorite poems. He would send these to admirers, usually with a personal message, and any schoolchild (or class) who contacted him could count on being so favored. One can only marvel at how he kept abreast of his correspondence and still found time to write his stories and articles. What was even more striking about Rutledge's gregariousness and sense of familial closeness, however, was his ability to breathe life into personal experiences in a fashion which makes the reader feel almost like "kinfolks." To join him, even vicariously, is to know something of that hospitable aura which typified Low Country Carolina of his day.

Reading books which focus on Rutledge's adolescence, most notably *My Colonel and His Lady* (1937) and *Tom and I on the Old Plantation* (1918), rapidly leads to realization that in many ways his lifelong love of camaraderie was rooted in an idyllic childhood. Wherever his career carried him, to Porter Military Academy in Charleston, Union College in New York, better than three decades at Pennsylvania's Mercersburg Academy, and finally full circle to the beloved environs of Hampton Plantation, there was fellowship and togetherness.

Rutledge is probably best remembered as a writer on nature and outdoor subjects, but many of his most appealing stories deal with family and friends. The best of these pieces are redolent of hearth and home—they set imagination's senses free with savory smells of country cooking, the warmth and welcome of a cheery hardwood fire ablaze, and the sounds of joyful reunion. In these tales the compassion and caring which were salient characteristics of the man shine through. His was a special ability to carry readers, employing simple yet moving scenarios, into his memory's rich storehouse.

In the selections which follow we join Rutledge as he shares hallowed memories—of holidays, festive occasions, and other special moments. In a warm, winsome fashion he resurrects a world we have largely lost. To accompany him into that world, traveling darkening yet delightful roads at a leisurely pace, is to understand something of the qualities he treasured in life. As we follow his literary footsteps we come to know him as a boy and as a man. And, thanks to the magnetism of his words, the magic of his world, and the mesmerism of his character, we are captivated.

My Colonel

He lives on one of the great rice plantations that lie along the Santee River in the coast country of South Carolina. His home was the headquarters of the Swamp Fox, the dauntless Francis Marion. On his visit to the far South, after the Revolution, the first gentleman in America, Gen. George Washington, breakfasted there. It has been the home of one of the most famous of Colonial Governors, and a second home to two signers of the Declaration. The noble old house itself looks like history. It has that alien yet generous majesty that is indefinably associated with the traditions of refinement. And because of this same spirit, which is in perfect harmony with the temper of its master, its hospitable doors are open wide to all comers. The old stage coach road from Charleston to Georgetown runs through the plantation; and even of late years, when travel on that route has been infrequent, my Colonel's old home has given welcome and shelter to half a score of belated travelers at one time. It has been known to have gathered under its kindly roof during a single evening such a list as this: a horse doctor, a wandering spiritualist, a bishop, a whiskey drummer, a Presbyterian minister of the old school, an insurance agent, and a bibulous hunter. (No sequence is followed in this list save that which its very incongruity suggests.) And all of these my Colonel delights to entertain.

That he is six feet tall; that one shoulder droops because of two wounds, one from Malvern Hill and one from Gettysburg; that his head is regal in its carriage, with its thin aquiline nose, its eyes the color of the blue morning sky, its strong and tender mouth, half

From *Old Plantation Days* (1921).

hidden under the heavy white mustache; that the cast of his countenance is noble and proud—all these are in a way descriptive; but it is
by suggestion that you come to know the real character of the man.

Every Negro in the county knows and loves my Colonel. In his
dealings with them he is not as other men; he is unique and picturesque to a high degree. At eight o'clock in the morning he will
exhaust his nerves and his expletives on the old reprobate, Wash
Green. (Once a year, when he votes, he is known by his full name:
George Washington Alexander Burnsides Green.) He will stalk back
and forth in a black rage, cursing the stupidity of the ragged Negro
who stands the fire well, and who keeps a cunning and humble
silence. He will pause anon to pull a flower and to look over his
beloved river and pine woods, while his eyes soften momentarily and
his face is illumined by tender memories. But his reverie is as short
as it is romantic. With double vehemence he descends on the lazy
miscreant; then finally he will stride into the house, fumble in the
harness-room over old buckles and broken chains, in the hall over
tattered gloves and an outworn rifle, wondering the while, with
growing contrition, whether he has not been too hard on poor Wash.
At length he will be drawn—and it is chivalric to consider this appeal
involuntary—to the great mahogany sideboard in the dining-room.
Here he takes what he calls a precaution. (Sometimes he styles it a
mild interjection.) This he accompanies with a silent toast: perchance
to some visionary memory, perchance to some fair lost face out of
the haunted past that lives in his heart. Then he will stretch himself
in the huge arm-chair, where the Swamp Fox once dozed, and soon
will be deep in a cherished copy of Kipling—the only modern poet
with whom he is familiar, although he used to be thoroughly versed
in the works of Burns, Byron, and Tennyson. He reads Fuzzy Wuzzy,
Gunga Din, and the Recessional. He knows this last by heart, and he
cannot sit still under its powerful influence. So he walks out on the
front piazza and down the steps, chanting the solemn and tremendous lines. There, under a big live-oak, with its gray, sighing banners
of moss, he comes abruptly upon Wash Green, who has been biding
his time. And now, indeed, the former things are passed away. For
an hour they stand under the great oak and talk of the old times
(being oblivious of the immediate and painful past). Then my Colonel,
with a certain air of mystery about him, goes back into the house.

Presently he reappears with his arm full of plunder. On closer inspection this would be seen to consist of a coat, two shirts, an old pair of leggins, and a plug of tobacco. His exit from the doorway is made somewhat surreptitiously, for more practical members of the family are apt to keep a hard eye on his generosity. But he reaches Wash in safety, and bestows his gifts with the old love in his eyes.

"W'ere iz I gwine see my Boss again?" queries Wash as he turns to go.

My Colonel's answer is a singular one; with the face of one reading the commination service he holds his right arm horizontal, with the thumb pointing dismally downward. Wash comprehends, and is convulsed; and as he crosses the field he breaks into shouts of laughter. Meanwhile, his master, humming happily the chorus of a love song, popular long before the War, returns to the dining-room and takes a double precaution.

As it is with Wash, so it is with all the Negroes. My Colonel knows by name, character, parentage and proclivities every little pickaninny on the nearby plantations. And as a rule they make splendid pigmy workmen. One of my Colonel's right-hand men is Three Cents, who is only eight years old. His mother called him that the day he was born. "Caze," she said, with more justice than mercy, "he made such a po' showin'." Another one of his diminutive protégés is Monk. After this fashion he got his name: his mother, casting about vainly for something to call him, was at length persuaded to wait until some marked proclivity of her child should give her a clue as to an appropriate appellation. When he was three years old he began to practise prehensile traits with his toes; he picked switches with them, and in climbing used them with remarkable skill; whereupon he was promptly christened Monk.

My Colonel is a lover of wild flowers; and the Santee woods are a paradise for them. On every hand in my Colonel's country Nature is riotous with her beauty and abundance. She is eager to retake what man has abandoned; and one by one the great plantations are falling to decay and desolation. Well she knows how to clothe a ruin, how to veil a cemetery, how to drape a tomb. And in this sweet silent land her flowers make lovely what were otherwise touched with the sadness of spiritual loneliness and pain. Yet, of these subconscious elements, my Colonel is hardly aware. He rides into the bay-branch and breaks a great fragrant cluster of snowy blooms for his wife; he reins in his horse to watch the humming birds at work and play; and he drenches his soul in the beauty of the pines, of the flowering thickets, and of the tender radiance of the blossoming fields. Of the flowers in the garden, he loves the red rose best; for half a centry ago his mother used to wear one in her hair. He even went so far in sentiment once as to write a little verse about a red rose; but he never showed it to any one, having always a deep regard for the sanctity of personal emotions.

My Colonel is the truest sportsman in the world. It is fifteen years since his youngest son, then but twelve years old, was so forgetful of his breeding one day as to shoot a quail on the ground. And to this hour his father cannot think of the incident without a profound feeling that the family has suffered shame and disgrace. One summer a neighboring rice planter shot a doe that had been destroying his pea field. Two days later a Negro who worked in the turpentine woods found the fawn starving and brought it to my Colonel. The Negro said that the old gentleman nearly cried when he saw the poor little creature; and he fed it himself with a bottle, covered it from the dew at night, and so saved its life. It finally grew into a three-prong buck that ate all the geraniums and kept the lawn shaggy; but my Colonel never regretted playing the Samaritan.

Touching matters of a religious nature, he is not self-conscious. He is reverent. He has nothing in common with those who say in their hearts that there is no God; for he has passed through many waters, and has found Him in their depths. He always says his prayers, though on cold nights he is apt to cut them short. His favorite prayer is that of the Publican, and he often repeats it with comforting contrition.

With very little persuasion he will tell you about the War—and, of course, there is but one war to him. Though he bears two wounds, he is free from any taint of bitterness of self-pity. "To the brave men on both sides," he will say, lifting his glass for a toast, "to the brave men who fought and the braver women who waited." And to him Gettysburg will always be the greatest disaster in history.

But best of all you will love my Colonel because of his genuine heart. He will meet you in a dugout cypress canoe, ten miles from the plantation; and at midnight in a pouring rain will take you off the stranded tug-boat. Before long he will tell you of the time when, running his Kentucky mare at full speed, he killed the two giant bucks as they jumped the road. It is his way of crowning you with his love and confidence.

His eyes will fill when he tells you good-bye. But as he stands waving to you from the desolate ricefield banks, you will catch the gleam of his eyes and the light of his smile. And you will remember him as a rare and true type of the Southern gentleman.

I Leave Home

After my boyhood years crowded with adventure and happiness, I began to have—sensing that the end of my old life was near—a feeling of adoration for Hampton House. Every time I came in the gate, my heart beat faster to see, across the wide pasture lands, happy in the light of morning or of noonday or of the setting sun, or gleaming in the orchid-glow of moon and stars, the white pillars, the glimmering windows, the great chimneys spouting smoke. The old home began to seem like a human heart—generous, understanding, unchanged by the years, wistful and thoughtful. I began to feel that it is a terrible thing to love a place—if one must leave it. Nor did the weeping beauty of Hampton's woodland setting make the thought of parting any easier.

I was to leave my family circle to go away to school, then to college. I was to leave Gabriel and Prince and Martha. The fields and woods I loved I was to desert. Was it well? The dogs and the horses and the cattle—these that had been my care—I was to leave these too. The sweet bays, the wood-violets; the pines and the cypresses and the hollies—these I was going to abandon. But my loyalty to all these was attested by the consciousness that they would always be kept beautiful in my heart.

Who was I to complain over my lot? I had had a full and joyous boyhood, with enough care and responsibility to deepen the experiences that were mine. Wherever life was to lead me, my memories would always be with me. I would always hear the music of those early years: the mockingbirds, the Carolina wrens, the calling of the

From *Wild Life of the South* (1935); also in *The Woods and Wild Things I Remember* (1970), with slight revisions.

wild ducks; the wind in the pines; the voice of my mother reading to me; and the voices of the Negroes singing "Jesus will fix it for me" and "Deep down in my heart." Yes, deep down in my heart these would always echo.

We were to leave Hampton early in May to spend the summer in the mountains of North Carolina. In September I was to go to school in Charleston. I remember my last evening as a boy on the plantation.

I stood on the white porch at Hampton, glimmering in the purple darkness. Faded was the pageantry from the west. But I could see faintly outlined against the sky the great oaks I loved, the lordly pines in which my dreams of strength and aspiration came true. Far off I could hear the Negroes laughing and whooping. A whippoor-will wailed in the fragrant woods.

Night had not only invested the earth, but my heart as well. All was the night's. I envied the Negroes who could stay at home. I envied the trees, the soil, now exhaling dewy odors, the birds asleep in the cassina bushes and in the oaks. I leaned against a white pillar and thought of my boyhood and its vanished days; of Prince and Hugh, of my animal friends, Ruby, Rowley, Nymph, and Music.

Over the oaks in the avenue the moon arose, argent, intolerable in pagan beauty, silvering all as in a picture of eternity.

Ringwood, one of our old hounds, discovering my loneliness and his own, came up the steps to me. I laid my hand on his head.

Those Were the Days

I am thinking of a time forty to forty-five years ago, and of some of the ordinary hunting and fishing experiences I then enjoyed. I am in some doubt as to whether those were the days or not. In contrast to these times, game and fish were, with some exceptions, abundant; so much so, in fact, that there could hardly have been that keenness of appreciation that one now enjoys in securing his quarry. It is generally true that the scarcer a thing is, the more deeply we appreciate it; a voluntary kiss from a man's wife is usually so rare as to be miraculous . . . But at any rate, here are a few of the experiences that, nearly a half-century ago, did not seem to me remarkable. If some of these same things were to happen to me today in the woods and on the waters, I'd surely think I was a liar!

In the year 1904, when I was twenty years old, I went from Washington, D.C., where I had been working on a newspaper, to teach in a school in the great Cumberland Valley of southern Pennsylvania. It was then, as it still is, a comparatively wild country, full of shaggy mountains, wild glens, limestone springs, trout streams. There a man can live where he can enjoy all the advantages of civilization; yet a half-hour's drive will take him into grouse, wild turkey, and deer country. Insofar as I can remember, trout fishing was then to me an entirely new and different kind of sport. I had never up to that time ever seen a brook trout. Reared on the Carolina coast, where the charr is unknown, I believe the whole business of trout-fishing was a closed book to me. I knew no more about it than an Eskimo knows of the Everglades.

From *Those Were the Days* (1955).

During my first autumn and winter in the grand Keystone State, I got acquainted with the hunting there. And among my best friends were the members of the outdoor fraternity in the little village in which I lived. Though I was a Rebel, and all of them were Yanks, we became as brothers. I was a stranger, and they took me in.

After the hunting season closed, I found, from haunting the hangouts of the Boys, that life would begin again with the opening of the trout season. Now, as I have said, I didn't then know a trout from a sucker. Like that of most ignoramuses about any sport, my interest at first was hardly more than mild. I guess you have to fall in love to understand what it means. I recall an old friend of mine, an inveterate duck hunter, who used to scorn and ridicule my deer hunting. He just couldn't see anything to it. At last I lured him deer hunting with me. Providentially, then he, with an 8-gauge gun, and at a distance of not more than thirty yards, blasted at and completely missed a whole herd of eleven deer. It was the making of him. After that he never wanted to hunt anything but deer. He came to be a pretty good shot at a buck; but to the end of his days he was haunted by the memory of the way he had utterly botched his first chance. His humiliation, I am sure, was accentuated by his having formerly characterized deer hunting as the most childish of all outdoor sports.

One year, when I was leaving for a Christmas vacation in Carolina, the headmaster of my Pennsylvania school, having heard of how I spent my leisure hours, asked me if I could not send him a little game from the plantation. He and his wife seemed to think, and with some justice, that the quality of the house party they were giving might be improved by the casual introduction of some venison, mallards, and quail. I promised not to disappoint him. Now mark that. Those were the days when a man *could* make such a promise and could keep it. It is many years now since I have made any similar promise.

I rather nonchalantly regaled that house party with venison, wild turkey, wild ducks, and quail. All were procured right near my plantation house with no especial effort. I remember sending twenty-six quail; and I believe it worth recording how I got these birds.

You know how all of us linger over a Christmas dinner.

It must have been at least three o'clock when I at length finished mine. On a brief mid-winter's afternoon, that does not give you very much time to hunt quail before dark. Yet, despite the waning day and despite the fact that I had no bird-dog, I decided to give bob-white a ramble. On my way through the yard I picked up two little Negro boys, Nebo and Cricket, to accompany me. They can often be very helpful on such a hunt.

At the time there was a great flood in the river; all the lowlands were deep under water, and their denizens had taken shelter on higher ground. Beyond the first cornfield that we crossed, there was a long low peninsula of broomsedge that jutted out into the yellow tide of the freshet. From a distance of at least two hundred yards I heard quail calling in that broomsedge. And it was not ordinary calling. It was as if several covies had gotten together, and were having a grand reunion.

And that is exactly what had happened. With my two little black henchmen close behind me, and my gun ready, I invaded the tall and tawny grass of the broomedge field.

The place was alive with quail; but they did not seem to be in covies; at least, they did not rise as such. Most of them got up singly or in pairs. I had hurriedly informed Nebo and Cricket that their job was to retrieve the birds I shot down.

The whole business lasted, I suppose, a half-hour. On that narrow hill above the waters of the flood there must have congregated eighty or ninety quail. The boys retrieved twenty-six for me.

At the time, the affair did seem unusual, but not especially remarkable. If it happened to me today, I'd be scared to tell the story of it.

It was during the time of that same flood that I saw the largest herd of whitetail deer I have ever seen together. There were twenty-eight. I counted them as they crossed a road just out of gunshot from me. No doubt the high waters had something to do with such a regular campmeeting congregation. Most of them were probably refugees from the flooded delta. In fact, they proved that they were strangers; for, though I was on the crossing they should have used, a crossing that all local deer residents would have used, they never came near it.

About five miles down the Santee River from my plantation home, rising strangely above the level of the vast delta country, there is a

sandy hill of considerable area known as Tranquillity. Fifty years a
Negro family lived there; and there it was that I used to get the kind
of duck shooting that now I just dream about.

The delta, some one hundred thousand acres in extent, had formerly been planted in rice; and the growing of this crop necessitated
a very complicated system of banks, canals, and ditches. Meandering
through the delta were some natural creeks. Now, in mid-winter,
especially with a sleety northeaster blowing, what could a wild duck
love more than these mazy marsh-hung creeks and canals, sunny
and warm and sheltered from the wind?

I remember leaving Tranquillity after breakfast one January morning with Charlie Lesesne, a Negro, who was to paddle me through
the lazy watercourses of the delta. At this sort of thing Charlie was
something of a genius. At the time I was only about twelve years old.
I had a single-barreled gun, and one precious box of twenty-five
shells.

Charlie paddled me for about four hours, holding to the creeks
rather than the canals; for, he told me, creeks had plenty of bends,
and our best chances of getting good close shots were as we rounded
the bends. Charlie warned me sagely: "Let him get that first jump
out of his system before you shoot; if you don't, you'll undershoot
him." I did undershoot several, but I made a good many doubles. I
shot nothing on the water. Charlie, who had been politely dubious
about me at first, seemed to gain confidence as the shooting pro-
gressed. At length I was down to my very last shell. As we eased
around a bend, about a dozen mallards flushed. I dropped three
green-headed drakes.

We were then some miles from Tranquillity. On the way back,
though we talked freely and paddled carelessly, I believe I could
have killed twenty-seven more mallards—that being the number we
had gathered in with one box of shells. I know it sounds incredible,
but the old days were sometimes like that. And when I think that my
father killed twenty-eight mallards at a single shot with an old Westley-
Richards muzzle-loader, my twenty-seven in twenty-five shots does
not seem remarkable. Later in my ducking experience I killed eighteen mallards with two barrels.

In contrast to big times those just described, I might say that only
a year ago I took a friend duck-shooting. He shot 33 shells, and did

not bring home a duck. "But I did hit one," he told me defensively. He is the kind of gunner who opens fire when the game first appears, whether or not it is a mile away. When I told him he should have waited, he countered defensively by saying, "If I had waited, they might not have come close enough."

I lived in the Cumberland Valley for more than thirty years. When I first went there, although there were plenty of fish, both deer and wild turkeys were very scarce. I saw the Game Commissioner, by stocking and by wise and salutary laws, bring them back. This undertaking would have been more difficult had automobiles then been in use. I used to walk to my hunting and fishing; and occasionally I hired a livery-stable team to go up Path Valley ten or twelve miles. There were not in those days, along the streams or in the hunting fields and mountains, any "foreigners." They came with cars.

I recall that a few years prior to World War I, I thought it not exceptional, at daybreak in the wild mountains of Franklin County, to count eighteen or twenty wild turkeys on the roost; or, in the course of a day's rambles, to come upon several flocks. It was an unusual thing for me then not to get my gobbler, usually on the first day.

Of course, when one thinks of hunting and fishing of the long ago, one is likely to remember the good and to forget the bad. Ammunition was not then so good. Transportation was sketchy. And then, of course, as always happens when you are dealing with wild game, there would be days when the woods appeared dead and the fields deserted. Fruitless hunts are by no means a modern invention.

Sometimes It Happens

N ext to getting a Republican to vote the New Deal ticket, the hardest thing known to me is to give a friend a shot at game—especially big game. Countless times I have failed at this. I remember posting a group of seven men on deer crossings, on a drive that had just those seven stands. I went away back in the woods and sat down to wait until the fireworks were over. And do you know that the only buck that was jumped came to me? Then, of course, the boys insisted that I had chosen the best stand! To tell the truth, the behavior of big game is unpredictable, and no man ought to make any promises to his pals about the certainty of getting a shot.

However, our hopes and plans are occasionally realized. Sometimes the thing does happen just as we hope and pray it will. As such occurrences are really rare, I thought it might be worth while to recount one that happened to me recently.

Two of my sons, one a surgeon and one in the Army, paid me a flying visit here at our old Carolina plantation. As they are great hunters, and as they could stay only two or three days, I was especially eager to give them some sport. The first morning my plans went wrong, for a fine 8-point buck came to me instead of to one of them. But they were generous, and genuinely glad that I got him. A little later that morning I had a peculiar adventure that leads up to the story I want to tell.

We were driving Peachtree, a deserted plantation, which belonged, in colonial days, to Thomas Lynch, Jr., youngest signer of the Declaration of Independence. I had placed my boys where I thought they would get a shot, while I went down on a long peninsula that juts

---

From *Those Were the Days* (1955).

into the great Santee River. The trees on this point are mainly dog-woods and liveoaks, and they had a heavy crop of berries and acorns.

I had gone but a little way through these wildwoods, trying to pick out a place where I could intercept a buck if he made up his mind to swim the river, when I noticed very fresh turkey scratchings. These are always readily identified from the pawings of deer and the bur-rowings through the leaves of squirrels. Wild turkeys really sweep the leaves aside; and if you look closely, you can see the long scratches of their toenails in the earth.

Looking ahead carefully, I saw the whole flock, about twenty of them—a grand sight. Of course, they had seen me first. They always do. And in such a case, as I had a shotgun and they were out of range, there was nothing for me to do. But they did something that gave me a chance. They ran down the gentle slope of the wooded hill into the dense wild marsh of an old deserted rice field.

It is perhaps characteristic of all wild game that is frightened that if it gains the shelter afforded by any kind of dense cover it will stop, at least momentarily. Changing my shells from buckshot to No. 2's, I dashed down the hill and straight into the marsh. As I expected they would, the turkeys had stopped. They were all around me, but most of them ducked off through the marsh.

One old gobbler took wing, and I hailed him down. Another one flew far across the old marsh and was killed by my son Middleton on his deer stand. The flock itself was badly scattered; and to a turkey hunter, that is the best news that is to be had. I knew it would be useless to hunt for them any more at the time; but after a few hours, when they began to call together, we might do something further to correct the meat shortage.

We hunted deer until about an hour before sundown, when I said, "Now, boys, I'll call one up to you."

We were all four in the same general neighborhood. My youngest son, Irvine, was with me, as was Prince, my faithful Negro hunter. My son Middleton was a few hundred yards away. About four hun-dred yards from the river, and jutting out into the marsh, there is a small but dense swamp, where the cypresses and tupelos are laden with Spanish moss. It's the very kind of place where wild turkeys love to roost. I well remember the time when they could be found roosting in bare trees; but that time has passed.

Game gets educated. Now turkeys prefer dense evergreen such as pines; and if they roost in deciduous trees at all, it will be only in those that are shrouded in moss, and usually have squirrel nests and bunches of mistletoe in them. They have a keen eye for camouflage. I suppose the most perfect roosting tree in my part of the country is the live-oak, which grows to immense size.

I put Irvine and Prince in the very heart of this little swamp, while I went to the border facing the river and began to call. By that time the sun was down, and a radiant afterglow suffused the lonely swamp and the wild river-marsh. After only a few minutes, on a huge cypress far across on the river bank, I both heard and saw a big gobbler go to roost. He was clearly outlined against the sunset sky. At such a time, when some distance from him, you can usually identify a wild turkey by the way he cranes his neck and turns his head and by the length of his spade-shaped tail.

As soon as I saw this old bird I made Irv' and my Negro change places with me. I wanted my son ahead of me when I called. From where I was sitting in the swamp I could still see the gobbler.

I had not called more than twice when he began to move on the cypress limb. Then he suddenly launched himself in our direction, coming like a black projectile straight for us. No surveyor can run a straighter line than a wild turkey if he is really coming to your call. It was a hard shot, but my son nailed him fairly, and the great bird fell almost in my lap. He was a grand prize. With these old veterans of the river swamps, I never use, and I never let my sons use, anything but 2's.

"It isn't over," I told my son. "They are just going to roost."

Ten minutes later I heard a great commotion behind me, and another gobbler took a tall tupelo almost over my head. I shot him down, but this meant little to me compared to the thrill I got out of calling one to my soldier son. As it was now pretty dusky, we headed for home. But I told my boys that night that we ought to try it again in the morning. I was dubious about our chances of going, for it had turned warm and had clouded over heavily.

The turkey call I use is one of my own invention, and for some reason its tone has a fatal fascination. Probably it is in the wood. I tried about twenty-six different kinds until I finally hit on common willow for the box and yellow locust for the cover. I have long since rejected both apple and cedar as too squeaky. I have a good call made of mahogany and curly maple, but the willow has a mellowness about it that apparently no other wood has.

With this call I have lured gobblers across the river, out of deep swamps where they had plenty to feed, and from the crests of giant pines and cypresses, where all night long they have slept in the silver privacy of starlight. In dealing with this bird, it is always a great mistake to call too much. If I ever get an answer, or if I ever have reason to believe that a turkey is coming, I never call again.

Well, so far I had given one of my sons some sport. If I could do the same thing for the other, that would be something. But, as I have said, it's not wise to make promises about getting wild and wary game to go to certain people.

The next day dawned wet and misty. By daylight we were at our appointed stations, but this time I had my son Middleton with me. We went to the wooded peninsula where I had originally run on this flock. The woods were still, dripping, shrouded. Putting him off to one side by an oak, I sat on a pine stump and touched my call. In a case of this kind, I give about three notes, and then wait five minutes or so before calling again.

On a dark morning, threatening rain, wild turkeys may stay on the roost until long after daylight. They dislike wet; and on a rainy day, when they do come to earth, they move about very little. I have found them at such a time either loafing in some sheltered place or following old roads and trails. Sometimes, instead of flying down, they will walk the limbs, or fly from tree to tree, talking all the while in subdued tones befitting the weather.

As soon as we were posted and I thought that the time was about right, I touched my call. Almost immediately I heard a turkey, directly in front of me and about two hundred yards away, fly toward me, from one tree to another. I knew it was coming, but to me—not to my son.

I therefore tiptoed toward him, making him stand in front of a big live-oak while I sat on the ground behind the tree and called again. I did not even look up. It was my business to call; the rest of the whole affair I left in his hands, knowing well that he could take care of the situations, as I had begun to teach him woodlore when he was only five years old.

Turkeys do not like to come down on any kind of day until they can see clearly all the surroundings on the ground. It was still rather dusky, and I did not know how long it might be before this wily old strategist would sail earthward. Strangely, I did not even hear him fly, for like a grouse a wild turkey can sometimes take wing with little or no noise. I was in the act of giving my most pleading call when Middleton's gun roared forth, and I heard him run forward. A moment later I saw him pick up a grand gobbler, which he had killed on the ground at sixty yards.

The extreme weight of one of these turkeys of the pure wild strain is about twenty-one pounds, and this one was as fine as they grow. No sooner were we headed for the car then the rains descended, and the floods came, and the winds blew. Gathering the other hunters, we got home safely, but in a perfect torrent.

In the firelit room of the old plantation home, eating our breakfast of mallards, grits, cornbread and coffee, we reviewed our little experience with that flock of turkeys. We had taken five, leaving about sixteen; all those we had killed were gobblers; the first two had been killed by fast maneuvers, and the other three had been called up. All three of us had had a share in the executing. The whole happening had been unusual and most satisfying—two of my boys had made a flying trip home, and I was privileged to call up an old gobbler for one in the twilight of the evening and another for my second son in the twilight of the morning.

Why I Taught My Boys
To Be Hunters

I have said that my hunting has often been solitary; but that was chiefly in the early days. During the last twenty-five years I have rarely taken to the woods and fields in the shooting season without having one or more of my own sons with me. Few human relationships are closer than those established by a mutual contact with nature; and it has always seemed to me that if more fathers were woodsmen, and would teach their sons to be likewise, most of the so-called father-and-son problems would vanish.

Providence gave me three sons, only about a year and a half apart; and since it was not possible for me to give them what we usually call the advantages of wealth, I made up my mind to do my best by them. I decided primarily to make them sportsmen, for I have a conviction that to be a sportsman is a mighty long step in the direction of being a man. I thought also that if a man brings up his sons to be hunters, they will never grow away from him. Rather the passing years will only bring them closer, with a thousand happy memories of the woods and fields. Again, a hunter never sits around home forlornly, not knowing what in the world to do with his leisure. His interest in nature will be such that he can delight in every season, and he has resources within himself that will make life always seem worth while.

Hunters should be started early. As each one of my boys reached the age of six I gave him a single-shot .22 rifle, and I began to let him go afield with me. For a year or so I never let him load the gun, even with dust shot; but I just tried to give him some notions of how to handle it, of how to cross a ditch or a fence with it, and in what direction to keep the muzzle pointed.

From *An American Hunter* (1937).

It was a great day for each youngster when he shot his first English sparrow with a .22 shot shell.

From the time when the first one was six years old, I could never get into my hunting clothes without hearing, "Dad, take me along!" Sometimes an argument was added: "I will shoot straight. I will put it on him!" To these winning pleas I have always tried to give an affirmative answer, even when I had to alternate carrying a played-out boy and a played-out puppy. But I knew that I was on the right track when I was trying to impress on the younger generation the importance of shooting straight. I directly applied to my own children that old copy-book maxim, "Teach the young idea how to shoot." I think the rod and gun better for boys than the saxophone and the fudge sundae. In the first place, there is something inherently manly and home-bred and truly American in that expression, "shooting straight." The hunter learns that reward comes from hard work; he learns from dealing with nature that a man must have a deep respect for the great natural laws. He learns also, I think, in a far higher degree than any form of standardized amateur athletics can give him, to play the game fairly.

Most of our harmless and genuine joys in this life are those which find their source in primitive instincts. A man who follows his natural inclinations, with due deference to common sense and moderation, is usually on the right track. Now the sport of hunting is one of the most honorable of the primeval instincts of man. What human thrill is there in lounging into a grimy butcher-shop and sorrowfully surrendering a hard-earned simoleon for a dubious slab of inert beef? Certainly any true man would far rather trudge fifteen miles in inclement weather just for a chance at a grouse. Even if he gets nothing, he will be a younger and a better man when he gets home, and with memories that will lighten the burden of the days when he cannot go afield.

A lot of good people, seeing me rearing my sons to be woodsmen, have offered me advice. "How can you love nature and yet shoot a deer?" "How can you bear to teach those children to kill things?"

These parlor naturalists and lollypop sentimentalists, whose knowledge of nature is such that they would probably take a flying buttress for a lovely game bird, are incapable of understanding that it is far less cruel to kill a wild deer than it is to poleax a defenseless ox in a stall. The ox has no chance; but the deer has about four chances out of five against even the good hunter. Besides, I have a philosophy which teaches me that certain game birds and animals are apparently made to be hunted, because of their peculiar food value and because their character lends zest to the pursuit of them. It has never seemed to me to be too far-fetched to suppose that Providence placed game here for a special purpose.

Hunting is not incompatible with the deepest and most genuine love of nature. Audubon was something of a hunter; so was the famous Bachman; so were both John Muir and John Burroughs. It has always seemed to me that any man is a better man for being a hunter. This sport confers a certain constant alertness, and develops a certain ruggedness of character that, in these days of too much civilization, is refreshing; moreover, it allies us to the pioneer past. In a deep sense, this great land of ours was won for us by hunters.

Again, there is a comradeship among hunters that has always seemed to me one of the finest human relationships. When fellow sportsmen meet in the woods or fields or the lonely marshes, they meet as friends who understand each other. There is a fine democracy about all this that is a mighty wholesome thing for young people to know. As much as I do anything else in life I treasure my comradeships with old, grizzled woodsmen. Hunting alone could have made us friends. And I want my boys to go through life making these humble contacts and learning from fellow human beings, many of them very unpretentious and simple-hearted, some of the ancient lore of nature that is one of the very finest heritages of our race. Nature always solves her own problems; and we can go far toward solving our own if we will listen to her teachings and consort with those who love her.

In the case of my own boys, from the .22 rifle they graduated to the .410 shotgun; then to a 20-gauge; then a 16; then a 12. I was guide for my oldest son, Arch, when he shot his first stag. We stalked him at sundown on Bull's Island, in the great sea-marsh of that magnificent preserve, creeping through the bulrushes and the myrtle bushes until we got in a position for a shot. And that night at the clubhouse, when I went to bed late, I found my young hunter still wide awake, no doubt going over our whole campaign of that memorable afternoon.

I was near my second son, Middleton, when he shot his first five stags. I saw all of them fall—and these deeds were done before he was eighteen.

I followed the blood-trail of the first buck my youngest son, Irvine, shot. He had let drive one barrel of his 16-guage at this great stag in a dense pine thicket. The buck made a right-about face and headed for the river, a mile away. He was running with a doe, and she went on across the water. The buck must have known that he could not make it, for he turned up the plantation avenue, actually jumped the gate, splashing it with blood, and fell dead under a giant live-oak only eighty yards from the house!

It's one thing to kill a deer, and it's another to kill one and then have him accommodate you by running out of the wilds right up to your front steps. That kind of performance saves a lot of toting. This stag was an old swamp buck with massive antlers. Last Christmas my eldest son had only three days' vacation; but he got two bucks.

Yes, I have brought up my three boys to be hunters; and I know full well that when the wild creatures need no longer have any apprehensions about me, my grandchildren will be hard on their trail, pursuing with keen enjoyment and wholesome passion the sport of kings. While other boys are whirling in the latest jazz or telling dubious stories on street corners, I'd like to think that mine are deep in the lonely woods, far in the silent hills, listening to another kind of music, learning a different kind of lore.

This privilege of hunting is about as fine a heritage as we have, and it needs to be passed on unsullied from father to son. There is still hope for the race when some members of it are not wholly dependent upon effete and urbane artificialities for their recreation. A true hunter will never feel at home in a night club. The whole thing would seem to him rather pathetic and comical—somehow not in the same world with solitary fragrant woods, rushing rivers and the elegant high-born creatures of nature with which he is familiar. Hunting gives a man a sense of balance, a sanity, a comprehension of the true values of life that make vicious and crazily stimulated joy a repellent thing.

I well remember the morning when I took all three of my boys on a hunt for the first time. I had told them the night before that we were going for grouse and had to make an early start for Path Valley. There must have been a romantic appeal in the phrase "early start," for I could hardly get them to sleep that night. And such a time as we had getting all the guns and shells and hunting clothes ready, and a lunch packed, and the alarm clock set! And now, nine years after that memorable day, we still delight in making early starts together.

That day, before we had been in the dewy fringes of the mountain a half hour, as we were walking abreast about fifty yards apart, we had the good fortune to flush a covey of five ruffed grouse. It was the first time that any of my boys had had a shot at this grand bird, which to my way of thinking outpoints every other game bird in the whole world, bar none. An old cock with a heavy ruff fell to Middleton's gun. A young cock tried to get back over Irvine's head. It was a gallant gesture, but the little huntsman's aim was true, and down came the prince of the woodland.

Arch and I were a little out of range for a shot on the rise, but ere long we flushed other birds, and I had the satisfaction of seeing him roll his first *Bonasa umbellus*. We were walking through some second growth, which was fairly thick. I had just been telling him that in such cover a grouse is mighty likely to go up pretty fast and steep to clear the tree-tops, where, for the tiniest fraction of a split second, it will seem to pause as it checks its rise and the direction of its flight, which is to take it like a scared projectile above the forest. I had been telling Arch that the best chance under such circumstances was usually offered just as the grouse got above the sprouts and seemed to hesitate.

I had just taken up my position in line when out of a tangle of fallen grape-vines that had been draping a clump of sumac bushes a regal grouse roared up in front of Arch. I could see the splendid bird streaking it for the sky and safety. At first I was afraid that Arch would shoot too soon, then that he would shoot too late; either one would be like not shooting at all. But just as the cock topped the trees and tilted himself downward the gun spoke, and the tilt continued, only steeper and without control. With a heavy thud the noble bird dropped within my sight on the tinted leaves of the autumnal forest floor.

Fellow-sportsmen will appreciate what I mean when I say that was a great day for me. When a father can see his boy follow and fairly kill our most wary and splendid game bird, I think the Old Man has a right to feel that his son's education is one to be proud of. I'd far rather have a son of mine able to climb a mountain and outwit the wary creatures of the wilderness than be able to dance the Brazilian busybody or be able to decide whether a lavender tie will match mauve socks. These little lisping men, these modern ruins, these lazy effeminates who could not tell you the difference between a bull and a bullet—it is not in these that the hope of America, that the hope of humanity, lies.

When Arch was thirteen, I had him up at daybreak with me one morning in the wilds of the Tuscarora mountains. From the crest of the wooded ridge on which we were standing we could see over an immense gorge on either side and beyond them, far away over the rolling ridges, northward and southward. It was dawn of the first day, and there were many hunters in the mountains. The best chance at a turkey in that country at such a time is to take just such a stand and wait for one to fly over or perhaps to come walking warily up the slope of one of the leaf-strewn gullies. We had been standing together for about fifteen minutes and had heard some shooting to the northward of us, three ridges away, when I saw a great black shape coming toward us over the tree-tops.

"Here he comes, son!" I told my youthful huntsman. "Hold for his head when he gets almost over you."

Three minutes later my boy was down on the slope of the gorge, retrieving a nineteen-pound gobbler, as proud as a lad could be, and entitled to be proud. It was all he could do to toil up the hill with his prize.

Irvine shot his first turkey on our plantation in Carolina. He was on a deer-stand when this old tom came running to him through the huckleberries. The great bird stood almost as tall as he did.

Middleton killed his first under peculiar circumstances. We walked into a flock together, at daybreak, and they scattered in all directions, but were too drowsy to fly far. He wounded a splendid bird, and it alighted in a tall yellow pine about a hundred yards from us. There was not enough cover to enable him to creep up to it, and the morning was so very still that I was afraid his first step would scare the gobbler from his lofty perch.

"I know what to do," he whispered to me as I stood at a loss to know what to advise." Don't you hear that old woodpecker hammering on that dead pine? Every time he begins to rap I'm going to take an easy, soft step forward. Perhaps I can get close enough."

"Go ahead," I told him, and stood watching this interesting stalk.

The woodpecker proved very accommodating, and every other minute hammered loudly on the sounding tree. Step by cautious step Middleton got nearer. At last he raised his gun, and at its report the gobbler reeled earthward. I thought the little piece of woodcraft very neatly executed.

If the sentimentalist were right, hunting would develop in men a cruelty of character. But I have found that it inculcates patience, demands discipline and iron nerve, and develops a serenity of spirit that makes for long life and long love of life. And it is my fixed conviction that if a parent can give his children a passionate and wholesome devotion to the outdoors, the fact that he cannot leave each of them a fortune does not really matter so much. They will always enjoy life in its nobler aspects without money and without price. They will worship the Creator in his mighty works. And because they know and love the natural world, they will always feel at home in the wide, sweet habitations of the Ancient Mother.

The Daisybank Table

It was sometime after our disgraceful behavior in the affair of Red Lightning before father would fall in very readily with any of the adventurous schemes that we proposed carrying through. And we had an especially difficult time persuading him to let us venture after the famous Daisybank Table. But our vital need of it finally overcame his scruples.

To be unable to give a wedding present to a person for whom we cared a great deal was painfully humiliating; yet it was the fall after the fatal storm of 1893, when every head of rice had been blackened and ruined by the salt tide that had submerged all the fields in the Santee country. Every one was "hard up." And it was at such a time that our nearest neighbor and one of our dearest friends had planned to be married. What in the world should we give her as a present? Her people, like ours, were plantation owners; so no gift characteristic of our picturesque life, such as a set of antlers or a barrel of plantation sweet potatoes, would serve. Moreover, there were no secrets between us; her mother knew all about our silver and china—having borrowed them on several state occasions; so there was no chance of our offering as a gift what had already become familiar as a loan.

After several family consultations, in which heirlooms were examined and rejected, our father at last suggested that we give as a wedding present the famous Daisybank table—if we could find it.

That table had a very romantic history. It was a beautiful piece of rosewood, and had been presented, about the year 1820, to Maj. Sydenham Desmond of Daisybank Place, in the Santee country, by

From *Tom and I on the Old Plantation* (1918).

the captain of a Spanish bark. It was a token of appreciation of the old major's kindness in having the captain nursed through an attack of yellow fever contracted in the coastwise trade. Later, the table was brought to our plantation and given to my grandmother by the major's son, who, according to tradition, might have been my grandfather, had he not fallen at the Battle of Antietam.

During the Civil War, the plantation was deserted, except for the Negroes. There was no fighting nearer than Charleston—forty-two miles away through the pineland; but wild rumors of advancing armies, of scouting foragers, and of pillaging marauders penetrated even to the pastoral retreats of the rice plantations. The Negroes stayed in their cabins, and looked after the crops as best they could without efficient supervision.

On several occasions, when rumors that the enemy were coming grew insistent, a few of the older and more trustworthy of the slaves went to the "great house," and bore from it into the woods the best pieces of furniture. The story is still told at home that old Peter McCoy, a veritable giant of a Negro, picked up, unaided, the massive mahogany sideboard, and carried it into the thickets by Spencer's Pond, half a mile away. Among the articles thus concealed was the famous and beautiful Daisybank table. Every piece except that had been recovered. We were given to understand that the table had been found in the woods by "a runaway Negro" (a criminal fugitive), who had taken it far up the river to Bear Wallow.

In the years after the war, no Southerner had time to trace lost heirlooms. Every man was trying to right the wreck of his fortunes, and to make some kind of living. Consequently, for a long time, nothing was done toward recovering the Daisybank table.

About 1880, my father went up the river to Bear Wallow, the strange Negro settlement about fifteen miles from home, for the express purpose of regaining his property. But evidently the man who had the table had got wind of his coming; although my father was met most respectfully, the answers given him were evasive, and he failed of his purpose. Yet he had noted a constrained attitude in the Negroes, and was convinced that one of them had the table. But he never found time and opportunity to go up the run again and try to find it.

All of us knew the history of the table; and on several occasions my brother and I had pleaded in vain for permission to go in search of it. I think the reason for the refusal was that there lived at Bear Wallow a Negro named West McConnor, who was a thorough desperado. He was a hunter and woodsman famous over three counties—a wild and ranging spirit, who was suspected of all kinds of lawlessness, and at whose door could be laid the evidence of three murders. Knowing all these facts, we had become rather reconciled to not going up the river, and were surprised when father himself suggested it.

"You boys are a good deal older than you were when you first asked me. I am willing for you to go if you take Prince. He is the only man in Berkeley County who can talk with West McConnor."

To take Prince meant that, whatever the success of the trip, we were assured of a comrade of good nature and good sense.

We wished to take the big .44 rifle, thinking that it might be an advantageous ally, but my father forbade it. He said we might take one of the light breech-loaders, if we liked, to shoot ducks in the river and squirrels in the cypresses along the banks; but we must limit our armament to that single piece.

We left the plantation at six o'clock on a warm December morning, taking the young flood up Warsaw Creek and out into the big Santee above Waterhorn place. The three of us were well balanced in the long, light, dugout cypress canoe; each of us had a broad-bladed paddle. We swept up the long reaches and took the frequent bends with a speed and a precision of which we were proud; for it showed how nearly in unison we could work. But after five or six miles, when we had come to a point in the river where the tide no longer helped us, we lost our pride, and settled down to hard work. Buckled down though we were to heavy paddling, we could not help noticing and admiring the marvelous country through which we were passing—a country that we had never seen, and one that few white men had ever penetrated.

The Santee was here a quarter of a mile wide; its waters were almost as black as those that drain a wood stream in the southern coast country. It was very deep, and flowed without sound or wave. So uniform was its current that the whole level expanse visible to the eye at any one moment appeared to move rather than to flow. The banks on either side were deeply wooded; and it seemed surprising that so far north of the equator the edges of a stream could show in winter such a dense growth of greenery. The cypresses prevailed; but there were many stately pines and cedars, hollies a hundred feet tall, and ancient live-oaks, massive and patriarchal. At some places we caught glimmering vistas between the stems of these trees; here and there canebrakes or tangled draperies of vines and creepers veiled from our eyes the mysterious forest beyond the river banks.

At last, about nine o'clock in the morning, when we were pretty well tired, we reached the landing place for the Bear Wallow settlement; and as we made the canoe fast, our hopes of regaining the Daisybank table rose high. We had at least accomplished the most difficult stage of the journey. From the rude landing the strange roadway, which seemed seldom used, entered the dark and forbidding woods, and was lost to our sight in their mystery and shadows.

"Prince, how far is it to Bear Wallow?" I asked.

" 'Tain't far, cap'n," he answered, gazing steadily at the dim opening in the forest; "it's only about two throws and a whoop."

"About how much?"

"If I throw a rock," the Negro explained, "then get that rock and throw it again; then get it again, and then whoop, them people in Bear Wallow can hear me whooping."

We took our way into the woodlands with some misgivings. By the time we had come to the end of the second "throw," the thinning ranks of the pines showed that we were nearing the settlement. Soon we came to a cabin or two, and heard the voices of Negroes; nor were we likely to hear any other voices there, for Bear Wallow was a Negro colony, and not more than a half-dozen white men had ever even seen it.

As we were going up the road, an odd thing happened. From their play in the sandy roadway, three little Negroes, innocent of clothes, seeing us approach, dashed frantically toward the cabins; but, prompted by some instinct of instant self-preservation, they dropped down in the tall grass beside the path. I have seen a fawn do the same thing. When we came up, there they lay, huddled in hiding. They had never before seen a white man, and they imagined we were specters. Farther on, we came to the settlement proper, and noticed one house that seemed especially large, and that occupied a central position.

"Dat's West McConnor's," said Prince; "and, boss men, if we gwine to find dat table, it will be right in dat house."

Having heard so much about the desperate character whose home we were approaching, this man who ruled the remote settlement with an authority as complete as that of the chief of an African tribe, we had expected to see an extraordinary figure; or, at least, a man powerful physically, who could rule by the might of his strength. When we approached the house, West McConnor came out.

We were amazed to find him a small, almost wizened, mulatto. He actually looked shy; but his countenance was inexpressibly cunning and crafty. I understood then, with something akin to disappointment, that his fame as a hunter must have been procured by his stealth and intelligence rather than by his strength and endurance. He made a rather sinister, but not impressive, figure as he stood in his doorway, waiting for us to come up.

He greeted us civilly but coldly, and was so unlike the Negroes we knew that we were completely baffled. With his sharp, shifting eyes, he questioned us searchingly, but his own dry speech was exceedingly uncommunicative. He accepted with grave thanks the gifts of tobacco, sugar, and coffee that we had brought; and even unbent so far as to ask after father. But it was clear that he wanted us to do most of the talking. That was just what we did not feel capable of doing; we were no match for this crafty little yellow man. So, while West stepped into the cabin for a moment to put away his gifts, we consulted with Prince.

"I tell you," Prince said, with a troubled look in his eyes, "you boss men go back of the potato patch there to see the big 'gator heads dat West throws out, and leave him to me."

We did as Prince suggested, crossed the narrow field, climbed the fence, and came to an open space under the giant yellow pines—and to one of the strangest sights I have ever witnessed. The whole of that open space, and it could not have been less than an acre in area, was strewn with bleached alligator bones. The Negro hunter, after taking the hide and a few steaks from the tail, had thrown the bodies out under the pines. We counted 119 skulls, and we did not count half of them. Some of the alligators must have been monsters, judging from the dimensions of their skulls. West McConnor had caught them from one end of the Santee delta to the other, and his toll had been heavy. From the innumerable teeth scattered about, we selected several dozen of the finest; then we returned to the Negro cabins.

Prince was standing where we had left him, but West was nowhere in sight. Prince had told us beforehand that West would never argue or seek to drive a bargain; he simply stated his terms, and then often disappeared, leaving the actual settlement to his wife, or to one of his sons.

"Well, Prince?" I asked, as we came up.

"West say," Prince answered, somewhat dubiously, "dat he never stealed dat table, but he got it in his house."

"Where is he and what will he take for it?" my brother asked.

"West done gone." Prince grinned; we understood that West did not care to tell just how he had come by the table.

"He say," Prince continued, "he will let you have the table if you will give him yo' breech-loadin' gun."

Tom and I looked at each other, and agreed to make the trade, although of all things, we hated to put another gun into West McConnor's hands. The gun was not an expensive one, whereas the table was invaluable. Tom handed the weapon to Prince.

"Take it in, Prince. Who's in the house? His wife? All right. And don't come back without the table."

Presently, from the cabin, Prince emerged, bearing before him the exquisite table that we knew at once must be the long-lost heirloom. We quickly saw that the little damage it had suffered during its thirty years of exile could be easily repaired.

Going home, we had the tide with us. We reached Hampton in safety; and what with the table and the wonderful assortment of alligator teeth we had brought, we were very happy.

So, after all, our loved neighbor got her wedding present. And she values it all the more because we told her the full story of its loss and its strange recovery.

My Favorite Hunting Story

For reasons that you will not find it difficult to understand, the great parable that Old Jim Alston told me is my favorite hunting story. Throughout the unpleasant episode known as the American Civil War, he was my father's Negro body-servant; and it was Jim who saved my father's life when, wounded and in a raging fever, he fell from his horse in the Potomac River during the Confederate retreat from Antietam. And the rescue was effected under the hot fire of Federal sharpshooters posted on the high rocky bluffs above the river.

After the war Jim was with us on the plantation for many years; but, being a Romeo of parts, he married or consorted with one dusky damsel after another. The last one took him with her to her own home, many miles from where Jim really belonged. My father never forgot Jim; and whenever they got together, they were like old cronies. I am afraid that I, being of a younger generation, forgot him. At least he had passed out of my mind for some years when one winter's day here he came, hobbling along with the help of a gnarled dogwood stick. He had walked sixteen miles—"all the way from Jeemstown," he told me.

Now, I knew very well that he had not come all that distance merely to see me. You know about these ulterior designs. But I made him happy and comfortable, and we had a good talk. Of course, I was expecting The Touch. But he had more legitimate business with me. The State of South Carolina, it seems, after discreetly waiting for the vast majority of her old soldiers to die off, had begun to pay pensions of fourteen dollars a month. I knew nothing

From *Those Were the Days* (1955).

of this; but Jim told me that the law had been in effect for about three years, and that he had not yet seen any of the money due him. He wanted me to get his pension, and to use some speed in the matter, as he did not have exactly a stranglehold on life. I promised the old man to go to work immediately, and I intended to do so. But I clean forgot.

Six months later, to my huge embarrassment, Old Jim appeared, driving in an ox-wagon this time. I told him the truth, and offered to lend him some money, promising at the same time to write the vital letter while he was with me.

He accepted the situation with that massive equanimity that a Negro alone possesses; and he had no word of blame or protest. But a light dawned in his fine old eyes, and he said, "Lemme tell you a thing."

We were sitting on an old bench in the plantation yard; and Jim, with his walking-stick drew sketches in the sand to illustrate his story, and also employed it to show how he used to handle his musket. Before he had gone to war, and for some years thereafter, he had been the plantation hunter and fisherman. His sole duty was to supply the Great House with fish and game; and I might add that such a life always seemed to me ideal.

"Some one mornin' in de fall, your Pa ride to my house; and when he used to come all the way to my house, I done already known I might as well hitch-up.

" 'Jim,' he say, 'Miss Elise comin' up from Cha'son, and Mr. Reginal', and Mr. Edmun', and they is bringin' friends. This is Thursday. We got to have two wild turkey for Sunday dinner. I would let you know befo', but the word just come.'

"I tell him not for worry. I done already know where a heaby gang of turkey is, and if I can't kill two, he ought to get another plantation gunnerman. I done tell him put his min' at rest; and I tell him he might as well tell that good-for-nothing Sallie gal what he got in the kitchen to mash up the peanuts for the dressin'. I been dat sho about the t'ing!

"Now, I been long time baitin' them turkey, but I say I better go right off and see if any feed left. I get my hamper-sack, I fill him with rice-tailin' and some broom-corn and some little rice. So I gone to the place. You know that high hill where Susie's cabin used to be, but the house burn down long ago? From there you hold for that long savanna where the Three Sisters used to be—them three big pines what been cut down when I was a boy. Well, sah, that is the place."

I mildly suggested to Jim that Susie's cabin and the Three Sisters were unknown to me, and that I doubted if I ever could follow his directions, even in thought. He eyed me quizzically. Then he smiled.

"Cap'n," he said, "you don't know enough for me to tell you anything. Howsomeever," he continued, "when I done get there, the pinestraw all rake up. They been there, but maybe two days before. All the feed been gone. I scatter all I had, and I say, I will come again tomorrow, and see if they find what I bring. Soon in the morning I gone there, and I wait. I gone in the blind and wait till sunrise, and here they come, 'bout forty eleven dozen wild turkeys. I been there a long time, until they done leave. So I say, "All right, I know you comin' tomorrow same time. If my hand be steady, the Big House will be full of turkeys!"

"That night, which was Friday night. I get ready. I get my ole musket down off the buckhorn rack. You know, Cap'n, you all is done got britches-loader. You just open the gun, slip in the shell, close the breech, and you all ready. But me, I got musket, and it takes time to load a musket the way I load him. 'Bout sundown it begin a jewin' rain. I say, 'All right. Ain't no rain gwine stop me!' I get my black power and I pour a heaby big load in a saucer on the table. Then I pour out the shot in a saucer same fashion. Then I 'xamine my caps, and lay two of them by the fire to dry out good. I gone outside and get some black moss, and I hang it by the fire to dry. I always used to wad my load with a strip I tear off my shirttail. But Ca'line—you know that wife I used to have what name Ca'line, that no-good 'oman—she say she tried sewing up what I done tear, and she says a man will tear up he clothes like no 'oman will do. That's why I use the moss for waddin'. Well, sah, I wipe off my ole musket, and I blow down the barrel, and the air come clear out of the nipple. I pour in the powder, a debbil of a big load. Then I wad him down with the moss what had done dried off by the fire. 'Bout that time Ca'line tell me it rainin' and we ain't got no wood in the house. So I put on my coat and gone after the wood. I get wet up, too, and I ask how come she did not set her mind on wood till night and rain done come down. But you better not start no argument with no 'oman. All is trickety, and when one begins to talk, a man have to stand back.

"When I rack the wood by the fire, I put the dry caps on the table. Ca'line ax me how come I ain't comin' to bed; so I gone to bed and drop sleep. But I can wake up all time of night, and 'bout the time all them hants and plateyes is creeping back to hide for the day, I been up. The rain been slack off, and ain't a wind stirrin'. I put one cap on the nipple, and one in my pocket, and I heist my foot from the turkey-blind. When I get there, day ain't clean yet. So I settle myself, and I make a peephole in the blind, and I wait, knowin' I ain't have to do a thing but take a straight aim at the whole flock and pull the trigger. Now, I been scatter the bait in a line what ran away from the blind. I like to shoot wild turkeys in the head; and if you make a trail, all their heads will be together when they is feedin'.

"After a while I hear something. Great God, here they come! Nothin' but turkeys, and they come from every side, and every turkey run on the bait. They begin to eat from both side of the trail. Their heads been as thick as black pepper. I know I can't miss. But I say I will have to go get the wagon for haul them home. Now, when turkeys is on the bait, you must wait no more. I ease my musket in the peephole; I lay the sight on the line of all them heads, and I squeeze the trigger.

"Wham-o-r-r! The black powder make so much smoke I can't tell how much I kill. But I ain't worry. I know I kill plenty. The air been full of turkeys flying away, but I sartain sure 'bout a dozen can't fly. I take my time and climb out of the blind. I begin to look 'bout. Ain't a God's turkey! Ain't a fedder! Salvation Days, what is this? Can't be I miss all that gang of wild turkey. But, same like I tell you, ain't a drop of blood, ain't a scale off a leg! And I wonder what yo' Pa gwine say; and wusser still, I wonder what that mean Ca'line gwine say. I think maybe I bline and can't see the turkeys lyin' all around. But no. Ain't one. Please God, ain't a smell of one. I 'fraid to go home. I say maybe somethin' done happen to my min', and ain't been no turkeys.

But the place been sandy, and I see all the fresh tracks. Must be I just ain't no gunnerman no mo'.

"Well, sah, I know they ain't comin' back for maybe two or three days. I been in a fix. So I gone home. Now, I been tell Ca'line all 'bout my plan; and when I get near the house, she been standin' in the door. Ever since we been married, she been tellin' me I been no-account. Now she looked as if she been satisfied she been right all along. I feel so too.

" 'I done hear you shoot', she say. 'Where the white man dinner?' I tell her the musket gone off accident-like.

" 'You miss, then you lie.' So she say. And I feel that way too.

"I walk by her and gone in the house. Cap'n, befo' God, the very fust thing I see is two saucer on the table. One been empty. The powder been in that. One been heap-up with shot. In the tarrigation with Ca'line 'bout the wood, I forgot to put the shot in my musket! I make that big fine plan; I ain't sleep much; I make high promise; I say I gwine show Ca'line what a man I is; I get in the blind, and the turkeys come right up to me, forty 'leven dozen of them. I get the dead bead on them. I pull the trigger. And ain't a God's shot been in the musket!"

Quite thrilled by this narrative, I asked Old Jim about the upset Sunday dinner.

"I gone out late that day and killed a little buck, but your Pa was disappoint. I tell him the same thing I done tole you, and all he say was, 'It isn't like you to do that, Jim.' I don't think he b'lieve me. I know it ain't like me, but still so I done do it. And it all come 'bout because I forget . . . You know why I tell you 'bout them turkeys?"

"It's a good story," I answered somewhat vaguely.

"No, sah, that ain't the reason why I tell you. You done understand now what happened to me because I forgot. A man must always remember. A long time ago, Cap'n, you promised me you gwine get me my army money. You forgot. Ever since your Pa suspicion me 'bout that thing, and ever since that Ca'line give me that sass 'bout it, I ain't forgot nothin'. And you must not forgot poor Old Jim Alston. You must 'member him."

A Plantation Christmas

In the rural sections of the South, and especially on the great estates and plantations, Christmas is probably as picturesquely celebrated as anywhere in the world. The Christmas found there has an old-English flavor; it is the jovial Christmas of Dickens. There are manifest the high spirit, the boisterous cheer, the holly, the mistletoe (not starved wreaths and single branches, but whole trees of holly and huge bunches of mistletoe) the smilax, the roaring fires of oak and pine, the songs, the laughter, the happy games, and all the festive enjoyments of the old-time Cavaliers. Whatever else may be said of those who settled the South from the court of Charles I, who, according to Edmund Burke, "had as much pride as virtue in them," they certainly knew how to make themselves happy at Christmas; and this characteristic they have bequeathed to their descendants. While their rollicking spirit may not be so nearly akin to that of the Original Christmas as the stern joy of the sober-hearted Puritans, their souls were warmer and their homes were happier and more picturesque. The Puritan had the lilies and the snow and the wintry starlight of mystic love and devotion; the Cavalier had the roses, the red wine, and the ruddy fireside of human affection.

To see how a typical plantation Christmas in the South is observed you must go with me far through the pine-woods that fringe the South Carolina coast, to one of those old plantations that lie along the Santee River delta. As we drive along the level road, the great forest will withdraw from us on all sides, disclosing magic vistas and mysterious swamp views, or perhaps a still stretch of water retired

From *Plantation Game Trails* (1921); also in *The Woods and Wild Things I Remember* (1970), with some changes.

mistily among the pines. In every water-course there will be elm-
and gum-trees, burdened with great bunches of mistletoe; while
beside the road, beautiful in their symmetry, their foliage, and their
berries lovely holly-trees will invite our fascinated eyes. And probably in the hollies or in the black-gums or tupelos of the swamp, but
surely darting swiftly among the tall pines, the light of the sinking
sun striking vividly on their scarlet breasts, we shall see a hundred,
possibly a thousand, robins, joyous among the delights afforded by
the Southern winter. Almost as friendly, though far less numerous
than the robins, are the cedar waxwings. Among the other birds
which give real meaning and cheer to the season are the wood thrush,
the Carolina wren, the cardinal, the mocking-bird, the catbird, the
brown thrasher, and many kinds of sparrows, notably the Peabody-
bird, which is so welcome a summer visitor to the Northern States.
Besides these common birds we may catch sight of a wild turkey, a
flock of bright-colored wood-ducks, or a giant black pileated woodpecker.

After our drive through the woods we shall enter the plantation
gateway, sentineled by century-old live-oaks, and overhung with
blossoming sprays of fragrant yellow jasmine. We drive past the
cotton-field whose dry bolls rattle and whisper in the wind, past the
clustered sweet potato banks and the tobacco drying-houses, until
beneath its ancient trees the snowy pillars of the great house come
into view. As we approach the steps we see a red woodbine festooned
over a cedar frame in the flower garden, and groups of rose bushes
laden with buds and blooms. The sun has now gone down behind
the dark pines, and the sky above them is softly aflame; and there in
that red setting the evening star glitters like a dewdrop on a poppy
flower.

It is Christmas Eve on the old plantation, and everywhere there is
an air of expectancy, especially among the Negroes, who like children,
feel most deeply the material joys of the season. And they share, too,
in the mystic meaning of the Holy Night. From far-off cabins, sunk
deep in the pines or across waste rice-land or on the open uplands,
there come sounds of singing, the melody of the Negro voices blend-
ing wondrously on the calm night air. Their hymns of "spirituals"
they can render with amazing feeling and felicity.

The Negroes have a pretty superstition to the effect that at midnight on Christmas Eve all the birds and animals go down on their knees in adoration of their Lord. I remember, as a little boy, creeping out to the chicken-yard with my brother in the dead of night to spy and see whether the wondrous thing would happen, really believing that it would. But we were forced to the melancholy conclusion that the fowls were agnostics; for though, seen by the blanching moonlight, they ruffled their feathers and stretched their necks, they did not take an attitude of reverence.

While we sit in the balmy air on the broad white veranda, listening to the singing as it floats softly through the night, the spirit of Christmas comes very near to us. There among the ancient oaks the wind through the swaying mosses breathes olden runes, while the Christmas stars above the solemn woods hold the promise of eternal light.

After the children have gone to bed in the great rambling plantation house, we begin arranging the Christmas presents; and these include not only the number for the family, but those for the servants, and the servants' families, friends, and visitors, and the friends' and visitors' friends, and so on. Many will come, and every one will get a present. There must always be a reserve store of gifts for cases of emergency in the form of Negroes who come unexpectedly. Many boxes for distribution come to us from the North, from friends who, having visited us during the hunting season, remember the needs of the Negroes and answer their silent appeals generously.

Early Christmas morning stealthy steps are heard along the halls; then there will be a soft knock, a shout of "Merry Christmas! Christmas gift!" from some one of the older servants; then peals of laughter from the delighted Negro and from the victim who has been caught napping. Often on the plantation we feign ignorance of the approach of some favorite servants just to give them the real delight that our apparent consternation affords them.

After the first surprises and greetings are over, fires—genuine Christmas fires—are kindled on all the hearths—fires that are soon merrily ablaze with that old-English cheer that none but the right wood can give. Southern fires do not have to run the dread gantlet of infant paralysis; nor are they dependent on newspaper, kerosene,

and other abominable means of tender solicitude. "Lightwood" suf-
fices for all their needs. It is the rich pine, full of highly inflammable
resin that does the work in an instant. The favorite wood for back-
logs is live-oak, which will burn for many hours with a soft ruddy
glow that gives out great heat. Scrub-oak or black-jack is more popular for general purposes because it is so plentiful; while tupelo, elm,
black gum, and sap pine fill in those gaps in the yawning fireplaces
between the kindling sticks and the giant yule log.

A Christmas breakfast on a Southern plantation is one of those
leisurely and delightful events that have no definite beginning or
ending, but which are aglow throughout with the light and warmth
of mirth, fellowship, and affection. Perhaps a cup of tea and a roll
and marmalade, with a bunch of fresh violets or a rose from the
garden on the tray, will be served first, as we gather on the piazza.
Later there will be an elaborate breakfast in the quaint old dining-
room, where, by the red firelight, and watched intently by the frieze
of deer's antlers festooned with holly and smilax, we shall pass two
happy hours. Among the truly Southern dishes most enjoyed are the
roasted rice-fed mallards, the venison sausages, and the crisp, brown
corn-breads.

After breakfast we shall all repair to the vast old echoing ballroom,
which occupies one whole wing of the house—a room with carved
wainscoting, waist-high, with tall, faded mirrors between the high
windows, and blue tiling of antique designs on the sides of the
fireplace. It is a room fragrantly haunted by memories of the past,
where the strains of the minuet and the courtly grace of the dancers
of colonial days would seem far more fitting than our practical
presence. But our coming to the ballroom has a real Christmas
significance, which is what most concerns us now; for it is here that
we give presents to the Negro children. They, dressed in their best
Sunday clothes, have been gathering for hours from our own plantation and from those adjacent ones whose sole occupants now are
their tenants. And now they come happily into the room through
the dark entryway at the back, the older ones, who recall the joys of
other years, leading and reassuring the tots who seem awed at the
expanse of the room and the light of the stately candles.

Their ages run from two to ten; their faces are remarkably bright
and appealing. There is little stolid dullness, but in its place we see

big bright eyes, rows of snowy teeth, and chubby black hands that will soon be filled with the generous stores of Santa Claus. Most of the children have a touch of color about their dress; one will wear a red necktie, one a string of blue beads, while a third may be the proud possessor of a favorite, though exclusive, mode of decoration, namely, a white or colored handkerchief pinned on the front of the shirt or dress or on the lapel of the jacket. As its secure fastening indicates, it is for purposes of ornament only.

On two long tables before the ranged rows of Negro children, their gifts are heaped high; and these include not only toys and trinkets and candy, but useful and durable gifts such as shoes and stockings, little dresses and suits, and many other kinds of apparel. Some of the children are too bewildered to appreciate their happiness; others in their joy will begin to dance (as this is the most spontaneous way for them to express their feelings), tentatively at first; but soon the whole crowd will join, and even the tiniest tot, clutching her gifts tightly, will lift her skirts and go through the swiftest and most intricate movements with great dexterity. This dancing is always a feature of a plantation Christmas.

Of course there is always a big deer-hunt on Christmas Day; though there is a proverb in the South that Christmas is hard on a hunter's aim. A Christmas hunting party is picturesque in a high degree. Gathering in a pre-arranged meeting-place, all the planters in that section of the country will appear dressed for the festival, each with his hounds trailing after him in the order of their enthusiasm. The presence of some planters who hunt on Christmas only, and who have never been known to hit anything, offers the wags of the party a rarer sport than deer could afford. About this company there is a spirit of irresponsibility, of holiday laxity that Southern hunters, who take their sport seriously, do not usually indulge in. As they ride away under the pines, to the winding of horns and the barking of dogs, they appear like some cavalcade of old, riding away into the shadows of the past. Into the woods they go, the wonderful woods of the Southern coast country, a company of merry gentlemen, light-hearted and—since the day is a festival—perhaps a little light-headed, too.

The return from the hunt is usually made about dark; and out at the barn the deer is unslung and the hounds begin to clamor for their share. By flickering lanterns and red-flaring lightwood torches the work is done. At the blowing of a horn the Negroes come from their cabins for venison steaks. Then will follow the royal Christmas dinner, served by candlelight. Rare merriment goes with hunters' appetites, and the house echoes with laughter that courses about the old-fashioned board.

Then once more we shall gather about the generous fireplace to hear the old Colonel tell how he shot the buck, recounting with delight that the Negro driver had shouted to his fellow-beaters, "Put on the pot, boys, de Cunnel is done shoot!" of how this or that dog conducted himself in the race; of how the sly old gobbler slipped away, and the whole series of adventures of the day.

And now the fire is very low; only the great live-oak log glows like a bed of rubies in the cavernous black chimney. The Colonel is asleep in his armchair, his favorite hound drowsing on the hearth at his feet. The room is hushed and the heavy curtains are motionless. The old stag's head gazes down with human wistfulness and the faded portraits seem alive in the soft shadows. The big clock above the fireplace intones the midnight in its mellow way. Christmas Day on the plantation is over.

PART II
CANINE COMPANIONS

Rutledge is seldom recognized as an outstanding writer of dog stories, yet his versatility and firsthand knowledge assured that he excelled on canine topics as in so many other subject areas. His best dog stories are a mixture of fact and fancy, all of them marked by the author's experience and understanding. Hunting dogs were an omnipresent feature of life at Hampton, as much a part of the plantation scene as plowed fields, lordly oaks, and rustic tenant cabins. Household pets had their place, but the animals Rutledge and his acquaintances truly cherished were "working dogs."

The nature of their "work" was about as varied as the lineage of the dogs. Rich or poor, most folks had several "yard dogs." These all-purpose canines served as perambulatory alarm systems, playmates for youngsters, sometime guardians of livestock, and self-ordained protectors of hearth and home. Although the description "yard dog" was occasionally used as a term of opprobrium, these animals belong to Southern culture as surely as cornbread and cow peas. Yard dogs usually ran free, and they were frequently used for certain types of hunting. Still, the distinction between these canines and true hunting dogs was as clear as that which separated yard dogs from household pets.

True hunting dogs were normally confined in kennels, largely because those allowed free range readily developed bad habits such as backtracking, abandoning the trail too quickly when they lost the track, and even such pernicious proclivities as egg sucking and raiding chicken roosts.

True hunting dogs, along with the odd yard dog acting as a surrogate, had a vital role to fill in Low Country sport. Most outdoorsmen owned a cur or perhaps a spunky fice for treeing squirrels. There would be pointers or a sprightly setter for the pursuit of partridges and retrievers for waterfowling. All of these had their place, but the lords of this canine world were hounds.

Low Country deer hunting was a sport of the chase, thanks both to tradition and to the fact that the terrain did not lend itself to stalking or tree stands. Often the difference between a prime haunch of venison on the table and a fruitless day afield was an effective pack of hounds. How Rutledge loved these deer hunts, and he rejoiced in the triumphs and tragedies of his dogs as nimrods have done since man first tamed wolves.

Rutledge's finest dog stories place him well to the forefront of those who captured countless hearts with tales of canine wizardry. He produced less work of this genre than another South Carolina writer, Havilah Babcock, and he is not as well known in the field as the notables John Taintor Foote and Corey Ford. Still, Rutledge brought together a baker's dozen tales of being afield with canine friends in *Bolio and Other Dogs* (1930), and there is a spicy sprinkling of fine material on dogs throughout his other books. That he knew and understood dogs is beyond debate, and he had an uncanny feel for the special relationship that can exist between a hunter and his trusted friend. Rutledge described this bond with insight few have matched. One has but to read his joyful descriptions in which dogs figure prominently to realize how much he loved them and how large they loomed in his sporting life.

When, for example, you read his words on the potential tribulations connected with training a puppy, you know that here speaks someone who has experienced both the heartbreak and wonder associated with doggy rites of passage: "Every puppy begins by conceiving his master to be a god; it is that master's business never to do anything to make that dog change his mind." The stories which follow are a mere sample, but they suffice to show that the wisdom contained in this quotation sprang from a man with deep empathy for his subject. To accompany him and the dogs he knew is to rejoice in that special bond which has always linked man to his faithful friend and unquestioning companion.

Boll-weevil Bores In

I really wasn't entitled to this particular hunt, for I had had my sport on the plantation and was headed northward again, where my work was waiting for me. Work has a pernicious habit of so waiting. But it is sometimes hard to get away from a remote plantation for more reasons than sentimental ones. From home I crossed two broad rivers and an alleged causeway that looked like the finished Panama Canal. On the farther side of the second river a man was supposed to meet me in a Lydia Languish of a Ford. After heroic efforts I got there. But he did not. I met a Negro, however, and asked him if he had seen or heard of the car.

"If you mean Mr. Johnson's car," he answered encouragingly, "I is sure that she tire done run off. She does do that for common."

I didn't want to go back home. All my things were packed up; all the good-byes had been said. Besides, there was the work ahead. Yet here I was stranded—and in a good bird country, yet without a dog. My car, I supposed, would be coming along after a while. How was I to pass the time?

"You live here, don't you?" I asked the Negro.

He grinned.

"I don't live no reg'lar place," he said amiably, "but my sister lives down the road."

"Does she have a dog?" I questioned. The query sounded to me foolish and forlorn.

"Boll-weevil is a dog," he said. "She got him."

"Boll-weevil," I repeated, hope dying in my heart. "I thought a boll-weevil was a kind of a beetle that bores holes in cotton-bolls. Why do you call a dog that?"

From *Bolio and Other Dogs* (1930); also in *Hunter's Choice* (1946).

"My sister calls him that because he's always getting into where he doesn't belong."

I tried by some frantic mental process to associate this quality with a good bird dog. My experiment failed.

"Will he hunt?" I asked.

"Anything," he answered. "He will hunt people or hogs or anything like that."

The chances for sport behind such a brute did not exactly appear rosy. Yet a man must be careful not to judge a dog by his name, nor by his appearance. I once knew a man named Bill Blood; but he was as shy and bashful as a husband is in his own home. Nor can we tell by names. One of the most worthless dogs I ever owned came to me under the proud appellation of Savannah Count's Maharajah. As a bird-dog he simply wasn't; but he might have made a good track man, for at the sound of a gun he would be off at top speed. On the other hand, one of the very best dogs I ever had was named Mike— just that. He was a grim-looking pointer, and I strongly suspected him of having hound blood in him. But he was a born hunter.

"What are you doing now?" I asked my Negro, thinking of hiring a guide.

"Nothing," he answered—at which, by the way, a plantation Negro is positively expert. "I don't no nothing reg'lar," he told me, with a faint hint of pride in such halcyon independence.

"Come along with me, then," I suggested. "Let's leave my bags at your sister's house, take Boll-weevil, and go for a hunt. Your sister can hail my car as it passes, and tell my driver to wait there for me."

"All right, Cap'n," was the cheerful response. Thus we set out to start something, with Boll-weevil as the starter.

My guide's name I learned was Chance Washington. I could not ascertain whether this first name was delicately indicative of his coming into the world or whether it was an abbreviation for Mischance. At any rate he agreed willingly enough to accompany me, and down the sandy road with my luggage we went, arriving ere long at a staggering cabin where Boll-weevil hung out. I looked hopefully across the paling fence, and in the corner I saw a mangy mass of yellowish hair half-buried in a pile of warm sand. It looked like a discarded duster of some kind. It was asleep, but its hind-feet raked its sides methodically. "An army travels on its stomach," some famous military leader said. That was one of the troubles with my new dog, that I now ruefully surveyed. He made me think of the two women, one of whom said:

"My husband's gone hunting today."

And the other:

"You poor dear! Never mind. I'll see if I can send you over something for dinner tomorrow night."

But slim chances often make great sport.

We arranged to leave our luggage, to have the car stopped, and to borrow Boll-weevil. The sad-eyed woman who called Chance her brother gave me this word of advice:

"You mustn't try to manage the dog," she said; "he has much sense, if you leave him alone. If you follow him, he will take you to something."

That kind of talk sounded sensible to me; indeed it might well be followed by a good many men hunting with better dogs than the one I now had.

Chance and Boll-weevil and I made a curious caravan. I doubted whether the Negro knew where he was going; I doubted my own sanity; and as for the dog, I doubted every blamed thing about him. He should have been in a hospital, except that things that are sent there seem to have some chance for recovery.

Down an old path through a broomsedge field we went toward the darksome edge of a tupelo swamp. I wanted to hunt the field, but Chance thought we had better follow Boll-weevil. He had now taken the lead; and while he had lost some of his forlorn inanity, he might still have posed for a statue called "Hopeless."

Halfway across the field the dog suddenly stopped. To me it appeared likely that he had simply played out. But he was rather rigid. His head was slightly tilted, and his tail had taken out of its undulating length a kink or two.

"He's pointing," said my guide.

Even as he spoke Boll-weevil gave a prodigious spring into the dense broomsedge. Out boiled a huge covey—twenty birds or more, and away they went for the shelter of the friendly thickets fringing the borders of the swamp.

I managed to miss one and to kill one; but Boll-weevil reached this latter before I did, and I haven't seen the bird yet.

"Does he eat them?" I asked Chance.

"Right reg'lar," the Negro said. "After this I'll try to beat him out."

I marveled at the brute's pointing; yet it was apparently no more than the crafty crouching of a wild dog before a spring upon its game. In that sense, even a cat will point. Yet he had undoubtedly winded the birds. My sport would be had, I reasoned, if I got up to Weevil before he flushed, and if Chance did some swift and masterly retrieving.

Myrtles and little pines grew on the margins of the swamp. Birds don't go far over such cover. I flushed one and got it. Boll-weevil came to a momentary stand on another. Briskly I stepped up, and was really in time, but my dog made so wild a jump into the bird's bosom that the quail gyrated crazily out of the brush, and since I could get no aim on him, I did not fire. The dog took a second airy leap, and this time the frightened bird started toward the tops of the tall tupelos, affording me a shot. Down he came, and Chance was on him as quickly as if he had been a ripe watermelon in somebody else's garden. Boll-weevil must have felt that he wasn't getting his share, for he began to ramble with fresh zeal, putting up the birds right and left. They seemed to know him—and I have no doubt that he had been after this same covey before. His pounces now were accompanied by little yelps, and their rises were made with frightened chitters. Yet, despite it all, the sport was rather fast and interesting. Certainly it was sporty. Normally a quail is a gamey target; it becomes verily a sporty one when it is hounded by a brute like Boll-weevil. But my business was like that of the ancient criminal prosecutors of England, who used first to execute the suspect, then investigate the case, then accuse the defendant. I shot the birds, and didn't bother much about investigating and accusing.

By the time our wild melee was over, I had a half-dozen birds, the dog had two, and Chance had my respect as a retriever. I complimented him on his agility.

"Boll-weevil teach me that," he told me. "When anything to eat is around, if I won't watch out sharp, he'll get it first."

The birds were now badly scattered, and it seemed wise to look for another covey. Chance said he knew where there was one in a cottonfield just beyond the narrow swamp. Thither we repaired; but just as we entered it, to our surprise Weevil set up an infernal racket. Then he fell silent, and the still air was pierced with the shrill squeals of a razorback hog that our dog had assaulted. A man generally hunts bacon in a grocery store, and I had no desire to found another Armour fortune. But as I looked at my guide, I saw with misgiving that he was positively radiating cupidity.

"I ain't had no ham this whole year," he volunteered.

Just then the circus calliope came our way. Through the brown and bowed cottonstalks a rangy old sow, yelling mighty murder from her bowsprit of a snout, dragged a yellow dishrag. The razorback having urgent business elsewhere, was running away with Boll-weevil.

"Now is the time," said Chance.

But I had hardening of the hearteries.

"Get him off," I answered.

Chance made a dive into the cotton, and after a struggle he emerged with our prize package in his arms. He carried the dog halfway across the field before he set him down.

Weevil, apparently roused by the variety of the sport he was having, actually began to hunt—not exactly as a highbred dog "makes game," but as if he were on the hot trail of a dinner. I followed fast; and in a few minutes I saw a covey running down the cotton-row in front of the dog. I was up with them when they flushed. Weevil tried to catch one as they rose, but his jump, though quite an honorable effort, fell short. On the rise I managed to make a double. One gets used to anything. Here were birds wildly flushed; but if the hunter expects such a rise, he can manage all right.

On our way after the birds, Weevil struck another trail; and he reached the end of this before I did. There was a sudden struggle in the cotton-stalks, and I caught sight of some huge black thing. Then "a silence fell," as the poets say. Chance and I reached the spot. I did not know whether to be more disgusted or amused: there lay Boll-weevil in sordid triumph on the body of a dishevelled old buzzard! I suppose the black scavenger had been shot down by some one, or had been injured in some other way. Weevil had promptly bored into him. Again Chance had to gather the dog to his bosom, and again we started after the birds. This covey had settled in some heavy boomgrass beyond the cottonfield. It was a clear hundred yards to the deep pinewoods beyond, toward which the birds headed as they rose. The shooting was really fast and sporty. Boll-weevil would point every bird; that is, he would make a momentary crouch, then a sudden spring to flush it accommodatingly. Being fairly well scattered, the birds got up singly. By the time we were through with them, we had, together with the others, fourteen. . . . It was enough. Besides, I was sure that the sounds of a gas-gobbler could be heard in the land. My Sagging Sallie was doubtless waiting for me.

Chance, Boll-weevil, and I paraded homeward. I know not what might have been the thoughts in the head of Chance, that lover of bacon who did no reg'lar work and who lived in no reg'lar place. Weevil's thoughts were also veiled from me. But I knew that I was thinking deeply about the strange ways of dogs and men. I didn't think that, in a highly civilized community, one could afford to keep a dog like Boll-weevil. Yet he had his virtues; he bored in—he was not afraid—he had a sort of nose—and if he was not fastidious in his choice of game, he was after something all the time.

My car was waiting. That was one thing it could do expertly. I asked the driver what had delayed him. He said he had no garage, and as a result left the car out in all weathers; "and my garage roof leaks sometimes," he explained. "Last night in that shower my spark-plugs got flooded."

I had a good bunch of quail to take with me homeward. I had besides memories of the good-natured improvident Chance, and more vivid memories of the curious canine Boll-weevil. There is no telling; that dog might have been a sweepstakes winner—if he had had the heredity and the environment. That, however, can be said of any failure. But I cannot call Weevil a failure. Suppose I had had Comanche Frank along? He, of course, would have done the thing in grand style. But I doubt if he would have afforded me better sport, and certainly not half the genuine diversion, of the lowly Boll-weevil. It was a chance hunt, a chance dog, a Chance guide. . . . And, as a general thing, the worse the chances, the keener the sport. Certainly I was never kept more on tiptoe than I was on that accidental outing by the humble and pariah Boll-weevil.

Poinsettia and Sparkplug

The first remark I heard about Poinsettia was unconsciously sinister. I had sent a Negro to bring her from the boat to the plantation. He arrived in "the dead vast and middle of the night," as any Negro will if you send him for anything; and his first words to me were:

"Cap'n, dis sholy is one fine houn'."

"Then, Cain," I said with cool discouragement, "you've brought the wrong dog."

"How come dat?" he asked. "Ain't no mo' dog been for bring."

"Hound?" I asked incredulously, peering into the darkness at the dusky shape crouched by Cain's feet.

"Houn', a fine houn'," the Negro assured him.

"Take her out to the kennel and tie her carefully, Cain," I said; "and don't put a slip-knot on her neck as you did on that pointer puppy. Her feed is ready. I will look at her in the morning."

I suppose the poet was right when he decided with a good deal of feeling that sleep is a blessed thing; yet he should have indicated what kind of sleep he meant—certainly it was not the kind in which I rioted and tossed until morning. I dreamed of hounds that pointed quail, and of bird-dogs that picked up a cold deer-trail; and of deer that retrieved dogs and brought them to me in well-broken fashion. Daybreak was a blessed relief to my orgy of imagination.

When I went out to look at my new dog, I had the feeling that at least it would be a relief to have the worst realized. It was. The dog came out of her kennel; and she was neither pointer nor setter. Nor was she hound. She just didn't seem to be anything in particular; but

From *Heart of the South* (1924); also in *Bolio and Other Dogs* (1930).

it seemed fair to give her the benefit of many doubts. I forthwith called her Poinsettia.

My other dog, a brash young pointer, Sparkplug by name, was meanwhile eying the stranger with as much interest as I did with misgiving.

"We three," I said, "are going to try the birds right after breakfast; and we'll take Cain along. I have an idea that Poinsettia will try to retrieve the live birds; and Cain can keep you, Sparkplug, from getting the dead ones. You brought seven home last week—inside."

This new dog, which a friend of mine in the city had sent to me, somehow made my breakfast hard to swallow. The dog had been highly praised; I was told she was an English setter; but as far as I could see, the only thing English about her was her head, which somewhat resembled, in shape, an English walnut. . . . But appearances in dogs are more deceptive than they are in men. The handsomest dog I ever had was the biggest booby in the field that it has ever been my disgust to witness. The sight of a rabbit would make him head vigorously for home; but he would not acquire his real momentum until he heard the sound of the gun.

For this day's sport, Cain and I were mounted; I had a little marsh-pony and he had a mule. I have ridden a mule—once. I took Cain because he could watch our mounts while I was shooting; and he was a pretty good Negro to locate coveys. He had been dipping the turpentine woods that summer, and he had found a good many broods of young birds; and every man who knows quail knows that they do not range very far from where they are hatched. Indeed, if conditions remained right, they would hardly ever be beyond calling distance from the place where they first saw the light.

As Cain and I rode out of the plantation gateway, we let Sparkplug run loose; he is the kind of a dog that you have to allow a chance to tire himself before he is of any account. Poinsettia, I led on a leash; most of the time I was dragging her. We came to where a fresh deer-track crossed the damp sand of the road, and she smelled it avidly, saying that she knew all about it. Her long and waving tail said so. Cain looked at the dog, at the track, again at the dog's waving tail, and last at me.

"A fine houn'," he volunteered.

"Yes," I reluctantly agreed. "I suppose we ought to hunt deer today. That reminds me of another dog I had that was death on field mice and moles. He was one of these fine dogs, too; all I had to do to be happy was to change my game. He was grand on dormice."

"But this dog hab a principle countenance."

On Sundays, Cain preaches; and into his conversation will creep high-sounding phrases. He meant that Poinsettia had a face which mirrored good principles.

Two hundred yards from the plantation gateway, while we were still in the live-oak avenue, Sparkplug ran into a covey of quail that must have been run off their roost early that morning. A broom-sedge field was near; and from there they had come into the woods. He flushed them, of course. Wildly they whirred over our heads, some of them lighting on the mossy live-oak limbs; others sailed down into the thickets of sparkleberry and holly.

"Cain," I said, "I'm going to try the gun on this new dog. I'll shoot one barrel and if she runs, I'll shoot the other at her. I have a feeling that we can test her as well here as anywhere else."

Sparkplug was plugging around in the brush like a bull of Bashan; and here and there I could get a glimpse of a flushed bird. I slipped the leash from Poinsettia. At once she stole forward, and it seemed to me that her walk was very catlike. Fifteen feet ahead of me, she drew to a point, her head high, with the nose pointed up. She was standing a quail in a low holly. The bird was flushed and shot; the dog retrieved it beautifully. But the young pointer was just running rings around himself. He pretended to be too excited to hear me calling to him; and that's a little deceitful habit many a dog has. I followed the wary Poinsettia. She drew to a disheveled heap of dead leaves. I looked closely. There was the bird—a cock, with his beady, bright eyes and the white throating showing. He was flushed, shot, and retrieved. Poinsettia stood again; but this time Sparkplug plunged in. A young pointer is often a clumsy brute, rushing in where genteel pups fear to tread. He flushed Poinsettia's bird. Then foolishly he bounded away after it. It corkscrewed out through a big laurel tree, and I couldn't fire.

Sparkplug bounded; but he was cut short in the bounding business. Poinsettia, overtaking him in a trice, leaped on him with a certain ferocity which, Kipling tells us, is of a variety far more deadly than is the ferocity of the male, and gave the youngster a good mauling. When she released him, the pup dashed off a few paces, stopped, looked back at me, and whined sadly. It had been his first encounter with the superior sex, and he was asking me who heaved the brick. He was all mussed up, body and soul—which is very good discipline for a youngster. I called him to me, told him to follow Poinsettia, and gave him to understand that my sympathies were with her. The clumsy pup fell in behind the older dog with a comical carefulness. I followed the two dogs into the thicket. There a bird detached itself from its perfect cover among the brown leaves, and began to run. But it ran round the side of the pointing dog; she warily turned her head to watch him. The bird kept skittering over the leaves, and his course brought him almost within jumping distance of the pup. He had been backing Poinsettia; but at sight of the bird, he got ready to do a Brodie into the bird's bosom. Poinsettia saw this maneuver; and she distinctly snarled at him! It was a curious piece of procedure to watch. The pup looked at Poinsettia, and straightway decided that he ought to keep on pointing. He did, to my amazement. The bird ran into the road, rose, spiraled over Cain's head, and gave me a fair shot. Poinsettia recovered it for me.

"You shoot mighty close my head, Cap'n," the Negro reminded me.

"It wouldn't hurt your head," I reminded him. "Cain, the poet had your bean and a bullet in mind when he wrote:

> 'We are two lions littered in one day,
> And I the elder and more terrible.'

Your head's the elder and more terrible. Get me?"

"Dat's so," he agreed, "dat's suttinly so."

"Let's go over for that cover by the spring, Cain. Well, what do you think of the hound?"

"For a houn'," he said, "she's a fine bird-dog. And she's so smart on training a pup," he added.

"She'll break Sparkplug for us, that's what she'll do. She just talks to him, Cain, as a woman does to a man. You get me? You know, 'Hell hath no fury like a woman scorned.' "

"And dat's the God's trufe, Cap'n," Cain agreed with something akin to personal feeling. "You done spoke the word."

We passed on down the pine-scented, dew-damp road; the air was clean and spicy, the undergrowth fragrantly fresh. It was good to be alive; and to be out in the pine-lands was all a man could wish.

When a hundred yards from the spring, Cain drew in his mule and pointed down to the sandy road. There, distinctly but peculiarly outlined, were the tracks of a covey of quail. When the birds walk in white sand that is dry underneath but has a thin surface of dew-wet soil, their feet pick up some of this sticky sand. But we knew that quail had been making the tracks.

"This is their highway," Cain told me; "they love for promenade 'cross this same road; and we can find them right ahead here."

The dogs had now come up with us, and we simply let them have their own way about finding the birds. The pup started off violently on the back trail. Poinsettia stepped to the edge of the road; and there she came to a dead point.

"So close?" I whispered, slipping from my mount and handing the rein to the Negro.

"I see them," Cain said; "they is under that little bush by the big stump. Cap'n, this is the big covey I been telling you 'bout."

I stepped past Poinsettia; a moment later I heard a scurry behind me, then a sudden yelp. The pup had blundered up, and was for going right on. But Poinsettia had stopped him.

"It beats my time," I admitted; "if her head is like a walnut, at least it isn't an empty shell."

A moment later the birds rose and made for a bay-branch two hundred yards off. It was indeed a big covey; there were not fewer than thirty quail in it. By good chance I doubled; Poinsettia brought me these birds. Immediately she began to range out freely, and I thought she was getting a bit wild. But her madness had excellent method in it. She was trying to keep between the birds and the pup. She knew very well where they were. Already I could see that she had a far-off wind of them—while the branch was distant some forty yards. She ranged widely; and she kept looking back cautiously, as if saying to Sparkplug, "Come on if you want to, but you must stay well behind me; and if you try to scare these birds that I am rounding up nicely here, I'll just repeat my little lesson of discipline with you."

The birds were running in the watercourse; that was one reason why Poinsettia got their scent so far. Cain and I sat our mounts

and watched this wonderful dog double-team it on the quail and
Sparkplug. When her head was turned to the birds, she was all eager
tenseness, all sporty delight; when she looked back toward the pup,
who was galloping, but rather guardedly, her expression hardened.

"Dat dog sholy is like a 'oman;" Cain said. "She kin turn a smilin'
face to she friends, and she kin turn a dangersome face to she
husban'."

"You talk like a man of experience," I said.

"Yes, Cap'n," Cain agreed soberly; "life done han' me out mo'
'sperience than anything else."

Poinsettia was standing now, and I tossed my rein to the patient
Negro. To my surprise, Sparkplug backstood the female. It has
always seemed to me that a young dog that would backstand an old
one was well on the way to being made. The birds flushed in little
bunches, and the shooting was clear—well above the bays and the
tangles of swamp-briar. Poinsettia did not break her stand until I
sent her after some of the dead birds. Then she went into the dense
cover and retrieved in perfect fashion. Cain, who had our game-bag
slung beside the pommel of his saddle, told me that we had eleven
birds.

"A good start," I said, "and we've taken enough out of each of
those coveys. Where next?"

"The dog's pointing up yonder," the Negro answered, pointing
far up the branch, where, indeed, Poinsettia was standing rigidly.

"A stray, I suppose; well, let's make it a dozen."

Just before I reached the dog, from a small, dense head of bays
that jutted into the broom-grass of the pine-land like a miniature
headland, there bounded a spike-buck! Jauntily he floated over a
few logs, his erected tail jerking from side to side. Soon he vanished
in the pines.

"Cain," I said, when the smiling Negro came up, "you win. She's
a hound."

"Dat wavy tail make me say 'houn' when I fust see the dog," he
said.

"Where's the next covey?"

"Right by the old pile of sawdust where the sawmill used to was."

We rode on through the sweet-smelling pine-lands. Bluebirds were warbling sunnily in the aromatic air. Woodpeckers were noisily calling and hammering. Behind us I heard the quail that we had been after, already calling together. High in the dreamy pines a warm wind murmured. All life seemed contented; I know that I was.

As Cain had said, the birds were by the old mill; and from this covey, by the aid of Poinsettia, we drew eight birds.

"Enough," I said to the Negro; "the sun's getting hot now, and it's after twelve o'clock. We have had a good day. As we go by Witch Pond, Cain, I'll shoot a blue heron for your dinner. I know you wouldn't bother to pick these little birds."

"Heron is mo' sweeter," the Negro agreed.

"Well," I said as we rode homeward together, "yesterday I had no dogs; now I have two. Don't you think the pup has learned a lot today?"

Cain laughed, as if the whole business struck him as very amusing.

"He will larn mo', too, befo' he done wid dat 'oman you call Poinsettia. . . . But, Cap'n, what is dat you done say 'bout a 'oman and hell?"

"Hell hath no fury like a woman scorned."

"Dat's his; dat's him."

"Why did you ask me, Cain.?"

"Dat's the berry thing for my sarmon on Sunday. I gwine use dat sholy."

"You'd better go easy with that stuff, Cain, in a mixed congregation. Remember what happened to Sparkplug today."

The Negro nodded thoughtfully.

"I will be careful," he said; "but I is a preacher, and I have to tell my people the gospel trufe."

Cain is, as he said, a preacher; nevertheless, he has his good points. For example, he isn't a half-bad companion on a quail-hunt in the Dixie pinelands.

Sarsaparilla

Of all the dogs that I have ever known, Sarsaparilla, an alleged hound, was the least promising in appearance. He was owned by one of the Negroes on our South Carolina place; and he was named back in those old days when patent medicines and soft drinks were first making their way into the remote hinterlands of the plantations, and when Negroes got a social kick out of naming their dogs, their children, and their mules Neuralgia, Asthma, Sarsaparilla, Ambrosia, and Dandruff.

This beast, Sarsaparilla, had other faults beside his effervescing name: he had apparently no sense at all, he was too tall, his head had no particular shape, his gait was an absurd walk. He gave one the impression of traveling on stilts. His color was a discord of mangy yellowish white. His facial expression was notably vacant. Sarsaparilla was simply ludicrous; he just wouldn't do. So, for a long time, I thought. But there came a day when I was to learn a mighty lesson about not judging by appearances. I was to learn that courage, like wealth, is solely a matter of the heart; and it took a yellow dog to teach me.

When great floods swept down the Santee River, they dislodged from the gloomy and impenetrable swamps above us a good deal more than mere sedge and drifting logs. Live things were in the flotsam. Deer came to our very backyard, shy wild turkeys, roving cattle, wild hogs of huge size and savage temper.

One morning when I went down to the stable-yard I was greeted by a shrill complaining from the hogs that were penned in the ample enclosure. Something was badly disconcerting them. When I came

From *Wild Life of the South* (1935).

up, I found that they had a visitor, a rangy wild boar from the swamps, a shaggy hyena-like creature, with gleaming tusks, alarming bristles, and a most truculent mien. I at once saw that he had jumped a low panel in the fence, and that, by setting two rails there, I could effect his capture. The thing was managed. But when I came to open the gate, he charged me, mouth wide, bristles high, tail erect. I got the gate shut not a second too soon. He checked his speed, champed his great jaws at me sullenly, and then turned back to torment the other dwellers in the yard.

Not wishing to shoot the boar, I decided to catch him with dogs. I therefore repaired to the nearby Negro settlement, where I gathered in seven dogs and as many Negroes, all of whom read between the lines of my story the glad tidings of Christmas bacon to be had for the catching. We had a motley pack: a bulldog, two hounds, an alleged collie, two plain curs of the most obscure antecedents, and Sarsaparilla. I remonstrated with Sarsaparilla's owner about bringing this soft drink to the slaughter. He laughed in a shamefaced way, as if he thought his dog were being taken along to be the clown of the fray. I recalled the boar's size and mien, looked at this burlesque on rickety stilts, and pity filled my heart.

Reaching the barnyard, we decided that an assault *en masse* was the proper maneuver. The dogs were to be the shock troops, and we were to follow up the advantage that they had obtained over the common enemy. We had sundry cudgels and ropes with which to belabor the victim.

The seven dogs went through the gate in a body; and the wild boar accommodated them by not permitting them to hesitate for a moment as to which hog they were after. Incontinently he rushed them. With great valor we watched the fray from the farther side of the fence, waiting until our chance seemed secure enough to enable us to cross the obstruction that protected us. Suddenly, hurled high over the fence, the bulldog rejoined us; all the zest seemed gone out of him. Then the two hounds fled across the yard and skulked into the stable; their attitude indicated that they carried no tornado insurance. The collie stood off and barked with hollow ferocity. The two plain dogs went manfully to work, but one was trampled by the boar. The other seized the monster's ear and hung on grimly. Yet the beast would rip him open, I knew.

Just then, Sarsaparilla, who had calmly and aloofly watched proceedings, stepped niftily in. He approached rather fastidiously, not from dismay but from a certain curious regard for finesse. Stationed behind the hog, he looked thoughtfully at the shaggy brute; then he quietly bowed his lunatic, dolesome head, mouthed the boar's upper haunch until he had a deliberate hold, sank his teeth, set his legs, and began grimly to shake his head.

The boar, I think, got one glimpse of what had him; he probably imagined it a saber-tooth tiger. Savagely shaking off the dog from his head, he squealed shrilly and turned to run. Sarsaparilla said quite firmly, "Not so fast."

The bewildered boar could not get loose. The other dogs came back. We jumped the fence, and soon we had the old marauder from the swamps securely roped. Sarsaparilla then stalked sedately off; he had condescended to help us; but he was not going to join in any of our puerile excitement.

"What kind of dog is that?" I asked his owner.

"God in he'ben knows," replied he, meaning no irreverance; "but he got *all* de sense. Sometimes I gwine change his name to Solomon."

That Night at Bowman's

A thunderstorm was rolling up from the southwest, and Bob Laval was hurrying about in the yard behind the plantation house, trying to get together the things he had to take home that night, and to put away what should be sheltered from the storm. He had a ten-mile drive before him; and as the mare Gypsy was very skittish about lightning, he was eager to get a good start ahead of the storm. He thought he could at least get through the first deep belt of woods before the rain came; and once out of the thick woods, he would not fear the lightning. The sudden coastal storms nearly always followed the line of the woods, and to be in the open was to be comparatively safe.

Gypsy was hitched to the buggy and was restless to start. Bob, whose second year of rice-planting on the Santee had made him look older than he should have looked at twenty years, paused on the steps of the old house, casting one inclusive glance around. It was Saturday, and he would not return to the plantation until Monday. He did not want to forget anything; for it is better for a planter to take a wetting that not to remember things of importance. He saw nothing further to keep him; so he stepped quickly down the steps toward the buggy. But as he laid his hand on the half-hitch to free Gypsy, he heard a lazy whine behind him. There at his heels was little Game, his young hound, waving his long tail and looking up at Bob with an expression of pleasurable anticipation.

"He'll want to follow, and I can't take him down to the village tonight. Alston knows about feeding him. But where can I tie him?"

From *Heart of the South* (1924).

As he was speaking, Laval caught the hound, who blinked dubiously over his master's haste and energy, and dragged him over to a decrepit shed under which lay a heavy log-drag. In its end was a ring and chain. The little hound was quickly fastened, and in another moment the planter was in his buggy and Gypsy's head was pointed toward home. And her pace promised to enable her to show a clean pair of heels to the onrolling storm.

When the rising tempest had blotted out the sun, a premature twilight had been shed over the plantation fields and over the dark forests of pine. But now the twilight of foreboding had turned into a night of storm and moaning darkness. Yet the mare Gypsy traveled famously, the planter giving her the reins; and three miles had been covered before Laval felt the first gust of rainy wind that made him turn up his collar and turn down the brim of his hat in the back. Then the great drops began to fall.

"Gypsy," he said to the mare, who was now more than ever agitated by her seeming flight before the reverberating thunder, "we're in for it; but don't you mind. I'll give you the best kind of a rubbing down when we get home. Just keep your head cool and your heels steady."

But Gypsy had a right to be frightened; for Laval had never seen a blacker storm. Familiar objects in the pine woods were lost to view less because of the sheets of lashing rain that now began to fall than by the strange eerie darkness that veiled the landscape. And even in the rush of the wind could be heard the sobbing of the wet-crested pines as they rocked in the blinded sky.

"Bowman's Run will be high," said the planter; "it was up a little this morning, and this will put it out of its bank."

This sluggish watercourse in the pine woods crossed the road four miles from Laval's plantation, and Gypsy's pace had brought the buggy now almost to it. As is the case with all the watercourses in the Southern pine woods, Bowman's Run was heavily wooded, and the edges of it which bordered the road were dense walls of bays, myrtles and gallberry bushes. The road widened here, and the stream proper flowed through the middle of a long waterslash, several hundred yards in extent. In most of this there was no current; just standing water varying in depth from a few inches to a foot or more. It was with something of a sense of foreboding that Bob Laval drew near this dank and gloomy stretch of road. The rain was falling very heavily, and several times lightning had struck not far off. Gypsy had behaved fairly well, considering her high-strung nature, but she was clearly becoming more tense; and as Laval was traveling with the storm, he was afraid that a sudden, close crash might make her break away. Through the roar of the rain and the wind in the pines he ·kept talking to her, urging her on steadily, yet checking her firmly. His strong brown hands showed white under the intense tugging on the reins.

Soon Gypsy began to splash into the waters of Bowman's Run. The lithe mare had never liked this place, for she had once smelled a rattlesnake here, and she remembered the disagreeable incident. This night her feeling was intensified by the terror of the storm. She stepped high in the water, and her neck was arched with the strange beauty and grace born of wakened fear. In a lull in the wind, the planter heard her blow out her breath in a nervous snort. But he thought he had her well in hand; yet as often happens, the weapon that is dreaded is not always the weapon that gives the deadly blow. Bob Laval was guarding her against being frightened by lightning; but he had not thought of another peril, nor could he have guarded against it if he had.

Suddenly, out of the wild and rainy sky, a heavy pine limb, snapped by a scudding gust of wind, fell hissing and hurtling on Gypsy's back. The mare broke furiously, reared, rushed forward at an angle that brought her against the rooty bank of the stream; and even while Bob called to her and sat back grimly against the reins, the buggy was hurled up into the air. It toppled over, and in the wrenching struggle, Gypsy broke away and galloped madly down the long watercourse. The mare was freed; but the overturning buggy had caught Bob Laval. And when the shock of the cold water brought him to complete consciousness and made him open his eyes, he knew that he was badly hurt. Gradually his pain began to center itself in his left arm and in his back. The buggy, which had no top, had turned completely over, and Bob was caught under the heavy seat, which rested across his back above the hips.

His left arm seemed useless; it was either broken or dislocated. Gypsy had probably done it, thought Laval, with the twisting wrench that she gave when she broke away. What happened to his back he did not know; but his position was an unbearable one. He was lying with his face in the water, and with his right arm he was trying to support himself. Several times he tried to turn to catch hold of one of the back wheels of the buggy to pull himself up; but he could not endure the agony that such a turn gave him. His back seemed to be in some fatal vise that was slowly and surely forcing him face downward into the water. For a time Bob could keep himself up by his right arm; but the waters of Bowman's Run were rising, and a man who is injured and pinned down in the water cannot count on his strength increasing, but must bravely face its waning, and attempt to substitute for physical exhaustion mental reserves of resourcefulness.

Laval's first fight was to keep from fainting; and only a grim resolution held him safe from that peril. Though at times utterly sick from pain, he warded off as if by a miracle the swoon that seemed inevitable. He kept telling himself that the time he fainted when the window-sash fell on his hand was because he had not had his nerve with him. But now he had a grip on himself. This he kept repeating and it reinforced him from sources of unknown power.

And it was not only against the water and the danger of fainting that he had to fight; he set his face like flint against an undercurrent of thought which sought to tell him that he might as well give up, that his position was hopeless. Frankly, Bob knew his chances were slight indeed; but he steadfastly refused to think of anything but that he would escape the peril that had so suddenly and so grievously trapped him.

He began to think that if the water came high enough, the buggy's weight might be released, and he might free himself. Once, when he lay for a moment with his head under water, he found that in that position he did not seem to be so tightly caught as he had supposed. He made a careful effort to catch with his right hand some purchase on the sandy road beneath the water, in an attempt to pull himself out. But the sand gave, and Bob came to the surface panting and sick. But not even then did he yield one inch to fear. If death was to have him, he thought, it would only be after he had fought to the last ounce of strength in body and brain. Never would he yield; he might perish, but he would not surrender.

The storm had rolled past now, and in the east certain clear stars were glimmering through the black-stemmed pines. Over the pinewood the tall pines still rocked and grieved, but they were now exhaling rainy aromatic odors that were borne to the young planter where he lay in his fateful position. All the sweetness of life, all that made life desirable and happy, seemed in that fragrant night wind to breathe; and all the darkness and bitterness of death stared him in the face from the black waters of Bowman's Run.

Those waters had now risen so that Laval could no longer, without holding his head under water, support his weight above it with his right arm; but the waters had not risen high enough to lift the buggy. The planter was fighting a good fight, but he had not won it. His strength was almost gone. Darkness seemed closing about him; not a darkness of the night or of the deep waters, but of eternity itself. In those last moments he looked for what he thought would be the last time at the great calm stars, at the mourning pines, and at the gleaming stretches of Bowman's water.

Through that water he fancied he saw some black object coming toward him. He thought it must be a drifting log. His eyes closed. When they opened the object was close to him. It kept coming on; laboriously it came, wearily; but it came steadily. At last it came up to the fainting planter. Its long ears were floating out on the water. Its great eyes were full of speechless love and devotion. It licked Bob's face.

It was the little hound, Game, that had come all the way from the plantation. And behind it was the huge live-oak log. Laval's tears started. He forgot for a moment his own peril in his compassion over the faithful little dog.

"You wanted to be with me," he said, "and you nearly killed yourself to come to me. Ah, little Game, what a heart you have!"

That the dog's struggles to pull the drag over the dark roads must have been desperate, Laval could easily discern. Its eyes were strained and wide; and it hardly seemed able to keep itself afloat. Having found its master, it seemed to think its mission accomplished, for it swam to the nearby bank and lay down. But its eyes were on the planter.

Bob Laval, to whom the coming of little Game had given undreamed hope, let the dog rest a few minutes, as long as he dared.

Then he called it over. When within reach, he unsnapped the chain from the heavy drag. Then he stroked the animal's head, talking to it the while intelligently.

"Game," he said "this isn't home. Let's go home, down the road there. But you'll have to help pull me out. Hi, boy, let's go."

The little hound understood the command and began to move out of the water. Laval, lying low in the water, with his right arm about the body of the dog, kept encouraging the little creature. The pull, straight away from the buggy and at a very low angle, enabled Bob to keep the position without suffering the agony that he had hitherto endured. The rising water, too, must have lightened the weight of the buggy, for Bob, with a thrill of hope, felt the vise-grip relax. Little Game seemed to understand, for he swam steadily. Slowly, slowly, the planter was drawn forward in the water. At the right angle, no great force seemed necessary to free him; but that force he himself had been unable to supply. But now Game had come, and with him rescue and life again; for in a few more minutes Bob felt himself freed. Yet he had dreaded this very moment, fearing that if it did come he would find his back fatally injured.

Cautiously, therefore, he stood up, and it was with a thankful heart that he regained his feet. For, save for a feeling of having been beaten and bruised, his back seemed not deeply injured. With his hand on the head of little Game, still swimming valiantly, the planter made his way slowly to shore. There he sat down on the bank and there Game curled up contentedly at his feet. There, too, the searching party from one of the plantations down the road, becoming aware of the danger that must be Bob's by having seen his mare Gypsy running wild, found the planter and the hound.

Bob soon recovered from his injuries; but Game never grew as large as he would have grown but for the terrible strain of that memorable night. He became, however, one of the greatest deer-dogs that the County had ever known; and if a stranger ever remarked on his small size, Laval would say, "His size, sir, is due to the fact that he saved my life." Then he would tell of what happened that night at Bowman's Run.

O Ringing Bells!

When Dave Mordaunt rose to the surface of those raving waters, instead of striking out for the sandy mound that jutted oddly out of the murky tumult of waves, he paused to look about him.

"Here, Bells!" he called. Though his eyes were anxious his voice was not excited. It was clear and well pitched.

For reply the rain slashed him savagely in the face, and the wind shrilled derisively in his ears. But his determination was resolute. He would not start for safety without Bells. Once more, treading the storm water, he called with shrewd clearness across the waves. Then a tousled white form appeared, baffled by the roaring elements. It struggled incontinently. But when she heard Dave's voice, the setter turned to him as the trembling needle sets steady and true toward the north. There came a happy yelp from the swimming dog. Ringing Bells was calling to her master.

"Come on, dog," shouted Dave. "It's pretty near time we were going," he added grimly.

Another glad yelp answered this; and in a moment the delicately molded head was swimming beside the grizzled face of her owner. Bells did not know where they were going. It was enough that she was with Dave, and that he spoke to her kindly though commandingly. And when, ten minutes later, the two came ashore on the only refuge on the storm-swept delta, the little English setter appeared ready for further adventures if Dave would but say the word. And Dave knew that there would be no trouble on that score; if Bells wished adventures, they were sure to be thronging in soon. As he sat down

---

From *Old Plantation Days* (1921); also in *Bolio and Other Dogs* (1930).

on the packed wet sand with his back to the tearing wind, he called her to him.

"Bells," he said, as she laid her head between his knees and looked up at him with reverent and adoring eyes, "do you know, girl, what's done gone and happened to us? We never had no business a-leavin' home when we saw them clouds making up in the northeast. Now we have done capsized, and that case of duckshot shells has done helped to sink our canoe. My gun's down there under that water somewheres. We got to this place all right; but how long the wind and tide are going to let us stay here is more than I know. We're a far ways from any other high land, and that I'm tellin' you.

The shrieking wind continued to drive in across the dim expanse of delta marsh, now almost topped by the vast tide that, sweeping in from the near-by ocean, was fast flooding the low-lying country adjacent to the river's mouth. The wind was full of gusty flaws that spat sharp raindrops keenly. Over Cedar Island, which stood as a dark coastal barrier between the waste delta and the sea, a strange yellowish light brooded in the dreadful heart of the on-rushing storm. A West Indian cyclone was coming up the Carolina coast in all its original and elemental fury and it boded frightful menace to all things in its path.

It lacked two hours to sundown; but a hurricane such as this one can merge day and night into swift blackness. To east and west of the wide delta, the mainland, where stood stately forests of pine, was first misted, then dimmed, then darkened, and at last extinguished. The wild tide, the dreadful cloud, the insane wind had their way with the delta. And the bleak rain connived to hide the desolation wrought. But as yet the mound on which the man and his dog had taken refuge remained above the waters.

This strange tiny island was a place little known even to the inhabitants of the country bordering on the delta. But Dave Mordaunt, having for a lifetime ranged those lonely regions of the river, knew it; and when the storm had cut him off from the mainland, he had straightway headed his canoe for the mound. Dave not only knew of the existence of it; he knew its origin as well. A half century before, when rice growing had been a flourishing industry of the delta country, there had existed the same menace from cyclones; and this great mound of earth had been erected near the center of the delta by a league of planters. The long years of erosion had worn it down to only a fraction of its original height; but it still remained the highest point in all that vast marshy region. When Dave Mordaunt and his dog reached it in this storm it was still about three feet above the water line, and the area of the part as yet uncovered was nearly half an acre.

"I'm glad to get on this place," said Dave, stroking thoughtfully the head of Bells, "but I'll be durn glad to get off here, too. She shouldn't rise no more than another foot; but," he added with grave uncertainty, "that's the yallerest cloud over Cedar Island that ever I seen."

It was not the first time he had lost his boat and his gun. But somehow this experience was going to be different from all the others. He felt sure of it.

"This thing," he mused sternly, "is gwine to be a hurricane. I smell it."

But as long as he continued to stroke the white setter's head, a legion of hurricanes could not perturb her.

Dave Mordaunt could never have been called an excitable man. He had sometimes found inaction better than action. Wherefore it was his nature to sit on the sodden mound of sand, barely rising above a waste of tossing waters, calmly stroking the head of his beloved dog while the rain drove like a sharp shrapnel against his broad back and the fiendish wind whipped him cruelly.

Having fought wind and weather for forty years, Dave knew the danger of his position; but he also had learned what is the graduating lesson in common sense—not to worry. He realized that he could hardly hope for some one to save him. The only escape lay less in the man's exertions than in an abating of the fury of the storm. And for this letting up of the hurricane, Dave Mordaunt, making Ringing Bells crouch between his knees for shelter, waited with grim patience.

But that waiting was vain. What brought Dave to a realization of this was a certain wild and eerie sight, more like a vision than a view of real things, that, during a strange lull in the rain, he saw to the southward. A sharp veering away of the cyclone between his refuge and Cedar Island had caused a dark line of trees to reappear on the seaward horizon—tall warriors they were, in black armor and in single file marching riverward. The man's eyes were now upon them, for they seemed like strong friends, bringing to him a reassurance. But even as Dave looked, the tall pines that had towered against the storms of a century, and that now seemed symbolic of a mastering strength, suddenly went down like a whisper. Through the seaward gap thus vividly made Dave could see the utter wildness of the ocean. All that savage and conquering wildness was moving resistlessly northward across the delta toward Dave's precarious place of refuge.

Already the man noted with a hardening light in his eyes that the sandy mound, which had been three feet out of water on his arrival, was now scarce one foot up. Though he had sat down with Bells on the highest point of the hillock, the waters were now upon them. Dave had to draw in his feet. The feathered tail of Ringing Bells was awash. Strangely, and it seemed to the doomed man very suddenly, he was left in a wilderness of waters. The pines of Cedar Island, drifting logs, floating sedge, had all vanished.

Standing in a crouched and braced position with his back to the howling storm, and with Bells standing with her forefeet on his shoulders and her head within the shelter of his breast, he made up his mind what to do.

"Bells," he said, "you have always been a good dog, and I've tried to be a good master to you, using you right. You have always minded me, and you will mind me now, I know. Now, listen, girl. Across the river yonder is home. You can make it. It's hard going, but you can do it. If you stay here, you sure will have to take drownin'. There ain't no use of your bein' drowned, Bells. I reckon I'll have to stay here and take what is comin' to me; but when I say, 'Go home!' I want you to go and go straight. . . . Understand me, little girl?"

More from the tone of the soft commanding voice than from the bitter driving of the wind and rain that whipped her flanks, Ringing Bells began to shiver. She always knew when Dave wanted her to carry out some plan of his. Dave Mordaunt lifted her weight from his breast and crouched low with her on the crest of the mound.

"Yonder's home," he said, pointing away to the westward. "Go, Bells! Go home, girl!"

The snowy little setter gave a yelp of understanding. A moment more and she had entered the wild waters. She knew the direction.

She knew what Dave had told her to do; and since the time when she had played as a little, white, innocent puppy at his feet, there in the humble home under the live-oaks overlooking the river, she had learned implicitly to trust and to obey the quiet hunter of the delta. He had never fooled her. He had taught her all she knew; and the greatest thing she had learned was obedience.

The man crouched on his desolate refuge, trying to follow with his weary eyes the swimming white form. But she had gotten away quickly; and now the scudding of the rain and the wild spume that was lashed up by the wind hid that desperate stretch of waters. Once, indeed, far off he thought he saw a white form suddenly glimmer and flash. But it might have been a breaking wave. Dave knew, however, that Bells would reach home. For one thing, her long and arduous training as a ducking dog had made her an excellent, hardy swimmer; for another, he had told her to go. And despite the apparent hopelessness of his own position, Dave Mordaunt had a gladness warming his heart. At least, Bells would be safe.

Though the larger waves were now breaking freely over the mound, the marooned man gave small heed to them. He was not afraid. The time had not come for him to think of himself; he was too busily thinking of little Ringing Bells and her valiant obedience.

It was in no foolish hope that her going might help him, that he had sent her home; for Dave Mordaunt was a lonely man, having neither wife nor parents, neither son nor daughter. His only relative was his brother Ben, a man much like him, who lived some two miles down the river from Dave's place.

"She'll get home," the man kept saying, "but I want her to get nigh there before I start; for if she knows I'm comin', she'll turn back. It looks mightily like drownin' for me; but leastways I can drown a little nearer home than this, and I can go down fightin'. I think the water will treat me better than this here crazy wind. When she ketches me to knees, I'll pull out; and though mayhap I'll founder right off there where my boat went down, it will not be just like standin' still and lettin' the tide come in and take me. It's a man's business, I reckon, to fight till he's done for. Anyway, the little one, she's safe . . . . And I'm coming after you, Bells."

It was not now a question of Dave's taking the water, for the water took him. Already the waves were breaking about his waist, and vehement currents were tugging at his knees, when he stepped down into the surging water.

There was now no gleam in the northern sky; and the only light was the disastrous and lurid glow that the hurricane cast. But this was as inconstant as the raving wind itself; for when Dave began to swim, it actually afforded him a glimpse of the farther shore; yet ere he had gone a rod a sudden darkness closed down upon the scene. He had a sense, though he had no sight, of the distant shore.

The lone swimmer, laboring on, rolled by the hurrying waves, smitten sharply by wind and driven spume, had one thought that glowed in his heart: he knew that Ringing Bells would have reached home by now. Even as he blindly swam he seemed to see the white setter making the shore, shaking her draggled coat in the shelter of one of the huge live-oaks, and then crawling into the snug bed of straw that her master had made for her under the cabin's high porch. Then another thought came to Dave.

What would become of Bells when he did not come ashore? His mind flashed to a cabin like his own down the river—his brother Ben's.

"He'll take her," he thought; "and he'll be good to her, though nobody will ever understand her same as I do. . . . He'll keep her to 'member me by."

Such were the swimmer's thoughts. He was a strong swimmer, to whom the breadth of the river would ordinarily have meant nothing. But now his attempt was to cross both it and the delta, and to do it in a storm. Not for a moment did he let himself think that the thing could not be done; but Dave Mordaunt was sane enough to realize, even in the unabating excitement of such an experience, that the odds were vastly against him. Yet that was the very reason he hardened his heart to do the desperate thing that had been forced upon him by the coming of the hurricane. He swam steadily with all his skill and with not more strength than he needed to exert; but what he needed was almost all he had.

There was no way for him to know of the progress he was making. He feared, indeed, that he had lost his sense of direction. The dim bulk of the sea islands, the blur to westward that had marked the river bank, the faint light in the sky over the delta to the north—all these were now shut out. But despite the fact that, for all he knew, he might be headed back for the mound, or northward up the river, or seaward under a blinding veer of the wind, Dave kept steadily on. . . . But not even a strong man can perform the impossible. . . . It was a half hour after he had left the inundated hillock that the swimmer felt himself going.

Though realizing the desperate nature of the battle he was waging, Dave Mordaunt would not admit to himself that he was drowning.

"Not yet!" he gasped, as, out of the black depths of the waters into which he had sunk, he rose to their stormy surface.

"Sink! Sin-k-k-k-k!" sobbed a great white wave, submerging him.

"Now! Now!" shrilled the mad wind in his ears as he went down.

"Not yet," muttered Dave. But his heart was sick, and his voice was no more than a wet groan.

"Soon! Soon!" shouted the crazy wind exultantly. And Dave knew that it was so. His thoughts went again to his dog.

"Bells," he gasped—"little Bells—Ben, he'll care for you."

The man's gnarled brown arms that had been wide for swimming, now swept convulsively together on the surface. The rude fingers met in a handclasp. Dave Mordaunt gave his soul over to God.

"For the sea is His," his heart said, "and He made it."

A moment thus he lay strangely on the surface, with waves rocking him not ungently; but then their forward rolling divulged his form no more. Dave had gone down; but his fight had been a brave one.

But the drowning man, far under the deep river's tide, felt a last hot rebellion against his fate. With terrible strength he beat his way upward out of the murk. He came to the surface all but unconscious.

Dave's unutterably weary eyes, heavy with the importunate summons of death's long sleep, opened dimly to the storm. But they opened wider as a strange object bulked in the grayness. It was portentous and black. There was something white on it. The man was not without superstition. He believed this to be the end.

Suddenly a sharp glad bark thrilled him, shocking him out of oblivion. Then a snowy form leaped from the black hulk. It swam toward Dave. Swiftly it came alongside, and over its warm strength the man dragged a dead arm.

"O God!" he gasped, "you done sent Bells for me!"

An hour later he was at home, lying on a rude couch before a crackling fire. On one side sat his brother Ben; and on the other, with her eyes never taken from her master's face, crouched Ringing Bells. Ben, a woodsman, bronzed until he was almost black, was a man of few words; but he could make his meaning clear enough.

"In the middle of the storm," he was saying to his brother, "Bells, she come to my house. And she made it plain that I must come to the river. Something was wrong, I knew. I come by here through the rain; and not finding you, I says to myself, 'More than likely he's over on yon mound, but he can't stay there.' By that time Bells, she was down at the river, barking. Three times she swam off, but I got her back. Then I took the twelve-foot oars and the big sturgeon boat—'tain't another craft could have come across that river—and we found you. Bells, she saw you afore I did," he added.

In the silence that followed, the snowy setter crept closer to the couch. Her eyes of utter faithfulness sought Dave's face. Dave's eyes were closed; but by instinct his hand moved toward her, searching. Ben understood his brother; for he took Dave's hand gently and laid it on the head of Ringing Bells.

PART III

NATURE'S WAYS

Any hunter who invests in Mother Nature's sound stock over a period of years is certain to reap rich dividends. To be sure, there will be a fair measure of disappointment and even sadness, but in the end the balance will solidly tilt to the side of gladness. Rutledge reveled in communion with nature, and it is important to remember that for him life in the outdoors transcended the narrow bounds of hook and bullet. He loved the chase and the incomparable hallelujah chorus of a pack of hounds hot on the trail of a stag, but the simple pleasures of observation were equally meaningful to him.

Over the years he spent countless hours, often at night, quietly watching the ever-unfolding drama provided by the myriad wild creatures that called Hampton home. His was a receptive, perceptive mind as he studied in nature's school. He would have agreed heartily with the pronouncement of Horace Kephart, the dean of American campers, that "there is no graduation day in the school of the outdoors." Yet there can be no denying that Rutledge merited advanced degrees in natural-history education. The stories that follow attest to his qualifications and demonstrate his ability to take real-life events he had witnessed and make them equally alive for his readers.

The Lady Was Kind

In a previous chapter I related a story entitled "Great Misses I Have Made," a piece in which I, with great candor, gave an account of some of my misadventures as a hunter. It might be as interesting to look at the reverse: to tell of certain of those times when Lady Luck was willing to be more than kind—when she acted like a girl who does the proposing.

Now, I do not want you to think that in these true tales I was setting myself up as a regular Deadeye Dick of a shot. You will soon discover for yourself that I personally had little to do with my extraordinary good fortune. And if you ask me how I happened to come home with far more than my share, my answer would be, "The Lady was kind."

While I was away from my plantation in South Carolina for most of the summer I kept getting frequent reports from Prince, my Negro foreman, of the game situation there. He had a lot to tell me about the deer; and as far as I could make out, I had apparently planted crops for them to harvest. He wrote me that whole herds would come into the peafield before dark. Deer have to be plentiful, tame, and hungry not to remain nocturnal in their habits.

On the last day of October I arrived on the plantation to spend the winter, reaching there in the late afternoon. After I had unpacked the car, I loaded my gun and strolled down the avenue a half mile long, toward the woods. The avenue was flanked on either side by the big peafield in which the deer had been banqueting every night. In the sandy road I could see hundreds of tracks, most of them

---

From *Hunter's Choice* (1946).

fresh. While most Negroes will lie just to please me, Prince had not lied. Big things had been going on here.

By the time I came within a hundred yards of the woods, the sun was down. But it had been a clear sunset, and a radiant afterglow suffused the whole world. Besides, at that time of year in the deep South, the foliage of the forest is at its height of color, and at sunrise and sunset the woods seem quietly ablaze. The leaves had not begun to fall.

To the left of the gate that is on a line with the edge of the woods, there is an especially dense thicket. Walking slowly, I was now within about sixty yards of it; that is, within gunshot. What was that yonder in the heavy patch of dogwoods and high-bush huckleberries? I couldn't really see body or legs. But I saw horns. Surely a buck, standing motionless there. He hadn't been hunted for ten months. For weeks he had fed in my field with impunity. Here I came down the sandy road, making no sound. Perhaps he did not even see me; certainly he never winded me.

Trying to walk up to an old buck is most uncertain business. Just as soon as I really made him out, I got my gun into position, at the same time edging a few feet forward. I probably was fifty yards from him when I shot. He acted as if lightning had struck him in the head. I saw him sink down, and I saw the glint of his horns as he lay dead on the ground. But I saw something else: a second buck, that before this I had not seen at all, jumped off as the first one fell. How close he had been standing to the first one, I do not know; but two old bucks that are consorting have a way of standing close together.

Slowly I walked over to the fallen stag. He was a fine one, and stone-dead. Somewhat idly I pushed my way through the fringe of the thicket, my gun ready. I was rather sure the second buck was gone; but sometimes when one falls, his comrade will stand around for some time. More than once I have seen two bucks running together; when one of them was killed, the other would stop.

A lot of wild creatures do not understand the meaning of the sound of a gun. In their natural haunts in the forest there are many familiar sounds loud enough to startle them, such as the fall of a tree. They don't like noises; they don't like a gun. But I often think they dislike it as a noise rather than as a gun.

In the twilight, on the open pond-edge beyond the thicket, I didn't see any wary buck waiting for his boy friend to join him. Of course, I was looking for a deer standing up, unharmed, and ready to bound away into the dusky forest. I wasn't prepared to see what I saw: the second buck lying dead between two cypresses on the edge of the pond! He too was a fine animal, and had been killed by two buckshot that had struck him high up in the back.

It is fifty years since I began to hunt deer; but nothing like this had ever happened to me before, nor is it likely ever to happen again. A hole-in-one is the ambition of every golfer. Well, this sort of thing is like putting a golf ball into two holes at the same time.

In my country, along the great delta of the Santee, especially in the lower reaches adjacent to the ocean, there are a good many duck hawks in the winter. While I take a certain kind of delight in their power and grace of flight, their perfection of physical stamina, unabated through the long centuries, and even in the swift certainty with which they take their prey, I must admit that they are very destructive. They are one of the few species, even among the predators, that kill for the lust of blood; they kill more than they need for their own immediate use. There is a primal and savage splendor about a duck hawk, but he is a merciless killer.

At daylight one morning, some years ago, I was shooting ducks in that deltaland, not far from the mouth of the river. A Negro was paddling me for jump-shooting through the mazy creeks and the old rice-field canals of the marshy wilderness. Every now and then my paddler, who knew about all that one ever learns about ducks, and who frequently advised me from the stern of the canoe, was given to muttering to himself, as if what he wished to express would be beyond my understanding. So when I heard him saying softly to himself, "Dat's too bad," I asked him what was too bad.

"I done see a duck hawk ahead of we; and where you see him, dat's bad. Look yonder now," he added as mallards and sprigs climbed the sky from the peaceful field. "He's coming dis way."

Up to that time I had not shot my gun, and it looked as if this marauder was going to ruin the morning's sport. If he came anywhere near, I would salute him. As the marsh was high on either side of the creek, and as the tide was rather low, I stood up in the canoe—a risky thing to attempt.

I was no sooner in that position than I saw a mallard drake flying straight for me, coming low and coming faster than I had ever seen a duck fly. He looked like a shell that had been shot out of a gun, and I was his target. I thought there was a second duck immediately behind him. I thought of the duck hawk, but there was not much time to think. Things were happening fast. Now was my chance to shoot.

The drake could not have been more than twenty yards from me when I fired at him, head on, and his momentum was such that I had to dodge his hurtling body as it fell into the creek beside the canoe. Hardly had it struck the water when there was a second splash, and the duck hawk lay beside the drake he had been pursuing!

I claim no credit for anything. It just happened, and at that moment Lady Luck was very kind. I had one duck toward the day's bag, and I had the general disturber of the peace.

While I have never made any deliberate attempt to do so, I have more than once killed a good many flying quail at one shot. On the edge of a wheatfield in Pennsylvania, early in the season, a huge covey of quail got up on my right and circled around to my left to reach a patch of woods. There were more than twenty birds, and they were not only flying bunched, but with curious deliberation. I felt certain of a double, and really didn't want to kill more with one barrel. But from that one shot I picked up eleven quail, and they were fine, full-grown birds. I did not honestly enjoy this experience; the Lady had gone too far in her generosity.

Another time, while coming down the mountain in the dusk, after a weary and fruitless grouse hunt, I heard a little scurry on the dead leaves. I was beside an old clearing near the foot of the mountain. Between me and the clearing there was a narrow but dense fringe of bushes and trees. The only real opening was a curious big hole through the heavy top of a red cedar, just such an opening as is made by the boys who string telephone wires. But there were no wires here. Although the light was low in the woods, I was facing the west, and the sunset sky was still bright behind the opening in the cedar boughs.

Almost as soon as I heard the noise in the leaves, a big covey of these mountain quail got up, and I thought at first they were going clear over the fringe of trees. I really could not make them out in the shadows of the woods. By instinct I brought my gun up to the opening in the cedar, and the whole covey converged into it. In that perfect concert which is one of the wonders of the flight of birds, they closed ranks and tore together through that funnel.

I just shot at the sky through the opening; and in the edge of the old field beyond the cedar I picked up six of those husky birds. They were, of course, true bobwhites; but when they live in the mountains, they seem to get larger and heavier. This curious piece of luck not only made my feeble alibi unnecessary, but it supplied me with a good story to tell, all the better because it was true.

Next to giving a friend a shot at a fine buck, one of the hardest things for me to do in the woods has always been to get a wild turkey for someone on a given date. I think it is the poet Browning who laments that we never get "the time and the place and the loved one all together." He, of course, was writing about human lovers; but the same thing is true when the loved and coveted one happens to be a wild turkey.

I have an old friend in Charleston who used to be a great hunter, but for years now he has been an invalid. About a week before Christmas he wrote to ask me whether I could possibly get him a wild gobbler for Christmas dinner. Now, that's a real order in these days. This business of timing the killing of wild game in the howling wilderness is a master problem. To complicate it in this case, my wife had also ordered wild turkey for Christmas. I was pretty hopeful about getting one; but two wild gobblers at the same time are about twenty times as hard to get as one. Well, here's what happened, and I had really little to do with the way in which it turned out.

I knew where some turkeys were, and it was within long walking distance of the plantation house. After dinner one day, at the critical period when I had to make good or go down in family history as an utter failure, I took my gun and slunk off into the woods. When it's turkeys you're after, you've got to slink. The woods into which I went are fairly open; there are plenty of oaks and pines, and here and there are big cypresses, growing on the borders of deep woodland ponds. Between the ponds are game trails.

It has been my experience that both deer and turkeys like to hang around water. Looking over the situation, I finally decided that I stood my best chance if I just picked a good spot, sat down and kept perfectly quiet. This kind of hunting has the advantage of being both restful and strategic. A man may happen to walk up to a wild turkey (his chances are best if the turkey happens to be deaf!), but the wisest move is to let the old boy come to you.

I sat on a cypress log, partly screened by a growth of blackberry canes. All the leaves were now down; the woods looked bare; there was no wind. It was an ideal time for hearing footsteps in the forest. I had not been waiting long when I saw great blue herons, weird anhingas, a raccoon on the edge of one of the ponds; but so far there was no game. A covey of quail trooped by me, feeding and talking. But I was listening for the man-like walk of a wild gobbler.

At last I heard what I had come to hear. And only a minute after I heard the sound I saw the great bird himself, looking very black and ponderous. He was going to walk the ridge between two of the small ponds. Unfortunately I was on a farther ridge. He would pass me, but it would be too far—perhaps a hundred and twenty yards. For a rifle, the shot would have been a perfect one.

This old bird was walking slowly, keeping close to the ground, just like a grouse, but every now and then straightening up to his star-tling height. What a bosom he had! And what a beard! He was one of these old swamp prophets. If I had seen him sooner, I might have dropped back and gotten over in front of his approach; but it would now be folly to move. Practically all the wild turkeys that are killed are turkeys that never see the hunter. To show yourself is to lose your chance.

As I was getting a little negative satisfaction out of admiring the splendor of this old monarch of the wilds I heard another sound. Glancing warily to one side, I saw a second old gobbler coming. This one must have been hungrier than the first one, for he was investigat-ing the possibilities of food along the edge of the pond. He looked as if he might come within range.

The first bird had now passed me, heading for the jungle-like thickets along the river. I forgot him to give all my attention to his burly partner. Once, when he was busily scratching in the set leaves, I got my gun up. On he came, but most deliberately. I had 2's in the left. When he got broadside, at perhaps sixty-five yards, and was as close as he would come, I knocked him down. He began a great floundering on the ground, and for a moment I sat still, waiting to see if he were really dead or whether, badly wounded, he would try to hide under the nearest brush pile. I have known a good many wounded wild turkeys to escape because the hunter ran in too hastily after the shot.

Rather idly I had loaded my gun again. By now the gobbler was still flopping, but not so wildly. Suddenly, to my amazement, while I was feeling certain that I had a fine bird for my friend, but that we would have to eat sausage for Christmas, the first gobbler came running back at full speed, jumped on his fallen and flapping comrade, and began beating him! You know how chickens act when you kill one and throw it down among them. For a second time within five minutes I eased up my gun; and when it spoke, two families had wild turkey for Christmas.

As to why the first bird, the one that walked past me, had not been scared off by my first barrel, I can only say, as I intimated earlier, wild game is by no means always scared into flight by a gun. It is usually startled, but it may not attribute the noise to the presence of man.

So while I have made some great misses during my days as a hunter—and it would be monotonous not to miss occasionally—I have had my share of good fortune. Yes, now and then the Lady has been very kind.

Babes in the Wildwoods

In those days when I lived on one of the most remote of plantations, one of my almost daily duties was the rounding up of stock
in the far greenwood that, like a gently rolling sea, stretched more
than forty miles southwest toward the nearest town. My great weak-
ness as a hunter and a finder of cattle was my tendency to digress: I
have always loved to watch wild things. A fawn has always meant
more to me than a calf; a baby wren more than a chick. Especially
have these little wild things engaged my affection and my interest;
these babes in the wildwoods. We nestle ours in downy blankets;
they have no enemies in the proper sense; the love that brought
them into the world yearns over their mere helplessness, with arms
to hold, with prayers to guard, with strength to shield, with tenderest
voice to sing. But how fares it with the elfin infants of the wild? How
do they get along in the huge foe-haunted forest, in the vast and
lonely swamp, upon the floods of great waters? Are they, too, guarded
by love? What are some of their tiny joys and sorrows? What are
their resources in times of peril?

Perhaps I can best answer these questions by relating simply some
of the observations I have made on little wild things. Nor has this
observation always been an easy matter; for these infants are precocious, and most of them have the elusiveness, the finesse of spirit of
patrician elves.

I remember seeing a flock of young wild turkeys on a day early in
June. I was driving along through the pine forest. From fragrant
thickets beside the road I heard vireos and parula warblers singing.
Suddenly I saw a wild turkey hen steal furtively into the road. As she

From *Wild Life of the South* (1935).

paused, ten or twelve tiny little turkeys trooped up behind her. They gathered in an expectant group, apparently wondering what was to happen next in this marvelous world.

I drew in my horse, slipped from my buggy, and walked forward toward the turkeys. The old mother at once darted into the bushes beside the road, where she immediately began to call with nervous excitement to her winsome little infants. The fairy-like children of the wild obeyed their mother's voice so swiftly and with so much precision that in a moment they vanished in the short grass bordering the road. I knew they had not run farther because there was a stretch of open sand ahead and they did not cross that. The mother in the meanwhile kept calling plaintively from the shadows of a watercourse some fifty yards away.

I sat down beside a pine, knowing that the little birds were all about me; and though I did not move, every one of them must have been watching me with beady bright eyes. For not one stirred from hiding. After at least fifteen minutes of vain waiting I began to walk back toward my buggy. Pausing to look over my shoulder, I saw the fairy-like fugitives running over the clear strip of sand toward their mother. A few moments later, as I drove by the place, the whole family was happily united, and my heart thrilled to hear music as sweet and appealing as any heard in the whole realm of nature: the treble elfin pipings of little wild turkeys, joyously rejoining their mother.

One day I came upon a nest of young wild rabbits, six in number. I discovered it through seeing some of the fur which the mother had pulled from her own breast sticking up in a patch of dead grass. Upon investigating, I discovered a shallow excavation lined with this fur. In this small pocket were the six palpitant little bunnies. I marveled that they could be comfortable in so small a place. I wondered also over the absence of the mother; for though I ranged the nearby woods carefully, I could see no sign of her. As I was obliged to pass by the same place late in the afternoon, I decided to watch for a little while to see if the mother would return home. My vigil was rewarded.

The first evidence of the approach of the mother was the violent upheaval in the hole itself; for all the little rabbits either heard her approach or else became occultly aware of it. I saw the grass heaving gladly, convulsively. The old mother stole up to the nest with a wondrous light in her beautiful gleaming eyes. With one front paw she gently drew aside the little mat of grass and fur that covered her precious babies. I knew, of course, that it must be suppertime, and I wondered just how the infants would be fed. To my surprise, the mother gently stretched herself over the aperture, lying there passively while her little ones nursed avidly. I do not know that I ever saw a sight in nature more appealing than that.

There is one more little incident that I should like to record. It has to do with the woodcock, one of the most beautiful and intelligent of American game birds. Every year a few pairs of these birds nest on the plantation; though it is customary for most of them to migrate before they breed. One pair that had a nest one spring in the dense shrubbery near the plantation house was a source of the rarest and most romantic interest to me. I watched it until the four young hatched and was highly amused to see how solemn these tiny fledglings looked, with their large heads, their big round eyes, and their very long bills, pointing almost straight downward. One day when the birds were about a week old, upon going as usual to investigate their progress, I was troubled at finding only two in the nest. Suddenly I heard a delicate music of whistling wings, and the mother settled on the ground near her babies. Nuzzling the young gently with her beak, she lifted one and flew away through the thicket. She held her baby in her bill just as a cat holds a kitten. The fourth baby was removed in the same manner. She was taking them to a safer place. My visits had become too frequent; this fact I guessed from the bright-eyed undetermined look she gave me.

Her flight took her across a marsh and into a deep swamp, and though I investigated, I never found the new home. But I am glad that she did carry her young away from what she considered danger, for it showed me that in the wild natural heart is the same love, the same protecting care, the same intelligent guarding of children that we find in human families.

A Forest Fire

Throughout my plantation boyhood I took a deep and solicitous interest in observing wild life during the disastrous forest fires that used to sweep the pinelands, not only over our own two thousand acres, but over an area of more than a hundred square miles. The conflagrations always afforded me a most unusual opportunity of observing the behavior of wild creatures under dramatic circumstances.

I believe a forest fire at night is far more destructive of wild life than is one in the daytime. For example, I have kept about a hundred yards ahead of advancing flames, which, unfanned by wind, were just eating their way redly along. The swath being cut, however, was a wide one, and as the fire was slowly burning, it was disastrously complete in what it did. I watched many wild things coming out of the smoke, and almost, it appeared, out of the flames. Their general aspect was one of discomfort and boredom rather than downright terror, such as many of them would have betrayed at the dread presence of man. I saw a group of five whitetail deer walking in single file, a huge stag leading. About every thirty yards they would pause to look and to listen; but it seemed to me that they were as wary of what might be the danger in front as they were of the peril behind. Indeed, they appeared to gauge sanely the nature of the fire. Apparently they had often seen fires before, and their equanimity was not greatly disturbed by one.

Many gray squirrels I saw, running on the ground and along logs. Some of these fugitives escaped. But squirrels, along with raccoons and other haunters of den-trees, are really the worst sufferers in bad

From *Wild Life of the South* (1935).

forest fires. At the first alarm they will make for home—that is, for a favorite hollow, and if that tree goes, they do, too. However, it is a fact that many of the ancient den-trees are among the largest of the forest, and for that very reason may survive a fire when scores of smaller trees go down. A gray fox I saw, stealing along in his artful fashion. He caught a wood-rat close to the fire—a fugitive ghoulishly taking advantage of a fellow-fugitive! Then there were rabbits and many other small creatures. As long as daylight lasted, I could not see among the wild things any panic; but, as I have said, this was a slow fire, burning leisurely through the forest. If the flames had been windswept and roaring along wildly, without doubt that element of incontinent flight would have been present.

The same fire was visited at night; and as my purpose was solely to watch the wild things, I gave that matter my full attention. I wish I could forget some of the sounds I heard. Clearly above the crackling of the flames and the soft roaring of the fire I could hear the mad screeching cries of the poor trapped squirrels. I was near a den-tree that was afire. Perhaps a dozen gray squirrels had taken refuge in it. At last the old patriarch went crashing down; and the pitiful cries I had heard from its beleaguered top ceased suddenly. Once on the ground, even in a dangerous fire, a squirrel has an even chance for safety. At other times at night I flushed quail and they seemed able to make off clearly. But the woods were dense with smoke, affecting painfully all the senses. In general, however, I do not believe many birds of any kind perish in forest fires. Wings afford a means of escape that nothing else could.

One afternoon, just about sundown, while I was in a section of the homeland woods that was then surrounded by a forest fire, an island of greenery in the sea of encroaching flames, I was attracted to a dense thicket of bays only ten square yards or so in area that occupied the center of the unburned tract. The fire, advancing somewhat slowly and softly on account of the damp chill of the coming night, with its attendant rise of dew, was about a hundred yards away in each direction. It appeared to me a place where wild life might be taking temporary but insecure refuge; therefore I approached it cautiously, from the leeward side.

No sooner had I come alongside than I heard, among the dry ferns and the dead leaves that covered the sphagnum moss of the place, a stealthy step. I say stealthy; and that kind of footfall made me know that it was no half-wild hog's that I heard, though many a one had been seen running along, squealing disconsolately over the general aspect of life. But this step was either that of a deer or a turkey. Dropping to one knee I listened intently for some further sound from the creature, or for some sight of it. For at least a minute it was still; and that is a long time when one is tensely listening. Then came another footfall, but attended this time by the crackling of the small dead branches of the sweet-bays. This told me that the creature was a deer. A wild turkey may make much noise coming through dead leaves, but seldom does it crack a bush on which it does not step.

These dead branches were being forced out of the way by a deer that was coming out into the twilight of the pinelands to browse and to roam. But, having drowsed all day in that thicket, he was coming out into a very different world from the one he had left at dawn. I wanted to see exactly what he would think of it all, how he would act. At last, out of the head of the little pond there appeared the graceful and sensitive head of a buck. His ears were set forward as for a moment he looked at the fire as it gleamed and crackled in the broomsedge. The picture of vividly alert intelligence, he suddenly decided on his course. Lowering his head, he stole forth noiselessly out of the thicket. To the west of us was the wide tract through which the fire had already passed, rimmed vividly on the near side by the oncoming flames. The buck, not the least disconcerted by the ring of fire in which he found himself, moved forward steadily in that eerie, effacing way that a deer has when undisturbed. He reached the fire, when, with one great bound and a show of his white regimental flag, he was lost to sight in the smoky woodland. I doubt if he had ever seen a real fire before; but he handled himself as if it were nothing for him to be trapped by a ring of flames. The very next afternoon, not far from that same place, I waked up an old, old stag that had been serenely lying in his bed in some small bay-bushes, while not a hundred yards to the left of him a forest fire roared terribly, and while all the woods were filled with acrid and blinding smoke. I believe that, lying close to the ground as they do, deer do not, when couched, get the full effects of smoke from a fire. Judging from the behavior of this second buck, a deer takes small account of a fire until it has literally run him out of his covert. This old stag, when I roused him, made off in long graceful leaps, his course taking him close to the high sheets of flame. When last I saw him he had passed through the fire and was rocking away safely through the distant forest.

In the swampy and pine barren country in which the particular fires occurred, there are many quail; the covies do not often number more than a dozen birds, but there are covies in abundance. When the fire swept their damp coverts and their sunny feeding-grounds in the broomsedge fields under the pines, these birds were in sore straits; for, though, as every sportsman knows, the quail can undoubtedly make good use of his wings, he is essentially a ground bird, and rarely takes wing except when disturbed. As quail are very fond of frequenting one small locality, they suffer from fire because their home is in fact destroyed. If unmolested, and if the nature of the cover does not change, these fine birds will remain year after year on a remarkably limited range.

As I walked through the burnt country, every few hundred yards I could hear the calling of quail. Once or twice a whole covey, strung out in line, with all the members of the family in plain view of one another, would set up the far-penetrating sweet gathering-call of the old mother. They were spiritually distracted. Many times I watched a covey running thus on the burnt ground, and heard the birds calling in a most pathetic and appealing way. But these birds were exceedingly wild, and appeared well able to take care of themselves. As my approach through the burnt and crackling bushes was noisy and obvious, they would flush at a distance of at least a hundred yards, and their flight sometimes carried them clear out of my vision. Two or three days after the fire had passed, all these birds had moved into a narrow strip of woodland that had been saved from the flames.

When such conflagrations come, all life is sure to suffer; and while, as I have related, I have seen wild creatures take small account of fires, it must be remembered that they were not terrific conflagrations, sweeping to death all before them. Such conflagrations are brought about nevertheless by small beginnings; by much material to be burned; and by a high wind. A single flame in a forest may well represent a primal force which, unleased, will mean utter devastation in its most hideous form to all living things of a vast surrounding region.

A Gallant Mother

One day when there was a great flood in the river, Prince and I went across to the delta to see if we could rescue some of the plantation stock that had been caught by the high waters.

The very first refugee we saw repaid us for our crossing of the dangerous river. The marvel of her really got me. That sounds romantic, I know. But of all wild mothers that have ever come under my observation, she was the finest and the ugliest. This fugitive from the flood was a full-blooded wild razorback—all bone and bristles and lean bacon. Her snout was so long and sharp that it gave her the appearance of smoking a pipe. Her sides were plainly slatted. Her *ensemble* was, for all her uncouthness, indescribably fierce. Her startling fringe of bristles was a sort of menacing triumph. Formidable indeed she looked—morose and vindictive—standing gingerly there on a sodden log, wedged precariously by the freshet tide into the low crotch of a water-oak.

Brush and sedge and the tree's limbs had made a tremulous islet that swayed in the rushing waters. Behind her, under her, quaking in the shelter of her mighty flanks, were her little ones—nine of them. She could easily save herself. But she would not leave them to perish. I wondered much what would now happen. These hogs, you understand, were perfectly wild; therefore we approached behind a fringe of cypresses, in order to watch their natural behavior.

Knowing that the old mother could swim miles to safety, I made up my mind to save at least some of the pigs. They were only about two or three weeks old; and in their present situation they looked to me doomed. . . . But perhaps no living thing is doomed as long as it has a mother.

From *Wild Life of the South* (1935).

You really ought to have seen this one. The waters were fast rising. The old savage creature knew well that she and her trembling brood must soon be dislodged from their quaking, frail support. About a half-mile away, across a clear stretch of water, there was some high ground known as the Pine Ridge. I saw her looking at it. She was appraising the risk incurred to reach it. She had, I knew, determined to swim to the Ridge. But she wasn't going alone. Lowering her hideous, formidable head, she tenderly nuzzled the pigs, one by one. To them she grunted deep and placid reassurance. She kept nudging them until all of them were in a huddle.

Then suddenly I saw her plunge off the log into the stormy tide. About thirty feet she swam—fiercely and with head high, as a hog always swims; then she headed around, and in a few moments had returned to the log. She climbed it, streaming. As surely as I was watching her, I believe that she was instructing her babies as to how the thing was to be done; and she was showing them how easy it was. Again she took gentle counsel with her nursery.

Slowly now, and with infinite caution and patience, she herded them down toward the water. She was actually in it, among the stranded sedges, for a moment or two, before she was satisfied that all her brood were with her. Then, grunting easily, very slowly she began to swim. She didn't swim like a hog; for she was now the solicitous mother. All her tiny pigs were in the lee of her great flank. Seeing to it that they started on that side, she broke the current for them, and they swam as if they were in a backwater. She did not appear to be trying to save her own life, but theirs. It was a beautiful sight to watch—that grim old monster mothering her babies across that stormy tide! Self-preservation is said to be the first law of Nature. But from the operation of that law shall we not have to make an exception of mothers?

An hour later Prince and I found our gallant old sea-going heroine on the Pine Ridge. She had every little pig safely with her. I looked with genuine admiration at the gaunt, grim creature.

Twenty Feet at Rimini

As yet the turbid Santee had appeared to me to be no higher or muddier than usual; but a word, moving more swiftly than ever surcharged waters can flow, told me that a great flood was coming down the river. The newspaper, in a perfunctory way, officially reported that the water at Rimini, which is more than a score of miles above us, was twenty feet above normal. Such a height at Rimini would mean with us a mighty flood; and in the time of such a freshet there are many strange and wild happenings in the vast and lonely delta of the Santee. As an almost boundless scope of wild and semi-wild country becomes submerged region above whose drowned habitations a thousand refugees struggle, on a contracted stage, and with man omitted, scenes of the deluge are reënacted. Because I knew the somewhat fearsome import of the telegraphic brevity of "twenty feet at Rimini," as soon as I had read the words I left the warm and cheerful fireside of the plantation dining-room, and walking through the hall to the back door, was there afforded a view of the river a hundred yards away.

The Santee did look rather more tawny than it had appeared a few hours before; but its aspect was not threatening. However, the alarming report of the newspaper was shortly to be confirmed in a manner which left me no possible reason for doubt. A dusky figure, having crossed the long ricefield banks which bordered the river, now approached me as I stood under a live-oak behind the house.

My visitor was Prince Alston, a Negro whose knowledge of the ways of the river is startling in its accuracy. I asked him what he thought of the condition of the Santee, knowing well enough that he

From *Days Off in Dixie* (1925).

had seen no newspaper. Unhesitatingly he gave as his opinion that a big water was on its way down to us. All the banks, he said, would surely be overflowed by the next morning; and by the following afternoon we could paddle in our canoe over the entire delta. He knew the river far better than I, and his ideas concerning its probable behavior carried more weight with me than the report from Rimini. The official there doubtless had gauges; but Prince had prescience, whose power transcends that of all things mechanical. Acting, therefore, on his belief, we prepared for a flood.

In meeting a somewhat similar emergency, Noah, I believe, built a boat. As we already had several boats, we merely drew these high up on the land and tied them to trees so far away from the water that it appeared impossible to believe that the river could float them. But during the long hours of darkness that were soon to follow, we realized that the wide and rather placid river, would be transformed into a wild and turbulent torrent sweeping in madness to the sea.

After all the boats had been made secure, Prince and I drove the stock into the barnyard, lest some of the cattle, wandering in the darkness near the river, might be caught and swept away, or drowned in the gross thickets bordering the swamps. After this task, as by now the dusk was falling, there was nothing we might do until the morrow. But more than once during the night I was awake; and I could not only hear the soft rush of the waters over the topped banks, but could actually smell the water; for when a freshet begins to overflow bottom-lands carpeted with leaves and trash, there is given off, especially at night, a pleasant, wild, fresh, rainy odor.

When morning dawned, the prophecy of Prince stood fulfilled. The river had risen ten feet in the night. The boats which we had dragged up so absurdly high were now afloat. The ricefield banks were flowed clear. All the lowlands were flooded. The delta—as much of it as was visible from the plantation landing—was an apparently endless stretch of yellow waters, out of which strangely rose tall trees, indefinably subdued by being partly submerged, waving cane-brakes, drowning elder bushes, and here and there a dry tuft of duck-oats or a futile wisp of sere marsh. From a window high in the house, a window which afforded me an unimpeded view of the wide river country as far as I could see, my eye fell upon the yellow waters, ramping wherever obstructed, the unnatural aspects of the perishing landscape, and the far weird vistas which pictured vaguely the stormy insistence of the mighty flood. Perhaps what made the scene most strange was the fact that the day was calm and bright and warm—a typical mid-winter day for that latitude; and yet there were visible those scenes which are usually associated with whatever is wildest in wind and rain. From what I saw I well knew that a day of excitement and strange adventure awaited me.

My first duty was to make sure that the stock was safely in the barnyard; and this matter had my attention. But as I began to walk along the edges of the freshet, one of the first refugees I espied stoutly swimming for shore was one of the many half-wild hogs that people the delta and that are supposed to belong to someone—usually the person who achieves their capture. This particular creature, a gray brute whose high back bristles showed, even as he swam desperately for his life, had come, I supposed, from Lone Pine Ridge, a small hillock standing a mile and a half away across the delta. Despite the heroic effort that he had already made, the hog was swimming with remarkable skill and strength; indeed, all my observation of these creatures as swimmers goes to confirm the belief that, although ordinary landdwellers, they are genuine experts in the water. Unless by mischance one becomes entangled in tough grass or in strong vines, or is wedged between trees, seldom indeed will one drown. Nor, in difficult places, are these hogs unable to perform masterful maneuvers. Once in a freshet I saw a herd of seven hogs, marooned on a canebrake hummock that bordered the river, plunge boldly and in concert into the terrible tide, swim upstream for thirty yards, and come safely to land on a much higher hummock. Considering the wild flowing of the waters, the feat was accomplished with cleverness, sanity, and great dispatch. The particular swimmer to which I first referred was halfway across the river before he saw me. I stood among the trees on the shore where he was intending to land, and seeing me, he turned sharply downstream; as far as I could see him, he held to the middle of the river.

Along the edges of the freshet tide there were many interesting, and some amusing, sights. It is always incongruous to see wild life in situations wherein normally it would never be found. In the damp

cotton-rows that dipped down to the water there were many Wilson
snipe; while in the tumultuous rootings of a potato field, in which
hogs had long foraged and steam-shovelled, there were woodcock,
squatting sedately and boring assiduously in the soft brown loam.
Thus two of the shyest, most secretive, and most intelligent of game
birds were, because of the exigencies fashioned by the flood, making
themselves absurdly common. In little briar patches and thickets
into which the waters were creeping with delicate sibilant whispers,
there crouched king rails, little black rails, soras, and swamp-sparrows.
Huddled disconsolately beside marshy tussocks and brown cypress
knees were scores of swamp-rabbits—gentle, limpid-eyed creatures
that appeared to have small fear of me. These swamp-rabbits, being
natives of the marshes and the bogs, are out of their element when
they come to land that is really high and dry. Two of them I caught
in my hands—a feat that was made possible by the little creatures'
inability to dodge cleverly, and by his proneness to run into obstacles.
In his native haunts he invariably follows well-beaten paths, in which
neither men nor other obstacles oblige him to dodge. And I believe
that his eyesight is not so good in the bright sunlight and in open
places as is the keen vision of his relative, the cotton-tail. Nor is this
defect unaccountable; for, since the swamp-rabbit is a dweller in
gross jungles of marsh and cane and wampee, his vision is adjusted
to half-lights. Into the dimness of his ordinary home even the bright-
ness of high noon will penetrate but wanly.

My sympathy for all these poor fugitives was heightened when I
observed that apparently they had escaped the flood only to fall
victims to predatory birds which now were afforded a cruel opportunity to attack them. In the delta of the Santee hawks and eagles are
always numerous and active; but they are especially in evidence
when there are fires in the pinelands or when there is a freshet in
the river. The marauders then concentrate. Both fires and floods
are allies of these hunters of the air. Either a fire or a freshet will
attract birds of prey within a radius of many miles; and by their
constant activity on the smoky borders of a conflagration or on the
boggy margins of a flood they appear grimly to rejoice in the suprem-
acy of their power. For my part, having a gun with me, I dispersed
some of these brigands with a curtain of fire, but I knew that my

protection of the refugees was imperfect indeed. The hawks and eagles would return as soon as I left, nicely timing their coming with my departure.

And my leaving for the house came sooner than I anticipated; for in the road leading through the cottonfield appeared Prince, paddle in hand. His approach meant my abandoning the freshet edges for the far more exciting diversions to be had in paddling for miles over the wastes of the drowned delta country.

Within a half-hour after my meeting with Prince we were seated in the twelve-foot cypress canoe and were pushing through the tops of the elder bushes on the river bank. We crossed the Santee, forthwith entering a country that might have represented the Pleistocene Age. I mean to say that some of the forms of wild life that we ran across there appeared to belong to the extinct species which haunted the earth thousands of years ago. Although the time was late December, and although with us the alligator is a creature that hibernates, I was not surprised to see sluggishly swimming on the surface of the waters between a canebrake top and a raft of sedge packed against a tupelo tree, a scaly monster with cold unblinking eyes.

As we were not twenty feet from this bull alligator, he was in peril; but he was too dazed and numb to regard us intelligently and to act discreetly. Roused by the waters of the flood, he had been forced out of his obscure winter den and now swam aimlessly on the surface—a drowsing dragon of medieval size and aspect. As I looked at him and considered his extreme discomfort in the chilly waters, I had an impulse to let him go; but then there came to mind the story of the Bengal tiger that, in a far country, swam ashore exhausted; and of how the man who discovered the creature did not delay in dispatching it—not for the harm it was then capable of doing, but because of the menace it would be when it had recovered its strength. I therefore shot the bull alligator; for while for the moment he might be harmless enough, throughout the long months of the coming spring and summer his reign over a certain part of the delta would have been a hideous festival of cruelty, with many a delicate fawn, many a gentle and beautiful wood-duck, many a lamb and kid falling victims to his voracity.

Beyond the place where the alligator sank, we came to a small grove of druid-like cypresses and let the boat drift rockingly in among the gnarled trunks that, fourteen feet from the ground, were of giant proportions. The age of such trees is a matter of centuries rather than of years; and I could not doubt but that this particular group had been growing there since before the time when the first white man had ever seen the great delta of the Santee, and when the Cherokees and the Seminoles cruised over the freshet waters as Prince and I were now paddling over them. Over the limbs of these trees massive vines of the muscadine had clambered, while the lithe supple-jack had so banded some limbs that the vines were like rings embedded in the soft wood. Such cypresses, we knew, would probably afford harborage to refugees from the freshet. Our little period of pausing under those great trees afforded us some of the most interesting observations of our trip. As was to be expected, on account of his faultless eyesight, the first discovery of note was made by Prince, and my failure to observe as quickly as he did might have had disastrous results.

I was just putting out my hand to rest it against one of the cypresses and steady the canoe, when Prince cried out in sudden warning. Instinctively I jerked back my hand, and not a second too soon; for, lying in an indolent coil on a small carpet of dead sedge drifted against the windward bole of the tree, was a five-foot cotton-mouth moccasin. His stout body, from long staining by river-mud, was like the sere color of the sedge. For a moment, however, as the wide jaws flashed open, a vivid patch of white was momentarily visible. So startling is this sudden flash of white that, since the snake has no other method of warning those who approach it too closely, I have long believed that the cotton of its mouth, if not designed as a warning, at least serves as one. This moccasin had no business to appear in that latitude in December. But, like the alligator, he had been driven forth from his sleeping-place to swim driftingly in the wintry waters and crawl benumbed on the sodden sedge.

I was curious to see whether its hibernating had affected its power to strike, or had reduced the normal portion of its venom. The big snake gave me immediate and convincing information about itself. It appeared sluggish in every way except in the matter of striking. The minute the snake was touched by the paddle, the broad and savage head drew back so quickly that the eye could not follow the movement; the wide jaws yawned; the yellowish-white fangs stood out almost straight.

We came across at least a dozen other moccasins on our trip, and all of them appeared to be in the same condition of torpor; but their drowsiness was of a type from which they could instantly be aroused. With that swiftness that is instinctive with wild life, they reacted to danger. Perhaps their hibernation in the latitude described is, after all, desultory and incomplete. The winter in the Carolinas is often a mere name. In Florida, there is no hibernation of reptiles. Indeed, one of the ordinary diversions of the tourist season in that state is said to be the thrill experienced upon stepping on a seven-foot diamondback rattler. In the pinelands adjacent to the lower Santee I can record seeing at least one great diamondback of the coastal wilderness lying before the doorway of his strange den, having been lured forth in mid-January by a spell of summer-like weather.

While I was engaged in testing the moccasin's striking powers, Prince suddenly gave a surprised chuckle of delight. I saw that he was looking up into one of the ancient cypresses and I knew what this meant, because the smile that wreathed Prince's face was the smile which he reserves for the discovery of a raccoon. In this instance the expanse of his expression of joy could hardly be commensurate with his exultance, for among the forks of the tree were five refugee raccoons! The flood had treed the whole family.

One might suppose that purely wild creatures discovered in the manner described would naturally want to climb higher, or to crouch lower, or at least to eye us sedulously. But the raccoon is the philosopher of the delta. With far more equanimity than a mortal can assume, he accepts all situations. He phlegmatically refuses to recognize a crisis. Being a "borrower of the night" for all its dark hours, he is a profound sleeper during the day; but even when awake and fully aware of approaching enemies, he betrays no emotion. Commonly he curls up in a hollow for his diurnal siesta; but when caught by a flood at some distance from his regular den tree, he will accommodate himself to circumstances. The crotch of a cypress is no mean substitute for a cozy hollow. One of the raccoons was so low down that my paddle could reach it. When poked with the paddle, it gave evidence of being very testy, but showed not the slightest sign of that swift alertness that we associate with the folk of the wild.

As it would have been a far more cruel thing—to Prince—for us to leave all the raccoons than it would have been—to them—to take all of them with us, I compromised with my paddler. He wanted the whole family; but we took the old male only. In thus abandoning four 'coons in one tree, I suppose my utter lack of financial considerations was shown, for raccoon hides are now worth twenty dollars apiece. But a man would have to sacrifice some qualities of his heart to take an old female and her young.

Leaving the cypress grove, we pushed off into a wide expanse of open water, and now for the first time we saw what the effects of the flood must be far down the river. One of these was to obliterate the feeding grounds of the migrated wildfowl. Overhead now, in the clear sunlight, flocks of ducks began to stream. All were heading northward toward the river swamps, where feasts of acorns awaited them. The distraction of the ducks was quite evident. They flew much lower than they should fly in full daylight over a man with a gun. In one flock I counted upward of two hundred. Another flock I estimated at a thousand. For a time scores of these flocks were in sight; but in about an hour most of them had passed us by. Other birds there were, flying somewhat aimlessly. There were yellowlegs and willets, Wilson snipe and gallinules, blackbirds in dark myriads, and solitary herons. Many a raft of sedge was black with redwings. Coming to a long canebrake, we followed its edge, and, peering into its green obscurity, I saw many a poor refugee. Rabbits seemed to be on every old stump, on the tops of bushes that were almost flush with the water, on the low-sweeping limbs of trees, and often swimming swiftly in and out of the vistas among the canes. Tiny marsh-sparrows, no whit dismayed by the high waters, sang merrily. Clapper rails rising with dangling legs and resembling nothing so much as bunches of old rags flew a short distance and then dropped, usually into the water. Many wild hogs passed us, swimming valiantly. Suddenly Prince exclaimed:

"Look yonder! Look yonder—making for the main!"

Far across the level waters my eye caught sight of a tall rack of white-tail deer antlers. A swamp-buck was swimming for the mainland. Even in a line more straight than he could swim, the distance was at least two miles; but the deer was safe in his strength. The declining sun of the afternoon glinted on his polished horns. Though swept somewhat out of his course by the irresistible tide, the swimmer held his direction, and the speed and the power of his swimming were superb.

Near the end of our canebrake we came upon two canoes whose occupants were abroad for the purpose of finding strayed stock. I do not think that they cared whose stock they might happen to find, their object being merely to capture what they could. Of course, they were after hogs. I was glad that they had not seen the buck. For my part, they were welcome to disport themselves after the razorbacks. For a career full of crises, commend me to hog-catching in a freshet—especially when the hunting is done from canoes which have but one natural bent, and that is to turn over. My greeting with these men was not over cordial, for we were above land that belonged to me. Whether, with fifteen feet of water submerging it, I could claim it, is a question for legal minds rather than for mine.

Prince and I were now seven miles from home, and the afternoon was waning. Besides, such a head-tide as we had would make our progress slow. Northward we turned, to skirt the dark edges of the line of trees on the delta-bank of the river. Northward we paddled, with many a sight of refugees in trees, on sedge, in rustling canebrakes. Always under our frail craft I could sense the mighty movement of the flood.

Dusk was falling as we reached the plantation. It was good to get home again. A cheerful fireside is never so appreciated as when one has come to it from the "tumultuous privacy of storm"—or flood. And a bright hearth meant peace to me after I had been made to feel, through a whole day, the full import of the apparently innocent words "twenty feet at Rimini."

PART IV
HUNTING JOYS

Hunting was an integral part of virtually all of Archibald Rutledge's life. Only during his final years, when infirmities kept him from responding to the hunter's horn, did he forgo the manifold pleasures of the quest. Hunting deer was probably his favorite sport, with America's big game bird, the wild turkey, rating a close second. Indeed, shooting sports of all sorts brought him great delight, as did the simple opportunity to be afield. Wild game figured prominently in the fare gracing the table at Hampton, and delicacies such as haunch of venison browned to a turn, roast turkey, and stuffed quail and mallards were considered essential parts of any holiday feast. Along those lines, it would be a mistake to come to the conclusion that Rutledge's lean, angular frame suggested indifference to culinary delights. Far from it. Descriptions of mouth-watering feasts are scattered throughout his writings, and his conservationist's blood saw to it that no portion of the game harvest was wasted.

In the final analysis it was the joy of the quest, with its camaraderie, manliness, and the sheer exuberance of being afield, which held his heart. In the stories which follow we see that both waterfowling and upland bird shooting held deep meaning for Rutledge. This was the more so because of a dearth of turkeys in Pennsylvania during his many years of residence there, along with the fact that methods of deer hunting in the state were ones he considered so dangerous that he declined to participate. There were consolations though, chief among them being the opportunity to hunt a bird Rutledge greatly admired, the ruffed grouse.

Pennsylvania had quail as well, but in nothing approaching the plentitude Rutledge knew at Hampton. Indeed, coveys of bobwhites and Carolina have long been virtually synonymous. Havilah Babcock's books, with bewitching titles like *Tales of Quails 'n Such* and *I Don't Want to Shoot an Elephant*, are set in the state he had adopted as home. Like Babcock, Rutledge put in endless hours afield after partridges, as quail were locally known. He knew every peafield and sedgefield where a pointer was likely to go "birdy." Overgrown back forties were as familiar to him as the keys of his battered typewriter, and many a winter afternoon would find him prowling lespedeza edges, those cafeterias for coveys of birds.

He was similarly keen on waterfowl, which were found in abundance in the abandoned rice fields and wetlands along the Santee. Whatever bird was the object of his efforts, Rutledge savored the experience and wrote of it with a zest which leaves little doubt about how he enjoyed bird hunting. Today the whistling of wings at dawn and the gabbling of ducks at dusk are but a faint echo of what Rutledge knew, and modern agricultural practices, together with a host of related adversities, have seen a dramatic drop in the numbers of quail. Still, we can know these sports as once they were by sharing them vicariously with Rutledge, and the six selections which follow offer a good cross section of the marvelous wing shooting he was privileged to enjoy.

Those Big Mountain Boys

The beautiful Cumberland Valley of southern Pennsylvania is really the northward extension, from the Potomac to the Susquehanna, of the Shenandoah Valley of Virginia. I lived in the former country for a period of thirty-three years, where I enjoyed some of the very best quail hunting then to be had in America. It was there also that I did my goruse hunting and my trout-fishing; but, as the saying goes, that is another story.

It must have been a happy hunting-ground for the Indians; for many of the names are of Indian origin—Conococheague, Conodoguinet, Taia Menta Sacta—this last being the name of a noble spring, and the meaning of the name is Never-Failing Water. There, too, I used to indulge my hobby of collecting Indian relics. I recall finding, in a brief afternoon's hunt, on a campsite at the junction of two streams, forty-seven arrowheads.

The Valley, some fifty miles long by twenty wide, used to be full of quail. They had everything a quail needs: plenty of good flowing water, countless fields of wheat-stubble, briared fencerows and brushy creek-banks. And if the winters were sometimes severe, there were dense pine thickets and honeysuckle jungles to which the birds could resort. I never thought much of going out on a brief November afternoon and killing fifteen birds or so. I hunted in the Valley, and did not tackle the hills unless I was after grouse. But it happened that, as I was working one afternoon on a covey in Jeff Meadows' pasture, he walked down from his barn to see me. We were old friends, and he let me hunt his place.

I showed him the three birds I had killed.

"Shucks," he said contemptuously, "them's babies."

From *Those Were the Days* (1955).

"What do you mean, 'babies'?" I retorted defensively.

Like the Psalmist, Jeff lifted up his eyes to the hills.

"If you'll take your dog up in them laurel thickets, you'll see quail as is quail—big covies, too—twenty-five and thirty birds. But they fly like mountain pheasants."

While, of course, I had always noticed differences in the size of quail, they seemed to me to be incident to age. A hunter frequently runs into a late-hatched covey in the autumn. Some of the birds may not be more than half-grown. However, the ones I had just showed Jeff were mature, and of standard size. The weight of such a bird will be about four ounces.

"This covey I have scattered," I told Jeff, "had about fourteen birds in it, and all were full grown. Do you mean to tell me there are bigger and better covies in the mountains?"

"There be," he answered simply.

"I reckon you saw them when you were tending your still," I suggested.

"No," he said with painstaking honesty, "that's over in the far woodlot."

"And you think I'll have some sport up yonder?" I asked, looking dubiously at the rather precipitous mountain slope.

"You can if you find 'em. Is that there dog of yours any good?"

It was his turn to look dubious; for he was looking at Mike, a regular mutt of a pointer, with plebeian written all over him. But though he had no social background, Mike was a tireless hunter and a game getter. I never owned a worse-looking or a better dog.

"Now, Jeff," I said, "that mountain is a big place, even for a good dog and a keen hunter. Have you any suggestions as to where I might find one of these giant covies of overgrown birds?"

"You see those four tall dead chestnuts away up yonder? There's an old sawdust pile there. That's where the mill used to be. A big covey hangs out around there, and in those laurel thickets above the clearing where the mill stood."

Without being sure of the entire truth of what he had been telling me, I took Jeff Meadows' advice. Calling Mike away from his unsteady point on a rabbit, I crossed the stream in the pasture, where shell-barks lay scattered on the ground amid the tattered gold of the freshly fallen hickory leaves. The aromas of autumn were in the air: the balmy fragrance of the dewy leaves; the tang of woodsmoke; the aromatic perfumes exhaling from the dying grasses, and from the shrubbery thickets along the lazy stream; the spicy scent from the dense pines that darkly fringed the base of the hill I was to climb.

I suppose the real difference between a hill and a mountain is a mere difference in height. These hills or mountains on either side of the Cumberland Valley naturally vary much in their individual elevations; but some of them rise to a height of two thousand feet—maybe more. I know that when I used to climb them, and measure them by the degree of my weariness, I thought that they were much higher than that.

As I ascended the slope by an old winding sheep path, my faithful Mike was busy with the bushes and the briar-patches on either side. I had called him away from a good covey in an open level pasture, and had brought him, without any explanation, to this rugged and unfamiliar country. But he came cheerfully, working all the time. Sometimes this same dog used to make me ashamed of myself; for I was his god, and often my behavior, especially toward him, was very far from godlike. But the only time he ever complained was when I would leave home without him.

I did not find it hard to follow the directions Jeff had given me. The four blasted chestnuts stood out vividly against the dark background of the mountain. The path was rocky and worn shapeless by erosion, but the ascent was gradual. And every now and then, as I turned to look back, I was repaid by a more and more spacious view of the Valley behind me.

It was one of those still and misty afternoons in November when, though it is not raining, everything seems dripping; and under such conditions a bird dog can do his very best work. And the bird hunter also; for he can hear anything. For my part, I have long since stopped hunting in a high wind. It's too distracting; and it is a great mistake to suppose that game can easily be approached in unfavorable weather. Rather it may be said that the wilder the weather, the wilder the game. Wind, especially, makes game skittish; for it knows well that it cannot hear an enemy approaching; hence is all the more on the alert.

When I came within a hundred yards of the dead chestnuts, I emerged into an old clearing; and I found myself on an almost level bench of the mountain. There were wild grapes here, sumac, blackberry canes, and dense little patches of mountain laurel. Ahead of me loomed a huge sawdust pile, weathered and tanned. Against an old stump was a bed of white sand; and I saw that quail had been washing there. It was the biggest wash I have ever seen. Maybe Jeff was telling the truth. There might be a big covey here; but I still doubted his description of the size of the birds.

As every hunter knows, coveys vary greatly in size: a normal covey rarely exceeds twenty birds; the average covey would be ten or twelve. Yet once in the deep South, in time of flood, when all the quail had to leave the lowlands, I found at least four coveys together. I know that I killed twenty-six birds out of what was, temporarily, one covey of at least sixty. I had that experience long before there were big limits on any kind of game.

All the way up the mountain Mike had been doing his best to find something, but not once had he had any luck. I have often thought that hunting can sometimes be dull for a good dog as well as for a man. But now, where a smother of wild grapevines made a canopy over some sassafras bushes, Mike began to show signs. I bore that way; but before I got anywhere near him, he was on a firm stand. As the place looked a good deal more like grouse than quail to me, I rather expected one or two of those tawny aristocrats to thunder up. But up to the time I came alongside Mike, nothing happened. I looked at him. A pointing bird dog, if he is certain, is really in a trance; and a faraway light is in his eyes. I knew from his aspect that Mike was not fooling. I thought I had better edge around the tumbled vines, on which clusters of misty blue fox-grapes were hanging. Mike, however, did not budge an inch.

Many a good bird dog is fooled when, after getting the full scent of the covey, the birds silently move off; and on a damp day they can do this with hardly a sound. I thought it possible that this had happened when suddenly the whole heavy jungle of grapevines seemed to explode. Out went one of the largest single coveys of quail I had ever seen. There certainly were not fewer than thirty—perhaps a few more. And they were as big and as fast as Jeff had told me they were. I was so surprised that Jeff had really told the truth that I got only one on the rise. When Mike brought him to me, I was amazed at his size. I compared him to those I had in my pocket. He looked almost twice as big and felt twice as heavy. As I have said, an ordinary Valley quail weighs only three or four ounces. This bird would go six or seven. Here, indeed, was a real discovery. To get two or three of these big boys would be like getting a herd-bull of a grouse.

When a covey of ordinary quail is flushed, all of them usually go in the same direction. They light scattered, but the individuals are not usually far apart. But these birds seemed to go in every direction except directly downhill. They fanned out over a wide and rough territory. There were plenty of rocks underfoot so that I had to watch every step I took; there were dense laurel patches, and, where a little stream trickled down, there were coverts of ferns and green-briars. Under the circumstances I decided to let Mike do the heavy work. The first stand he made was a full two hundred yards from where I had flushed the covey. This was a single, which corkscrewed into the tree-tops like a grouse. I managed to get him. Up and down those slopes, through dogwood and sumac and locust thickets Mike and I worked our way. By the time it had begun to get a little dusky, I had killed seven of these mountain quail. Homeward we then turned toward the Valley with its lights beginning to twinkle.

This had been angle shooting, hillside shooting, brush shooting, perhaps a little more difficult than grouse shooting except that these birds lay better to the dog than grouse would. The climbing was hard, the footing uncertain. A good many birds got away before I had a chance to shoot. And I missed several. But it was great while it lasted.

The people of the Valley believe these are just Valley birds that withdrew to the mountain on the approach of winter. I doubt this. These birds are different. Besides, here they have plenty of water, food, shelter, and strange as it may seem, there are probably fewer predators on such a mountain. Certainly there are more hawks in the Valley and more skunks; and there are plenty of roaming house-cats, perhaps the very worst enemy that quail have close to civilization. I think these birds live in the mountains, and their wilderness environment accounts for their superior weight and size.

I revisited that place in the winter, during a time of deep snow, carrying some food. About a quarter of a mile from the sawdust pile I found the covey in a natural rock shelter—just the sort of place that Indians took advantage of in the winters of their faroff day. It was easy to tell that they used this place regularly in rough weather. Here was a highly intelligent selection of just about the only place that would make them independent of the rigors of winter. By studying their tracks in the snow, I could see that they had been finding sufficient food, including haws, the fruits of the wildrose, and some buds.

Ever since that experience, whenever I have my choice of hunting for the small quail of the Valley or the big boys of the mountain. I head hillward. And I have been wondering whether what I found in the Cumberland Valley of Pennsylvania may not be generally true wherever one has valley and mountain topography. Perhaps the best way for a hunter to find out whether these noble birds are in his part of the country is to ask a native as honest as I found Jeff Meadows to be.

Snipe of the Pinelands

While occasionally a bird-dog will stand a buck in the pinelands, the thing is not to be exactly expected. When I go abroad with my setters and pointers I usually anticipate quail, and an occasional woodcock. Yet so varied is the wild life of the great wooded coastal plain of the Carolinas that the hunter, in pursuit of one kind of game, often finds another. It was so that day I ran into the great flight of snipe, far out in the lonely woods.

If I were to see a picture showing that old slaveholder and secessionist Abe Lincoln gallantly leading the armies of the Confederacy against that arch-traitor, the haughty cavalier U.S. Grant, I certainly should not be more amazed than I was when, craftily edging my way to a deer-stand through the dewy broomgrass and little gallberries on the damp edges of Montgomery Branch, I suddenly flushed a regular flock of Wilson's snipe, not fewer than thirty in number. A few steps farther on, more got up in their frantic, enigmatic way. My gun was loaded with buckshot.

"Steve," I said to the Negro with me, "what do you make of all these snipe out here in the pinelands? They belong on the delta."

"God A'mighty in heben knows" was Steve's elaborate disclaimer that he held the solution of the mystery. "An' if we ax dem why dey is here," he continued speculatively, "dey ain't gwine say a thing but 'Snipe! Snipe!' Make you don't shoot some, Cap'n?"

"Does a snipe weigh two hundred pounds?" I retorted in a scornful whisper. "Does he carry horns? Is his haunch big enough to fill up that cavern that you call your belly? Talk sense, Steve."

"But if it happen so we ain't tumble no buck," the good Negro persisted, "we ought to come back here. You would have big fun."

From *An American Hunter* (1937).

The buck we were after was there, all right; but you know the definite difference between locating one and tumbling him. He slipped out of the wrong end of the drive, and we were left lamenting, as the poem says.

"Steve," I said, "you've got snipe on your brain."

"Yes, sah," he admitted guiltily. "I always did like to hear 'Snipe!' *Bam-or!* 'Snipe!' *Bam-or!*"

"All right," I agreed as we walked together toward the place where we had flushed the birds. "You stay here while I go up to the car and get the right ammunition."

Steve was good at staying. He subsided in the sunny broomsedge while I went after some 8's. On my return he was fast asleep.

While I was on this expedition I kept wondering what in the world could have lured the snipe from their perfect home on the vast and lonely delta of the Santee, where they had all the marsh and mud and similar delights to satisfy a snipe's heart, and to come to this comparatively dry stretch of wildwoods. I could only think that someone must have been banging away at them on the delta; that perhaps the hawks were pretty bad there over the more open stretches, where I have seen even the lordly bald eagle strike at an English snipe; or that they had by chance discovered better food and better shelter in the pine woods. At any rate, here they would not have to compete for a living with wild ducks rooting up and shoveling up everything in sight. Ten thousand mallards foraging right constitute a vacuum-cleaner squad against which it is very hard to hold one's economic own. At any rate, here were the snipe; and I believe that when an unusual chance presents itself to a hunter, he should not stop to ask any questions but wade right in.

As I had no dog with me except Steve, I knew that I'd just have to walk the snipe up. Anyway, a dog isn't much good on snipe; or rather, snipe seldom give a dog a fair chance. They are very skittish, and it is not likely that their scent is satisfactorily heavy. Also, the fact that they abide in bogs, where the general dampness carries many scents, makes a dog's pointing of them a rather unusual affair.

When I got back to Steve, he was snoring. He would be. He just lay there in the sun and glistened. I tickled his ear with a long straw of the broomsedge, whereupon he muttered "No, Liza, I ain't been gwine wid no yaller gal." Liza is his wife.

I shot the gun off over his head, at the detonation of which he sprang up bewildered.

"I thought that was Liza," he said, with vast relief when he saw that it was only I.

"Now, Steve, you got me into this snipe business; you'll have to see me through. What I want you to do is to mark down the dead birds—if I kill any; likewise watch where the others light. I want you to pick up the dead birds, but always stay behind me. You have a good solid head, but I am not so sure of its chances against lead at close range."

"I onerstan'," said Steve with a grin. "I is for be de dog."

"Why, naturally," I responded cheerfully.

And in my part of the country, such is the complete fellowship, under a strict caste system, of the white man and the Negro that this kind of talk can go on with high good humor and with no self-consciousness or hurt pride or other bunk.

You snipe-hunters know that while this game little bird is in flight a zigzag flash of lightning, he usually presents a clear target against the sky-line. You don't have to figure on the brush as you do with the grouse and the woodcock, and often the quail. A bird of the bogs, he often lies close; sometimes he keeps darting along the ground from one marshy patch of cover to another, his gleaming eyes fixed on the approaching hunter. But when he gets up, he is usually clear. Yet I do not know a more difficult target. His scared sharp cry, his flashing speed, his craxy flight—all these make him as game as any bird we have.

On one occasion the manager of a big hunting club said to me: "We have had no duckshooting this week on account of the warm weather. If you go down on that old rice levee that leads out to the duck blinds, for heaven's sake don't shoot that one jack-snipe. He's been furnishing sport for the club members for about ten days."

There's a tribute to a bird as is a tribute.

As Steve and I turned our attention to business, the country that lay before us looked birdy for quail but not for shore birds. There was a normal stand of great yellow pines. Off to the left was the dark and fragrant thicket which we call Montgomery Branch—that happening to be its name. Under the pines was a dense growth of knee-high grass and bushes, the grass chiefly broomsedge and the bushes huckleberry, gallberry and the like.

Here and there in a damp spot there would be a cluster of tupelos and gums, over the low branches of which smilax made a cool canopy. On several occasions I have walked up an old stag from under just such a canopy. As far as I could see, the country varied little. The snipe were everywhere ahead of us, and my faithful henchman and I simply had to keep on going to walk them up.

"Now don't get ahead of the gun, Steve," I warned again. "That's what the snipe are supposed to do."

Fellow sportsmen, wherever you may be who read these lines, if you have tears, prepare to shed them now. Get a bucket ready, and a sieve to strain out the pearls.

You remember I said that I had gone to the car for 8's with which to bang the birdies. Even so. All the barrels my gun had were loaded with this dusting material. You remember also that I had awakened Steve from his guilty dreams by taking a chance shot over his head. You'll see that such a noise in the woods does not always have the effect it is supposed to have.

About eighty yards ahead of us was one of the smilax four-posters, rising beautifully from a particularly dense little islet of greenery. Though it was late December, the dampness and the sunny shelter had kept the grass green there. Toward this Steve and I headed, sure that there must be some snipe near such a place. There were!

When I was within about thirty yards of the tiny thicket, three snipe got up under my feet, whirling away in wild and wayward flight. I missed with both barrels. To complete my disgust, out of the greenery ahead, with easy grace, rocked a great full-antlered buck, presenting a perfect broadside to me.

"O my Pastor!" muttered Steve behind me, an exclamation that he never uses unless he is pretty far gone emotionally.

Under the circumstances there was nothing to do but swallow hard and retain my religion. But it did seem a strange thing that we had missed that bedded buck on our first part of the hunt, when I was all set for him. And when I had crudely awakened Steve, the deer had not budged.

"He hab a haunch same like de butt end of a sugar barrel, and jes' as sweet," Steve lamented.

At that moment a snipe got up, crying "Scaip! Scaip!" I shot him spitefully and feelingly. Steve proved to me his faultlessness as a retriever.

On the other side of the deer bed a flock of perhaps twenty snipe got up together, and I managed to get three out of the crowd. We felt better, Steve and I, especially as I bagged a big wood bunny a moment later.

By this time the sky was dotted with scared snipe. You know how they act; go way up yonder as if they were Lindberghs, heading for Paris; then take some swift circles that bring them lower; then sweep earthward to nose-dive under some cover. But they don't actually nose-dive, having a fairy-like, graceful way of staying in flight, lifting their wings, dropping their legs, and alighting with extraordinary daintiness and precision.

I now had two chances to shoot: there were the birds that flushed, and again the birds coming back to light. Shooting became fast, and I found Steve invaluable. He would keep saying, "Mind on your right, Cap'n," and "Some comin' back behind here." He had torn a rag from his shirt, which loss left him wearing a regular bathing-beauty costume, and with this he tied up the birds.

It was a strange sight, to one familiar with seeing snipe over creeks, marshes and inlets, to see them miles from water, in the clear sky above the towering yellow pines. The particular stretch of woods we were hunting maintained the same character for a space of about six hundred yards by two hundred; and this territory the birds did not seem to want to leave. However madly they tore out of the greenery and however frantically they scaled the sky, going as if they had a date with the reigning beauty in Hong Kong or somewhere equally far, and being late on the start too, they nevertheless inevitably slanted back homeward. By the time I had walked up a fresh lot, those I had previously flushed were all about me, veering down to cover.

About this time I had a chance to make a rather peculiar observation on wild life. Roaming far from his lonely haunts on the delta, a great bald eagle beat his way over the lofty pines. His head glistened in the sunlight; his body looked black. A king in the air, he was nothing if not illustrious. Yet as one of the Wilson's snipe darted by him he turned in his lordly course, quickened his majestic pace, and actually struck at the fleeting little game bird. Perhaps the gesture was more one of annoyance than a deliberate attempt to capture prey.

I now asked Steve how many snipe he had, and he told me fourteen. That seemed enough, though we had certainly flushed more than a hundred, and if we had had a mind to do so we could easily have doubled our bag. But we decided that we had done enough. Yet, as often happens, hunters get chance shots on the way to the car.

To my surprise we flushed a brace of woodcock out of some swampy ground under a growth of sweet myrtles. These we collected, Steve remarking that they looked like "little gobblers," which seemed to me a very happy description. As the good Negro brought these up to me he suddenly turned his head, listening. "A houn' is runnin'," he said thoughtfully. "He comin' dis way. Put in a buckshot, Cap'n."

I did as I was told, and we sat down on a log. Far off we heard the faint, deep voice of a trailing hound. He was a mile off, but he was coming for us. At any moment we might see a fugitive deer skulking our way, for where we had stopped is a famous stand.

Nearer came the dog, but no deer hove in sight, and I began to think that he might be running the cold trail of one of the two bucks we had started. He was now almost within sight.

"I see de dog," said Steve disappointedly. "O my Pastor, no!" he whispered excitedly. "Turkey!"

He told me later that what he had taken for the dog's tail, visible above some bushes, was in reality the head and neck of a gobbler.

The loads in my gun troubled me—one 8's and one buckshot. But I had nothing else. As yet I had not seen the turkey. There was no doubt that it was his track which the hound was running. When fresh and when the air is damp, such a bird will leave a scent that any good dog will run.

"He is comin' through dem little pines on your lef'," Steve informed me, "an' he is runnin' like de debbil."

Such a crisis, as you know, is soon over. In a twinkling I saw the great bird, got my sight on him, and let him have the buckshot at fifty yards. His behavior would lead one to believe that he had been struck by lightning. He had been. His neck had managed to interfere with the hastiness of a single buckshot.

"Dat's dat," muttered Steve. "Bless God A'mighty!"

"You're loaded," I said. "I'll retrieve this one."

He was a fine bird, with hardly a feather ruffled—a gallant old scout of the wide pinelands. He would not scale less than eighteen pounds.

Steve and I reached the car heavy-laden. It was a happy drive we had home, with the winter sunlight streaming softly through the quiet woods and the hale odors of the wild, free forest coming fragrantly to us. But dearer to the heart of my humble companion were certain imagined odors: those which were wont to set his soul on fire when that cloudy mountain known as his Liza prepared his evening meal of corn-bread, fried rabbit, and snowy, steaming rice.

Paddling Them Up

While there are all kinds of ways of shooting ducks, my favorite is paddling them up. Almost always the character of a country determines the kind of hunting one should do there. As I live near the great delta of the Santee, an area of one hundred thousand acres, all of which was formerly banked and intersected by canals and ditches and creeks for the growing of rice, the way to have a real sport here with the ducks is to get into a canoe or a small bateau, handled by an experienced Negro paddler. Such a man, if he is good, is peerless.

This is a region of fresh tidewater; and the best time to paddle them up is when the tide is high, flooding all those little nooks and crannies in the marsh which ducks delight to investigate. And when they are off the main stream of water, silent paddling makes approach easy.

But first I ought to give you an idea of the nature of my country, and of the habits of ducks there in the winter.

The observation of wild life having been, even from the dawn of my childhood, an absorbing passion with me; and Hampton being ideally located for an indulgence in this fascinating diversion; I have lost few opportunities to study the children of nature.

Most observers of the flight of wild ducks are handicapped by the fact that, being themselves concealed, their vision is badly circumscribed. They can see the wild fowl that pass overhead, but very few others. At Fairfield on the Santee, four miles below Hampton, it is different. There one may stand on the tall sandy bluff overlooking the river, a site that affords him an elevation of thirty-five feet above the water, and watch at his ease and with the widest possible vision

From *Hunter's Choice* (1946).

the myriads of ducks that come pouring into the waste rice fields that lie immediately beyond the Santee's yellow tide.

There are many wild life observations that I have always delighted in making; but this one was perhaps my favorite. Possibly the environment of extraordinary natural beauty had much to do with my enjoyment. At this point the great river flows northwest and southeast, and the observer has an immense view of its lordly sweep in both directions. Its melancholy fair shores are dim with a certain enchanting loveliness that increases as those shores recede. To be specific, the foliage on the overhanging live-oaks is always lustrous; the coloring on the water-oaks is brightest in mid-winter; the cypresses and tupelos and gums are festooned with Spanish moss, and with riotous plumy sprays of smilax and yellow jasmine. Here and there along the shore are glimmering sandbars, dim receding bays, estuaries retiring mistily into alluring thickets of sweet myrtle, towered over by momentous pines. It seems a country untouched by the ravages of the woodsman's axe, a region as romantic in natural beauty as it must have been when the caravels of Columbus first tossed and plunged their unknown way across the Atlantic.

That the Santee country was then inhabited I have no doubt; for even today one finds an occasional arrowhead chipped from flint by the Cherokees or the Santees or the Sewees; and I have an exquisite Indian pipe that was found buried under a stone on Fairfield. On the estate immediately to the southward there is an immense mound, supposedly of Indian origin. No one has ever disturbed it, though within it may lie countless treasures, perhaps of a character so striking as to supply the key to an understanding of this lost civilization.

Beyond the Santee from Fairfield lies a mighty reach of the famous Santee Delta. About fifteen miles above its mouth the river divides, and the two streams flow practically parallel to the coast. The distance between them is from a mile to a mile and a half; but the actual distance to be traversed in crossing the delta is usually much greater. At one point at which the marshy peninsula is only about a mile wide, boats go through Six-Mile Creek, the name of which indicates its meandering nature.

The extreme northern portion of the delta is a deeply wooded swamp; the southern tip is an idyllic barrier isle known as Cedar Island. On nearly all of the intervening land, rice was formerly planted; indeed, there was a time when this region was the most important rice-growing center of North America. These ancient abandoned rice fields have, of course, grown up; and the intricate systems of canals, flood-gates, check-banks, quarter-drains, trunks, and river-dikes have degenerated. That they have not been utterly obliterated is due to the natural dredging of the tides, which has the effect of keeping most of the waterways open, so that what was in the old days artificial has now become natural. A canal which formerly was nothing but a big deep ditch has now become a respectable waterway. At high water all these vast fields are flooded to a depth of from a few inches to a foot or more. Here the wild ducks can get shallow, still, water, thousands of acres of wampee, duck-oats, and lotus in which to feed; immense stretches of reedy, watery mud, havens of refuge from cold and wind; ideal feeding grounds; miles upon miles of placid canal water up which to float; countless flats upon which to loaf and bask and preen. Is it any wonder that widgeons and wood ducks, teal and shovelers, ruddy ducks and canvasbacks, black ducks, mallards, and bluebills delight in this wildfowl Riviera?

The habits of these ducks during their winter residense on the delta and on its spacious environs vary only with the weather; and usually there is a certain regularity that is independent of weather conditions. On fair and balmy days they leave the rice fields at dawn, spending the entire day in the salt water at the mouth of the river, on the semi-tropical sandbars glistening there, and in the brackish, limpid ponds of the coastal islands. If the weather continues warm and fair, they do not return to the fields until twilight. On cold stormy days they are inclined to stay in the quiet fields and sheltered creeks and ditches all day; and those that leave return early. In sleety weather, with the wind blowing and with the temperature hovering near the freezing point, all day over the delta the ducks can be seen lighting, myriads of them; and occasionally when a great flock is startled, the roar of its rising and its darkness against the sky remind one vividly of a thundercloud. From late October, when the ducks arrive in full force, until early March, when they begin to feel the rapture of the mating instinct, and when therefore they begin their migration, they follow with regularity the daily routine mentioned.

I think it no mean sight to behold, streaming in from the unseen vastness of the ocean, squadrons and flotillas, and detachments of these splendid wild fowl—all sentient creatures, all beautiful, all swift and deft of wing—thronging the rosy afternoon heavens, and with boisterous joy calling to their comrades in the air and to those already settled in the waste fields beneath them. Standing on the bluff at Fairfield, a bluff sheltered by live-oaks, wild oranges, and huge patriarchs of the magnolia grandiflora, I loved to watch the black, gigantic spearheads of ducks streaming like comets northward, now veering, now turning, now scattered almost like a burst rocket in the swift grace of a speedy alighting. The black ducks and the mallards outnumber all the others. Geese are wholly absent, although on one occasion I counted at this very point on the Santee a flock of fifty-six, the largest number ever recorded as having been observed in that region.

I have always loved to watch wildfowl, even though I am not hunting them, and I have watched them at night.

The world of nature that awakens at twilight is another world—a dewy domain, a starlit country; and in it I have discovered fairies. Creation is of darkness as well as of light. To me, since earliest boyhood days, there has been a magic and a mystery about the life of nature at night that has always had a deeper charm that what we observe in the obvious daytime. Then it is that fragrant shadows form a glamorous background, and are as veils marginal to sidereal loveliness. Then starlight spangles earth's beauty; then it is that far musical voices haunt the purple night. And it is then that many of the warier and more beautiful wild things come forth to roam the velvet lands of darkness.

It was early in March, a time of the year when the great coastal country of the Carolinas is beginning beautifully to respond to all the sumptuous purpose of the spring. Leaving the plantation landing long before daybreak, while the full moon was yet high above the sleeping oaks and pines, I paddled alone down Warsaw Creek, misty and wan in the moonshine, and so out into the pale luminance of the Santee River. A breathless hush was over the world, a tranced stillness that seemed expectant of a miracle. The great river flowed soundless out of mystery into mystery—out of the mouldering cypress swamp to the northward, toward the tremendous delta country to the southward, and thence into the lordly Atlantic. Thousands of

stars were mirrored in the river's ample bosom; there was a communion as deep as love between the river and the sky.

My purpose in coming into this primeval loneliness at night was to
watch the gathering on the river of the mighty host of wild ducks, on
the eve of their departure for their summer homes in the far North.
I had come to watch the fairies in the moonlight. To these beautiful
children of nature the almighty voice of love had begun importu-
nately to call; to the very heart of life itself it called, and they heard
it, and would obey.

I paddled to a tiny island in the very center of the river, and there,
hiding my canoe in the marsh, I went ashore and climbed into a low
fork of a cypress, from which vantage point I had a commanding
view up the glimmering tide. I knew from previous observations that
just before daybreak these ducks, leaving their feeding grounds in
the old abandoned rice fields of the delta, would congregate on the
river about a half-mile above my island, and then, in a vast and
festive concourse, would drift downward on the lambent waters
toward the sunrise. Almost as soon as I had settled myself, I heard a
flock of mallards pass overhead, the thin sweet music of their wings
in harmony with the primal quiet of the scene. It is almost impossible
to see these voyagers of the night, flying birds, except at certain rare
angles in the brilliant moonlight. Coming down out of the hidden
swamp I heard flocks of wood ducks—the eerie musical cries easily
distinguished them. Few of them migrate, but they seemed to want
to join the gathering hosts. The moon now was nearing the crests of
the great pines to the westward; its sad and beautiful light flooded
the old plantations, the dreaming river, the solitary delta. In such
beamy silver radiance there is no bush or tree or clod, however,
obscure and unknown by daylight, but to virginal marble is wrought.
In lily-white stone it is tenderly statued.

And now the silvery heavens were alive with joyous wings, joyous
cries; and I could hear the soft splashing of the ducks as they alighted
on the water. Soon the first of them began to come into sight, sporting on the gleaming tide. in their gorgeous nuptial plumage they
drifted idly, alert yet serene, with that indefinable air of highborn
elegance, that every true game bird displays. In the moonlight I
could not distinguish their colors; they all looked black on the silvery
waters; and only by their size and by certain characteristic attitudes

could I distinguish the different species. Now the moon burned softly into the pinecrests; and now the great river, for as far as I could see, was black with ducks—a living raft that drifted delightedly down the stilly tide. There could not have been fewer than ten thousand ducks in that splendid company; and I knew that I, in these modern days, was viewing a scene such as must have been common to the Santee and the Sewee Indians, who roamed that region before the coming of Columbus to the New World. Past my little island in pairs, in tiny groups, in great communal gatherings drifted these fairies in the moonlight. Not one seemed solitary. They dove, they splashed, they rose partly out of the water and flapped their wings in an ecstacy of happy relaxation. The glint of some sheen of plumage I could occasionally catch as they turned in the moonlight. Subdued, and yet excited converse, I caught, as if they were well aware of the momentous journey to be performed, and of the meaning of the mysterious joy that stirred every heart. And now the moon was down behind the forest. The morning star throbbed resplendent above it. The cast was whitening; its dark amethyst had turned to pearl; now momentarily it became azalea; and soon it would be rose. The magic moonlight was no more. My fairies of the silver light were now wild ducks—but not less beautiful, if less mysterious. So the purple night had passed, and I had been privileged to share a part of that beauty.

And here is another observation of ducks. Between four o'clock of an afternoon and dark, wood ducks would come thronging into the old fields of the delta from their daytime haunts in the swamps, the lagoons, and the placid black ponds in the woods. At the juncture of four fields beloved of these ducks, there stood a bald cypress, the only tree of any size for a considerable distance about on all sides. Though no wood duck to my knowledge ever built in this cypress, I always called it the wood duck tree. The reason for this appellation was a good one; apparently regardless of the direction from which a duck came, and regardless, also, of the place where it had determined to go, it was practically sure to pass over this gnarled sentinel.

I can recall vividly those days when, to watch this curious phenomenon, I used to leave home early, and, with the dusty August sunshine beating like golden hammers on my back, repair to my cypress, far back in the lone waste lands. As a feeder of stock, I distinctly left a good deal to be desired. But when wood ducks are flying, who can remain absorbed in hogs and cattle? At that time of the year the young ducks were flying, and it used to amuse me to see how the old mothers would lead their streaming broods.

Until after sundown I would watch this aërial performance, while the sky bloomed like a vast flower; until the distant pine forests took on an airy, poetic aspect, visionary and glimmering; until the silent arrival of the stupendous; mystical night. So tranced was I of that wild delta, those speeding wildfowl with their sweet, ghostly calls, my ancient cypress toward which all of them converged, that I used to look back until the great tree was no longer visible; until on two slender spires of the cypress the full moon would rest like a crystal sphere poised on the fingers of a magician.

One September a storm blew down the patriarch tree. The following summer the ducks were as plentiful as ever, but they had abandoned the practice of steering by the old landmark. I can have no reason for their changed behavior save that they had lost their natural guidepost.

Instinctively we do as they did: we steer by stars, mountains, trees, the gleam of a river, the soft subsidence of a valley, the outpost of a hill. I never go into mountain wilds without having a certain peak or gap carefully located in relation to the road I have come. Is it unreasonable to suppose that Wild Brother, so infinitely more keen of senses than we are, and so much more of a traveler, should count on landmarks to guide him, just as we do?

One of the best Negro paddlers I ever had was London Legree. Negroes were often named for cities: I have known a Lisbon, a Boston, a Havana, and a Paris—whose surname was Green!

London lived on the vast and lonely delta, on an island in that marshy wilderness. Tall and spare as an Indian, he knew the delta, and apparently had solved all its mysteries. Although I had many a day's sport with him, there was one I especially remember, for reasons that you will understand. That December morning tide was high at ten o'clock. At nine we left London's place in a dugout cypress canoe. Said as we settled ourselves, "We must not talk. I will paddle, and you will shoot."

In this kind of sport you rarely jump a big flock of ducks: singles and pairs—that is the rule. Nor have I found that the firing of the gun disturbed many of them. The day was chilly and overcast, with a keen wind out of the north.

My experience with this kind of shooting has, I suppose, been identical with that of all hunters: there's no sport in shooting a duck on the water; all the sport's in getting them a-wing. And the best way to kill a jumping duck is to wait until he gets the jump out of his system. It is exceedingly hard to cover him on his swift initial rise.

Through the mazy windings of Atkinson's Creek we went. At a sharp bend, a canvasback drake arose, and we collected him. I then missed a pair of blue-winged teal. Two black ducks and a mallard drake we added to our bag; then a pair of widgeons at a single shot.

I had brought with me only a single box of shells; and as the sport increased, I became interested in seeing whether I could take home twenty-five birds. Remember, this was back in the days when such a bag was legal.

After about an hour and a half of London's matchless maneuvering, I had twenty-three ducks and one shell. Then for the first time London spoke.

"Wait for a double," he said.

I passed up several easy singles; at last, at an old canal mouth, six mallards rose. I doubled two drakes. As I had made several other doubles, my shooting had not been remarkable. But there was solid satisfaction in having taken out one box of shells, and having brought to bag twenty-five fine ducks.

Adventures with the Black Prince

As I have been saying, the mature whitetail stag, fairly taken, is a prize of which any sportsman may justly be proud. Unless the hunter has just run into a piece of dumb luck, the killing of such an animal represents genuine skill in woodcraft and in accurate shooting. However, I think a slightly greater skill in both is demanded by grouse hunting in the mountains. Where I do most of my following of this superb patrician of the wilds, the day's bag-limit is two; and if I secure the limit, I am always satisfied, even though I have roamed the rocky hillsides and the shaggy glens from daydawn until dark.

As I understand the business, the Black Prince of history was not really black; neither is this prince of mine black. In each case, however, the name carries the proper suggestion. It is good enough. Imagination does the rest.

Which game bird is your favorite? Many a hunter will call the wild turkey his lady love; others will profess a soulmateship for the canvasback, the mallard, or the brant. The bobwhite has his lovers, and even the demi-domesticated ring-necked pheasant.

To me, the finest bird that ever beat a wing is the ruffed grouse. If he isn't a prince, then all the royalty of this world is dead and gone. His presence in any woodland gives the place a magic tone. He is what the beauty of the wildest forest means. With him comes wonder; in his flight, sorcery departs. I know of no other bird that has so poetic a spirit. He is both the Ariel and the Apollo of the fairy forest world.

Although I have been following the Black Prince for a matter of twenty years and though he is by now a fairly familiar object to me, I

From *An American Hunter* (1937).

get the same old romantic thrill every time I see him. I am just like a woman who happens to be in love with her husband. Certain of my meetings with the ruffed grouse have always haunted my memory. These I shall give in the hope that they may arouse an interest or re-awaken similar recollections in the minds of my fellow-sportsmen.

It was the night before the last day of the season in southern Pennsylvania. I wandered down into the village to see if I couldn't get a hint from some of my cronies as to the best place for a last chance. Often, at the very end of a season, hunters will begin to divulge secrets about game that they have sacredly guarded for weeks and months.

Fortune favored me. In a shoe store I met an old mountain man who looked like Christmas. He had been telling certain listless listeners of the hogs he had butchered. (Butchering is the height of social éclat in rural Pennsylvania.) Try as I will, I cannot get interested in butchering. The real reason is, I suppose, that the party of the second part has no chance.

After a while I managed to ask a casual question about ruffed grouse. People enamored of hog-killing sometimes miss the atmosphere of romance in which the Black Prince lives and moves and has his being. The mountain man's audience began to melt away. But I stayed, for he seemed to comprehend my question.

"Was you ever to Burnt Cabins?" he asked. "I was there a week ago, come last Friday. The mountains there break away, you know, and them steep little hills come walking right down in the valley. I was up one of them piney gullies, and I jumped six mountain pheasants. If you was to go up there, I can't say as you would get any, but you'd shoot your gun.

"I seen an old hen-mother in the woods last summer," he went on, "and she had eight chicks with her—little pheasants, you know; little grouses, I reckon you'd call 'em. And do you know, she bustled up to me just like a man's wife when she's real riled and she plumb scared me. And all the while she was just foolin', 'cause her little 'uns was in danger; and I reckon her heart was a-going worse than mine. Yes, sir, I know them birds, and I has had a liking for them ever since I was a boy."

Here, I thought, was a friend indeed; a sportsman at heart, too, slightly damaged by too much swine-slaughtering. To be a sportsman,

I take it, a man has to move in an orbit slightly outside that of a mere killer.

Having thanked my friend, I returned home under the sparkling November stars. Burnt Cabins, that desolate hamlet which hitherto had never awakened in me any halcyon dreams, had suddenly become the goal of my most roseate ambitions. And those little hills coyly parading into the valley—I could see them, and their piney slopes, and the sunshiny silence of their hollows, and the Black Princes that they were said to harbor.

Before the stars of that November night had set, I was on my way, "lizzying" northward some fifteen miles. Though it was clear daylight ere I reached Burnt Cabins and though I was driving through an utter wilderness, there was danger that I might pass the place without seeing it. Burnt Cabins perhaps was; possibly it may be; but, O my brother, at present it simply isn't.

But here was a wreck of an old mill; here were two staggering farm-houses; and here were the little meandering hills. On second thought I recalled that I really shouldn't look for the fabled cabins. The Indians burned them nearly two centuries ago.

A mist hung over the hills, a tingly frosting of the earth and sky. Fresh, dewy scents were in the air, such fragrances as one never gets, I think, save in mountain lands at daybreak on November mornings. I prefer a November morn to a September morn. I scented hickories, wet oak leaves, frosted wild grapes, damp pine needles, and all sorts of other luring, delicious things. I was in a new country, yet these delights were old and well-loved ones.

Before me now were the little hills that my friend had described, and the piney gullies. I saw sumac, scarlet oak, clumps of greenbriers. It all looked to me like Black Prince country.

To hunt in a new country, all alone, is in itself something of an adventure. As day broadened fast, tingling the hillcrests, I could tell from a general view of things that I was to be strictly alone; seldom had I seen a more solitary country. But it is in just such a place that the Prince delights to reign.

A hundred yards up the first dusky gorge a cock grouse got up ahead of me from beneath a tangle of wild grapes. He dashed off behind a pine, threading the mazy thicket in that deft way of his which has all the thrilling precision of the highest intelligence. I followed the bird warily, only to have him, a hundred yards from where he had first been flushed, hurtle thunderously out of a hemlock. He "pulled a fast one," as they say; and my second possible chance went glimmering.

At such a time, a hunter may take a sober inventory of himself, asking whether he isn't getting too old for this sort of thing. He notes that he minds the hill-climbing, too. Then, says the devil of discouragement, the ruffed grouse is a much better bird alive than dead. He fourflushes on disconsolately until, from a green-brier tangle, up goes a gorgeous rocket.

It happened to me just that way, at that moment. I love a grouse to rise to the tree-tops and to lay plans to shoot amazingly off from that advantageous elevation. Such tactics, I think, afford the gunner something like a chance. This big cock shot skyward; full against the morning he rose, climbing actually above a big white oak.

I held on him fairly, but the shot was too far. However, I never hunt this superb fellow without being prepared for long shots. Some of my friends ridicule my loads; but I can stand their taunts. I know what those loads will do.

I shoot larger shot than most men use for grouse and I want all the powder I can get. I know this combination is heavy for grouse, but I want it heavy. When most of the shooting has to be done in heavy cover through which the shot has to smash; when the birds are so educated that they allow a man no kind of a shot except a far one; when a load will do its work cleanly at long ranges—why, I say use that load.

As the sound of my gun awoke the immemorial silences of the Burnt Cabins country, the proud cock whirled in the air and spun down into the dewy covert. Another kind of inventory the hunter takes under such circumstances. He isn't so old, after all; and as for this business of hill-climbing, why he's as fresh as a daisy.

And what a thrill it is to kill fairly this lordly bird! The head-band on the hunter's hat cracks wide open. If a skunk came his way, he's so joyous and gay that he'd feel like patting it. . . . I have had all these feelings; and I don't believe that they're the least original with me.

By the time I had retrieved my grouse, I was at the head of the gulley. I crossed the ridge and dipped down into another tiny vale, all shimmering now in the early sunlight. There are glinting lights and reticent shadows in such a place that are never seen anywhere else. A half-mile went, with no other wild life sight than a big, burly mountain rabbit that bounded away among the piles of leaves.

I came to a flat where the little birches and pines were very thick. Moss carpeted the ground, and it was as green as if a spring rain had just fallen. There were many chestnut sprouts, and down to the left a brook brawled lazily.

Suddenly I saw something coming. It was a second grouse that something had evidently startled far up the hillside on my right. I saw him coming lower. He dipped into the brush. Not thirty yards from me he came to ground. I was surprised to notice with what difficulty he cleared his wings in alighting among the saplings.

For a second I lost sight of him, and that meant forever. I mean that I could not a second time distinguish him on the ground. He was there, and close to me; but his color was too much like the tawny shade of the fallen leaves. I thought I saw his black ruff, but there was no certainty of this.

For fifteen minutes I tried to imitate a statue. I wanted to see him walk, perform naturally. I love to watch a wild thing that is unaware of my being close. But never a feather did he stir. It was for me then to stir him. I'd walk him up, and perhaps get a shot at him as he rocketed off through the tall sprouts.

Naturally, there are all kinds of thrills in hunting—from the one a man gets when he walks up an old antlered stag, to the one he feels when the yellowlegs begin to draw to a good stool. For me, there's hardly a greater thrill than in walking up a ruffed grouse, especially when you know he's there.

Ten yards I advanced. He did not stir. Another five I went. Then up he got, with no preliminaries at all. He appeared to have an urgent business engagement down-town. He seemed to have an appointment with a lawyer who had a legacy for him. Over a hemlock he sped, taking an opening between two graceful top branches with unerring deftness.

I caught him at the height of his rise, and he fell like a plummet. When I reached him, he lay in an old trail, his fantail spread wide. God might have made a handsomer bird, but I'm sure He never did.

After this second adventure I went to the brook and followed it for more than a mile. Bear signs I saw, and deer-tracks; trout darting in the sunny shallows and in the purple pools. I came to an old drumming log—a mossy old monarch that, as a sapling of the long ago, must have seen the redskins skulking in these very thickets. I saw signs of grouse on the log. Ahead of me was a brambly gulley, full of wild raspberry canes, sumac, teaberry, and fox-grapes.

A white pine was growing in the gulley—a stocky, dense affair. A grouse hunter has to keep his eye on such a tree. His game loves nothing better than to dodge behind such an obstruction. But I was not prepared for what happened to me. From the dusky shelter of the low sweeping boughs, under which, I suppose, the birds had run for cover, three grouse rose. I did not see one, but I counted the rises. Directly behind the pine they went, and straight up the narrow gorge.

The chance looked good to me. Under such conditions a ruffed grouse usually flies about two hundred yards. I think much depends on the nature of the country. In dipping, mountain country he goes much farther, especially if he is flying down. Some men claim that he will not go so far if shot at. I don't know. I am certain, however, that he will not go so far if he is shot at and hit!

I am dubious about this business of shooting at game to make it lie close. It may stick tight sometimes, but so watchfully close as to be excessively wary. I have often heard deer hunters (who had badly missed) claim that they had "just shot to turn the deer." I never heard a hunter who had killed a deer say that he had shot to turn him.

Shooting to turn game or to make it lie close is, at best, a wild and hazardous performance. It is one of those devices to be classified with salting its tail and catching it by holding a bag open for it in the dark.

A good stiff drink (from the brook), a settling of my hunting coat, a pause to look the situation over carefully—and I was off after my three friends. A hunter after a grouse is engaged in a most ancient game of hide-and-seek. I have never hunted grouse with a really good dog. My idea is that a very old dog with a superb nose and the slowest pace imaginable is best.

Two hundred yards I went, taking the place in slowly and stopping to investigate fallen tree-tops and brushy little patches, old logs and young evergreens. Not a bird could I flush. Two young white pines stood in my path, and between them a dogwood tree, partly hidden in their fragrant green embrace. I stooped under this dogwood tree and emerged on the farther side of the pines.

I stood there puzzled, worse so than I had imagined, for out of the dogwood dashed a grouse—downhill this time, and completely sheltered by the dense evergreens. He was gone clear, and he deserved to have his life and liberty. . . . The other two I never saw again.

I ranged onward until I came to an old logging road, down which I wandered. There is peace of heart that comes from such a walk; and I guess, after all, that is what we most want in this life. I felt that the trees and the stream singing away from the roadside thicket, and even the sandy road itself, were my friends.

On a smooth stretch of damp sand I caught sight of a track. The Black Prince again! He had crossed but a short time before. I could even see in the wet sand the delicate etching made beside the tracks by the booting feathers of this wildwood patrician. I turned to follow the trail, which, of course, was lost as soon as it left the road. But at least I had the direction.

My walk took me under tall hemlocks and great oaks—a stretch of virgin timber. Gnarled old giants they were, massive and splendid. Rather open, the country looked, for grouse. But a man can never tell.

Suddenly out of a smallish evergreen a Black Prince hurtled. I got my gun up; I thought I had it on him. But don't you know that guilty, deep-in-the-heart feeling that you are not holding true? I had it. And it did not lie. The bird went clear, despite the manful blaring of my pet gun. I couldn't look such a gun in the face and blame it.

It is a fine thing for a man to miss occasionally. He puts a more just estimate on himself. "The shell didn't pattern," some men will explain. Perhaps it is better to confess the fault cleanly. I heard this ingenious alibi on one occasion: "How can you expect me to hit a deer like that? I held right for it, and it jumped over the shot."

Perhaps a mile farther on I came to a dense pine-thicket on a cleared hill. Such a place is often resorted to by both deer and grouse. I saw grape-vines in the shadowy fastness, and these looked promising.

Soon I was lost in the dusky silence of this strange grove. None of the pines were much taller than my head, but for that reason they were all the more thick. A trail ran through them, and down this I stepped warily.

Some six yards from the edge I heard a grouse get up and go roaring off toward the ravine below the pines. I ran to the edge of the thicket, got my gun up, and fired at the bird just as he was clearing the tops of the hardwood trees on the brink of the gulley. Down he came—a fortunate shot, I later discovered when I dressed him, for but one pellet had struck him and that in the back of the head.

I often think that, in shotgun shooting, however accurate may be our aim, the business of actually placing the shot is always a matter of pure chance. I saw a man shoot a wild turkey with a rifle one day. The bird was standing with his head held high. As the rifle cracked he suddenly stretched his neck downward, and the ball took him fairly in the head. The hunter, who was shooting with a peep-sight, was very proud of his work; but I always had an unspoken suspicion that if the turkey had kept his head where he had it, the bullet would have missed him by six inches.

Burnt Cabins, three grouse, the little hills that leave the mountains and parade into the valley, the winy fragrances from fallen leaves, the brawling brook—all these come back to me. If I should be told that I was to have a really Last Hunt and that there could be no other this side of some preserve in Paradise, I am sure that I'd want to choose to go once again after the Black Prince.

Prince of the Woodlands

While individual deer seem to develop rare intelligence, that sort of wisdom appears to be the possession of every member of the ruffed grouse tribe. I have known some deer to be simply dumb; some to be awkward and lumbering; some to be so curious as to be downright stupid. But in country where he has been long and persistently hunted, I have yet to see a ruffed grouse that is not always a shrewd tactician; and of course he is ever an aristocrat.

Oh, I have missed them—plenty of them, missed them coming and going, fore and aft. But since only the hits are history, I should like to record eight instances in which I have killed grouse—the whole constituting a kind of a case book . . . Reading some of the very admirable articles on grouse by other sportsmen, I shall not be obliged to trespass on their preserves; for, while we have been after the same matchless game, my experiences have been radically different from theirs. For example, I have never had the privilege of shooting a grouse over the point of a dog. Our grouse in southern Pennsylvania are so scarce and so wary that they will hardly lie to a dog, however slow and cautious he may be. Our grouse seem on edge all the time; they are always wanting to go places suddenly in high gear. Our grouse shooting is practically all in the mountains, in heavy thickets, where tangles of grapevines riot over the lower trees; where old lumbering operations have permitted the second growth to make a wilderness of things; and where the footing is usually on slippery rocks . . . All my grouse I have killed by walking them up; occasionally getting one on the first rise, but usually marking one down and following him with the greatest caution. Once in a long

From *An American Hunter* (1937).

while I get a shot at one that another man has put up . . . Well, here are the stories—true, even if I do happen to be the teller.

I. The Prince in the Golden Palace

Leaving my car in Johnson's Lane, which skirts the eastern edge of the Tuscaroras, I took a woods trail into the mountain about three o'clock on that golden autumn afternoon. The whole world hung like a ripe russet apple, and it smelled that way too. The air was still, damp, aromatic, fragrant with the scents of hickory-leaves, wild grapes, dewy mosses. The mystery of Indian Summer was over the world; and the woods were a golden palace, hung with gorgeous banners of flaming leaves. As I walked almost noiselessly up the old sandy trail that wound mazily into the mountain, I marveled at the beauty of it all; everything seemed saffron, and softly gleaming. Leaving the path, I followed upward the course of a little stream that had great green curtains of briars clothing the bushes and the lower trees on its banks. Of these berries grouse are very fond; and so dense is the cover that these vines afford that it is often possible to approach within twenty feet of a bird sheltered by one of these emerald canopies. But there were no birds in these briars that day. I turned aside into a golden dell, on the farther shoulder of which was a low growth of rock-oak and kalmia. While I paused for a moment to watch a gray squirrel, I heard a telltale chitter in the low laurels on the little hillock to the left . . . Then I heard a grouse-note that was entirely new to me: it sounded like a soft yet distinct "Kruck-kruck-kroo-kroo." Then there came the inevitable little run in the strewn leaves, and my prince beat his way down the mountain.

In such a case I try with all the power of my sight and my hearing to get the bird's exact direction. When the woods are still, the hunter can often hear him alight. When not badly scared, and if the brush is fairly thick, a grouse may not fly a hundred yards; but he may go two. I have found that when he flies below the tree-tops, he likely will not go far. But if he once tops them, he may be bound for foreign lands.

I heard this one alight. Starting back toward him about twenty yards to the right of his course downhill, I found myself in an old road. By trying to keep a grouse on his left, the hunter will usually be afforded a better chance when the bird flushes. Two hundred yards I went, but nary a prince did I see. I turned and started back. I came on slowly and rather nonchalantly. Trying to creep often arouses this aristocrat's suspicion.

But my hope was almost gone when I came within fifty yards of the spot where the grouse had first risen. I stopped to look about. Somehow I had missed him. As I was peering to my right, from behind an old chestnut stump on my left he got up, starting straight away. There was a tattered screen of gold between us. I just had a vision of that splendid tawny form hurtling like a projectile through the tinted woods. I saw that broad fan-tail with its beautiful banding of black. The only possible shot I had was one that depended for its effectiveness on co-ordination that was automatic. I must have covered the bird; for, while I did not really see him when I shot, I heard him fall. It was a lucky example of "dead reckoning."

I found him lying on the gorgeous bed of leaves, a gorgeous thing himself—princely, unruffled of plumage. And I always recall that incident as a golden kind of thing—all golden—the woods, the plumage of my prize, and the nature of my good fortune.

II. A Wanderer

I suppose every grouse hunter remembers best the remarkable things that happened to him in following this superb game bird. One of the surprises of my life was the time I killed one when hunting quail. I was in some low brush along a creek, full four miles from the mountains. Quail were scattered in the cover. I had just crossed a wire fence and had turned toward the place where my dog was working when a grouse tore out of a patch of briars almost at my feet. I shot him almost before I realized what he was. How came he to be so far from his home in the hills? The creek flowed from the mountains; and undoubtedly, attracted by the abundant food and the good cover along its borders, he had wandered away from his habitat. That one bird in my bag meant more to me as I went home than the ten quail I had. In a sentimental way, I think a grouse outweighs a wild turkey.

III. The One I Tracked

It is easy enough to track a grouse in the snow; and to do so with killing intent is perhaps to take unfair advantage of him. But it is a different thing to track one across a sandy road. That October day it rained softly and insistently. About two o'clock the showers stopped. I drove out to the mountain and walked a little way down the sandy road that sags amiably through the brush at its foot. The road was still glistening from the rain, and from the bowed trees the water dripped heavily. Coming to a very clear stretch of sand, I saw where a grouse had apparently just crossed. He had been in the thickets next to the fields and was heading into the mountain. The little serrated fringes on his toes make a grouse's track readily identified. I studied carefully the exact line of his walk, and then looked into the forest on my left to see what cover might look attractive to my bird. Near the road great arras of greenbriars wept over a fallen cedar tree; a little farther on I saw lustrous bunches of wild-grapes hanging above a tangle of vines. A grouse will hardly pass up two such places.

But he was not in the briars. I recall feeling morally certain that he was under the grapes . . . Grouse do not always fulfil one's ideas as to where they ought to be. But this one did. And he executed a maneuver against which the hunter always has to be wary. Instead of rocketing off in his customary slap-dash but unerring fashion, he elected to take the air in a peculiar sliding and almost noiseless way. If I had not been certain that he was there, I never could have made the shot. As it was, I had to let drive through the tangle of vines, and I did not know the verdict until I picked him up on a carpet of vivid green moss some fifty yards from where I had shot. However, so great is this bird's momentum that his pitch often carries him many yards forward from that point in the air at which he is struck. I have known claims to be made of ninety-yard shots which were not, for the reason given, more than sixty-five or seventy.

IV. Old Transcontinental

Along certain stretches of our Conococheague Creek (which is respectable Indian for God knows what) there are few crossings. One reach of three miles offers one bridge only—and that a teetery, hold-my-hand affair. Yet beyond it is the best deer, turkey, and grouse country of all our mountains. Just beyond the bridge is a bare meadow; then fringes of alders and dense briars; then the open forest, sloping gradually upward. Game in these lowlands is very wild; not only because so many hunters cross that single bridge and go after it with early-morning zest; but because so many likewise, having bad luck higher up, and not caring much for those Mt. Everest expeditions, spend their time lazily combing these thickets. And it was here that, for a matter of three seasons, dwelt Old Transcontinental, a cock grouse that had furnished sport but no dinner to scores and scores of hunters. We christened him as we did because of his habit of flying farther than any other gouse that we had even known. Pitching out of the gloomy recesses of a shrouded hemlock, that bird has flown full three-quarters of a mile—and I have seen him do it. Occasionally he would resort to the higher ridges, and launching himself from one of these, he would rocket down the mountain-slope at a speed and for a distance that were amazing. This was not only an excessively wary and far-traveling grouse; he was over-sized as well . . .

Coming one day out of the turkey-woods with no gobbler slung manfully across my shoulder, walking rather wearily down an old road that ran through the lower thickets in which this matchless prince made his haunts, I was startled by having him hurtle suddenly from beneath a grapevine tangle and tear through the woods toward the meadow. It was only a hundred and fifty yards to that open stretch; and such a fly was far too short for this old champion. Yet it did not seem likely that he would pass the cover of the thickets. If he stopped short, he would be in the low alders and tall briars on the meadow's edge. It looked like a chance for which I had waited in vain for three years. There was no mistaking his identity: he was too big, and this was his home.

I followed the road until I came out into the clear meadow. Then I turned to the left, keeping to the open. The bushes and briars that formed a margin to the woods were not over eight feet high, and they extended out into the meadow for a distance of about twenty feet. In this fringe my wily old voyager must be lurking. Out of the bushes at a rather critical place there rose a scarlet oak, the branches of which wept in characteristic fashion to the ground. Through that dense tangle of limbs I never could have made a shot; yet I had the feeling that Old Transcontinental would surely take the air just as soon as I got directly behind that obstruction between us. But round it I safely passed. If he got up now, I had a clear shot . . . So few are the clear shots in our country at grouse that the chance for one is positively disconcerting. As in every other sport, in wing-shooting there is such a thing as being too tense . . . Suddenly he roared out of the briars, executing a sort of spiral, the beveling of which gave him terrific momentum. Instead of going down over the briars, he headed straight into the dusky woods. At such a time there's always an aperture for which the bird is heading; and if the hunter is lucky in guessing *which* aperture, the game is his. I managed to cover a likely hole just as the cock did, and he plunged headlong. This was a magnificent specimen in full plumage; yet my triumph was tempered by the thought that I had robbed those woods of a real personality.

V. The Orquic Valley Ghost

There's game of ghostly beauty—albinos; and they appear in practically all forms of wild life. But I had never seen a snow-white grouse until a forest ranger told me of one that haunted the hemlock-hung hollows of Orquic Valley, which lies just outside the Buchanan Game Reserve. For at least two seasons this extraordinary bird had been reported; and after I learned of his existence I was told by hunters that they had been after him in real earnest. But like most other birds or animals of this spectacular coloring, this grouse was so shy that he was rarely seen and more rarely shot at. One man told me that he had seen the bird in a pine tree, but had taken it for an owl. When he was fifty yards past it, this prince in ermine rocketed down the long lonely valley away from him, its glimmering form at last fading from sight against the distant tree-tops . . . Such a bird seemed to me worth an especial trip into the wilds of Orquic, which is typical Pennsylvania deer-country: a primeval vale between two immense ridges, strewn to the very top with boulders. Yet despite the rocks the place is heavily timbered. Down the laureled gorge dashes a trout-stream . . . For many miles there is no human habitation.

This adventure represents a thing in hunting that all experienced sportsmen have found to be true: however wild your game may be, if you stay with it, your great chance will surely come. The only question is, How long can you stick?

My trek after this grouse of the snowy plumage was an all-day affair, and I must spare details. About two miles down Orquic Valley, some three hours after I had begun to hunt, I jumped him out of a wild melee of old logs and grape-vines . . . Now, while he was the very thing I was hunting for with all my heart and soul, let me confess that when he jumped, I did not even shoot at him. You know how it is: sometimes the mind plays queer tricks. Occasionally mine tells me, at the critical moment when my gun should be in action, that, at last, the game is *found* . . . Meanwhile he is getting away on burning wings. I just stood there and watched with amazement and something akin to awe the bewildering beauty, grace, and speed of that patrician of patricians . . . I almost forgot to mark where he was going!

I flushed him on one slope of the broad valley; his flight took him clear across to the other ridge. I thought I saw him go down by a clump of burly rock-pines . . . In that neighborhood, gentlemen, all over those treacherous rocks, under and over logs and smothers of vines, up and down dale, even across the immense ridge I faithfully rambled. But the prince with the ermine coat I utterly lost. He was either a smart bird or I was a dumb hunter—probably both. During my milling around I flushed a half-dozen other grouse. These I passed up, and then, as my Great Hope began to wane, I cursed this practice of passing things up.

The sun had begun to stretch out the hills when I turned home-ward. As a hunter often will, I decided to go back by the place where I had first roused my game . . . I might find a white feather to take home. He had certainly burst through those vines with vigor enough to strip himself of all plumage . . . At last I came to the wild vineyard. Certain sere leaves on the rock-oaks were whispering, and that natu-ral sound must have deadened my footballs. I came to the very tangle out of which my snowy bomb had exploded . . . I foolishly and vainly peered in the place for sight of a feather. This I was doing when the albino bird itself burst from the dense vines out of which I had started him seven hours before. He went off at a crazy tangent, and I led him about two feet. To my surprise he fell at the shot; and when I retrieved him, he entirely fulfilled all my ideas of a dream-prince. This bird is always aristocratic and immaculate. What shall be said of one whose plumage is like new-fallen snow? Of all the wildwood trophies I have ever secured, this one was the handsomest, and secured under the most peculiar conditions.

How had he come back to his starting point? In this part of the country grouse are in the habit of flying to their favorite feeding-ground; and while I had been searching for him half a mile away, unseen by me he had flown back across the valley to his beloved grape-vines.

VI. The Prince in the Pines

In the wilds of Path Valley, where the mountains lie on either hand in mighty folds, there's an immense old field, in the center of which is a pine thicket some five acres in extent. These trees are not more than twenty feet high; many of them are half blown over. Going through them is like trying hard to get lost. Such a place is often resorted to both by deer and grouse. I saw grape-vines in this shadowy fastness, and these looked promising. Soon I was lost in the dusky silence of this strange grove. A dim trail led through this fragrant sanctuary, and down this I warily walked.

Some six or seven yards from the farther end I heard a grouse get up and go roaring off toward the ravine below the pines. I dashed to the edge of the thicket, got my gun up, and fired at the far-fleeing bird just as he was clearing the tops of the hardwood trees on the brink of the gully. Down he came—a fortunate shot, and pure luck, of course. I later discovered when he was dressed that just one shot had struck him, but that was in the back of the head.

VII. A Wily Patrician

One day I was hunting at Webster's Mills with two of my sons—that place being within a few miles of Hancock, Maryland. The Mills perhaps have been or may be, but at present they aren't. My boys had gone ahead of me, greatly excited over the fresh spoor of a bear. I was sitting on a pine stump, the mellow sunlight filtering over me and through me. Suddenly I heard a grouse get up. The boys had flushed him, and he came straight back for me. I saw him hurtling headlong toward me, and was about to get out of his way when he banked and came to earth just about twelve feet from me. I have noticed that when a grouse alights after having been alarmed, he nearly always runs for the nearest shelter. In this case he dodged in beside an old log. He was out of sight, but there he was. And there I was. I figured that he had not made me out. What to do in such a case is a little puzzling. The place was thick, and the chance for a deft get-away exceedingly good. But to my right were hemlocks and birches and a stream. It was toward them that the bird had been headed. When flushed again, he would doubtless take up his old route. For five minutes I studied the situation, trying to put myself in the place of the bird. At last I made up my mind just where he was going . . . Oh, Man! Never make up your mind that you know what an intelligent wild critter is gwine do. What keeps him alive is his ability to keep you guessing. I rose from the stump and was ready for a right-hand shot toward the hemlocks. But no. That grouse slid off the ground with hardly any more noise than an owl that had just had his hinges greased would make. He just snaked himself off, very low to the ground, deftly threading the glimmering thicket. I let drive hopelessly, but he fell. It really wasn't fair. He had fairly outwitted me, but had lost the game . . . I remember that grouse because he always makes me think that to kill this bird the hunter should make an especial study of its styles of flight. There's an infinite variety— from the stormy explosive rise to this eerie, moth-like performance; but always there is a kind of dizzy precision and a high-gear speed, even in the thickest timber, that puts this bird in a class by itself, and will thrill the heart of any hunter, however seasoned.

VIII. The Prince in the Mist

I was turkey-hunting behind Hogback Mountain. It was just daylight, but a radiant mist was over the world, and in the deeper hollows it was still banked in mysterious folds. I had both barrels loaded with chilled 2's. Coming to an ancient charcoal hearth, which in the Pennsylvania woods are favorite places for both hunters and game to reconnoiter, I stood there looking out over the wild valley, with the immense rocky flank of Hogback to my right. No one knows why those things happen so, but this one did, and is now a part of my hunting history. Across the gleaming vale I saw a shape coming at lightning speed; another, even swifter, was following. It was a big cock grouse, with a goshawk after it. They were at least seventy yards up, but were coming almost over me. I just had time to get my gun up. Leading the grouse almost a yard, I touched the trigger; then gave precisely the same attention to the tawny pursuer. By some miracle both birds plunged downward; and when I found them they were not ten yards apart. I suppose I should have let the lordly grouse go; but in hunting, as in most things mortal, instinct is stronger and more immediate than sentiment.

Such is the true history of eight of the princes of the woodland that I have secured. If I were to record the tale of those I had missed, my story would be much longer.

A Unique Quail Hunt

We were just about halfway through our plantation Christmas dinner, which is no mean kind of an entertainment, when a Negro bearing a note for me shuffled to the door. I took the letter and read its brief contents. A friend in the city was having a house-party of a dozen guests. As yet they had enjoyed no game. Would it be possible for me to secure and dispatch immediately about twenty-five or thirty quail? The writer assured me that I knew where the birds were, and all that; and that he would not trouble me, but that he knew how much I should enjoy getting the bag for him. But unless they could be put on the mail Christmas night they would arrive too late for the aforesaid purpose. Gentle reader, have you ever had a friend who knew nothing of hunting ask you to get game for him? He thinks he is conferring a privilege on you; for he honestly believes that on a big plantation shooting quail is just like picking cotton, and bagging a wild turkey is just like going into the garden and cutting off a cabbage—just like that!

But this friend of mine, however uninformed on some matters, is a man whom I like to please; therefore during the remainder of the dinner I was honestly planning how I might accommodate his wishes. To do this would, in the first place, require quick work, for the sun was hardly two hours high. Moreover, to another friend I had lent my only bird-dog for a Christmas Day hunt. Unless a man has two or three coveys of quail shooed into a coop, and has the lid clamped down over them, how is he going to produce them suddenly at a friend's mere wish? But in hunting as in most things it pays to try.

Leaving the rest of the company discussing juleps and the like, I emerged from the house just before the sun had begun to burn the

From *Plantation Game Trails* (1921).

tall pines to the westward of the plantation. Seeing several little Negro boys who had already had a share of dinner, I impressed them into my service. We crossed the cotton-fields, heading toward a long stretch of broomsedge that bordered the creek. In this dense yellow grass there are always quail, but to find them without a dog would be difficult; yet there were my dusky henchmen to help. Pausing once to look the situation over, I heard, coming from a far edge of the field, where an extraordinarily high tide had begun to back the water into the grass, the carrying-on of two coveys of quail that had run into each other. The voluble gossip that they were engaging in was sweet music to my ears. And there was little lost motion in my getting to where the birds were.

Telling my small trailers to stand close behind me so as to give me a chance to shoot, I began walking up the birds. They must have been having for themselves some kind of a Christmas festival or dinner-party, for they were as loath to rise as some friends I had just left had been unwilling to leave the table. I never saw birds rise so scatteringly; not if I live until the League of Nations or the millennium or something like that comes off, do I expect to see more quail in one place. I said that two coveys had come together. That was all wrong. The thing I am telling is a true thing; and when I say that, standing almost in one place, with birds rising almost continuously, I was enabled to kill eleven birds "on the rise," you will understand what kind of a camp-meeting I had invaded. Nor did the birds, even after much shooting, fly wildly. They must have been too deeply engrossed with social engagements to consider me. From the grassy edges where I had flushed them they swung to the left, settling about in the tall broomgrass on a little hillock that rose softly from the dead level of the old field.

The little Negroes retrieved all the shot birds, and we now began to walk up the scattered ones. The sun was down behind the pines now; and the brightly lighted sky gave most excellent visibility. To walk up these fine birds and to have them go whirring off toward the fading sunset afforded me as fine an opportunity for quail-shooting as I have ever enjoyed. The crippled birds were gathered in for me by the small boys, who performed very creditably. They also carried the game, so that all I had to do was to flush the birds and shoot.

They were not followed for the third rise, both because they were by that time widely scattered, and because, on pausing to count heads, I discovered, to my surprise, that we had twenty-eight. They would be enough. The house-party would be supplied. Nor, strange to say, had the matter in this instance been much more difficult than picking cotton. I got the birds off on the mail that night, and learned later that they had arrived in time to render festive the occasion for which they had been gathered in.

There remains, perhaps, a word concerning the remarkable size of this bunch of birds that it was my good fortune to encounter. I have seen at other times coveys numbering as many as thirty-five or forty birds, and these undoubtedly consisted of two or more bevies that had come together. My accounting for this particular covey is this: that on account of the very high water prevailing in the creek, which had flooded the marshes and bottom-lands, two coveys, possibly three, that had been used to roosting in the marsh, had come late in the afternoon to the broomsedge field, and there had met another covey. They were discussing the situation when I heard them; and the fact that they realized that their regular haunts were flooded kept most of them in the broomgrass. In all, the hunt was a unique one, not the least interesting feature of which being my new type of retriever that proved his worth on that memorable occasion.

PART V

CHIMERAS

Rutledge was endlessly intrigued by the dangerous creatures in the woods and waters around Hampton. There was something about the mystical dread of these chimeras, as he liked to style them, which attracted his interest and stirred his creativity. In a sense, however, his choice of the word *chimera* was erroneous, for it suggests imaginary or fanciful monsters. No one loved a good story better than Rutledge, and certainly he was not one to let a bit of embellishment stand in the way of a good presentation. In fact, imagination runs rampant in some of the stories which follow, but there was plenty of real danger in the world around Hampton as well. Creatures of the Santee wilds—rattlesnakes, cottonmouth moccasins, alligators, wild boars, sharks, and the like—were all too real. They lurked, hidden and dreaded, ready to punish the careless or unwary intruder. Rutledge and his black henchmen knew them well, because they sought sport and observed nature in the domains frequented by these creatures.

There is something in that elusive quality we call human nature which draws us inexorably into conflict with chimeras. At Hampton perhaps it was that trait common to many outdoorsmen, an subconscious desire for an element of danger to add spice to their pursuits. Certainly Rutledge never allowed fear or the potential presence of dangerous beasts to interfere with his sport. In fact, as the tales that follow suggest, he sometimes seemed to relish dangerous encounters, and where personal experience did not provide them, his fertile imagination created them. Unquestionably chimeras gave him plenty of story material, and the six selections offered here are but a sampling of the many he wrote about them. They are uniformly well done, and even at second hand the sensations associated with the evil beasts he describes fill us with dread.

Today's student of natural history might not agree with Rutledge's evaluations of certain species as worthy of little more than condemnation and killing whenever possible. Yet much of our inclination to leave nature's balance alone is the product of remoteness, of being so distant from real dangers as to think them virtually non-existent. Rutledge lived, so to speak, on danger's doorstep, and he never considered avoiding or fleeing from dangerous creatures when he encountered them. To some degree at least his determination to kill them was understandable, because alligators and wild boars did not mix well with prized hunting dogs, nor were deadly serpents to be welcomed where people and domestic animals regularly trod.

Mainly though, as we read these selections, it is with strong awareness that the author had a flair for high drama. The sinister, scary denizens he describes fill us with loathing even as they exert the same appeal which draws a moth to the flame. The ability to create that type of attraction is one mark of a fine writer.

A Great Serpent

Witch Pond is one of those sudden and spectral bodies of water that are found in the pinewood districts of South Carolina; lonely, forbidding, black-watered, and heavily grown with silent straight tupelos and weeping cypresses. This pond is about half a mile from the old plantation gateway, on the left of the road as one goes out. At this point, immediately on the right of the road, is Spencer's Pond; originally these two had been one, but a causeway having been laid and heaped with sand, the road leading into the plantation was like an isthmus between two ponds. In time, trees and shrubs took root on the sides of the road, and through the screen of these, the passer-by could see the dark waters on either side glimmering.

This causeway was at the entrance to what we called the Pasture Woods, which were virgin, dense of growth, dark and fragrant. Beyond, the great pine forest began to come into view—airy, full of sunshine, silence, and aromatic breezes.

Coming home from a ride or a drive, our horses would never quicken their pace, as horses do when they realize that they are nearly home, until they came to Witch Pond, when they invariably broke from a walk into a trot or from a trot into a gallop. Naturally our imaginations associated these accustomed actions with some sinister aspect of the mysterious ponds, of which the horses' instinct made them cognizant; and not without a cause did we believe thus. Twice I had killed big alligators in Witch Pond, and once, when our hounds took a deer across Spencer's Pond, they returned to us cowed and silent, while the deer never again reappeared. We supposed that

From *Wild Life of the South* (1935).

a 'gator had caught the deer, and that the hounds had witnessed that tragedy of the wild.

One March morning, in the year 1894, when the warmth of the early springtime was flushing into bridal bloom even the ancient live-oaks and the patriarchal cypresses, I was riding happily through the Pasture Woods, and had come almost to Witch Pond, when my attention was casually attracted by what I supposed to be a log lying across the causeway. There had been no storm; but I easily accounted for the log's being there by supposing that the dead shaft of a pine, standing long by reason of the strength of its solid heart, had at length given way at the bottom, and had been tumbled across the road. Hardly a month before I had found such a tree in the road near the avenue gateway.

There was a freshet in the river; and this had caused the water of Witch Pond to rise, so that now it was trickling into the deep sandy rut on the left of the road. The smallest incident of life is unique, and is often impressive even when not accompanied by vivid circumstances. I can remember the exact appearance of that particular spot as it looked forty years ago.

I was riding a young horse whose habit was to keep an unnecessarily sharp vigil for objects at which to shy, and I knew that he saw the log; but I paid no particular attention to it, except that as we reached it I tightened rein so that my mount would not stumble.

As the horse put his right forefoot over it, I glanced down—and I saw the dead tree move! I was aware, in a sudden shock of dazed understanding, that the huge body spanning the road was a part of the length of a great serpent, whose identity was for the moment unknown to me. At the same time, the horse winded it, and probably saw it move, for he gave a tremendous bound, almost unseating me. For fifty yards he ran like the wind, snorting and tossing his head; then I got control of him. Turning him, I looked back and there saw that the serpent had turned, and was lying his full length in the road, his head toward me.

In our life on the plantation, I had an unusual variety of experiences with snakes and reptiles of many kinds; and with the assistance of a quaint old book entitled *Reptilian Life in the Carolinas* we had identified a large number of species. We knew well the rattlesnakes and their pilots; the beautiful king snake, which we used to call the thunderbolt; the deadly cotton-mouth moccasin; the harlequin snake; the black racer, and many others. As far as our knowledge then extended, and we have since become assured that in that (solitary) particular it needed no supplement, the largest snake in the Santee country was the great diamondback rattler of the deep swamps. Occasionally a huge moccasin would be killed; but the most venomous variety of this species does not grow large.

This Witch Pond serpent that now lay in the road before me literally dwarfed the great diamondback which some Negro lumbermen had brought out of the Laurel Hill swamp. It was so much larger than any snake that I had ever dreamed could be found in those woods that I turned my horse this way and that, so that I could be really sure that I was seeing what I saw. My survey satisfied me fully: there could be no doubt of the proportions of this monstrous serpent which, unaccountably, had invaded the peaceful woods through which I had long been accustomed to ride.

At any rate I dismounted, tethering my horse to a pine sapling; I used a light half-hitch tie, so that if necessary I could free him in a moment.

Then I took a short turn in the woods in search of the right kind of a pole with which to attack the reptile. I rejected stout young hickories that would amply have sufficed for any snake of my former acquaintance. I eyed a stately-shafted yellow pine, wishing that I had the prowess to wield such a bludgeon. I half hoped that when I returned to the road, the serpent, with a wisdom in keeping with his size, would have presaged my attack, and would have disappeared. But on my return to the road, armed with a twenty-foot pine pole, there lay the Witch Pond serpent; apparently waiting for me.

The weight of my weapon was so great for a boy ten years old that I decided to lift it into proper position before beginning my attack, and to advance on the snake with the pole poised above me. This I did, walking slowly down the road, ready to strike if he should make a move toward me, and fully ready to run, should my blow prove ineffective.

The great snake did not move, but I could see him watching me sleepily, with a dull light glaring glazedly out of his metallic eyes. I had long since learned, from an experience with a rattlesnake pilot, to distrust the sleepy look of a snake, and I was not deceived now.

At last I came within striking distance; I must have been about fifteen feet from the head of the reptile. This was as near as I ever got to him, and I measured him carefully with my eye. And I knew then that whatever might be the success of my venture, I should have a marvelously strange story to tell those at home, and I wanted to be sure of my facts.

The head of the snake was as broad as a man's hand, and shaped not unlike it; in length, I took him to be ten feet; his body looked to be a foot in circumference; his coloring was as uncertain brown, with hints of brighter shades, which the swamp mud through which he had crawled had discolored and partly concealed. I did not wholly identify him until I saw his sheaf of rattles, held a little off the ground. As I came up, he whirred them softly; their arid murmur was a song of death.

Being, as I conceived, within a vital distance of the snake, I decided to strike the blow that I knew would create instant and wonderful developments; but there was one result for which I was wholly unprepared, and that was the only one that happened.

With all the force that the falling weight of the pole and that of my own strength could give, I brought my weapon down on the broad head of the serpent. The blow rebounded as if it had been dealt to a huge ball of rubber; the snake itself, instead of writhing in pain, appeared simply to be slightly annoyed, and lifted its head and three or four feet of its body several inches from the road. If I were to describe the expression that I believed I then saw in that snake's face, I should call it bored disdain, touched with awakening menace.

The blow had been fair, and I had no reason to believe that I could give one more effective than the first one had been. Besides, under the circumstances, it was not very hard for me to persuade myself that it would not be right to be late for the mail just for the sake of a snake. So I tossed the pole over into the bushes, turned, and ran down the road toward my horse. I had to make myself walk before I reached him, because my excitement excited him, and he came very near getting loose.

When from his back I again looked toward Witch Pond, there lay the serpent in that strange position of indolent menace.

One of the real regrets of my life is that I rode away that morning, leaving my fell antagonist in possession of the field. Not long afterwards, however, near the same place, a Negro turpentine worker killed a great diamondback rattler, eight feet in length. I have always believed that this chimera and my Witch Pond serpent were one and the same.

Serpents of the Trail

For more than an hour I had been seated in the delightful sunshine of the Southern woods. My back was against an ancient live-oak; indeed, I was retired among the huge convolutions of the old monarch's high-heaved roots. I had seen some interesting things in wild life: half-a-dozen gray squirrels disporting themselves among the dead leaves on the ground; a covey of quail trooping out of the woods toward a broomsedge; and one lone wild gobbler beginning to roam in that purposeful and significant manner which shows that he feels the coming urge of spring. Suddenly, off to my left, there was a flash of black and white falling; then came a heavy thud which was followed by the sound of slow scuffling. I quickly went over toward the scene of this encounter of the wild, and was rewarded by a strange sight. A king snake, which had been basking in the mellow sunlight on a horizontal live-oak limb some ten feet above the ground, had dropped from that height upon a glass snake, which, as I came up, was in the snake-killer's fatal toils. The maneuver was characteristically clever on the part of the king snake, or what we call the "thunderbolt," which on this occasion justified his latter appellation.

On another day, near the same spot, I saw a great king snake pursuing another reptile; I did not catch sight of the victim, but I felt sorry for him; for never have I seen a pursuer appear more in earnest or more certain of accomplishing his design. With a lithe, rocking motion, and with his head and forebody held high off the ground the beautiful harrier moved swiftly through the woods, threading the secret pathways with eerie assurance and with all the speed and alertness of the most crafty of hunters. The end of this chase I did not witness; but on another occasion I saw the behavior

---

From *Days Off in Dixie* (1924).

of a king snake when his prey was taken from him; and the reader can judge from that incident, now described, that the thunderbolt can hardly be robbed of his kill.

A party of us had been deer-hunting in October, the worst month for snakes in the pinelands of Carolina. As we gathered in the road after a drive, one of our number bore over his shoulder a long pine pole, and upon the pole a strange burden. Wrapped in final and in fatal battle were a rattler and a king snake. They were of about the same proportions; the killer was slightly longer, and the rattler slightly bulkier in the body. This was a timber rattlesnake, and not a lordly diamondback. When this sinister burden was deposited in the road, we separated the snakes with poles; and a difficult feat it was to drag them apart. One man of the group suggested that we have a race; and to this we agreed. We lifted the rattler across the roadside ditch and gave him a quiet chance to crawl away. Indeed, we were obliged to give him almost a half-hour before we were sure that he had made any kind of getaway. At the end of that time we set the thunderbolt down on the trail of the rattler. I shall never forget with what intelligent alacrity the king snake followed the slot. We followed also; but we had some difficulty in so doing. About two hundred yards from the road we came upon the combatants. Once more they were locked in grim and gorgeous battle. It appeared to me that they had exactly the same "hold" on each other as they had had when first found. This second encounter we did not try to terminate. And it could have but one end, for the king snake is complete master of the rattler. However, I doubt if any king snake could handle one of the huge old diamondbacks that it has been my dubious privilege to encounter—regal serpents, not only of dreadful venomous power, but also of superbly formidable muscular development.

During my plantation life I have not had many meetings with the true diamondback; nor, indeed, with his humbler relative, the timber rattler. But such encounters as have been mine have impressed me greatly. These reptiles I respect highly, and I have the natural and common dread of them. It is, however, a remarkable thing that so few persons are actually struck by the rattler; and of those struck, the majority recover. But let it not be thought that the rattlesnake's venom may not prove fatal, as a New England schoolteacher lately contended with me. I was asked to show a single instance in which the rattler had killed a man. It happens that for many years I have carefully collected data on this somewhat gruesome matter, and I can report several authentic instances. I can in each instance give name, date, and exact circumstances of the tragedy. I will comment on two only. The first occurred near Arden, North Carolina, in the summer of 1894. I was within a mile of the scene of the accident. Two mountain children were picking blackberries along an old fence row. The elder, some yards from the younger, heard the latter talking to something. Then suddenly there was a cry. When the elder child reached the younger, the rattler had struck it twice upon the neck, the most dangerous place. The child soon lapsed into unconsciousness and never recovered. The snake in this instance was not killed; but it was undoubtedly a regular mountain timber rattler.

The second case I do not give without hesitation, yet it is well for every man or woman who ventures into snake country to be aware of the possible peril. Only by that caution which comes from being intelligently informed can danger be avoided. Less than a year ago, on a plantation not far south of Savannah, Georgia, two brothers were inspecting some pine timber on one of the wilder parts of their estate. Both of them were standing on a huge fallen log, which rested in a bed of ferns, huckleberry bushes, gallberries, and the like. They were talking in that absorbed fashion which is the result of the mind's being busy with appraisal when one of them stepped down from the log into the underbrush. He was instantly struck, and with no warning, by a huge diamondback. The wound was directly in the femoral artery; and so instantaneous was the effect of the venom that the victim fell to the ground. He swooned and within four hours he had passed away without ever having regained consciousness. The snake, a most formidable chimera, was killed.

But rattlesnakes, especially the monster diamondbacks, are not anywhere very common; the Southwest contains more than any other region. And from about the latitude of Savannah northward reptiles hibernate from November to March, which are the very months when sportsmen are most likely to be abroad in snaky haunts.

Now, if the reader will permit me, I shall descend from the dreadful to the amusing—or shall rise, perhaps. For it is a fact that there are certain features about snake life which render it humorous—at least from the human standpoint.

One day I was fishing in a big rice field canal, which is no mean place for large-mouth bass. I had a Negro with me. Getting a somewhat sluggish strike, I tried to hook the fish, but instead, my line became fastened about a submerged snag. The Negro offered to loose it for me. He made his way down the bank; he stepped into the edge of the water, holding my line gingerly in his hand. Drawing it taut so that the direction of it into the water would locate the old snag for him, he reached down with the other hand into the depths of the muddy water. Meanwhile I waited somewhat negligently, expecting nothing interesting. Suddenly the Negro cried out wildly; and he had the best reason in the world so to cry. He had managed to pull the line loose, but as it came free there emerged from the water, fast hooked, a huge rusty cotton-mouth moccasin; and it swiftly wrapped itself, tail first, about the man's bare arm. For a moment we should have been in the movies. I was on the bank, holding the line sufficiently taut to keep the snake from striking the Negro, but not at all anxious to have the moccasin suddenly released and thrown into my shirt-front. But in a moment it was over and the man was freed. Yet it took the two of us some time to get rid of our dangerous prey. I may add that in Southern rivers, in reserves, in rice field ditches and canals, moccasins abound. Several times, in high water, I have had the cotton-mouth drop into my boat from overhanging aquatic bushes, on which this snake loves to bask.

Not once, but several times, I have come upon one snake in the grimly amusing task of swallowing another snake. The contest enters the championship class when the sizes of the two reptiles approach equality. I remember seeing a moccasin trying to "get away" with a common water snake that was almost his own length. When I found them, they had entered a difficult stage of the business. Taking proper precautions, I pulled them apart, but it was not an easy thing to do. One serpent appeared to me to be feeling about as badly abused as the other; but what surprised me was the fact that the water snake was not yet dead. Nor did he die then. I killed the cotton-mouth, which is a deadly brute, but the other snake I let go. It is harmless, though many observers take it to be a true moccasin.

When Solomon—or perhaps it was David—mentioned the way of the serpent upon the sand as passing strange, he might have made the matter more concrete had he said the way of the water snake with the bullfrog. The enmity between these two is a ludicrous thing. The mature bullfrog is a pompous, vain, bumptious fellow; and he is an enormous coward. From the borders of a lagoon I love to watch the military maneuvers of frogs and their arch-enemies, the snakes. The largest frogs are, I think, safe from attack; but their safety does not seem to reassure them. The most impressive and manly bellowing will cease; the frog will shrink and cower, he will ease himself off, or he will make the leap of his life if a water snake comes his way. I do not blame the frog. But I do find amusement in his Falstaffian ways. I remember coming one day on the margin of a rice field upon a sight so strange that I found myself wondering if I were really awake. A tremendous water snake had caught a medium-sized frog, but he had not by any means subdued him. The snake had the frog by the front of the head, just as I have seen a snake take a nine-inch brook trout; but the frog was using his legs to good advantage. I studied the expression on the face of the reptile: it was crafty yet disturbed, malicious, grim, catlike. There was a lively tussle, sure enough; and throughout the whole performance the bullfrog kept "bulling" in a painfully muffled fashion down the very throat of his would-be murderer. But I had come in time to act as the victim's deliverer.

One of the most curious little reptiles I know is the hog-nosed rattler, a diminutive reptile but a genuine rattlesnake of which I have spoken before. Another curiosity is the coral snake; an anomaly in nature. It is almost as spectacular in coloring as the Gila monster, and it has not a single resemblance to any other venomous reptile. It is slender, shapely, round, and has a small head, weak jaws, and a very small mouth. But it is a true venom-carrier. I have not seen many coral snakes; and of those I have observed, most had been ploughed up in fields bordering woodlands, for it spends a good deal of its time underground or under shelter. I suppose that this habit is largely a matter of precaution, for his gorgeous bands of black and red must make him a brilliant target for enemies. This snake is a strange creature; it appears half asleep most of the time, and has never appeared to me to have any definite personality, with which, for example, the blacksnake is well supplied.

Such are a few glimpses of these children of nature that are classi-fied as sinister, and for which the human race certainly has an ancient antipathy—an aversion which probably is not all on one side. And besides man the reptile world has many dread enemies. In the region of which I write the snakes are preyed upon by eagles and hawks; they are destroyed in wholesale fashion by forest fires; particularly when they are hibernating in old logs and stumps; and they are devoured by hogs. Deer also kill snakes, especially rattlesnakes, by springing upon them. And even a small harmless snake is hardly safe from the average man, whose revulsion at seeing it is such that he does not know how or care whether to distinguish between the evil and the good.

As a race, I think, most reptiles are disappearing; and perhaps it is to be expected, for at least to me they appear to be survivors from the lost ages of the flying lizards and the monstrous amphibians which once made the world no place upon which man could with decency dwell.

A Demon of the Jetties

Along the entire reach of the Carolina coast there is, perhaps, no more favorable fishing ground for black sea-bass than the jetties off Charleston. The Charleston bar is narrow; and the distance between Sullivan's and James Island is no greater than the width of the average coast inlet, although this opening is the outlet for the Ashley and Cooper rivers. Several years ago, in order to allow the tides to dredge the bar, rock jetties were built up from the opposing points of the adjacent islands, and these extend in parallel lines some distance out to sea.

The rough rockwork of the jetties attracts many kinds of fish; and among them none is dearer to the Southern sportsman than the black sea-bass, for it is not only an excellent fish to eat, but it furnishes rare excitement when taken on a small rod.

One September afternoon Ray Haskell went out to the jetties to fish for black bass.

"You had better come with me," his friend Arthur Rhett urged, as they were crossing the harbor in Rhett's yawl. "You'll catch more red snapper on the banks in half an hour than you will catch bass on the jetties all the afternoon."

"But no one fishes for snapper with a rod, Arthur; besides, I want to try the bass with my new tackle. Leave me on the jetties, and pick me up on your way home. Next time," he added, smiling, "you'll stop there with me."

"Well," his friend replied, "that may be so. At any rate, it will not take me long today to run out and back, and I don't care to fish more than an hour. You will have had enough of it by that time, too, I think."

From *Heart of the South* (1924).

After a half-hour's run with the ebb down the harbor, the two young men reached the jetties, and Rhett brought his yawl up into the hurrying tide and put his friend out on the granite bowlders.

His boat swung swiftly in the outgoing current; her sails filled with the soft breeze, and she swept gracefully over the bar and out to sea.

Haskell jointed his rod, selected a favorable point near the seaward end of the jetty, and began to fish. The tide was running out strong, and he did not expect the black bass to strike well until the flood; however, he kept his line in the water, hoping for luck. At last the running of the tide slackened somewhat; the eddies no longer whirled about the rocks; in quite corners the water was glassy and still. The flood would soon be coming in. But the period of the slack water is the poorest time for any kind of fishing, and Haskell grew weary of catching nothing. He laid his rod down, and sat on the rocks near the brink of the lapping water. He watched the tall, dark pines on James Island, and the sea gulls rising and dipping, and gazed at the noble proportions of Fort Moultrie on Sullivan's Island, and the memorable and historic Fort Sumter. Afar to the northwest the city sparkled in the clear sunlight. Haskell looked everywhere except in the water immediately before him.

Out of the channel waters there now came stealthily, waveringly, a long dark arm that felt its way along the smooth, wave-worn rocks. Other arms were just below the surface, half hidden by the murky water. The lone fisherman did not guess his deadly peril until two of the powerful tentacles of the octopus suddenly laid hold on his ankles. One coil whipped itself about his knee, and the hundreds of cup-like suckers on the under sides of the tentacle set like blind teeth against him.

The shock brought Haskell to his feet, but the creature's strength unbalanced him, and he sank down again. With fierce strength he grasped the smooth, muscular arms, but he could not move them from his legs. Other dark arms, lines with red-mouthed suckers, were waving above the water. Another one gripped Haskell, and he felt it start the blood.

On a beach or on a sandy shore he might have thwarted an attack from such a creature; but here on the rocks this demon-like monster had everything in its favor. The water beyond the rocks was thirty feet deep. Among the submerged granite bowlders, the octopus could get a grip with its tentacles that would enable it to draw down its prey. Haskell braced his arms against the cruel strength that was trying to dislodge him, and looked about for help. The same sea gulls were rising and dipping; the same two forts were looking sternly out to sea; the same distant city flashed in the sunlight. The only sail that Haskell could see was that of a sloop, far across the harbor and headed up the Cooper River. Rhett would not return from the banks for at least two hours. It was most unlikely that any other fishing boat would be coming past the jetties at that time of tide. Several hours before, scores of the "Mosquito Fleet," as they are called, had gone out to the "fishing drops" off the bar; and several hours later they would be thronging in past the jetties. But now not one was passing. Haskell realized that he must fight his own battle with this grim and terrible antagonist.

The octopus was waving its arms less restlessly now, and had withdrawn some of them beneath the water; Haskell surmised with dread that they were gripping the rocks, in order to get a more powerful purchase against him. As yet he found himself in no great pain, although his legs were strangely numb. Presently, however, the pressure and the pulling of the tentacles became more intense, and the sucking of the mouths grew painful.

Then suddenly, as if the creature were tired of playing with its victim, and had determined on a bold move, it began to move down the sunken rocks into deep water. To his horror, Haskell found himself being dragged irresistibly down. Struggling desperately, he grasped the rocks, but his hold was feeble against the brute strength of this monster. The grip of his hands slipped. He turned over on his stomach, and caught a big bowlder with both hands. He knew that he must hold on; and he held. The slow movement of the octopus ceased. There was a momentary pause in the struggle. But even while Haskell lay panting against the rocks, he felt another tentacle, then another, come tap-tapping about his back, and he shuddered as the long clammy arms groped for a hold. He could do nothing against them, for he dared not loosen his grasp on the bowlder for a moment. The tentacles that were fastened about his legs had in no way relaxed their tenacious grip.

Plans of escape passed through Haskell's brain in feverish succession, but he discarded them all. He knew that in his plight he must not waste his precious strength and energy in futile attempts; he realized that he could not tear himself loose from the tentacles of the big octopus; and he was certain that the creature would not relax its hold. He had with him no weapon of any kind. If he had had a keen knife he might have been able to sever the smooth slippery, muscular tentacles. But his bare hands and his wits were his only weapons. At last a plan of escape came to his mind that seemed to have a small chance of succeeding. The creature had moved once of its own accord, Haskell reasoned; might it not, under gentle persuasion, move again, and this time upward? If he could get the octopus high enough on the rocks so that the front of its head would be above water, he might crush it with one of the granite bowlders.

The warm flood-tide water was now flowing up the channel; and probably on account of that, and because the fisherman did not struggle, the octopus ceased to strain against him as at first. Gently, inch by inch, Haskell pulled himself up on the rocks, moving so slowly that he did not seem to be moving at all. Doubtless most of the wild things that the octopus caught struggled to get away; and the creature, sure of its hold on the man, felt certain of its prey, and so, giving a little with the incoming tide, moved with Haskell up the rocks. But when the man reached the position from which the octopus had first dragged him, the powerful beast set its anchors firmly, and held. Haskell tugged and strained in vain; his back and arms ached cruelly with the struggle. Where the tentacle mouths pressed against his flesh, he felt the warm blood flowing freely. His heart was filled with despair, but he did not give an inch of the ground he had gained. He was at least as immovable in his position as the octopus was in its. Finally, when Haskell realized that his strength was failing, and that he would soon be forced to loosen his hold, he felt his enemy give way slightly, grudgingly. A fraction of an inch at a time it came up on the rocks of the jetties. Haskell saw the wavering shadows of its tentacles on the rocks. Still he strained on up the jagged slope. The higher he could get the better would be his chance of dealing the octopus a stunning blow.

At last, when he found himself higher than he had been since the creature seized him, he laid both hands on a rough heavy rock, and turned on his back. With an effort he raised the rock over his head, sat up, poised the weapon, and hurled it fiercely at his grim adversary. The upper part of the octopus's body was resting on the side of a submerged rock, and offered Haskell a fair target. He hurled the granite bowlder at it, but the rock struck too low. The only effect of the blow was to make the octopus lift other tentacles, as if in warning, and tighten the grip of those that held its prey. Again Haskell felt himself being drawn down with terrible sureness. Haskell knew that the creature would not now pause until it had taken him into deep water.

With wonderful poise and mental clearness he seized another rock, and waited until the two powerful tentacles that held him were taut over the rough ledge of a bowlder; then he leaned forward, and holding the rock in both hands, smote the tentacles with quick, fierce blows that severed the terrible arms from the creature's body.

The octopus sank beside the rocks, leaving behind it the two tentacles. Haskell tore them from their horrible grip. In the flood of the channel a red track marked the creature's course, as it moved away under the water.

An hour later Rhett came in from the banks, and ran his yawl beside the jetty, in order to pick up his friend. "Well, any sport?" he asked.

"I don't believe I should call it sport," Haskell replied; "but it was about as near danger as I ever care to be."

Then, on their homeward sail over the harbor, Haskell showed Rhett his wounds and told him of his perilous encounter with the sinister demon of the jetties.

The Specter of Tiger Creek

After passing the winter on the plantation, we moved, in the spring, down to a house on the coast, where we spent the summer, safe from malaria and other swamp-fevers. It was there that we did our salt-water fishing, and there that we had this adventure with a huge shark in Tiger Creek.

One of the most popular forms of fishing along the Southern coast is the taking of mullets at night, either with a cast-net or with a gill-seine. They cannot be taken with a hook and line, and only rarely can they be caught in the daytime with a net.

One day in August my brother Tom and I, on our return home from a trip after school-bass along the marshes, ran into a big school of mullets near the mouth of Tiger Creek, a deep estuary that withdraws from the main channel and winds a sinuous way up into the marsh-fields. We could do nothing with the mullets then, but we reasoned that they might be there on the next flood, which would be about midnight, and we decided to try for them with the gill-seine.

At eleven o'clock we left the glimmering shell wharf and dropped silently down on the late ebb.

We had a ten-foot cypress bateau, light but steady, and capable of carrying a good load. Tom rowed, and I well remember that the starlight and the silent ranks of green cedars on the shore and the strange noises in the marshes made us feel very adventurous.

A pull of half an hour down the channel brought us to Tiger Creek, the surface of which glittered frostily in the starlight with the myriads of small fish that were playing on it. By this time the young flood was beginning to creep in; so, running the boat up under the

From *Tom and I on the Old Plantation* (1918).

lee shore, we waited there, and listened with pleasurable assurance to the telltale thudding of the water—a certain sign of mullets. As we had expected, they were going into Tiger Creek; we had only to wait until they got well up the stream before stopping the mouth with the seine.

When it was evident that the school had passed us, we rowed quietly up the creek for a little distance. Then, while my brother pulled slowly, I staked one end of the seine and paid out the length over the stern. The creek was forty feet wide, and our net only thirty; so we staked the boat at the short end, which made an apparent, although not a perfect, shut-off.

As I was the younger, it usually fell to me to run the fish down, while Tom tended the net; but this time he asked me, much to my delight, if I would not like to take the fish out when they struck the net. Making me promise not to let the big ones get away, he splashed off through the marsh with an oar over his shoulder.

Having made the boat fast between the seine and the shore, I let myself down into the warm, sparkling water and began to feel my way out along the seine. I wanted to make sure that the corks were all floating right side up, and that the lead-line was set true. The water was not so deep as I thought it would be, for it came only a little above my waist by the boat and at the middle of the net; but the bottom was very soft and sticky, so that several times I had to take hold of the seine to pull my feet out of the mud. Consequently, I did not venture so far as the narrow channel that ran close to the shore at the other end of the net. There, I knew, the water was deeper. I found the net hanging right; and as it was a new one, with no holes and no weak places. I felt sure that we would make a large catch.

Before long I heard Tom begin to shout, and then came the sound of his oar spanking the water near the head of the creek. Soon I heard mullets jumping; then the water about me began to murmur, and a big fish struck the seine and gilled himself. The corks bobbed and the water foamed, while I waded toward the fish, took him out, and threw him into the boat. Before I could turn, several had gilled themselves, and one had jumped into our bateau. The hurrying fish, fleeing for open water, bumped against me. They rushed here and there, huddled against the seine, jumped over it, gilled themselves, or buried themselves in the mud beneath it.

I was so busy and so eager to reach a certain fish that was making a great froth near the middle of the seine that I did not at first notice the decided lull in the general noise, and, anyway, my ears were pretty well engaged with Tom's shouting and his pounding with the oar. But I soon realized that something unusual in the water had frightened the mullets even more than our seine. Yet, well as I knew the salt creeks and the real dangers that lurk there, I did not move from the spot where, with my feet bogged in the sucking mud, I was feeling out along the seine and lifting it here and there to take out the fish that had gilled themselves.

I was holding the seine up with my right hand, and my left hand was hanging by my side in the water, when I suddenly felt a big wave rise to my shoulder, and in front of it, moving sluggishly past me along the downstream side of the seine, I saw the fin of a great shark. He had come in with the flood, and was prowling about for the kill.

Of all the creatures that infest salt waters, none are more sinister than the sharks, especially the hammerheads and the tigers. Moving like shadowy specters just beneath the surface, they appear suddenly, seize their prey, and rending it with their needle-like teeth, dart away to devour it. They are crafty in their movements, usually cowardly about noises, sinister in their silent and deadly approach.

The hammerheads never grow very large in those waters, but the gray, racing body of the tiger I had seen as long as twelve feet. The shark that was now so near me was—as I guessed from the height of his fin and the size of the wave it carried—ten feet long.

Just now he had turned away from the seine, and was making a semi-circle in the creek. It is said that when a shark begins to circle on the surface, with his fin cutting the water faster and faster as he turns, it is time to look for trouble. That is exactly what I saw there on the surface of that placid creek, and I believed I knew what it meant. He had wind of me, and was circling to find and close in on me. There was something fascinating about his bloodhound tactics; sometimes he would stop as if listening, or as if thinking the puzzle out in his crafty mind; then he would move deliberately off with insolent assurance.

At first I was merely surprised that such a big shark should be near Tiger Creek, and provoked that he should have spoiled our seining, for there was now no sight or sound of a fish anywhere. But when I saw the alertness of the creature, the terrible intensity in that rigid fin, that sweeping hither and thither of the lithe body, my feelings changed; I wanted to get out of his way as quickly as I could. There was nothing between us but open water, for I was on the outside of the seine.

Having stood so long in one place, my feet had gradually become set in the heavy mud, so that when I tried to move toward the boat I could not take a step. Hitherto, with the help of the seine, I had pulled myself along; but now, although I tugged vehemently, the only result was the giving of the stake on the farther shore. I could not budge an inch. I think the rapidly rising tide, now well up toward my shoulders, kept me from getting the proper leverage with my knees. At any rate, I was as fast to the bottom as if I had been tied.

Meanwhile, Tom, eager to get down to the seine, where he imagined I was having great sport, had ceased his shouting and beating. He was still a good way off, and I could hear him tramping along through the crackling marsh. I struggled with the dull trap that had locked its soft jaws on my feet, but I only made my knees ache with the strain, and apparently sank myself deeper into the water.

The shark had now come up to the end of the seine next to the boat. He stopped for a moment by it, evidently puzzled. But I felt certain that his next turn would be toward me. With that, losing my nerve, I shouted for Tom, and heard him answer me. He was having a tussle of his own trying to cross a boggy inlet that the incoming tide had filled; evidently, he thought I was calling him to hurry so as to help take the mullets out of the net.

When I heard him floundering in that mud-hole, I gave up the idea that he could help me out of my difficulty. Perhaps it was better so; for when I felt entirely thrown on my own resources, when I knew that, single-handed, I must try conclusions with the huge creature that was hunting me, I knew that I must act, and act at once. Weapon of any kind I had none. I was alone and defenseless, in water almost up to my neck, and a ten-foot tiger-shark was within two boat-lengths of me, looking for me. For the first time since I had been fishing in those waters I was unnerved.

But my thinking was clear enough until I saw that big creature turn slowly away from the boat and come toward me through the dark water. Then I lost my head. I cried out wildly for Tom. I beat the water with my hands and screamed at the shark. But he came steadily on. His deliberation was more terrible than his swiftness would have been. I felt that he saw me standing there helpless. He was coming straight toward me now, with no sign of uncertainty in his movements. I saw his fin rise higher out of the water, as if he were summoning all his savage strength for the final rush, and I grew sick at his brutal assurance.

He was only ten feet away now. Whatever fate was in store for me would, I thought, be immediate. Every chance of escape seemed cut off. Yet even in that dark moment an inspiration seized me. Catching the seine violently, I lifted it as high as I could, ducked through the water under it, rose on the other side and dropped the net into place. I had put a defense between me and my pursuer!

But how frail was that defense against the giant strength of the ruthless, cold-blooded creature! Yet for a moment it separated me from his terrible jaws. Now I felt slightly protected, but I could not move from my position, for my feet were still firmly embedded. The shark had already rushed by, and, baffled and perplexed, was circling swiftly. But now again he saw me, and came head on for the seine. I knew that it would not withstand his great weight and dreadful momentum. On he came, literally charging me. But before he struck the net he swerved, so that he did not break through, but turned swiftly along it.

My fascinated eyes followed him. He swam up to the end of the net next the boat. With the flow of the flood, the boat had swung on her moorings. It now lay up the creek, and thus left a clear gap of ten feet, through which the shark, suddenly accelerating his speed, spurted fiercely. He was on me now; there was nothing between us. One wide circle in the creek would give him his bearings—then he would rush on his prey.

But with the coming of my enemy, my brother Tom also approached. I had forgotten him in my delirious fear. Now I shouted to him at the top of my voice, crying wildly, "Shark! Shark! Help me, or he'll get me!"

I saw him pause; then, catching my words, he broke into a full run. Leaping into the boat, he jerked the painter loose and shoved out rapidly.

Straight as a well-sped arrow the great gray shark raced down upon me. I steeled myself for the sickening shock. But Tom's powerful hands gripped my arms, and he lifted me into the boat. There flashed by the stern the tall knife-fin of the tiger, and the huge creature tore his terrible way through the net as if it had been a cobweb.

Dangerous Beasts

Every man who goes into the wilderness takes chances with the beasts that he may encounter. I know some men who are so scared of wild creatures that they will never venture into the woods or on waters; I know others who take a manly delight in ridiculing the idea that anything in American forests or waters can hurt a human being. The first attitude is hardly necessary, for one is often safer in the woods than he is on the highway or on the city streets; the second viewpoint is distinctly foolhardy.

What, then, is the sane attitude to take? I believe it to be this: if a wild thing is capable of hurting you, whether or not he or any of his kind has ever hurt anyone before, whether or not you think he may, take no chances with him. In the first place, remember that you are dealing with wild strength, which, pound for pound, will be far superior and far more savage than your own; and remember that you will be dealing with wild stamina also which may prove to be dangerous to you.

Perhaps I can best get my idea across by telling of some personal experiences and also of some experiences that friends of mine have had. By no means all the accidents to hunters and fishermen come from the careless use of firearms, or from getting snagged on fish hooks, or from rocking the boat. I claim that there are other definite dangers when one invades nature's primeval country.

I knew a man who wounded a buck. Followed by hounds, it took refuge in a small pond. The dogs ringed the water, yowling, but they wouldn't go in on the stag. It is a rare thing, indeed, to find a deerhound or a foxhound that will pull down a wounded buck.

From *Hunter's Choice* (1946).

They will follow him valiantly; but when he turns to bay, they keep their distance. Their zeal is tempered by a wholesome respect for his hoofs and horns.

In this case the hunter, a man weighing more than two hundred pounds, used no caution at all. Laying down his gun, he waded into the shallow water, thinking he could "take on" the stag without danger to himself. The buck promptly charged him, drove a tine of his antler clear through the palm of the man's hand, jerked him sideways, and threw him down in the water, all the time striking at him savagely with his lance-like fore feet.

Fortunately for the victim, another hunter arrived and shot the stag. The man who had been attacked spent about three weeks in bed and had to get a new hunting suit. His right hand is still crippled.

Once when I shot down a buck, a Negro driver went up to him too soon. What followed was about as frantic a struggle as I ever beheld. When man and beast finally separated, the man had practically nothing on, he was cut in twenty places, and he had had enough of fighting bucks to last him all his life.

I was telling some of these stories to a deer guide in Canada, and he listened to me respectfully, but, I thought, with growing incredulity. Finally he told me that in the Canadian wilds it was practically a law of hunting that no man should ever approach a wounded buck. If the stag was down but not dead, he was always dispatched with another bullet. The guide went on to say that, among the men in his territory, a wounded buck deer was always considered a very dangerous animal.

Having actually witnessed a good many encounters of this sort, I cannot say that the danger may be attributed to the stag's ferocity; more likely it is due to his swiftness, his strength, his love of life, and his wild effort to escape. I once knew a hunter to be run over by a crippled stag; he was very seriously injured. But I do not think the buck charged him. He just happened to be in the way.

There are times, of course, when an unwounded stag may be dangerous. For example, if he is cornered, and you happen to be standing in his chosen avenue of escape, he's going over you or through you, not around you. At times, in the mating season, deer and other similar wild animals appear to lose much, and occasionally all, of their natural fear of man. At such a time the keepers of deer parks are often attacked.

I have known a stag, a huge twelve-pointer, to threaten some Negro children on their way to school. This was in October. At any other season of the year, a buck will run from even a baby.

When wild things are wounded, are mating, are cornered, or just happen to be in a certain mood, be careful. I take it that their behavior is sometimes unpredictable. It is mighty foolish to say dogmatically that a certain species will do this and will not do that. Therefore you can't always tell. Many of them have surly and truculent moods, and certain individuals may act in a manner utterly alien to the common behavior of his tribe. Man, the Goliath, occasionally meets a David in the wilds.

To illustrate definitely what I mean, let me say that, while the cougar is commonly considered cowardly, as far as man is concerned, and the wildcat cowardly as well, yet there are authentic instances of attacks upon human beings by both these great cats. Now, the meaning of the word *attack* may have to be modified somewhat, for it may be that the mountain lion or the bobcat mistook the human being for legitimate prey.

I knew a man who was calling a wild turkey. Suddenly, to his consternation, a forty-pound wildcat landed on his back, all ready for business. It does not seem to me to make much difference whether the wildcat mistook the man for a turkey or not; nor did the doctor think so when he saw his wounds; nor his wife, when she tried to sew up his shirt and coat. A puma or wildcat is fully capable of doing considerable damage to you; therefore be circumspect about him. It will pay always to recognize in him the possibility, if not the threat, or trouble. And the same is true of practically every living wild thing—even of a squirrel.

Hunting squirrels with a friend, I saw him shoot one, and then walk over and pick it up while it was still alive. It sank its teeth clear through the thumb of his left hand. When he, dazed with pain, tried to shake it off, the weight of the squirrel tore its teeth out of the finger, leaving a deep and ragged wound that bothered him for a long time.

Nor should it be forgotten that wounds received from wild creatures render one liable to infection. Although I have had no personal experience with lions, tigers, and leopards, I have been told by African and Indian hunters that the danger of infection from one of their bites is great. The same is true of the bite of a non-poisonous snake. He has no venom, but he may admit poisonous bacteria to your system.

When it comes to venomous serpents, a man cannot be too careful; yet I have seen men, otherwise sensible, take foolish chances. I learned early not to take liberties with snakes, even when they were apparently dead. When but a barefoot boy, I was driving to the plantation one September morning at daylight. A wagon had gone just ahead of me.

Near the plantation gate I saw a huge diamondback rattler that the wagon had just run over. His head was in one rut, his body spanned the road, and his tail was hidden in the bushes beyond. By the time I had quieted the horse I was driving and had tied him, there was light enough for me to see that the snake's head had apparently been crushed by a wheel. Going closer, I saw that the tail carried a wonderful sheaf of rattles. These I just had to have.

Although my fingers would not meet around this old monster's body, I took hold of him about two feet from the tail. This was with my left hand, my intention being to pull the rattles off with my right. But I did no such thing; for, with a contortion so swift that I had no chance to escape, the serpent reared upward and struck me full on the back of my left hand. The blow hurt me, and I was covered with blood—whose, I did not know.

Running down to a pond, I washed my hand, could see no punctures, and did not seem to be dying very fast. The snake had struck me, but his fangs must have been broken. He did me no harm. Since that day, nearly fifty years ago, I have never been enthusiastic about picking up any kind of snake, dead or alive. In fact, I believe that there are some things that a man is not supposed to pick up.

As to the danger from snakes in North America, I do not consider it very great if a man will be cautious. A good deal depends on where he is. Wherever he is, he should be familar with the venomous serpents of that locality; and if they haunt certain places, he ought to steer clear of them. He ought to be careful about laying his hands on bushes, logs, ledges, or fallen treetops.

Both rattlers and copperheads often lie well off the ground; and, of course, the cotton-mouth is at home in a bush over the water. Especially should a man be careful about investigating old logs, stumps, piles of stone, old racks of wood, and hollows. Such places are favorite dens. Leather boots not less than twenty inches high will give your legs good protection. For very thick country, hip rubber boots are better; they have the advantage of being higher and of standing away from the leg.

Ordinary hunting boots sixteen inches high will not give you proper protection from a big diamondback. A friend of mine was struck four inches above the knee. Always it should be kept in mind that the snake may not be lying on the ground.

Of course, the dread of snakes may be overdone. It seems to be ancestral. Hardly one person in a million in America is struck; and of those that are, only a small percentage die. The factors which determine the nature of the injury are these: the size of the snake, which determines the amount of venom delivered; the location of the wound; the physical condition of the person, and the kind of treatment given. Immediate and powerful suction of some kind, to keep the venom out of circulation, is the oldest and best treatment. Later, serum should be injected.

Fortunately, snakes hibernate, except in the extreme southern parts of our country; therefore sportsmen who go abroad in the autumn and winter, after the first hard frosts, need have no dread of reptiles. Anyway, most men, even hunters and lovers of nature, keep out of the deep woods in the summer. Stay away from snaky haunts, and likely you'll be safe.

Aside from venomous snakes, there is another reptile of America for which I have a profound respect: I mean the alligator. Now, many a man who should know better ridicules the idea that a 'gator will hurt you. True, there are few authentic records of a man's being attacked by this great saurian, a survivor of the Age of Monsters. But he lives the life of a grim marauder, is well able to kill a man, may not recognize a man in the water as the same biped he fears on land, and is altogether not to be trusted.

I have had one bull alligator make an unprovoked charge at my canoe. When I shot him, he was not more than five feet away. I have known a 'gator to kill a cow, and known one to pull down an eight-point buck. My common sense tells me that any creature who can thus perform is dangerous, whether or not you may consider him a coward.

The alligator often uses his tail as a powerful bludgeon to stun his victim before seizing it in his capacious jaws. Because he can hurt me, I am taking no chances with him, and consider alligator-infested waters dangerous. And we must always remember that the kin of our 'gators, the cayman of South American waters, the crocodile of Africa and of India, and the huge sea-going species of the great isles of the Pacific are all man-eaters.

When it comes to the shark, the same general principle of being careful should hold true. Even the sight of one sends some people into a panic. On the other hand, I have had a scientist of national reputation tell me that there is no record of a human being having been attacked and killed by a shark. Either he is posing as a man of superior courage or else he is an ignoramus.

I have seen what was left of four human beings after sharks had attacked them, and that sight remains to me more convincing than any armchair arguments as to the shark's innocence. True, the most dangerous species are commonly found in tropical waters; yet these same terrors of the deep travel far north in the summer, and have been captured off the New England coast. The great white shark is usually considered the true man-eater; but to me, any good-sized shark certainly can, and may, do you damage.

One of my hands still shows the deep lacerations of a shark's teeth—a shark that I ran afoul of while tending a seine at night in a tidal estuary. I never identified my attacker; but there was no question of his design on me, and even in the darkness I felt the brute power of him. With such a creature, whether it be a white shark, a hammerhead, or a great fish of any other kind, it is not wise to take liberties. The fact that he can torpedo you should be enough to deter you from considering him lightly.

When it comes to bears, I believe that the only two American ones that are considered dangerous are the grizzly and the Kodiak; to these should be added the polar bear, though few men are ever likely to encounter him. However, he would be a formidable antagonist. Not all grizzlies show fight, nor all Kodiaks; and for a brown, a cinnamon, or a black bear to defy a man is a rarity. Yet always, it seems to me, in dealing with these mighty old men of the wilds, there is always the possibility that you may meet an individual that is a bad actor.

Wounded bears are treacherous; and an old grizzly with cubs is fighting motherhood personified. As far as you are concerned, it makes no difference how many people have been attacked by bears; perhaps in one locality there may be no record of any such attack. Yet keep in mind that you may establish the record. Most bears flee at the scent or sight of man; but when you are in the wilds, a combination of circumstances may serve to reverse ordinary behavior.

As I have said before, but think it well to repeat, creatures with young, those that are mating, those that are cornered, wounded, or just in a cantankerous mood may act as you would not expect them to act. Remember that you will be safest if you will always recognize the potentiality of brute strength and the variability of brute temper.

You know how it is, even with domestic creatures. A horse or a cow, a bull or a hog, a cat or a dog may unaccountably turn savage; and what is true on the farm is likewise true in the woods and on the waters. Caution is life insurance to every man who deals with animals, whether tame or wild.

During a time of a flood, we had captured on my place a wild boar out of the river swamps. He was a brigand if there ever was one, and savage to the tips of his bristles. I had him in a heavy pen in the stable-yard. One day, after six weeks' vain attempt to tame him, I went down to the pen to dispatch him with a rifle. Whether or not he sensed my design, as I stepped into the stable-yard and closed the gate behind me, he suddenly, with main strength, forced the heavy logs of the pen apart and came charging for me, a mad projectile of evil fury. He was so close to me when I shot him that his rush upset me, and for a few minutes I did not know who had had the worst of it.

I remember as a boy having an old Negro hunter tell me, when we were hunting deer near the haunt of a great wild boar, that if the boar came out I was to let him pass, as he would charge me if I merely wounded him. I obeyed orders, but ever since have regretted that I did not let drive at the huge hulking brute that passed me at thirty yards.

If a man is hunting, and brings down wild game that can in any way hurt him, he should promptly dispatch it before going up to it. This is both wise and merciful. If he is not out to kill things, he ought to be careful not to provoke a charge.

While I think it is usually true that every living thing in America, if given a chance, will withdraw from a man's presence, yet there are times when there are creatures in moods of which this general truth does not hold. Therefore it is well to guard against the exceptional as well as the ordinary. And it certainly should be remembered that you yourself may have a highly original experience with a wild creature. The fact that old woodsmen have never had such an encounter is no proof against its possibility, even against its likelihood.

The Killer of Hell Hole

I am telling you a good deal about deer-hunting; but don't thereby imagine that there is nothing else to hunt in the old plantation regions. There are, for example, the wild boars. These hulking hyenas I have seen grow to a size and attain a ferocity hardly equalled by the huge wart-hogs of Africa and the burly boars of the German forests. An adventure I had with one of these old brigands seems worth recording.

Hell Hole is one of my favorite haunts. You'd be surprised to see how pretty a place it is. Probably some amateur woodsman long ago got mired in a morass there, and out of spite gave this lovely wilderness its hateful name.

I know a place in Pennsylvania named Paradise—one of these model home towns, full of rotary clubs, home brew and other forms of uplift. I prefer Hell Hole.

Said Net Port to me—Ned being the Pluto of this same nether region—"Bring your dogs an' your niggers over next Sat'day. We're goin' to try to kill the ole wild boar of Satan Swamp."

Reader, would you have gone? Satan Swamp in the heart of Hell Hole! It doesn't sound very virtuous.

"I'll be over, Ned," I told my ancient, grizzled friend. "Now, remember not to shoot me for a revenue officer when you see me coming."

Early that memorable Saturday morning I got my two packs ready—canine and African. The leader of the former was Ranter, ably supported by Yelping Maid and Gleeboy. The leader of the latter was Steve, having in his train Paris (with the surname of Green) and Anchovy. There was nothing poisonous in the character of Paris,

From *An American Hunter* (1937).

or especially spicy in the personality of Anchovy. You have to take these plantation Negro names as they come—whether they be Sarsaparilla, Dandruff, or Neuralgia.

Having no money and no prospects, a Negro will usually marry. All mine were married. And their wives were glad to have them depart on this wild-boar expedition, partly because such a daparture would bring on a general domestic armistice, and partly because dreams of bacon, even from a wild boar, never lose for a Negro their tremendous glamour.

Steve was mounted on his mule Emma, while Paris and Anchovy walked. They were barefooted; but they didn't mind rambling the woods that way. Plantation Negroes develop on their feet masterful pads of callus, which protect them though do not contribute to their beauty. If you will stick a toothpick upright in a watermelon seed, you will get an idea of the way Steve's foot looked on his leg.

From home it is about six miles to the borders of Hell Hole. Steve and I decided to go by the road, taking the dogs with us. Paris and Anchovy were to cut through the woods, meeting us at Ned Port's still. At the compass-minded business of cutting through the wildwoods a plantation Negro has few equals.

As Steve was about to get Emma underway we heard a voice behind us calling. It was Amnesia, Steve's much larger and better half. At that commanding tone, Emma relaxed comfortably, while Steve sat up uncomfortably.

"Wah dat 'oman want now?" he asked.

Down the road from her cabin Amnesia came hurrying. Warily Emma batted back one ear. Long since had this dumb, sagacious brute recognized most of her master's trouble.

Amnesia nodded pleasantly enough to me, but her attitude toward Steve was militant. I could not help overhearing her charge to him.

"You gwine for hunt. Well and good. But we ain't got a God's t'ing in de house for eat. Now, 'member, you ain't gwine for hunt fun; you gwine for hunt dinner. Eider bring home dat hog, or find some home an' 'oman where you can live without work and without eat. Is you onnerstan' me, Steve?"

"I onnerstan' you, Amnesia," Steve admitted readily; "but you mus' 'member dat wild boar ain't so easy for ketch. He kin run like

de debbil; and if he done make a stan', he hab tush in his head sharp
as a razor at a frolic."

"Ain't you kin run too?"

Steve laughed in his barbarous, frank way. "Runnin' ain't all I kin
do if a wild boar git after me. Gal, I'se gwine fly."

Amnesia did not share in her husband's mirth. "If you fly, don't
fly to me. I ain't done eat right since two weeks las' Sat'day."

"You ain't want dat bo' hog to kill me, is you?"

"Not 'xactly," Amnesia admitted grudgingly." Least way, not 'fore
you done brung him home."

This parting shot did not leave my dusky henchman in a very
glamorous mood. Sawing with the rope lines to get Emma into action,
he called to the hounds. Together we set off down the dewy morning road, flanked on either hand by endless reaches of glimmering
pine timber. Steve was silent for a long time, and I did not break in
on his meditations until we were halfway to Ned's place.

"Amnesia is very much in earnest about your bringing her some
bacon," I ventured.

"If I ketch de bo' and de sow all two, same-fashion all de pig,
Amnesia wouldn't satisfy. Cap'n, is you know when a 'oman is satisfy
right?"

I confessed ignorance on this vital matter.

"She satisfy," said Steve with the melancholy certainty that comes
from experience alone, "when she got a man, and got him scared."

Having delivered this oracular pronouncement, Steve smote Emma
with both his heels at once, with some fury of emphasis. But Emma's
only response was a slight switching of her patient tail.

"In that case," I said, "Amnesia ought to be satisfied with you,
Steve."

"Cap'n, you ain't done know Amnesia," was his profound reply.

Leaving the main road, we now struck through the margins of
Hell Hole—a strange, wild region of virgin forest, where gigantic
pines climbed the sky and gigantic vines climbed the trees; where
stretched many a mile of shimmering greenery, between the denser
reaches of which we could see dark-red swamp water gleaming; a
region of beauty and silence, of immediate stillnesses and far cries,
of mystery and pagan solitude. A perfect abode for wild life it is; for
deer, turkeys, foxes, wild hogs and an occasional black bear.

Until you have been into a place like Hell Hole, you have not come rightly to understand the fascination of the Low Country of the Carolinas. And until you see the pack of a white pinelander like my friend Ned Port, you have never rightly understood what things may be called dogs. Our approach to Ned's woodland abode was suddenly announced by a furious attack that one of his curs made from the roadside bushes upon the innocent Emma. She sidled, bided her time, and then implanted upon the eager face of the intruder such a placement kick as I had never seen executed upon any gridiron. The dog hobbled away into the bushes, having lost all interest in the matter of biting mules.

Coming from under a dense canopy of live-oak limbs, heavy with packed foliage and bannering moss, we saw Ned's place before us and Ned himself standing by the gate, dressed for the woods and the hunt. However, Ned is normally dressed for the woods; but when he has hunting guests, he does the company the honor to wear his grandfather's hunting-horn.

This horn never amuses me except when Ned wears it. It's too big for him. When you see them together, you hardly know which one is wearing the other. Ned's grandfather was a regular giant, and his hunting equipment ran to things Gargantuan. This horn, I have heard, came from a regular elephant of the Texas wide-horned breed. With it on, Ned looks like a flivver equipped with oversize cords for a truck.

He met us with a quiet smile. "Is them dogs any account?" he asked with that refreshing ingenuousness that a woodlander is likely to have. He indicated my pack—Ranter, Yelping Maid, and Gleeboy—at the same time turning an eye of satisfied appraisal upon his own prides and joys behind him. A rangy, mangy, piratic crew they were, looking as if the ethnic pot had run over and spilled some scum.

"What do you call them, Ned?" I asked, knowing well his love for appropriate and picturesque names.

"That pair," he said, pointing to two dogs of that undetermined breed known in Carolina as "just plain nigger dogs," I call Smut and Smoke. This one lying here is Jailbird. That's Angel by the fence there—she that's got the tail bit off and the frazzled ear what a wildcat chewed; and yonder by the house are the best of all, Do and

Don't. You see," Ned explained, "one of them is always right about a trail; and if one won't ketch a hog or a steer, the other will."

"I see," I admitted, making a mental note of the fact that every living human being should have a pair of helpers of some sort that would act in the perfect concert of Do and Don't.

"I brought Steve with me," I said, indicating my dozing rider on his dozing mule, "and I have Paris Green and Anchovy coming through the woods. They'll be here soon."

Ned smiled again. "They been here a long time," he said. "My wife done gave them breakfast in the kitchen. They're sleepin' in the sun by the barn now."

After some effort we awaked our huntsmen, Paris and Anchovy. Then, with Ned, his pack, and Old Testament, we hied us into the lustrous, glimmering heart of Hell Hole, toward that bourn of the forbidding name—Satan Swamp.

"How about this wild boar, Ned?" I asked my host. "Have you seen him lately? Is he as wild and as ferocious as you thought he was last year when he got away from you?"

Like a true backwoodsman, Ned considered his answer before he spoke. Any honest sportsman is grave when he talks of dangerous game.

"I didn't make no mistake," he said. "This is the boar that killed them two fine hounds what Mr. Hutchins paid fifty dollars apiece for. This is the same hog that cut up Ephraim Garrett, that nigger that lives down the road here. One of his little dogs cornered it, and he went in on it like a fool, and the boar ripped both of his legs wide open."

Surreptitiously I glanced at my henchmen to see the effect of this story upon them. Paris had not heard it; but Anchovy's eyes were bulging, and had in them all the telltale lights of readiness for flight. Steve feigned indifference, but I could see him kicking Emma nervously, and he muttered to himself—a sure sign he was getting very uneasy.

As for Old Testament, he tucked in the ragged fringe of his shirt and gave his trousers a hitch, fastening them more tightly with a stick thrust through a buttonhole. His general air, though ancient, seemed to me one of an athlete stripped for the course instead of that of a warrior girding for battle.

"I see this boar last week," Ned told me, while all the Negroes, fascinated, closed ranks to listen, "and he was walking about on that high ridge in Satan Swamp just like nobody's business. His tushes are as long as your white hound's tail, and have that same curl in them, and sharp! Do you remember that long knife what Judge Seabrook had them show in court the time they tried Snake Wiley for killing Jim Hampson? You remember how he made ribbons of Jim—regular streamers? That's how sharp this boar's tushes are."

"Great God!" I heard Steve mutter, as if for the first time the horror of the thing into which he was getting had begun to dawn upon him.

Is you sho', Old Testament," I heard Paris ask this ancient man in a voice of incredulity and awe, "is you sartain sure dat dis is a hog what is meant to hunt?"

"Is some things in dis worl' what ain't meant for people to hunt or to worry," Old Testament admitted.

"Ghos' is one thing," Anchovy supplied, at the sound of the very name of which he suddenly glanced back fearsomely.

"Howsomeber," Ned's old man admitted, "dis bo' ain't 'xactly kill no man yet."

"Well," was the feeling rejoinder of Paris, "if I can help myself dis day, I ain't gwine to give him no chance to kill no man. Far as I concern, he ain't gwine kill no man. I'se rather go hongry dan have a hog big as a mule—"

"Big as a mule?" quoted Old Testament scornfully. "Boy, what you talking 'bout? Dis bo' stan' mo' higher than Emma."

At this Steve pulled up Emma shortly. She was especially good at stopping and standing. "Hog tall as Emma?" Steve asked in a whisper. The thing had seized his imagination. "Hog big as a mule ain't for hunt; he for let 'lone.

"If he ever git a man on he tush, he will wave him round same like dem school-chillun wave dem flag."

"Same fashion," Old Testament confirmed fervently.

The fascination of terror is, of all fascinations, the one that really gets a Negro where he lives. Its hold on him is far more instant and tenacious than any blandishing caress of glamour could possibly be. And it now had hold of these children of nature that Ned Port and I were taking into the beauteous wilds of Satan Swamp.

The reference of Paris to the waving of flags entered and painfully haunted the soul of Anchovy. The fact that he had on a red and white shirt may have been additional tinder to his imagination, suggesting to him that the great boar of Hell Hole might discriminate nicely when it came to this waving business, choosing him for artistic rather than for personal reasons. In fact, as the thought developed, Anchovy, pretending extreme warmth, hunched out of the flaming shirt, and with more craft than unselfishness tied it behind the wreck of wood and leather that Steve called a saddle.

"Ain't gwine wave me," Anchovy kept muttering, starting a soliloquy that, in feeling and in profundity, would yield nothing to any asides of the melancholy Dane himself. "How he gwine wave me? Ain't I got me two foot? Is I gwine hab pyralysis and stan' like I was nail on de groun'? Paris!" he called, as if he wanted some one to reassure him by answering some of his solemn queries, "what you gwine do if dat bo' hog start for you?"

Paris spat in scorn of so foolish a question.

"Is you 'member dat gang o' cars what bruk loose from de engine and run down dat hill by de ole sawmill? After dey git gwine right, ain't dey trabble? Boy, you done see dem trabble; but you ain't done see no real trabblin' till you see me set sail wid a bo' hog with tush wide as a oxen horn comin' for me."

"I glad I got Emma," Steve said. "Dat keeps me off de groun', anyway."

At this Old Testament seemed silently convulsed. At last his mirth vented itself in curious, little, ancient chuckles.

"How come you laugh?" asked Steve, somewhat aggrieved.

"De las' time we been out here," Old Testament informed us, "de bo' ain't bodder wid de mans on de groun'. He make right for de man on de horse. An' mule is wusser," he added.

"Great God!" muttered Steve, and the next moment he was on the ground, leading Emma.

Ned, who was heading our procession, suddenly came to a pause; and with him, more suddenly, paused every Negro, twitching and looking about with an appraisal of places of retreat and exit.

"The place is right yonder," he said, pointing to a deep and most mysterious part of the general wilderness. "Right by that bunch of pines yonder that we call the Seven Sisters is where Dead Man's Ridge begins."

Steve, Paris, Anchovy, and Old Testament looked at one another significantly. Anchovy, even without his shirt, perspired freely, from causes mental rather than physical.

"It was right off there that Ephraim Garrett was cut to pieces," Ned told us, as if he were a realtor recounting the pleasant traditions of the place. "Down that abandoned road to the right is the spot where old man Cain shot his wife and mother-in-law to death."

"Why he shoot he wife?" whispered Paris.

"Dey say he didn't know what else to do wid her," Old Testament answered.

"Come on, boys," Ned went on briskly, "we're pretty close to the fun now. Hold up!" he said suddenly in a different voice, at the same time pointing to the wet sand in the road. "This is the track of the killer right now. Here, you niggers," he commanded, "look at this if you want to see a real hog-track."

Deeply incised were the monstrous prints of a gigantic hog. It seemed to me, indeed, that they might be those of a heifer or a young bull; but I did not wish to question Ned's word in the presence of company.

"What you t'ink, Steve?" asked Old Testament, a certain local pride tingeing his tone.

"Dat may be a hog," Steve admitted, "but he ain't no hog for ketch."

"He meat would be mighty tough," quoth Anchovy, in a voice that showed a retreating tendency in his mind.

"Dey don't grow dat way back home," Paris said thoughtfully; "but is he is ketch, my Jehoviah, what a ham!"

At this comforting observation there was some licking of lips, and it seemed to me that the morale of our little party looked up a little.

"I think," said Ned, "that we'll make a start right here."

A little to my surprise and much to the childish delight of our dark huntsmen, Ned solemnly unslung his mighty hunting-horn and began to sound it like the blast of doom. At the sound thereof Smut and Smoke, Do and Don't, Yelping Maid, Gleeboy, and all the other hounds began to howl amiably and miserably, as if the citadels of their souls were being captured by angelic devils. Some of them sat down to go through this mournful rite correctly. Gleeboy by mischance sat suddenly on a sharp stick, and his quick, unabashed yelp rather jarred upon the grieving harmony of the chorus of wails.

"A horn gits to a houn'," Ned said rather breathlessly, "an' makes him think of bigger game than fleas. We'll turn them loose on the trail right here."

"How are we to follow them, Ned? By any set plan?" I asked.

"We scatter out among the woods hereabouts; and when the dogs round up the old bo' and bring him to bay, why, the nearest one to him goes in on him."

"Saviour in hebben!" ejaculated Steve. "What you mean, Cap'n Ned, when you say 'Goes in on him'?"

"I mean go for him, jump on him, throw him down, and hold him until the rest of us get to you."

Steve grinned in an abashed way, as if Ned were honoring him too highly.

"A local man," he observed sagely, "like Old Testament here, ought surely to go in on him first."

"Dat's so," Anchovy and Paris chimed in.

"He say," Paris added, "dat we is to scatter 'bout in de woods. I'm thinking I is better at scatterin' dan at goin' in."

"Put them dogs on the trail and let's ketch this killer," said Ned with assumed testiness. "If you boys is so scared of a hog, I wonder what you would do if the dogs happen to run out an ole b'ar."

"I ain't los' no b'ar," said Anchovy quickly.

By this time the dogs had begun to trail off into the bushes, yowling out sweet tidings that they had settled to a trail that was a trail. Yet no one, not even the hounds themselves, dreamed that their tremendous game was so close. Even while we were gingerly and, with remarkable tenacity for each other's company, tentatively "scattering," two hundred yards ahead of us in the heart of a dense thicket of sweet myrtle and smilax vines a bomb exploded. Some monstrous thing started a mighty rush through the tangled greenery, while the dogs in full cry let us know that the boar was up and on his way.

A glance at our Negroes showed the four of them standing so close together that they seemed welded.

"Yonder he goes!" shouted Ned excitedly, pointing to a high open ridge in the pinelands, down which raced a gray shape of formidable size and cyclone speed.

Here was no mere wild hog, but a true wild boar of savage aspect and huge size. Here, indeed, within our sight was the killer of Satan Swamp.

"Come on! Come on!"cried Ned. "They'll bring him to bay, and we ought to be up with them. Hey, what are you all standin' there like that for?"

Reluctantly the four Negroes came toward us.

"Cap'n," said Steve soberly, "we done see dat thing, and we don't think we can ketch dat hog."

"If de dog can ketch him, well and good," Paris explained, as if he did not wish completely to back down; "but if they have a bad luck, we ought to ketch something else."

"Cap'n Ned," asked Anchovy, "ain't you got no smaller hog in dese woods? If dogs can't specify with a hog, how can man specify?"

To these queries Ned's only reply was a triumphant "They've got him now! Now's our chance!"

Toward the far-off melee we now ran, through bunches of huckleberry bushes, over old logs, down long yellow savannas of broomgrass. We were making so much noise ourselves that we could not ascertain accurately by the sounds ahead just what was happening in our van. The Negroes kept very close to us, but were by no means eager to pass us. They kept close to one another also, running almost as one man. Even Old Testament, the senior by many years of the other three, was right with them.

Our first intimation of how the battle was going came with dramatic suddenness. We did not come to something—something came to us. Before us the bushes parted wildly, and toward us rushed our frantically demoralized pack—how many dogs I could not at first distinguish, but a crowd, and all of them scared to death. Behind us they took scurrying refuge, and at once began whining, whimpering, licking wounds and giving other evidences of having lost heart in the fray.

Ned began to examine their wounds, and I looked to the wounded feelings of my huntsmen.

"We didn't get up in time," I explained.

Steve laughed the laugh of relieved terror. "De dogs git there in time," he said, "an' look what done happen to them."

"What's the next move, Ned?" I asked.

"My dog Angel ain't come back," he said, "and I can't hear her baying."

Anchovy began to snicker. "She is sure bayin' an angel song 'bout now, Cap'n."

"Let's go to where they bayed him," Ned proposed.

Forward we went, all of us sharing to some degree in the general uneasiness of the situation. The dogs followed us tentatively, seeming to marvel at our boldness. Nor were their looks lost on our followers.

"When I look at Gleeboy," Anchovy remarked, "he done seem to say, 'You gwine pretty fas' and happy to be gwine where you is gwine.' "

"Yes," Paris agreed; "we start out wid one dog we call Don't and now we has a whole pack named Don't."

Ned, the leader of our not over-valiant van, now came to a halt on the pine ridge ahead of us, and we saw him gazing ruefully at something. As we came up we saw that it was all that was left of Angel.

"She is done been make a flag of," Steve said, with that curious lack of feeling a Negro sometimes displays. It is not so much a lack of emotion as it is the conviction that the time for a display of emotion has passed.

"Now," said Ned, "here's another reason why this killer has got to die. I ain't letting no bo' hog kill up my bes' dog for nothin'."

"Dat's so," Old Testament agreed.

"You feel dat way, Cap'n Ned," Steve ventured; "but kin we git dem dogs to jine in dat feeling'?"

To my surprise, the pack returned to the trail, but dutifully rather than enthusiastically. They headed for the darksome, haunted borders of Satan Swamp. We followed, some of us vengefully and some of us because we didn't care to be left behind.

Down Dead Man's Ridge we went, the dogs warming on the trail, and to Bloody Creek we came—a deep woodland watercourse appropriately named from the leaf-stained color of the mysterious water. We had to hunt for a crossing-place, and eventually found an old fording, kept in use by wild creatures. There was a considerable bluff on the opposite side, and in this there was a small aperture—evidently the opening of a little cave.

Steve happened to see on the sand-bar tracks that he took for those of a 'possum. They led to the tiny cave's mouth. Here, indeed, was rare good fortune. Was not this a chance to appease Amnesia without encountering the dreadful killer? While the dogs crossed the creek and trailed into a little thicket nearby Steve followed the 'possum to his lair. Coming to the opening, he paused to consider. Nor did he escape the sarcasms of his fellows.

"Le' me hol' yo' hat," said Anchovy.

"Gimme dat pants, Steve. You ain't gwine need him no mo'."

"Burying you ain't gwine cost Amnesia a cent. You done been real considerate, and die in a hole already done dig."

"Steve," whined Old Testament, "don't forget to say yo' prayers, boy, befo' you go in dat place."

Steve would never have gone, but he had nicely estimated chances. If he could get a 'possum, he would be safely heeled. It would be far safer to "go in on" a sleeping 'possum than to go in on a ramping wild boar, his tusks still bloody from recent execution.

We gathered about the cave's opening while Steve crawled through the aperture. Inside, he complained that he could not see very clearly, and he asked us to stand from the front of the mouth so as not to cut off the light. So Steve groped his way back into the darksome place after the 'possum.

While he was so engaged, and naturally shut away from outside sights and sounds, things of a wild and confused nature began to happen with us. First, we heard the dogs in the dense thicket up on the creek-bank begin a frantic outcry. There was a rocking of bush-tops; sounds of a desperate rush; a sudden lull. Then, sliding and plunging down the creek-bank not twenty yeards from us, came the Killer himself—a monstrous and ferocious creature. After him yelped, bawled and whined the pack—somewhat emboldened by the fact that they seemed to have their enemy on the run.

The grim fugitive, having slid to the sand-bank bordering the bed of the creek, paused for a bickering moment, head high, bristles up, tail up. He champed his jaws in slantwise fashion. He saw us, and came head on for us. But he seemed to be more concerned about the dogs, which now came in a huddling gang to the top of the slide above the great beast. I saw the boar cut his little fierce eyes upward at his pursuers, which were none too certain of the wisdom of their course.

In the excitement of the moment I had failed to take note of the effect of the boar's coming on my dark huntsmen. Now, when I looked for them, Ned alone stood by my side.

"Look out!" I heard him say sharply. "He's comin' for us!"

When a wild boar means mischief, he makes his run with his head down. It is by a sudden thrust upward of his tusks that he does his deadly work. When he charges with his head high, he probably means that he just wants gangway. This beast charged us with his head up, nor did he come all the way. Suddenly he turned abruptly toward the opening of the little cave into which Steve had gone, 'possum bent. Toward this aperture the boar plunged with a rickety, veering rush.

"My Gawd!" yelled Ned. "He's gone after Steve!"

To do him justice, Ned was steady of nerve. Now he too made a break for the gloomy aperture. As I followed him I thought how treacherous all caves look. Their mouths seem carnivorous.

The boar reached the opening first and tried to dash inward. But he was rather too big for such a doorway, and he did not have time to sidle in. After a confused moment, Ned and I found ourselves trying to hold the boar, while he, half inside and half outside, was frantically trying to kick loose. I had one of his big feet a dozen times, but he always knocked me loose. Ned had a gallant grip on his tail.

This was a silent struggle. As a rule, when a hog squeals, he is beginning to admit defeat. This boar hadn't begun to fight. The dogs meanwhile had halted at some distance behind us and were giving a few feeble yaps. They seemed to be more than willing for us to finish this woodland picnic.

Despite the intensity of the struggle, there was practically no sound, so that suddenly we heard a subterranean voice from the darkness of the cave.

"Who done darken dat door?" Steve complained. "Ain't I done ax you all don't darken dat door?"

Ned shouted, partly to Steve, but mostly to the wide, wide world. "If this bo's tail pops, you'll soon know what darkens that door!"

"Ned," I gasped, "where are all the niggers? If we had them, we could hold this thing."

"I reckon they done been home some time," he answered. Then, "Oh, my gosh!" he cried.

The boar's flight had really never been delayed by me. Ned had held him manfully until his tail, probably weakened by some old wound, pulled off. Into the darkness and into Steve the mad monster plunged. We stood aside to give Steve a clear track. I was looking for him, but I didn't see much of him. A streaming meteor shot by us—a projectile that, as far as I could tell, hurricaned straight ahead without once touching the ground.

There was a big, bare sweet-gum tree on the far side of the creek, and toward this Steve instinctively flew. He seemed to take the wide dark creek, to catch one of the higher limbs of the gum, and to make a giant swing to safety, all in one motion. Then he scuttled upward like a frantic squirrel.

Then it was Ned and I discovered that this same tree was literally draped with brave Negro Killer-killers. Ensconced there was Anchovy, thirty feet from the ground. Six feet higher, tightly wedged in a crotch, sat Paris. Thirty feet higher, stretched out on a limb like a black fox-squirrel, lay Old Testament. He didn't want that boar even to see him! Ancient, crafty man!

"Come on down here, you buzzards!" yelled Ned. "Ain't no bacon up there."

"Cap'n," called Steve, "can you done block up dat hole I done left open just now?"

Our other pack had meanwhile utterly lost interest in the chase. They were lolling about, idly licking their wounds, lapping up water and giving fleas the bum's rush.

Ned and I together carried an old log and thrust it into the cave's opening, thus blocking a too sudden exit by the boar. At sight of the barricade our henchmen began warily to clamber down the gum-tree. Gingerly they came over to where Ned and I stood on the sand-bar.

"We've got him now," said Ned. "All we have to do is go in on him."

"That's all," I confirmed lightly, in a tone in which I intended to convey simple manliness, readiness in a crisis, and all that.

Steve, Paris, Anchovy, and Old Testament looked at one another. There was unanimity in their glance, but not of the stuff of which heroes are made.

"Are you ready?" asked Ned, taking a step toward the cave.

"Cap'n Ned, you'll have to 'scuse us dis time," Paris said. "Steve and me and Anchovy done have a meeting' ob de Sons of Pharaoh's Daughter on Choosday night, and we can't miss dat."

"No, sah!" the other two chimed in.

"How 'bout you, old man?" asked Ned, turning to Old Testament. "Is you scared too?"

"I ain't scare," he protested, "but I done promised my wife Neuralgia I won't go in no scare place."

Ned looked at me in despair. "You and I'll go in," he said. "We'll show these triflin' niggers how to act."

Once more we advanced on the cave. With some caution, Ned and I lifted away the blocking log. Glancing behind me, I saw our four men backing away toward the creek.

Ned stooped to peer into the darkness of the cavern. Weirdly, with silent speed, a great gray shape suddenly filled the fateful opening.

"Look out!" yelled Ned, making a break for it.

I clambered up the bank with an ease and a spirit that amazed me. By the time I looked round, the charging boar was nowhere in sight. But every Negro was perched in the tall gum-tree exactly as he had been before. And next to Old Testament was Ned himself! We exchanged shamefaced grins—he from the tree and I from the bank.

After this collapse in our morale, we called off the hunt, collected all the dogs but Angel, corralled Emma, and started homeward.

"Steve," said Ned, "do the flies bother Amnesia much in the summertime?"

"Yes, he do," Steve admitted, doubtful of the import of such a question.

"Well," said Ned, "you have to take something home to her. Tie this on a stick and tell her to use it to brush flies."

And he handed to Steve the sole trophy of our hunt—the frayed tail of the Killer of Hell Hole Swamp.

PART VI
TALES TALL AND TRUE

As will be abundantly clear to the reader long before reaching this juncture, Archibald Rutledge was a masterful storyteller. Indeed, virtually all of his many books of prose are made up of collections of stories as opposed to being extended narrative treatments. One explanation for Rutledge's preference for short works may have been monetary in nature; it was more rewarding in material terms to publish a piece in a magazine and then use it as a chapter in a book. And make no doubt about it, matters of an economic nature mattered a great deal to Rutledge. His salary as a teacher at Mercersburg was probably adequate at best, and as his boys grew toward manhood there was the additional burden of underwriting their college educations. Then too, visions of a restored Hampton were constantly in his mind, and while he knew loving hands could accomplish much when it came to bringing the plantation home back to its former magnificence, ample funds would also be essential.

The fact remains, however, that these financial considerations are not the principal reason for the bulk of Rutledge's work taking the form of short stories or real-life cameos. In truth, he chose this literary medium because it suited him. The genre fit him comfortably, like a well-worn hunting coat, and from all accounts his prowess as a writer was matched by his flair for the spoken language. Countless visitors to Hampton were held enthralled as he related one story after another with a verve and vivacity that clearly gave him as much pleasure as it gave his audience.

For the five pieces which follow I have chosen the section title "Tales Tall and True" for the simple reason that it fits. All of the selections appear, at first glance, to be fiction. But Rutledge, like all good storytellers, drew heavily from personal experience, and one suspects that an appreciable degree of fact underlies each story. Certainly they will ring true to those familiar with Low Country ways and mores.

Congaree

They had told him very plainly that if he came back into Tabor Swamp they would kill him. Old Ben Burley told him so, and all the men of the Burley clan had seconded the grim threat of their leader. Into the wild and melancholy domain of these fierce white men the Negro Congaree had followed one of his stray cattle; when the swamp men had come upon him thus searching, they had summarily issued their dread warning. Without any words in reply, Congaree had desisted from his search and had returned to his humble home.

"I ain't meant no harm," he kept saying to himself as if mildly justifying his having visited the monstrous swamp that lay northward from his tiny clearing on the brink of the vast sea-marshes. "I ain't meant no harm," he repeated aloud; and then over and over he kept puzzling in his mind what he had overheard Ben Burley mutter to himself: "We are in big trouble out here, and we don't want any strangers prowling around."

What could that trouble be? On the faces of the men who had driven him out Congaree had seen stamped the image of a haunting and disastrous fear. Perhaps, thought the Negro, the men of Tabor Swamp had good cause for telling him to clear out. The whole business seemed mysterious, dangerous. And it was. Indeed, the affair was heartbreaking. And it involved all the Tabors and the Burleys and the Minots, the three families, closely related by marriage, which owned or controlled the immense tract of semi-wasteland known as Tabor Swamp. Upon all of them now strange and deep trouble had suddenly fallen; and out of it there appeared no way.

From *Heart of the South* (1924).

And the dread secret that had been kept from Congaree was that Rosalie Burley was lost.

The tiny golden-haired daughter of Ben Burley, a child not quite three years old when all this happened, had vanished from her home far back in the Tabor Swamp wildwoods. It being March, when the first white lilies of the forest are in bloom, she might have gone down the pathway from her home toward the edges of the deep swamp. Her father had shown her some lily buds near the spring there. It was on that pathway that she had last been seen. Tuesday evening that had been; it was on Wednesday forenoon that the swamp men had encountered Congaree. They were then searching for the lost child; and their tempers, always proud and sensitive, were now on a desperate edge. Rosalie was what joy and beauty and innocence meant to these rough and savage but not ignoble men. They loved her with a fierce, pathetic tenderness—these raw and hulking woodsmen. To them "Rosalie" was a fit name for the child whose wild-rose loveliness reminded them of happy flowers. As nothing else could, she inspired their purest and deepest love; as nothing else could, her disappearance roused them to a pitch of wild and incredible dismay.

When Wednesday afternoon came and all their careful search of the swamp had proven fruitless, the men had held a solemn council. At this Ben Burley presided.

"She's gone." he said with blunt pathos: "we can't find her. All we got was the little blue ribbon hanging on the myrtle bush. What can we do now, boys? We can't stand to give her up."

"The little blue ribbon," muttered one of the other men desolately, "and the tracks in the sand by the spring."

"Do you think, Cousin Ben," asked Jim Tabor—tall, spare, hawk-eyed Jim—"do you think anybody could have kidnapped Rosalie? She was *that* pretty," he ended with mournful emphasis.

The dreadful word "kidnapped" was a foreign one to the remote community of Tabor Swamp; but now the suggestion that had been made took hold of the wary, anxious, and baffled party of men.

"Only rich people get their children stolen," Ben Burley objected. "Ain't none of us rich," he added with decision.

"But, Cousin Ben, you was mighty rich in having Rosalie," Jim Tabor suggested.

"Anybody would want to have her, same like we do," another member of the group said.

"Hold on now," spoke out old Amos Burley in his slow authoritative voice, "didn't we run that Negro Congaree out of here yesterday? What was he doing away over here on our side of the swamp? What kind of a man is he anyhow?"

"He's the only stranger who's been here in a month," Dick Minot interrupted.

"Don't nobody know who that fellow is," old Amos continued. "He just dropped down into this country. He took possession of Sambo's deserted place on Owendaw Creek. And those boats that take the inside passage come right by his door. He sells provender to strangers," he ended.

"Maybe he's selling more than provender," Dick Minot broke in again.

"What if this Congaree is our man?" Jim Tabor asked sternly, his gray eyes glittering vindictively under cavernous eyebrows. "He might steal the child for somebody else—gypsies or tourists or the like."

To Jim and to all other members of the clan all people not within the circle of their families were strangers and liable to suspicion. Even Congaree, though he had been at Owendaw for six years, was to them a stranger. He lived outside the swamp; and he was not a Burley, a Minot, or a Tabor.

"Amos and Jim, they done struck the trail," growled Asher Minot, a huge, bearlike man, black-bearded, deep-voiced, and menacing of aspect.

"I believe you're right," Ben Burley blurted out. "Congaree lives right by the creek where all those house-boats pass. He has dealings with strangers. He sells them things."

"Are we ready to start?" asked young Dick Minot sharply.

"We're ready," Jim Tabor answered. "Six miles it is, but not half of that straight through the swamp."

"We'll be going," said Ben Burley with grim decision.

"Congaree will tell us," the formidable Asher Minot muttered; "we'll get it out of him."

Thus it was that, impelled by what seemed to be a reasonable certainty, eleven men set forth through the dusky pathways of Tabor Swamp, their goal being the humble cabin of Congaree, huddled

obscurely under a great live-oak which overhung Owendaw Creek, a
deep tidal estuary which formed a part of the inland waterway system along the lonely coast.

Between Congaree's house and Tabor Swamp there was a wide
reach of melancholy marshland, a waste of reedy morasses, treacherous bogs, whispering stretches of mazy sedges. Beyond the cabin lay
the creek, then sea-marsh, glimmering and still; then the ocean. A
solitary place it was; and Congaree lived alone. Yet sometimes the
passing craft stopped at his staggering wharf and there took on
fresh water and occasionally such vegetables as the Negro's tiny
garden would supply. But these craft seemed always to belong to
another world than Congaree's which was a lonely one.

It was after two o'clock in the afternoon when the men of Tabor
Swamp set out for Congaree's home; and it happened that just then
the Negro was entertaining an old acquaintance, Bram Jackson. To
him Congaree had been quietly recounting his experience in the
swamp; and wide grew the eyes of Bram, while on his dusky face
Fear made her sudden throne. Something akin to genuine terror
was on his countenance when, ere his friend had completed his
story, Bram drew furtively from a pocket a tiny calico sunbonnet. It
was torn and crushed.

"I find dis in the swamp," Bram said. "I been after a wild turkey.
Don't this belong to a w'ite chile?"

Congaree looked grave. Was this the deep trouble of which Ben
Burley had spoken?

"I hear dat a little chile lost in the swamp," Bram went on. "Maybe
this is her hat," he suggested, holding up the pathetic thing. One of
the blue ribbon ties was missing.

"You is a fool to carry it wid you if you look like dat," said Congaree
bluntly. "Folks'll think you know something 'bout dis chile. Where'd
you find it?" he demanded.

"Right back here on Hickory Ridge."

"To-day?"

"Soon dis morning. Congaree, I must be gwine now. I'll leave dis
hat here," he added craftily; "I might meet somebody."

"Leave it," said Congaree in a tone which had a depth of meaning
which Bram did not fathom. Taking the tiny sad relic, he laid it on a

bench beside him on the porch. "I'll take it to Mr. Burley tomorrow," he said.

"You better not!" exclaimed Bram, his eyes starting with apprehension.

Congaree looked at him coldly. "A man," he said, "better always do what he oughter do."

Bram did not answer; but from his shifty step and his furtive look, he might have been judged to be a beliver in always doing the easy and politic thing. Moveover, his anxiety to be gone showed that a great fear was upon him.

When Bram left, the sun was two hours high. Congaree glanced appraisingly at it; then he gazed thoughtfully toward Tabor Swamp.

"They should know 'bout dis little bonnet tonight," he reasoned. "I'll drive in my cows from the marsh. Den I'll go."

Southward down a bypath from his cabin turned the Negro. The sunlight flickering upon him through the live-oaks showed his stout, strong frame, his alert and easy step, his erect and manly bearing. A quiet independence was about him. Such was Congaree, the man whom the dwellers in Tabor Swamp believed had stolen away their exquisite little sweetheart.

Almost as soon as the Negro had rounded the first bend in the marsh-pathway he began to call up his cattle. Plaintive, soft, far-reaching was his voice; it was as though he were singing them homeward with a lullaby. Congaree's call was answered by the secret birds of the marsh and by an ancient owl, wildly sequestered in the moldering swamp. On went the Negro, along brackish rivulets in the marsh, by tall ranks of whispering sedge, following the winding cattle-track. At last he heard a cow low; and soon he came within sight of a greedy old Jersey, up to her knees in mud, scything with her curling tongue the succulent tops of the young marsh which was just beginning to spring. But his two other cows Congaree could not see.

"I wonder now," he mused, going forward slowly and examining the tracks in the damp salt sand, "I wonder if them other ones—"

Suddenly the Negro caught his breath; then he eased himself down on one knee to gaze at a footprint, a tiny one—and of a kind that he had never seen in the marsh before.

"A little chile," he said, rising and looking about him. "She ain't been gone long from here."

Again the Negro called; and after that he shaded his eyes with his hand and looked across a very peculiar stretch of sand. From the marshland proper it had been carefully fenced off. Congaree and the other men whose stock ranged on this reedy moorland had united in building this fence. Up and down the coast this place was known as Tarleton's Deep. Since Revolutionary days a legend had persisted that three of Tarleton's roving cavalrymen had gone down in this dreadful pit, half quagmire, half quicksand, and most dangerous. In it grew certain fair flowers—wild flags, wampee, water-lilies, and white lilies. Its moisture, coming from the swamp rather than from the sea, was fresh; and vivid greenness of the water-plants growing in it had often allured cattle to stray into its fatal grasp. Then the fence had been built; and Congaree, as the man among those interested in it who lived nearest to it, kept it in repair. Near the north end he always had in readiness a small roll of barbed wire.

It was along the north side of the fence that Congaree had now come; and again he paused to call and to look for the mysterious tiny footprint.

But hardly had he given his first pleading and mellow whoop when behind him he heard some one running rapidly. Yet ere he turned, fifty yards away he saw a sight which gave him a sudden thrill—a little child had struggled through the wire. Now, with baby arms extended, she was running toward Tarleton's Deep. Already she was on the very brink of it. Certain white lilies were before her. She loved them, and she must have them. Coming out of the darksomeness of the swamp and out of the silent mystery of the marsh, she saw and recognized something she loved. Toward the dread quicksands Rosalie was running—toward death on joyous feet was speeding the little lost sweetheart of the fierce men of Tabor Swamp.

"Congaree! Congaree!" a frightened voice yelled to him from behind. "Run fo' yo' life! Dem men is to yo' house right now. Ain't you done leave the little hat on the piazza? They'll get you. Run, Congaree!"

Shouting his warning, Bram Jackson passed Congaree almost like a storm. Whirling away down the marsh path, he turned a bend by some cedars and vanished into the swamp. Then from the direction whence Bram had so hastily come, Congaree heard the rising of an angry tumult. He knew that in a few moments, taking his track, the men would be upon him.

The Negro was looking at the child. "She's gwine sink and drown," he said simply.

Then with a swiftness directed by a sudden and importunate purpose he ran along outside the fence, reached a roll of rusty wire, jerked the end free, stooped through the fence with it, raveled it until he had a long stretch free; then he took a turn with it about a post. Grasping the other end, he ran after the imperiled child. The wire tore Congaree's hand, but he heeded not the wound. Unless he had the wire, both rescued and rescuer would surely sink in Tarleton's Deep. He was now close to Rosalie.

The child was among the lilies. She was so intent on their beauty and on gathering two great lustrous ones that she did not know that she was sinking. Yet the sands had her. Already their cold lips were fondling her rosy knees. Amid beauty, amid a marsh stillness, in the quiet evening the monster of Tarleton's Deep laid its chill and fearful claim on Rosalie. In the ancient swamp through which she had come there had been no danger to compare with this one. But Congaree was now near.

"Don't you be 'fraid," he said gently, apprehensive lest she try to run and in struggling should sink from sight. "You pa's lookin' for you. You must let me carry you out of the water."

Congaree himself was now deep in the quagmire. He had shifted the wire to his left hand. Struggling forward, he reached far out with his right to grasp the child. Just then his footing seemed to go from under him. Almost to his waist he sank in the chill and eager sands. Yet from his purpose he did not desist. Rosalie, too, was fast sinking. But now Congaree's strong arm reached her. Out of Tarleton's Deep he lifted her, out of the jaws of death.

Holding the child carefully, with pain and the anguish of a mighty struggle he began to pull himself out of the grim grip of the deep. His hand torn and bleeding, all his power put forth, knowing that his worst danger would have to be faced when the men from Tabor Swamp appeared, Congaree toiled on. And Rosalie was so interested in arranging into a pretty cluster the few lilies she had gathered that she hardly seemed to notice that the Negro was bringing her to safety.

When, the child in his arms, Congaree had almost reached the fence, a group of eleven almost frantic men came rushing down the pathway. Old Ben Burley was in the lead; after him came gaunt Jim Tabor, Amos Burley, black-bearded Asher Minot, and all the rest. Murder, swift and relentless, murder that is vengeance, was in their hearts and on their faces. In his right hand old Ben gripped his rifle; in the other he had crused with the strength of his despair Rosalie's sunbonnet. From his bronzed hand the blue ribbon dangled strangely. Dick Minot, impetuous and wild, was shouting in his mad anger. Thus they rushed upon Congaree.

The silent Negro, never pausing in his approach, reached one side of the fence just as the men reached the other. Across the barrier he lifted Rosalie gently and laid her safely in her father's arms. And into the father's eyes Congaree looked with the calm strength of fidelity.

"I wanted more flowers," Rosalie explained, "but he carried me out of the water." And more she told them in her elfin fashion of her wanderings in the swamp, where she had slept, of her finding the lilies.

One by one the men were convinced; and one by one to the tacit Congaree they came, solemnly shaking his hand. When a swamp man does that, he pays a mighty tribute. In simple fashion the Negro told them how the sunbonnet had come to be on his porch. They believed him; and his quiet manhood moved them much—that, and the recovery of Rosalie. Nothing proved this more clearly than the strange heaving of the vast shoulders of Asher Minot as he wept as a strong man does.

And thus it was that Rosalie found the white lilies after all; and thus it was that the undying affection of the fierce clansmen of Tabor Swamp was won by the Negro Congaree. One has to love a man who is great of heart.

A Pair of Mallards

After several years of disastrous experience as a rice planter on the Santee River, Maj. Blythe Biddecomb, who had returned to his "stale, flat and unprofitable" law practice in Charleston, wrote his friend, Col. Jocelyn, that he was homesick for a pair of rice-fed mallards. Now, whenever any one mentioned game to the colonel, he took it as a challenge to his skill and as a high opportunity for gratifying his generosity. So the day after the major's letter came he started down the river in a little dugout cypress canoe for Murphy's Island at the mouth of the Santee.

Col. Jocelyn took with him his fine old English gun, a few boxes of 4's, a small basket of provisions, and—more for companionship than for help—Three Cents, a little Negro, who, although he had a Christian name, had long worn that mercenary title. And his bright ways and his diminutive figure went far toward establishing the fitness of it.

Col. Jocelyn and Three Cents were great "chums." When the boy was four years old, he had remarked stolidly to his father, the coachman, "Pa, you didn't currycomb dat horse right." Word of this rebuke came to the master of Mayfield, and he chuckled in great glee, and decided thenceforward to make Three Cents his chief counselor.

For several years this comradeship between the white-haired old gentleman and the pickaninny had continued; in fact, the colonel became quite dependent upon Three Cents, and the boy looked to his patron for everything.

So it happened that they set out together in the canoe, and headed for the mallard paradise—there where the great river lost itself in the greater sea, and where, by day and by night, clouds of wild ducks, wintering on the coast, rolled over the shimmering beaches and the yellow river mouth toward Bird Bank.

It was a twelve-mile paddle down from the plantation; but the tide was ebbing, and both occupants of the canoe were swinging cypress

From *Old Plantation Days* (1921).

paddles; so the long, slim craft shot swiftly by the shadowy banks, by tall, sighing growths of tawny marsh, by pebbly strands where the tide washed languidly.

Once, standing spectrally transfigured against the pale afternoon sky, they saw the grim, bleached skeleton of what had once been a proud house that fire had devoured. Then they passed a prosperous place where, in happy contrast to the recent scene, a turpentine still was sweetening the air with soft aromatic fragrance. Then the plantations ceased and there began the long waste stretches of marsh that extended clear down to the mouth of the river.

When they had at last landed on the back beach of Murphy's Island, they repaired to the best of the duck ponds, which was situated a good mile across the island. On their way they were aware of the long lines of ducks that frequently darkened the strip of sky above their reed-grown pathway.

Coming at last cautiously to the edge of the pond, where the colonel expected to hear a great clamor of feeding ducks, they were met by a telltale silence. Then, far across the stretch of water, they saw a bald eagle poised on a dead tree; there would be no duck shooting where the monarch ruled.

"Look here, Three Cents, that old rascal has every mallard within a mile flying for his life!" the colonel exclaimed. And to himself he muttered, "Blythe's dinner won't fly here this evening!"

"Maybe, sah, we might find Cedar Island mo' bettah, sah," the little Negro ventured.

Col. Jocelyn did not answer; but from the hopeful look that stole into his face you might have guessed that Three Cents had solved the problem. He looked quizzically at the sky, with its few ragged clouds scudding eastward. He had fully made up his mind; but on matters of hunting the colonel always thought it wise not to accept another's judgment too hastily. Hesitation implied doubt, doubt implied thought and knowledge, and the old gentleman was not above the gentle vanity of wishing to be regarded as learned. "Well," he said at last, "there isn't any place to sleep on Cedar Island, and here we could spend the night in the old clubhouse; but, at that, I guess Cedar Island is our only chance."

"Yes, sah," echoed Three Cents, as if the idea were his master's, "dat's de only chance."

Retracting their steps, they soon came to the canoe, which they launched and headed straight across the river for Cedar Island—a long, low sea island, with heavy delta marshes behind and with a wooded point that faced the ocean. It was a famous place for ducks, but because of its remote situation sportsmen rarely visited it.

As the line of cedars on Murphy's Island sank into the sea, Col. Jocelyn and Three Cents gained fair headway toward their goal; but behind them the ashen clouds in the west were hiding the low sun. Moreover, the paddle across the river was a long one and difficult in the cross sea that was running. The colonel was on the middle seat; his henchman swung his paddle manfully from the stern. The going was not very rough, but with every stroke they felt the lightness of their craft and the majestic power of the sea that paced beneath them.

When they were halfway across, the colonel knew that he had made a mistake in trying to reach Cedar Island that night; Three Cents had known the same thing some time before, but he had not expressed his doubts. There seemed to be no immediate danger; but it would be dark before they got there, and the west wind over the salt water was growing very cold.

With those thoughts in his mind, the colonel glanced over his shoulder with a smile intended to cheer Three Cents; but the bullet head of the Negro was buried between his shoulders, and his paddle was flashing doggedly from the murky water to the chill air and back again.

"He's all right," the colonel assured his conscience, which was accusing him of bringing a child out into danger.

The sun had now set and the sweep of the ebb grew slower. Tint by tint the colors faded from the sky, and the counterglow in the east died swiftly. Over the river the incoming ducks began to fly. The dull roar of the surf on the outer beaches sounded insistently. The shore lines faded, vanished—and it was night.

"Boss," asked Three Cents, through lips that were stiff with the briny cold, "is we headed right? I b'lieve, sah," he added respectfully, "we is too far down de ribber."

Had the colonel shared that opinion there would have been less cause for apprehension; but the old gentleman thought they were too far upstream. That meant that they did not know where they were. Above them they could hear the whistling music of wild ducks' wings. Vaguely, to the south and east, they heard the booming of the surf. Darkness was before them and behind them; and darkness covered them.

The colonel, old hunter that he was, began to feel uneasy—chiefly on account of the presence of Three Cents. An hour before it had seemed simple to reach either island; but now the blessed sight and touch of dry land seemed indeed remote possibilities.

There was no moon. There were no stars. The canoe seemed to have changed its course; and the high, smooth waves that she was now riding moved with the strength and dignity that they gather only in the ocean. The cold salt spray began to break over the gunwales, and it froze as it fell. The two paddles were already coated with it. The wind was slowly rising, and with it came that bitter, bitter sea cold that cuts into the marrow. For the first time in his life Col. Jocelyn felt powerless to fight the forces that appeared to be leagued against him. His hands were almost as stiff from cold as the paddle. His legs and feet were losing their feeling.

Suddenly, with a jerk of decision, he laid his paddle along the thwarts in front of him and, steadying himself on the gunwales, turned himself in the boat so that he faced Three Cents. Dimly he could make out the pitiful little form. The colonel's strong arms reached out, took the Negro child by the shoulders and lifted him down into the bottom of the boat. He had to wrench the paddle from the boy's hands; it was frozen to the palms.

"Oh, please, boss," the little fellow chattered, "don't lemme freeze! I 'speck I is a goner dis time; but I ain't sorry, sah, dat I come with you." Then Three Cents nestled up between the colonel's knees.

Colder grew the wind, and the waves broke heavily against the boat. Three Cents moaned and trembled. There was nothing to cover him with. Col. Jocelyn lifted one of the little Negro's hands and slipped it up his own sleeve. "Can't let the child die!" he muttered.

With that he fumbled with the buttons on his coat, loosed it, and quivering in the piercing cold, slipped it off and laid it over his little comrade.

Under his coat Col. Jocelyn wore a low-necked jersey. Through that the stark wet wind cut like a saber. He tried to grip his paddle in his numb hands; if he could only get started, he thought, he might be able to warm up. But his hands, coated with ice, refused to respond to his will; so blindly he tried to steer the canoe, and tried to keep her before the wind so that the waves would not swamp her.

Three Cents had dropped off to sleep, but he was still moaning and shaking; and once he shook with a violent chill. The colonel tried to fix the coat tighter about the boy, but he could not manage it very well. Then he tried to cover the little Negro's feet with the loose straw in the bottom of the boat, but the child woke up, crying. Clinging to the colonel's knees, he begged him to make a fire in the boat!

For answer the colonel unbuttoned his jersey, slipped it off, and wrapped it closely about the little black boy whom he was literally giving his life to save.

The child felt instant and grateful relief—the man, acute agony. The fiend of cold seemed to lay icy hands on his very heart. The wind felt scorching, and he thought himself intolerably burned; but he slowly realized that he must be freezing to death. There in the darkness, there in the treacherous inlet, he would meet his end! Antietam or Gettysburg, he said, would have been better than this.

Then a monster, blacker than the night, rose out of the water before them; it rushed down upon them; and the bow of the canoe ran high on the shore—of Murphy's Island!

Somehow, he forgets how, the colonel and Three Cents crawled to the old clubhouse, where they built a roaring fire. And before its huge comfort and cheer they ate the provisions from the basket, and slept.

On the way home the next morning the colonel shot two mallards, and he sent them, with his regards, to Maj. Blythe Biddecomb.

Two days later Maj. Biddecomb was entertaining at dinner.

"Mallards?" he replied to a question concerning their number on the Santee. "There are millions of them there, sir. Now, my dear personal friend, Col. Henry Jocelyn, sent me this pair; and I'll warrant you, sir, that he wasn't on the river long enough to make a shadow. In fact, for a man so robust as I am, mallard shooting is just a little tame; but Henry, dear fellow, could never stand the cold and exposure as I can, God bless him!"

What Scared Kitty

The very first intimation Maj. Meriwether Bohun had that anything was wrong was the tremendous bound that his mare,
Kitty, gave. Had he not been an expert horseman, the little thorough-
bred's sudden dash would surely have unseated him; but he managed to keep his saddle and to pull in the mare.

"Whoa, girl!" he said gently, gathering in the lines with his left
hand and patting his mount soothingly with his right. "What is it
that scared you, little one? There's nothing on this old swamp road
to frighten any one, Kitty."

But there evidently was; for the mare was trembling and blowing
her breath spasmodically through her wide, quivering nostrils. Maj.
Bohun knew from those signs that Kitty's keen senses had detected
some danger on that narrow, dark, lonely pathway.

It happened on the old road leading from Maj. Bohun's plantation in the Santee country to the neighboring plantation of Wedgewood, which, except for a few Negro tenants, had long since been
deserted. Moreover, it happened at night. The major was sure that
his mare had scented danger of some kind. Her nervousness was
increasing every moment; she kept fidgeting, and then began to give
unmistakable signs of intending to bolt.

"One of the girth buckles may be jamming her," the major said to
himself. "I'll get off a minute to feel if everything is all right."

He dismounted and led the frightened mare forward a few paces;
then he stopped her and his hands began to fumble over the buckles
of the girth. For the moment, he let the lines fall loose on the horse's
neck. In that moment, whether the mare realized that her master

From *Old Plantation Days* (1921).

was off his guard or whether some stray wind had wafted to her another scent of her peril, she whirled suddenly and, snorting loudly, galloped back down the black passage of the road along which she had come.

There the major was left standing, three miles from home and three miles from Wedgewood. He was on an elevated part of the road, on what had once been a causeway; and that particular point was near the heart of the swamp that separated his own plantation from Wedgewood. Yet, strange as it may seem, Maj. Bohun's presence in such a place at such a time had come about in a perfectly natural way.

That afternoon he had promised to go over to Wedgewood to see a sick Negro. The day had been hot; a thunderstorm had come up just as the major was about to start on his ride, and for more than an hour a wild tempest had shaken the tall magnolias and swayed the great live-oaks that stood round the major's house. The sun was setting when at last the rain ceased.

With the major a promise was a promise. He had sent word to the Negro that he was coming, and nothing would have kept him from fulfilling his obligation. The major was a proud man; yet his pride was productive of the highest virtues—generosity, courage, hospitality, and gallant adherence to a fine code of honor. There was no man of his county who had suffered more or who complained less, who had had more cause for tears yet who had preserved more genuinely his light heart, his merry smile, and his ringing laughter.

Behind his rambling old plantation house, many parts of which had acknowledged the triumph of time to the extent of leaning dejectedly, stood a little brick building. It had been a smoke-house, but the major had fitted it with benches and a fireplace. There the many Negroes who came to see him could have a warm and sheltered waiting place. From there, as soon as the storm had abated, Major Bohun had called Will, his ancient Negro servant. At the foot of the steps Will had stood, with his battered cap in his hand, and with the last fine drops of the heavy shower falling upon his gray head.

"Will," the major had said, "I want you to saddle Kitty for me. It's stopped raining, and I'm going over to Wedgewood to see poor Joe Wilson."

Maj. Bohun made his tone final. He knew very well that Will would be sure to object to his plan. Long, faithful service had given the Negro the privilege of advising his master on all matters.

"You gwine there to-night, Mas' Meriwether?" he had asked, with strong disapproval in his tone. "Dat road is so bery slippery after dis rain, sah, and Wedgewood is a long, lonely way off, sah."

Although the objection was dutifully made, the Negro would really have been disappointed if the major had not kept to his word. It would have been the first time it had ever happened; and the dusky servitor was not at all beneath appreciating a delicate point of honor, and of considering it as his own as well as his master's.

"No; I must go, Will," the major had answered at once. "I shall be ready as soon as you get the horse here."

Down at the stable, while Will was adjusting the bridle and saddle on Kitty, he kept muttering proudly to himself, "'Cose he gwine! I done know he wouldn't bruk his wud! No, sah, not eben to a sick nigger! Bruk his wud?" he asked himself with scornful incredulity, to afford himself the satisfaction of stoutly denying such an absurdity. "Not him! Dat's about all we got left on dis ole place now; but we ain't gwine to lose dat! No, sah, not so long as me and Mas' Meriwether libes. You hear dat, Kitty?"

Meanwhile Maj. Bohun had been taking stock of what he could spare for the sick man at Wedgewood. The bundle that he finally tied up consisted of sundry little packages of groceries, the waistcoat of an old suit of evening clothes, a flaming red tie of antique design and a woolen muffler. It was an odd assortment of gifts for an invalid; but the major did not trouble himself about that. The gifts would carry his affection; and that was the most that any gift could carry.

It was an hour later, when he was riding along the lonely swamp road, that something had frightened Kitty.

After his mount had galloped off in the darkness, Maj. Bohun stood doubtfully in the black gulch of the road. The package for the sick man he had stuffed into one of his greatcoat pockets, and he now put his hand on it reminiscently.

There was everything to take him back home, it seemed: this danger, whatever it was, should take him back; the fact that he was now on foot should make him turn rather than go on; it would take him more than an hour to walk to the Negro cabin at Wedgewood, and he well knew how uncomfortable he would be when he arrived. But in spite of all that Maj. Bohun did not hesitate. His mind had made him pause, but his heart had had only a single purpose. He would go on.

All the dark and lonely way to Wedgewood the major puzzled over Kitty's fright. There were several things that might have caused it. Out of the lonely vastness of the monstrous swamp might have come a roaming black bear; it might have been a Negro fugitive from one of the county chain gangs; it might have been a rattlesnake, the sinister and penetrating odor of which will make even the best horse unmanageable.

Before the major started forward he had listened intently for a sound that might betray the identity of the creature that had frightened his mare; but except for the lonely wind grieving through the towering pines the silence of the moldering swamp was unbroken.

Once, indeed, he heard the far-off and melancholy note of a great horned owl; but it was so weird and remote that it seemed a tone of the deep woodland wilderness itself rather than the voice of a living creature.

"I don't know what it could have been; I give up," Maj. Bohun muttered to himself; "but it certainly gave Kitty a bad scare. She'll go into the stable lot at home. I hope Will doesn't find her to-night; he would worry a good deal about me."

An hour's walk through the silent, cavernous woods brought the major to the borders of Wedgewood, and soon afterwards he came to Joe Wilson's cabin.

Matters were worse than Maj. Bohun had anticipated, and he was heartily glad that he had come. From the dim couch beside the dark fireplace where he lay, the sick Negro looked up at him with grateful eyes.

"I knowed you would come, sah," he said, rousing himself to make the effort of speaking. He tried to sit up in the light of the smoking lamp, but he had not the strength.

The major busied himself to make Joe comfortable. The invalid was alone in the cabin, and was too weak to help himself; but Maj.

Bohun knew what to do. First he conferred his gifts, and that lightened the Negro's heart. Next he made the fire blaze brightly. He
then unwrapped the groceries he had brought, and used the paper
to stuff up a drafty crack above the Negro's bed; then he put on a
few old pans and began to cook some of the food. And all the while
he kept talking cheerfully to the stricken man, whose only reply was
a reiteration of the solemn statement:

"I sholy would 'a' died dis night, Mas' Meriwether, if you hadn't 'a'
come."

When the sick man had had his supper, the major began to prepare to return; but there was such a dumb appeal in the Negro's eyes
that he speedily came to a different decision.

"Joe," he said, "I believe I'll just stay here for the night. Kitty got
away from me, and I don't want to walk all the way home in the
dark. I'll just sit in this chair by the fire. You go to sleep now, Joe,
and I'll be right here when you wake."

The Negro could not thank him, but he sighed with deep content
and closed his eyes peacefully. The depth of his gratitude became
articulate in his dreams; for once he cried out poignantly, as if in
protest, "No! No! He done say he would come!" and then subsided
into deep slumber.

When morning came, Maj. Bohun was still sitting beside Joe; and
when the Negro woke, refreshed and much better, he saw the old
planter's kindly face.

Joe's fever was gone, and his brain, he said, was clear.

"You had a good night, Joe," said the major. "You are going to get
well now. I'll send Will over with some things for you this afternoon;
and to-morrow I'll come again myself."

Into the radiant dawn of a golden September day the major
stepped; and as he walked briskly down the plantation road, he
squared his shoulders and hummed blithely an old love melody. He
loved the woods; and this walk home through the dewy freshness
and glimmering beauty filled him with pure joy. On all sides the
marvelous beauty of the Southern forest withdrew into rare beauty;
the vistas, in ending, suggested a diviner loveliness beyond them.

It was, indeed, so beautiful that Maj. Bohun did not think of the
sinister experience of the night before until he came almost to the

place where Kitty had deserted him. Then he remembered; and he was not at all surprised to see the faithful Will coming down the narrow causeway to meet him.

"He's found Kitty with the saddle and bridle on her," said the major to himself, "and has come over to see what has happened to me."

But suddenly Will stopped abruptly in the road; then he gave a shout and jumped back. Maj. Bohun came up quickly; Will was calling to him to be careful, and was pointing to what lay on the causeway.

Spanning the road between him and the Negro, Maj. Bohun saw the thing that had frightened Kitty. It was a monstrous reptile—a diamondbacked rattler of the swamp. Its massive body could not have been less than nine feet long.

It lay at a peculiar, awkward angle; but its broad, malignant, spade-shaped head was alertly raised, and its cold, yellow eyes glittered ominously. About the grim and terrible mouth there was an expression of savage cruelty. The lips were pallid, drawn, deadly; but the huge rattlesnake seemed to have control of the forward part of its body only. It could strike, but it could not coil. Its back had evidently been injured. Yet, partly because of that very injury, it was the most dangerous and formidable monster of the lonely Southern swamp.

The Negro made a detour through the bushes, and now stood beside Maj. Bohun, who told him of Kitty's breaking away.

"And there's what scared her," he added, as they gazed at the hideous rattler; "no wonder she bolted from me."

"But dat snake ain't been lyin' here all night?" the Negro asked, staring, fascinated, at the dread reptile in the roadway before them.

"I believe I know what happened," the major replied. "Kitty shied when we passed the snake. She winded him, but she did not know where he was. Then, when she broke and galloped back, she ran over him and injured him. Yes, he has lain there all night. What a monster!"

It took the two men the better part of half an hour to cut long poles in the swamp and to kill the powerful rattlesnake. The major then counted the rattles; there were twenty-nine. He also saw where the mare's hoofs had crushed the back of the reptile.

"See here, Will," he said, pointing to the deep wound, "here's where Kitty scored. This snake must have been maddened by such trampling," he went on, half to himself, "and would have been wild to strike after such an injury. Now if I hadn't gone on to Wedgwood," he mused aloud; "if I had turned back. The road is so narrow here, and it was so dark—"

Maj. Bohun cleared his throat slightly. The Negro, whose eyes were wet, said hurriedly and in a tone of assumed assurance, "But you didn't been in no danger, sah, 'cause you had done promised Joe to come to see him. And we don't neber bruk dat Bohun wud, sah."

Judge Napier's Sentence

It was only after a desperate struggle that Julian Broderick, a state policeman, had mastered the fugitive. Broderick could not remember having ever had so stern and prolonged a chase and so sudden and fierce an encounter. The affair happened, too, on a peculiarly lonely stretch of beach between the solitary pinelands and the waste sea-marshes. Broderick knew that had the struggle ended differently many a day would have passed before his friends learned of his fate—if they ever learned of it. After the posse had abandoned the pursuit, Broderick had dogged his man through swamps and across the rivers until at last he had come upon him just as the fellow was about to cross a deep tidal estuary. In the clash that followed the law had triumphed, and as soon as Broderick had handcuffed his man the two began the toilsome march to Sellers, the nearest settlement.

The prisoner was Jason Jones, a powerful Negro, whose reputation in his community at Rosemary up to the time when he robbed Ashton, the storekeeper, had been good. Jones had fled on the night of the crime. The deed had been done on a Friday. It was not until the following Tuesday that the robber was caught; in all that time, Broderick felt sure, the silent man who now marched before him had had hardly a mouthful to eat. Compared with Broderick, Jason Jones was a giant; and the state policeman felt that he should have had small chance against so formidable an antagonist if the man had not been exhausted by the pitiless and protracted pursuit. Broderick was sorry for the fellow, and he intended when they reached Sellers to see to it immediately that the man was decently cared for.

From *Old Plantation Days* (1921).

The two men arrived in the seacoast village at sunset, but a strange sort of darkness had already set in. A sharp misty rain, driven by an insistent east wind, had been falling for an hour. The huddled houses of the small settlement showed lights in them. It was an evening to be indoors. Broderick, weary physically and mentally, at last brought his captive to the post office. Sellers was the kind of village that has only one officer of the law, who serves as constable, storekeeper, and postmaster, and Broderick was an old friend of this man, whose name was Jim Laws.

"Jim," he said, "I've got a man here with me. Guess I'll have to ask you to let me keep him here to-night."

"Right, Julian," the other answered, gazing with interest on the powerful form of Jason Jones. "Tell me what you need, Julian."

"I must take this man on the truck to the city the first thing in the morning. We've had nothing to eat, Jim, for a good while."

The postmaster busied himself behind the counter; and soon cheese, crackers, canned salmon and ancient gingerbreads were forthcoming. These he set before Broderick.

"Jason," said his captor, not without kindness, "I'll take the cuffs off now for a while so that you can eat your supper." The Negro muttered thanks.

The postmaster, who had been about to close up shop when the two men arrived, slouched into his overcoat.

"Stormy wind coming up," he remarked; "if it doesn't get too bad, Julian, I'll have my wife send you up a pot of hot coffee. I'll tell Dave Janney about stopping for you in the morning." In a lower voice he added, "Come to the door." And when Broderick had complied, the postmaster whispered, "Julian, do you want any help with this fellow to-night? I can come back if you think you might need me."

"No, I can manage him," Broderick replied. "There's no reason for you to come back."

The door, which the storekeeper now opened, was blown violently against the wall. The two smoky lamps in the room flared convulsively. Broderick shot an apprehensive glance toward his prisoner.

"Regular storm," he said by way of farewell to the postmaster, who stepped forth into the rain and the night.

To be left alone for a night with a prisoner was no new experience for Broderick; he took the situation as a matter of course.

"Jason," he said, raising his voice somewhat in order to make himself heard above the wind, "there's a bench over there, where you can get some sleep. I'll put the cuffs back on you, that being according to orders and regulations."

The Negro made no protest. In his silent way he seemed to be sensible of the kindness that Broderick had shown him. When the handcuffs had been adjusted, the fellow went obediently to the rude couch and lay down. There was something resigned about his manner, as if he had realized that there was no use trying to escape the hand of the law.

Jason soon slept, though the night was no night for sleeping. In a chair tilted against the counter sat Broderick, trying to read by the dim lamplight a week-old paper. Outside the wind had slowly increased until now it was almost a cyclone. The watcher was sure that he heard a great tree go down. The frame building began to creak and groan.

"No chance for Jim to send that coffee," he kept saying to himself. As the hours wore on toward midnight, the violence of the gale increased. Jim Laws' store was especially exposed to the force of the blast. The storm was coming from the east. There was nothing in the village of Sellers between the sea-marshes and the post office. A small lumber yard was to the north. The few scattered dwellings were a considerable distance away on the landward side. The post office had to take the full fury of the tempest.

About an hour before midnight Broderick, now thoroughly alarmed, went to the window on the leeward side of the building. In the darkness a storm-lashed tide was raging before a seventy-mile gale. The salt water was already under the building. Knowing the ways of coastal storms, Broderick realized that this was a hurricane out of the West Indies. At any moment the rising tide might sweep from its foundations the rickety structure in which he and his prisoner were sheltered. Crossing the room to the windward side, he saw that water was already on the floor, and that salt spume was driving in through the cracks in the building.

Broderick hurriedly set three mail sacks and certain boxes of store goods on the counter. He would try to keep what he could out of the wet for Jim Laws. There was no chance that the postmaster would get back, for he and his neighbors, too, would be fully occupied in getting their families out of their endangered houses to places of safety. Broderick and his prisoner would have to shift for themselves.

With Jason, exhaustion had had its way; he was sleeping through the storm. His huge form lay cramped on the small couch. Broderick was glad that the man should rest, but the time had come to awaken him. His decision to arouse him was hastened by a grinding crash, which was followed by a heavy down pour through the roof. A live-oak tree had fallen on the building.

"When live-oaks go," Broderick muttered, "it's time for us to leave!"

Even after the fall of the tree through the roof the Negro slept; Broderick had some difficulty in awakening him.

"Jason, sit up and listen to what I have to say."

Broderick waited until he was sure that his prisoner had full possession of his senses.

"Jason, we are caught in a storm—you understand? You and I have to leave this place. Now, I want to give you the best chance I can to get away. I am therefore going to take the cuffs off. You are to stay with me as long as you can, Jason. If things get so bad that you have to save yourself from drowning, look out for yourself. But when the storm is over, you are to come back to me. Is it a fair deal and agreement?

"Yes, cap'n, more than fair." the towering black man replied, evidently impressed by Broderick's quiet manner, which was in high contrast to the howling gale.

At that moment there came a heavy thudding against the windward side of the building, then a smashing, splintering blow. A heavy stick of pine timber, drifting from the sawmill nearby, had been driven like a ram through the side of the building. The waves drove it farther in, and twisted it, so that now through the gaping hole the sea water rushed. The spumy salt tide rushed also through the door that Broderick opened. On the threshold the two men stood for a moment. The white man was afraid that the Negro might not be willing to venture forth. He turned to call to Jason, and at the same time took a step downward into the wild tide-race.

"Take my hand, Jason; let's try to get through this together."

Even while he was speaking, he was thrown violently against the building, and the hand that had reached out for Jason's was clutching the air. With a groan, Broderick sank into the seething black waters. A heavy timber, companion to the one that had rammed the building, had been driven against him. His leg was broken near the thigh; he could neither swim nor stand; he would surely drown.

Into the wailing darkness came the huge form of Jason. His bulk loomed monstrous in the doorway.

"Cap'n, where is you? he shouted.

With his feeble fingers trailing idly against the side of the building, with his breath almost gone from another savage thrust of the cruel timber, Broderick called back faintly. "Here Jason! But I'm done for. Save yourself. Keep the wind at your back, and you'll get into the woods. Save yourself."

In the oblivion that surged down upon him, the doomed man in the water was hardly aware of the giant form that towered above him in the storm. But great arms were under him, lifting him. A voice of hope spoke to him. A strength to master the strength of the storm had come to shield him.

It was noon of the following day; and though the wind was still high, the clouds were breaking. What had been the village of Sellers was now a desolation. Three miles inland, in a pinelander's stout cabin, lay Broderick. Jason had brought him there through the storm, and the first object the aching eyes of the state policeman caught as he opened them was the huge form of the Negro, seated near the fireplace.

"You've come back, Jason." said Broderick, "as you promised. You are a man of your word."

"I didn't never gone, cap'n," the Negro responded simply.

Then the owner of the cabin told of the exploit of Jason. In ending he said with some show of feeling, "He carried you just like a woman would a baby, Julian; and he would not rest till he had you as comfortable as you could be made. He must be a mighty faithful man of yours."

"He is," said Julian Broderick.

That was a strange trail which, two weeks later, was called in the courtroom of Judge Trevelyan Napier in Charleston. Jason Jones, accused of robbing the Ashton store in Rosemary, was at the bar of justice. The judge had heard the evidence; and in his charge to the jury he had suggested that, if the twelve gentlemen found a verdict of guilty, he would see to it that the punishment met the offense. He intimated that the robbing of country stores was a practice that, so far as he could effect it, would have to cease in Charleston County.

"Jason Jones," said Judge Napier, addressing the prisoner, "the law gives you the right to make any statement you may wish to make; do you wish to say anything for yourself?"

"Please, sah," the Negro replied, "make my fine as light as you can. I'se mighty sorry I done broke in the store. My wife is dead, and I has seven head of chillun. I broke in the store 'caze they been hongry."

At that moment there was a stir in the courtroom. Broderick, lying on a cot, was brought in. The doctors at the hospital had not yet permitted him even to use crutches. From his bed of pain he told with evident effort the story of the storm. Through it all the listeners were spellbound. Judge Napier cleared his throat suspiciously.

"Gentlemen of the jury," he said at the conclusion of the policeman's story, "retire for your verdict. Find according to the evidence."

In a few minutes the men returned with the verdict of guilty.

"Jason Jones, stand up and hear your sentence," said Judge Napier. "We find you guilty of robbing the Ashton store. But we also find you guilty of saving your captor's life at the great risk of your own, and you stayed by him as you had promised to do. The amount of damage that you did the store is about five dollars, which I, in an unofficial capacity, will make good. The account of the law against you is cleared by your late conduct. Jason, you are a free man. May you be a good one. Return home now and work hard for those seven children. Mr. Broderick, here, and certain other gentlemen in the room have thrown together and now hand you this little gift of a hundred dollars. Jason, I am convinced that you are naturally a brave and good man. Be brave and good always. You may go. You are free."

A Wildwood Christmas

I

The high-bush huckleberries were in bloom. Wild yellow daisies starred the level floor of the great pine forest. But for faint aeolian airs sounding in the lofty crests of the huge yellow pines, the woods were still. Had it been nearer the river, many birds would have been singing on that April day; but this was the wild pinewoods country, and few birds are found there. Between Montgomery Branch and the Green Bay, the country is silent and solitary; one might imagine it almost bare of life.

But life was here in its most wonderful form—life reproducing itself. On that benign Carolina springtime day, a white-tail doe had given birth to a fawn. To a wild creature of her physical perfection and native vigor, birth was natural and unattended by fear of pain.

Seven months ago she had mated with the great ten-point stag from Fox Bay. Now her hour was past, and the burly little buck was surprisingly wide awake. He lay curled in the broomsedge bed under the fragrant myrtles.

The mother stood over him, licking him, cleansing him, loving him. Her whole attitude was a blessing and a caress. Her liquid eyes were tender with affection. They should have been wide with amazement for the fawn was unlike any she had ever seen before. Her baby was black—a perfect glossy black, strange and beautiful.

Once in the wilds of Wambaw Swamp she had seen a spectral white buck; and a spotted half albino had come across the river the previous summer. But her baby from the tips of his ears to the points of his tiny gleaming hoofs was solid ebony.

From *Those Were the Days* (1955).

With the tall, rocking pines for sentinels, with the bright sunshine warming the dewy wilderness, and the peaceful sky above, it did not seem a baby deer could so soon be in danger. But he was not an hour old before he was in peril of his life. His watchful mother knew what to fear in those lonely woods, and she was alert to every sight or sound or odor that might threaten her fawn.

The first premonition of trouble came to her as an odor. With a start her head lifted, her eyes were set forward, and her body became tense. Her black nostrils widened apprehensively and defiantly. This odor was not unpleasant, but the doe dreaded it; it was animal, yet seemed vegetable also.

Depending as she did on power of smell more than on eyesight to identify anything that approached, the doe now took a step forward in the suspected direction, her nostrils flaring. She knew the character of this ancient enemy, but as yet she had not seen him. She glanced back at her baby; then she moved clear of the bed of grass in which she had given him birth.

The black fawn lay in the dappled sunlight, happily drowsing and blinking. He knew nothing about death. When he was first born, he had been chilly; but now the genial sun was warming him, and he was beginning to feel at home in his new world.

His mother advanced a few yards towards the clump of sweetgum bushes that grew about a huge yellow pine stump. All about the stump the trash and leaves had been strangely cleared away, leaving a circle of clean white sand. Years before a forest fire had burned some of the stump roots deeply into the ground, leaving a cavernous black hole there. And now, coming out to sun himself was the evil creature that the doe had winded, a great diamondback rattlesnake nearly six feet long, the serpent terror of the western world.

Moving with lordly deliberateness up the sandy incline from his den, the banded death came into the sunlight of the sweet spring-time world. It was as if a chimera from another and sinister planet were invading the wholesome realm of earth. And for all the horror of his wide-sunken eyes, the sullen droop at the corners of the mouth, the cold pallor of thin lips, and the powerful jaws, the huge serpent was beautiful. There was majestic rhythm in his movements, and the spirit of power was in him, and the spirit of awe went before him.

As soon as the doe saw the rattler, she stopped, and all her hair stood out slightly so she looked menacing and larger than natural. Mingled emotions of hatred and anger gleamed in her eyes. She had seen many rattlers before, and she had killed some. But none were so large as this. There was but one way in which she could kill him: that was by springing on him with her forefeet drawn lightly together like a sheaf of spears. Her polished, sharp hoofs made deadly lances. But to kill a rattler a deer has to have his enemy fairly in the open.

The fawn's mother now waited. Restlessly she stamped one forefoot. She looked back to where her baby lay. And when she turned her head, the monster saw her. Only about a yard of dread length had cleared his hole; only his great spade-shaped head and the extreme forepart of his heavy body lay on the white sand—that circle he had cleared about the old stump.

The rattler saw the doe and he was afraid. He lay there looking at her with his cold, basilisk-like eyes. Then he swung his head slowly, turning back into his darksome den.

When he disappeared the doe knew that, for the moment, the danger had passed; but she knew also she could not leave her baby where he was. It was not, of course, that the reptile would have considered the fawn his prey; but such a serpent is extremely irritable and considers anything that moves near his den an enemy. Yet the mother would have to stay with her baby until he could walk.

Still trembling a little, she nobbled at the tender green shoots of grass. Then, with head low, she returned to her strange little black fawn.

The mother, bending above him, now pushed him with her nose, now moved him with one of her front feet. She was trying to see whether she could get him to stand up. At last he did, but his legs were very wobbly, and they seemed much to long and slender. The doe now stepped forward, bleating softly, until her full breast was directly above her baby. He began to nurse, indifferently and uncertainly at first; but when he found how good the milk tasted, he spread his legs, sank his tiny hoofs into the sand, and went to work in real earnest.

When he had had all he could hold, he took a few teetery steps; then lay down, and his mother lay beside him. Little Roland slept; but his mother kept untiring watch.

After the black fawn had slept three hours, he awoke. Already he was stronger, was growing, and developing an air of naive intelligence. If she had not seen an enemy coming from under the old pine stump the doe would now have left her baby, and have gone to the lush savannas and the misty green watercourses to feed. But she would not leave him near the den of a diamondback. It was not that this dreaded serpent would deliberately attack the fawn. But he might be attracted by its odors; the monster might approach; the fawn, in moving from him, might touch or alarm him. Then he would strike. Perhaps the mother did not think of all that. Perhaps she knew only that the diamondback means death, and that she must get her baby out of danger.

Standing up, she gently nuzzled the fawn until he swayingly took his feet. The with her black nose she pushed him forward slowly, step by step. Sometimes she would go a little way ahead to make certain all was well; then she would coax him forward through the grass and ferns.

When they reached a dense clump of gallberries on the edge of a savanna, she let him lie down. They had come a safe distance. She tucked him into his wildwood cradle. And the fawn slept; that is, as much as a deer ever really sleeps—more daydreaming than slumber, drowsing and blinking, relaxing and resting. It is perhaps worth noticing that all herbivorous creatures sleep lightly whereas the carnivora slumber profoundly.

The doe, satisfied now that her baby was safe and happy, stole swiftly away from him and began to feed on the tender grass of the savanna. At any other time of the year she would not have fed until twilight, then on through the night; but now, partly because the woods were thick with greenery, and chiefly because her baby had to have his milk regularly, she ventured abroad in the day light, in the retired security of the wild forest. She knew her fawn would not stir from where she had left him; and there was now no danger near.

Especially did she feel safe from men; they rarely came into the springtime and summer woods. Not until the beginning of autumn would the forest be clamorous with their shouting, the blare of their guns, and with the tumult of hounds and horns. But men, she knew, were strange creatures, of uncertain habits and disconcerting irregularity of behavior, and sometimes they appeared when they were least expected.

II

"Maisie, if there is going to be preaching on Sunday, we ought to have some flowers for the church and our own ain't nothin'! Where did you find those white wild lilies last year? Maybe you might find some more. But if you go a-lookin' for 'em, you must watch out for snakes. A day like this will bring the rattlers outen their dens. I would like to go with you, but I can't go into the woods like I used to."

Maybelle Mayhew regarded her daughter, tall and slender and boyish at sixteen years of age. She was beautiful to an unusual degree, blooming like a wildflower in her pineland home.

"I know where them flowers is," said Maisie, in a voice that had bird notes in it. "I just go down the road a piece; then I cross Montgomery Branch as you are headin' for Boggy Bay, where we used to pick all them high-bush huckleberries. There's lots of lilies there, and they would sure look pretty in the church Sunday."

"Well, child, be careful. Take a stick with you and beat on the bushes ahead of you as you go along. That's the best way to tell if a snake is there. And keep on the path if you can. And don't be too long-a-waitin' to look at a lot of other flowers and at birds' nests same as you allus do."

Bareheaded and barelegged, Maisie ran across the sandy yard of her home, and out into the woodland road that passed the Mayhew farm. She paused for a moment to break a chinaberry shoot. She would use this to investigate the snake situation. Then she sped on down the road, her feet making clear imprints in the damp sand.

Having a woodsman's uncanny sense of direction, from the road she presently turned into a dim game trail, just a narrow path strewn with pine needles, and overhung by a careless disarray of little bushes, huckleberries, gallberries, and tiny sweet bays, now in bloom, their snowy chalices gleaming.

Maisie tapped the brushes ahead with her stick. Once she heard it give a strange klink, and then she laughed to see the glossy back of a land terrapin. Once something scuttled away at lightning speed, and she heard it run up a pine. She knew it was a wild skink, a lizard of gaudy, almost poisonous, colors, and gifted with truly amazing speed.

Into the hushed and fragrant twilight she went, into the dimness and the dewiness of Montgomery Branch, where wampees shed the water like quicksilver, and where were fan palmettoes and great purple flags. Wading the stream, she started suddenly when a patriarch bullfrog plunged from the grassy bank into his favorite pool.

From the cool shadows of the watercourse Maisie climbed the low hill to the level pineland floor. She did not know it, but when she paused there, she was standing within twenty feet of the diamondback's den. But he lay hushed and hidden in his ashen coil, and she tripped gaily onward toward the savanna. The white wood lilies always grew in a damp place, and this was the place she had found them the year before.

"Those same ones will be blooming again this year," she said. They don't seem to mind if I take their flowers. They just keep blooming away. I wish I could be like a wood lily," she went on idly to herself—"always pretty and white and clean."

Searching the pathway ahead with wary eyes, she came to a heavy clump of gallberries, and struck it sharply with her stick. Then she thrust it into the green privacy of the shadows.

Something stirred there; said Maisie, whose eyes were keen as those of any other wild thing, saw a black shape, not much bigger than a coiled rattler.

"Laws-a-massy!" she exlaimed. "Now ain't that som'thin'! And I nigh stepped on him. I hain't never seen one so black before!"

With the end of the stick she separated thick, low branches. The sunlight flooded through the aperture, and there before her wondering eyes lay the tiny black fawn.

"Great Christmas!" she exclaimed. "Hit's a baby deer, and he's as black as the inside of a chimbley! How come he here?" she asked herself. "I wonder where his ma is. His pa, he don't ever mind him; but his ma, she ought to be about. And she might fight me on occasion of him."

Maisie could hardly take her eyes off this dusky woodland elf. When she did look up, there was the doe, only a few yards away; and it was amazing what emotions her mien and her attitude expressed; dread, courage, anger, terror for herself and her baby, boundless affection for her little black fawn, and what looked to Maisie like a pathetic appeal from one woman to another.

"Don't you mind me," Maisie said to her gently, "I wouldn't hurt your baby. . . . But ain't it funny," she added to herself, "that he's black all over? He hain't got nary a spot. Iffen you ask me, that is something I never hoped to see."

The doe kept stepping nearer, hesitatingly, menacingly. The scent of man was of all scents the most dreaded, much more than that of a deerhound, an alligator, or a rattlesnake. A doe will not actually fight a human being in defense of her young; the most she will do is to come near, perhaps feign to threaten, and certainly to look imploringly at the intruder.

"I wish he was mine," said Maisie. "I sure would like to carry him home. But the doe, she wouldn't have no more this year, because deer have a baby only once a year. And she would grieve mighty hard if I took this one. My, but he do look cuddly and cute!"

She had almost forgotten about the lilies. Softly now she stepped away from the doe and the fawn. As soon as she had gone a few yards into the green savanna, the wild mother stole up to her black elf, carefully investigating him to make sure he was safe.

Maisie found her lilies; and with a bouquet as large as she could carry, she set out to return home. But she made a wide circuit about the doe and fawn.

"I know just how she feels," she kept saying to herself. "I'd feel that way if I had a little youngun, and me scared it might come to some hurt. Won't Rodney be surprised when I tell him! And I guess he'll tease me and say it ain't so, same as he allus does. Maybe I won't tell him at all," she reasoned with girlish craft. "As sure as I do, he'll be for hunting him. A little black deer! Rodney won't believe it. He'll be for saying I saw a coon or a cooter, I know him."

When she came to the open road she dropped her stick. "I don't mind snakes when I can see 'em plain like and open. It's steppin' on 'em unbeknown that I don't hanker after."

Soon she was within sight of the clearing in the pinelands that was the home of the Mayhews. She saw her father plowing in the cornfield, her mother sitting on the porch where she had left her. Standing near her in the yard was a third figure. Maisie's eyes brightened at sight of him.

"Hit's Rod," she said, and instinctively she touched her hair with her free hand and smoothed down her dress. "Shall I tell him or no?"

As she came up to the gate, looking at her flushed, excited face, Rodney Magwood, a lean young giant, black-browed and handsome in a backwoods way, said in his drawling, bantering fashion:

"You seed more than flowers where you been. Is you been findin' bird nests again?"

Maisie gave the lilies to her mother. Then she took a womanly moment to compose herself.

"Rod Magwood," she said gravely, "What I seed you ain't never seed before."

Rodney laughed. "Maisie, you see plenty what I don't see, and you see plenty what ain't here to see."

"All right then," said Maisie, sitting down on the top step. "I won't tell you; but and iffen I tole you, you'd be s'prised."

"Uh-huh," Rodney grunted indulgently.

"What did you see, child?" asked her mother.

"A black deer," Maisie announced boldly.

Rodney threw back his head and laughed loudly. Then as suddenly he became silent and thoughtful.

"Look here, Maze," he said, "is you sure it warn't one of them wild black hogs out of the Big Ocean Bay, or maybe a b'ar from outen Hell Hole Swamp? They git over this a-way every so and again."

"It was a baby deer, and as black as your houn' dog Bugle; and you know that houn' ain't nothin' but black, same as midnight."

"War you close to him—a little fawn?"

"I was up on him, and his ma, she war right there lookin' at me. I war right sorry for her, she was that worried."

"Did they run from you?"

"He couldn't, and she wouldn't. He is a little and weak but awful purty."

"Do tell," muttered Maisie's mother.

"I do remember," Rodney said, "come to think about it, Ned Parler, he tole me he seed a black buck onct. And he didn't shoot at him. It was a thick place and he thought it was an Angus steer what had got away from some place. But when it hit the hill, he saw the horns, and it was a deer."

His tone was changed. People of the back country of the pinelands are superstitious.

"Do youall reckon hit could mean anything—Maisie seein' that black deer, and the moon comin' full tonight? You know the likes of such things are sometimes tokens."

The mother looked at her only daughter with a light of strange fear in her deep-set eyes.

"Like as not it was just a plain deer what Maisie thought was black. Yet I seed a white one onct."

Both Rod and Maisie remembered also; for it was hardly a month after she had seen the albino buck that her only son had died.

"I hope this one is a buck," said Rodney. "I sure would like to kill him when his horns get growed."

"I hopes you never see him," said Maisie with a maternal protective instinct. "Maybe," she added with a child's strange cunning. "Maybe he is a token, and then it would be bad luck to kill him. He might bring us all bad luck, Rod, if we trouble him. The likes of him should be let alone."

"Child, how you talk!" said her mother. Rodney laughed softly, but there was a faint uneasiness in his merriment. Although he could not have defined it, he had a premonition of danger, all the more disturbing because it was vague.

III

Eight years had passed since that sunny April day when Maisie Mayhew had come upon little Black Roland. Time had brought its changes. Maisie and Rod Magwood had now been married five years: they had their little home in the wilderness, and two babies had been born to them, little Rodney and Lucy.

As for Black Roland, he was now a huge, twelve-point stag, hero of many an adventure. So hard had he been hunted by the Nimrods of the backwoods that he had crossed the Santee River and for more than three years had lived in the moldering solitude of a huge swamp in the heart of the wilderness.

He lived on Mound Ridge, which is near the western end of the great Santee Delta in coastal Carolina, a place probably as primeval as any left in North America. Magwood did not live on the Ridge, but he spent much time there, his chief reason being Black Roland. With ordinary white-tail bucks he had an intimate and life-long acquaintance; but this deer was unlike any he had ever seen.

Roland was so very different that the first time Rodney saw him the backwoods hunter was not sure what the creature might be. For this great swamp stag was coal black. It was not only his color that made him remarkable, but he carried a rack of palmated antlers that Magwood knew to be a record, even for that famous deer country. And they were as black as Roland's glistening hide.

For three seasons Rodney had followed him; each season he had seen the buck; once he had picked up one of his dropped antlers. But the hunter's chance to kill this wary king did not come until the time of the great flood. Those wild waters which were to inundate hundreds of thousands of acres of land, began to rise during the first days of the week before Christmas.

For several days Rodney, whose little home was over in the Cedar Hill country on the mainland west of the river, had been reading in the daily paper of the coming of big water. As it had a long way to come, nearly three hundred miles, it took some days to reach his place.

When the swollen river strikes tidewater, the whole delta is deeply submerged—a region sixteen miles long and from two to three miles wide; and at such a time all wild life in that vast wilderness of bog, marsh, and swamp has a precarious time. Deer and turkeys, snakes and alligators, rabbits and king rails, wild hogs and cattle—all gather on the high timbered ridges; and if these ridges are submerged, the refugees have a swim to safety elsewhere.

"Maisie," said Rod to his little blue-eyed wife that December morning, "the river is up, and I aim to go acrost to the Ridge. First thing you know, Christmas will be here, and we don't have no venison. I can't let that happen to us. I might even see that old black buck we call Roland. John Souther seen him last month. He thought he was a black steer! I know hereabouts he lives." He almost whispered, afraid of betraying the secret even to his wife.

"Don't you take no chances in a freshet," cautioned Maisie. "Mound Ridge is a bad place, even without a big water. That's where you had trouble with that wounded buck—him what made me spend a week mendin' your clothes what he plum tore off. And that's where the Parler boy got struck with that big diamondback rattlesnake what kilt him."

"You ought to see that buck what I mean," said Rodney, ignoring his wife's calling up, none too rosily, the reputation of Mound Ridge. "I've done seen all the big deer horns in this country, but none like his."

"Well, don't you take no chances with him, either. I don't trust no big wild thing, especially if he's got horns."

Rodney laughed at her fears.

"And what would you think of me if I stayed home because I was scared?"

Maisie smiled.

"We do need the venison," she confessed.

"I'll be home afore sundown," he said. "Don't you worry Ain't nothing on Mound Ridge worse than what I am."

Magwood's two hounds, Creek and Mate, howled dismally because he did not take them.

"I don't need you dogs," he drawled. "You ain't no 'count in a freshet. All you'd do would be to get drowned."

Making his way down to the river, Rod shivered and turned up his coat collar. It was a raw day, misty and close to freezing. The wind off the river was bleak. Coming to his dug-out cypress canoe, he got into the frail craft, laid his gun carefully beside him, steadied himself, and then pushed off.

Now he could see the freshet waters creeping up, flooding the land. Soon he was on the great river itself, wide and stormy, rushing to the sea.

As the flood had already engulfed the vast delta lying between the North and South Santees, the whole expanse of wild water now before his was almost three miles wide. With stormy strength the huge tide rushed oceanward, bearing upon its tawny bosom rafts of dislodged sedge, swimming wild creatures, old logs, and tons of natural refuge. All about the hunter was an atmosphere of lonely danger.

"Maisie knowed when she tole me to be careful," he muttered. "This here river sure is gettin' wild. But it ain't so far to Mound

Ridge," he comforted himself. "Right yonder at them tall pines on the delta—that's her. If ole Roland ain't already swum to the mainland, he'll have to be on the Ridge. He's a marshy deer; but you can't see no marsh now. He couldn't stay where he generally stays—'less he's a submarine."

As he paddled, he noticed the many fugitives swimming by, heading for high ground: swamp rabbits, razor-back hogs, a huge bull alligator that must have been washed out of hibernation; a burly wildcat, tawny as the flood itself, swimming for life; and once an otter, alone of all the wild things undismayed by the flood, heading gracefully upstream, as if the gloomy might of the down-rushing river were merely a challenge to his sporting instinct.

A hard paddle brought Magwood across the river, and he entered the comparatively hushed country of the drowned delta. All the wooded river banks were deeply submerged. The great marshes were covered, though here and there tall spears of yellow duck-oats showed. Out of a moss-shrouded cypress the hunter flushed an old wild gobbler. Huge and black, he beat his way powerfully across the stormy waters toward the mainland.

"If I don't kill a deer," Magwood said, "I might come on him yonder where he's goin'. Maisie would like him for Christmas dinner."

A mile away, across the comparatively open water of the inundated delta, towered the dark pines of Mound Ridge, the only dry place left in that exceedingly wet country. The intervening water was not nearly so rough as the river had been, but Rodney had his troubles: constantly he had to be on the lookout for half-submerged logs. A canoe such as his could easily be tipped over by the heavy momentum of these pieces of flotsam.

Before long he neared Mound Ridge, and when his paddle could touch bottom, he pushed his canoe very quietly up to the Ridge and ran her nose on shore. Sitting perfectly still, he scanned the land ahead of him. Fugitives great and small crowded it. He saw a wild cow; myriads of swamp rabbits; several razorbacks; king rails that kept stepping on and over cottonmouth mocassins, he saw a doe and her twin yearling fawns.

Then, far on the western end, he saw a strange black shape, glistening in the sleety drizzle. He saw the turn of a regal head; he saw the noble antlers, faintly glinting. It was Black Roland!

"I got him at last," he whispered to himself. "If I work it the way I ought to work it, he ain't got no chanct to get away this time. Lawsy, can this boat carry him and me?"

Southward the waters stretched sixteen miles to the ocean; northward the country was widely flooded for an almost equal distance. Both to the east and to the west lay a mile and a half of open water. Rodney opened his gun; he carefully examined his shells. On the inside of his coat he wiped both his gun and his hands.

"This here," he said, "is one shot I mustn't miss. I got a chanct I have waited four years for. But I got to be careful. A deer is a deer. The old buck that gets away is generally the one you cornered. Sometimes he knows a trick worth two of any a man has.

"I know I can't walk up to him," he continued. "I must come up on his righthand side, and maybe get up to him that way. If he takes the water, I got a boat. I done tole the boys I seed a black buck, and they laughed at me. Now I'm going to show 'em."

Very cautiously he pushed his canoe along the eastern side of the Ridge. Many of the fugitives moved ahead of him, but some turned back. All seemed disinclined to take the water. Familiar with the wild life of that country, Rodney marveled at nothing but the great black stag, still standing warily on the far end of the Ridge. As he came near the doe and her fawns, they plunged in and struck eastward toward the faint outline of the distant mainland. He knew they would have no trouble reaching it; deer are lithe and powerful swimmers.

True to his buck nature, Black Roland carefully weighed his chances. In time of peril, a doe and her young will go anywhere just to get out of trouble. But it is not so with a buck. He fixes a certain sanctuary in mind; and when he has made his decision, he heads for it with all speed.

Magwood remembered the time he had tried to get a Negro to drive a buck to him; instead, the buck, having another plan in mind, almost ran over and trampled the would-be driver. When Rodney had protested about the Negro's failure to carry the scheme through, the wise man said:

"Ain't you know a buck? He gwine where he gwine."

The wilderness hunter was now within very long gunshot of the black buck. Some deer, often shot at and long-experienced, seem to know what that vital distance is. Roland had seen the doe and fawns head eastward. He would go west. Almost deliberately, even while Magwood was beginning to lay a strangely trembling hand on the grip of his gun, Roland waded out into the water, and in a moment was swimming evenly and strongly for the western mainland, mile and a half distant. And he had to go on; for there was no place between the Ridge and the mainland where he could stop. For a short way, a deer can often distance a man in a boat; but in a light canoe, if a man is a good paddler, he can always overtake a swimming deer in a long pull.

As soon as the black buck was in the water, Rodney threw off all reserve. Pushing and paddling desperately, he rounded the north end of the Ridge before Roland was out of sight. But the deer was some two hundred yards ahead, only his great antlers visible. Behind him the hunter settled down to grim effort; yet he could not paddle as if he were on open water. Roland was swimming through the flooded swamp; and both he and Magwood had to maneuver among the trees that stood in the water.

In this maneuvering, the buck had the advantage, since he merely had to swim through the best openings. If it had been a race over open water, there would have been no doubt of the outcome; but under these conditions the black stag had a chance. Rodney's main hope was to keep in sight and fairly near until they reached the clear water of the river.

Once when his canoe became momentarily wedged between two tupelo trees, Magwood stood up, gun in hand, to take a better look. There was Roland, eighty yards ahead. And far beyond the hunter could see a brightening of the dim swamp, and he knew it was the wide and open river.

Magwood now made his plan, "I'll follow him across the river, keeping up right clost; then I'll shoot him as soon as ever he touches the mainland. If I shoot him in the river, I couldn't manage him in this boat. He might get swept down and clear out to sea like that buck I shot in the river five years ago. The way he is swimming, he is coming ashore right by my landing. Maisie will be surprised when she sees what kind of buck I got this time."

The sweeping tide became swifter as it was less obstructed by trees; the light ahead increased; the river, tawny and wild, came within sight. Roland cleared the swamp a hundred yards ahead of the hunter; but soon Magwood had gained fifty yards, then twenty more. The deer was now at the hunter's mercy. Oblivious of the waves breaking into the canoe, of the driving sleet, the hunter concentrated on Black Roland, swimming valiantly just ahead, his mighty crown of antlers huge above the yellow flood.

"Ain't no deer like this been killed in this country since a hatchet was a hammer" muttered Rodney. He could count the points of the craggy antlers. He was sure there were twelve, perhaps more.

"Maisie, she laughed when I told her about this buck; but she won't laugh when I get him home. And Check and Mate, their feelings is going to be hurt for not being in on a hunt like this."

The black stag and the man were now near the middle of the river; Magwood had paddled within a few yards of him, and was so intent on watching him that he was not watching anything else. This was a very deep and dangerous part of the river. The mainland lay three hundred yards ahead, misty and wild. Both Black Roland and the man, hunted and hunter, longed to reach it.

"If nothin' happens," said Rodney, with melting sleet running off his cap and into his eyes, blurring his vision, "it will all be over in a few minutes."

But something did happen.

Swept from an ancient mooring by the mighty flood, a huge cypress, branches, monstrous bole, and scraggly clutching roots, all half submerged, swept down the middle of the shrouded river. A massive root caught and partly turned the swimming deer. Another, lifting from the water as the tree rocked upward on the flood, caught the frail canoe, and over it went.

Magwood's gun shot downward to the bottom of the river. The canoe, half its side torn away, drifted swiftly off. Rodney, baffled, hemmed by the roots, turned and began to swim around the obstruction, clutching frantically for anything that was near. He saw something. Grimly he caught and hung on. For a moment he thought he had hold of the floating cypress. But, recovering from his shock, he was in for an almost equal one; he had Black Roland by the horns; but his position was precarious and awkward. He turned in the water, righting himself. He lay flat on the deer's back, both hands gripping the great bases of the buck's horns. And Black Roland was swimming for his life toward the mainland.

When he felt a little more sure of himself, Rodney let his left hand slip for a moment to his belt. His long-bladed hunting knife was still in its sheath.

"Ain't like I planned it," he muttered darkly, "but since my gun is gone, my knife will do."

In the countless ages during which that great river has rolled to the sea, no doubt many strange sights have been seen on its bosom; naked Indians, picturesque Spanish sailors, French Huguenot refugees, Negro slaves, Tarleton's men hunting vainly for Francis Marion in this gross wilderness. And many a strange scene of wild life this river must have witnessed; but perhaps no stranger sight than Rodney Magwood, the pineland hunter, minus his gun and canoe, riding toward the shore on a great black stag he had set out to kill.

"The hide on the neck of a buck like this," thought Rodney, "is about as tough as a bull alligator's hide. I got a knife; but maybe a good knife ain't enough. Howsoever, it's all I got, and I'll give him what I has."

Valiantly but laboriously swimming with his heavy burden, Black Roland was now within fifty yards of the coveted shore. Just ahead of him, and leaning far over the water, was a huge holly tree, its leaves glistening and its scarlet berries gleaming in the sleety rain. The old buck saw a little strip of white sand beach just below the holly. There he could land.

Gripping Black Roland's left antler with his left hand, Rodney cautiously loosed the grip of his right hand; then he began to open and close it to get rid of the stiffness. He wiped the rain and water out of his eyes, then he softly reached round to his belt, got hold of the hilt of his knife, and drew the blade from its sheath.

As he brought the knife round on the righthand side, it gleamed dully under the water. Such a feat as he contemplated depended largely for its success on proper timing. It would not be long now—merely a matter of seconds. The man himself had been brought so near the shore he was practically safe; and Black Roland was closer to death than he had ever been in his life.

Curiously, for the first time, as the noble buck, blowing now from weariness, his splendid stamina nearly exhausted by his double effort of saving both himself and his enemy, Rodney saw Roland's left eye as the stag turned his head slightly; and the buck seemed to be glancing back at him.

Beneath him Magwood could feel the heaving of the deer's flanks. With the extra weight of the man, and perhaps from fear of the burden he carried, he was having a real struggle to make the short distance.

Again Rodney saw that attentive black eye, wary, wild, pitiful . . . He thought of Maisie waiting for him, and little Rodney and Lucy. He even thought of his hounds, and of what a clamor they would set up if he could bring a buck like this home. He thought of the emptiness of that Christmas Eve if he returned with nothing— with indeed less than nothing since his boat and his gun were lost. He looked toward the shore, and the huge holly caught his sight. . . Holly and Christmas and peace on earth and good-will to every living thing.

In the last few yards before they gained the shore Rodney's feeling toward Roland changed. To reach shore meant life to him, but it meant death to the black stag, after his dauntless battle. Rodney was a hunter of the wilderness, and he had killed many bucks. But no deer had ever before saved his life.

He had a desperate moment of mental struggle; if he did one thing he would go home in triumph, and he would have a story his friends would ask him to retell as long as he lived; he would make Maisie happy, and the children, and they would have plenty of fresh venison for Christmas. If he did the other thing, he would have nothing except the feeling that he had been merciful and generous.

Black Roland was very tired now. His feet were about to touch the sandy bottom of the river shore. As soon as he struck land, the deer, Rodney knew, would break out of the water and race into the forest.

More slowly than he had drawn it forth, but with equal determination, Magwood thrust the knife back into its sheath.

Black Roland's feet struck a sand bar. Rodney slid easily from his back, and as the great buck sprang forward, the hunter gave him a friendly slap.

"Go on, you old rascal," he said, "and don't you let me catch up on you no mo'."

As he waded slowly out of the water, Rodney stopped to break a bough of the brilliant holly; and this was all he carried homeward.

Hatless, and without his gun, but with a strange new light in his eyes, Rodney Magwood appeared at his home.

"Why, Rod," said Maisie, as he handed her the holly, "you have been overboard. Where is your gun? I was afraid you might get into trouble. But nothin' matters so you got back safe. I got your hot coffee all ready."

Drying off before his open fire, Rodney told his wife and his two wide-eyed children the whole story.

"Now what ever come over me to act like that?" he asked.

Maisie's eyes were bright. Pineland people are not demonstrative. But she came over to his chair and her hand stole to his shoulder.

"You done all right," she said. "To let him live was a real nice Christmas present for that old black buck. I reckon, too, he growed from that same little black fawn I seed when you was a courtin' me, Rod. I never did want him kilt. Some of the boys, they was a-huntin' this morning, and they done brung us venison and a wild turkey. We'll have a fine Christmas. . ." Then her shy and loving heart spoke openly as she said, "Rod, ain't many hunters would have been man enough to do what you done."

Bibliographical Note

All of Rutledge's major prose works were consulted in the prepa-
ration of this book. A list of these is given below. Those denoted with
an asterisk are books from which stories included in this volume
were taken. In addition, several books and articles were useful in
providing background information and biographical details. Irvine
Rutledge's warm, winsome memoir of his father, *We Called Him
Flintlock* (1974), proved invaluable. *Hidden Glory: The Life and Times of
Hampton Plantation, Legend of the South Santee* (1983), by Mary Bray
Wheeler and Genon Hickerson Neblett, is a carefully researched
history of Hampton which offers information on the plantation and
those who lived there over succeeding generations. It includes a
chapter entitled "The Poet: Archibald Hamilton Rutledge (1883–
1973)."

While there is no full biography of Rutledge, Idella Bodie's *The
Story of Archibald Rutledge: A Hunt for Life's Extras* (1980), written for a
youthful audience, is interesting. A number of shorter biographical
pieces are also useful. These include Virginia Ravenel, "South
Carolina's Poet Laureate," *Sandlapper* (October 1968) 47–51; Benton
Young, "The Squire of Hampton," *South Carolina Wildlife* (September/
October 1983) 16–21; and Rob Wegner, "Flintlock: A Dixie Deer-
slayer," *Deer & Deer Hunting* (June 1990) 23–44. Wegner's article also
appears in his seminal work, *Deer & Deer Hunting: Book III* (1990).

Another noteworthy source is an obscure pamphlet, "Ceremonies
Honoring Dr. Archibald Rutledge, Poet Laureate of South Carolina,"
issued when Rutledge was accorded special recognition by the South
Carolina General Assembly in 1956. Rutledge is listed in many of the
standard biographical directories. Among these, the most useful are
Who's Who in South Carolina (1934–35), *The Reader's Encyclopedia of*

American Literature (1962), *Who Was Who Among North American Authors* (1976), *Contemporary Authors* (1966), and *Southern Writers: A Biographical Dictionary* (1979). George Bird Evans has penetrating short sketches of Rutledge in two of his books, *Men Who Shot* (1983) and *George Bird Evans Introduces* (1990).

Finally, Rutledge himself provides the best information on his life. Virtually all his prose works carry some autobiographical elements, and his papers in the South Caroliniana Library at the University of South Carolina in Columbia, while disappointing (one wonders what became of the massive correspondence he conducted), are important. His "Bright College Years," published in the *Georgia Review* (Summer 1967), and subsequently in the *Charleston News and Courier* (9 July 1967), with the title changed to "Years in College— Remembered," is an overlooked reflective piece of great value.

Books by Rutledge Consulted

*An American Hunter (1937)
Beauty in the Heart (1953)
The Beauty of the Night (1947)
*Bolio and Other Dogs (1930)
*Days Off in Dixie (1925)
The Flower of Hope (1930)
From the Hills to the Sea (1958)
*God's Children (1947)
*Heart of the South (1924)
Home by the River (1955)
How Wild Was My Village (1969)
*Hunter's Choice (1946)
It Will Be Daybreak Soon (1938)
Life's Extras (1928)
Love's Meaning (1943)
A Monarch of the Sky (1926)
My Colonel and His Lady (1937)
*Old Plantation Days (1921)
*Peace in the Heart (1930)

A Plantation Boyhood (1932)
**Plantation Game Trails* (1921)
Sanctuary (1920)
Santee Paradise (1956)
South of Richmond (1923)
**Those Were the Days* (1955)
**Tom and I on the Old Plantation* (1918)
A Wildwood Tale; A Drama of the Open (1950)
**Wild Life of the South* (1935)
Willie Was a Lady (1966)
**The Woods and Wild Things I Remember* (1970)
The World Around Hampton (1960)